YOU DESERVE EACH OTHER

—

Sarah Hogle

G. P. PUTNAM'S SONS
New York

PUTNAM
— EST. 1838 —

G. P. PUTNAM'S SONS
Publishers Since 1838
An imprint of Penguin Random House LLC
penguinrandomhouse.com

Library of Congress Cataloging-in-Publication Data

Names: Hogle, Sarah, author.
Title: You deserve each other / Sarah Hogle.
Description: New York: G. P. Putnam's Sons, 2020. |
Summary: "For fans of *The Hating Game*, a debut lovers-to-enemies-to-lovers
romantic comedy about two unhappily engaged people, each trying to
force the other to end the relationship—and falling back in
love in the process."—Provided by publisher.
Identifiers: LCCN 2019046872 (print) | LCCN 2019046873 (ebook) |
ISBN 9780593085424 (trade paperback) | ISBN 9780593085431 (ebook)
Subjects: GSAFD: Love stories.
Classification: LCC PS3608.O48268 Y68 2020 (print) |
LCC PS3608.O48268 (ebook) | DDC 813/.6—dc23
LC record available at https://lccn.loc.gov/2019046872
LC ebook record available at https://lccn.loc.gov/2019046873

Printed in the United States of America
14th Printing

Book design by Ashley Tucker

—

For my husband, Marcus, and for our children.
You're my happy place.

—

PROLOGUE

I think he's going to kiss me tonight.

If he doesn't, I just might die. It's our second date, and we're parked at a drive-in theater pretending to watch a movie while sneaking looks at each other. This movie is two hours and five minutes long. We have spent one hour and fifty-five minutes not kissing. I don't want to sound desperate, but I didn't contour a third of my body with this much highlighter to not get any of it on his shirt. If all goes according to plan, he's going to be limping home tonight with ravaged hair and enough shimmer powder on his clothes to make him reflective to passing cars. He's going to smell like my pheromones for a week no matter how hard he scrubs.

I haven't been shy with the hint-dropping, drawing attention to my lips by licking, nibbling, and idly touching them—advice I got from *Cosmopolitan*. My shiny lip gloss was developed in a lab to magnetize the mouths of men, effective as fanning peacock feathers. Nicholas's primitive instincts won't be able to resist. It's also a magnet for my hair and I keep getting the eye-watering taste of extra-hold hair spray in my mouth, but sometimes beauty requires sacrifice. On top of all this, my left hand drapes across my seat palm-up for maximum accessibility in case he'd like to pick it up and take it home with him.

My hopes begin to wither when he looks at me and then quickly away. Maybe he's the kind of person who goes to the drive-in to actually watch the movie. As much as I'd hate to consider it, maybe he's simply not feeling this. It wouldn't be the first time a smooth-talking charmer dropped me off with a good-night kiss and ghosted right when I thought things were getting good.

And then I see it: a signal that eating my hair all night has not been in vain. It arrives in the form of an empty mint wrapper sitting in the cup holder. I subtly sniff the air and heck yes, that is definitely wintergreen I smell. I check the cup holder again and it's even better than I'd thought. Two empty wrappers! He's doubling up! A man doesn't double up on mints unless he's preparing for a little move-making.

My god, this man is so handsome I'm half convinced I somehow tricked him into this. I like every single little thing about Nicholas. He didn't wait three days to call after the first date. All of his texts are grammatically correct. I have yet to receive an unsolicited dick pic. Already, I want to reserve a ballroom for our wedding reception.

"Naomi?" he says, and I blink.

"Huh?"

He smiles. It's so adorable that I smile, too. "Did you hear me?"

The answer to that is no, because I'm over here admiring his profile and being way too infatuated for it being so early in our . . . I can't even call this a relationship. We've only been on two dates. *Get it together, Naomi.*

"Zone out a lot?" he guesses.

I feel myself flush. "Yeah. Sorry. Sometimes people talk to me and I don't even register it."

His smile widens. "You're cute."

He thinks I'm cute? My heart flutters and glows. I give an inner thank-you speech to my false eyelashes and this low-cut (but still classy) blouse.

He cocks his head, studying me. "I was saying that the movie's over."

I whip my head to face the screen. He's right. I have no idea how the movie ended and couldn't tell you what the major plot points were. I think it was a romance, but who cares? I'm much more interested in the romance happening here in this car. The lot is now deserted, granting us enough privacy to make my imagination go wild. Anything could happen. It's just me, Nicholas, and—

The pink cardigan folded neatly on his back seat, which obviously belongs to a woman, and that woman isn't me.

My stomach drops, and Nicholas follows my gaze. "That's for my mother," he says quickly. I'm not quite convinced until he shows me a HAPPY BIRTHDAY card beneath it, which he's signed and added a personal message to. *Love you, Mom!* I inwardly swoon.

"That's so nice," I tell him, acutely aware of how isolated and intimate it feels in his car. I'm a mess of nervous butterflies, and the discarded mint wrappers keep snagging my eye. The movie's over, so what's he waiting for? "Thanks for taking me here. Not many drive-ins left these days. Probably only a couple in the whole Midwest." It's even rarer to find one that operates year-round. Luckily, we were provided with a complimentary electric heater to offset the insanity of doing something like this in January. We've got a few blankets spread over us, and for an out-of-the-box winter date it's been surprisingly cozy.

"There are eight left in the state, actually," he says. The fact that he knows this piece of trivia right off the top of his head is impressive. "Are you hungry? There's a frozen yogurt stand near here that has the best frozen yogurt you've ever had in your life."

I'm not a fan of frozen yogurt (especially when it's cold out), but no way am I being anything but agreeable. We don't know each other that well yet, and if I want to score a third date I need to come off as low-maintenance. I'm easygoing Naomi, fun to hang out with and *definitely* fun to make out with. Maybe after the frozen yogurt he'll kiss me. And possibly unbutton his shirt. "That sounds great!"

Instead of fastening his seat belt and driving away, he hesitates. Fiddles with the radio dials until static fuzz tunes in to an upbeat indie song called "You Say It Too." It hits me that he's fallen so quiet because he's nervous, not disinterested, which surprises me because up until now he's exhibited nothing but confidence. There's a charge in the air and my pulse accelerates with intuition of what's to come. The rhythm of my blood is a chant. *Yes! Yes! Yes!*

"You're beautiful," he says earnestly, turning to face me in full. His eyes are hesitant as he bites his cheek and I'm stunned that *he's* the nervous one here. My heart skips as he leans toward me an inch. Then another. His lips part, gaze dropping to my mouth, and just like that I can no longer remember any other men I've ever dated, he's eclipsed them all so utterly. He's intelligent and charming and perfect, absolutely perfect for me.

My heart is now lodged firmly in my throat. His fingers stroke through my hair, tilting my head up to meet his. Nicholas leans in that final inch and lights up my world like a shooting star, anticipation and wonder and a feeling of tremendous rightness barreling through my veins. He kisses me and I'm a goner, just like I knew would happen.

What a magical, extraordinary night.

CHAPTER ONE

ONE YEAR AND NINE MONTHS LATER

What an ugly, crappy day. Rain pelts off the windshield of my coworker's likewise crappy car, which smells like cold McDonald's French fries and pine trees. Leon taps his fingertips on the steering wheel, leaning forward a bit to see out. His windshield wipers are stroking back and forth with all they've got, but the rain is pouring like someone slit the sky down the middle and an ocean started roaring out.

"Thanks again for the ride."

"Sure, anytime."

I roll my lips inward and inhale a bloom of pine. Whatever he misted in here before I got in is going to follow me around for the rest of the day. I don't know too much about Leon, so it's fully possible there's a corpse in the trunk and the pine spray is to cover it up.

"Raining pretty hard," I say. Brandy couldn't take me home because her sister picked her up early. Zach took his motorcycle today, which I bet he's regretting. Melissa offered to give me a lift, clearly hoping I'd decline, which is why I did. I kind of hate myself for still wanting her to like me. She's been unreasonably prickly toward me ever since I set her up with my fiancé's friend, who turned out to be a serial cheater. She thinks Nicholas and I knew he was the cheating type from the get-go and shredded her trust in men on purpose.

"Yeah, it's supposed to rain all week."

"That's too bad for the trick-or-treaters."

Leon turns to face me for a moment, before his eyes slide back to the road. Or what he can see of it—frankly I don't know how he's still inching along because I can't see a thing. We could be mowing through a field for all I know. It's the tail end of October and forty degrees. Last week I was wearing shorts. The week before that, it was so cold that it almost snowed. Autumn in Wisconsin is a joy.

"You passing out candy?" Leon asks.

The answer should be a given. I love candy and I love kids, especially obnoxious little boys because I think they're funny. I also love the fall. All month I've been using the shimmery copper pan in my eye shadow palette, trying to give my eyelids the same glow of sunset gently slanting over a pumpkin patch.

My bedroom floor is a mess of soft pullover sweaters that make me feel like a sea captain, knee-high boots, and infinity scarves. Every meal contains some hint of pumpkin spice. If I'm not ingesting pumpkin, I'm breathing it in like an addict, lining every available surface of my home with candles that smell like food. Apple pie, pumpkin pie, pumpkin spice, apple pumpkin.

My aesthetic is aggressively, unapologetically basic. Some of it stems from a lady at a MAC counter telling me I'm an autumn, because of my amber eyes and long, stick-straight hair the color of pecans, but I know in my leaf-ogling, beanie-loving, pumpkin-gorging soul that I'd be a basic bitch even if I had neutral undertones. It's in my DNA.

And yet I don't feel like passing out candy on Halloween. I haven't even decorated, which used to be one of my favorite things to do at the start of a season. I might end up spending the evening alone in sweats, watching bad TV while Nicholas is off playing *Gears of War* at a friend's house, or we might turn in before nine p.m. after passing out cheap, travel-size toothbrushes and floss to disappointed children.

"Maybe," I say at last, because I no longer care what I do. I could be riding a roller coaster or writing a grocery list and my enthusiasm level would look the same. The thought depresses me, but what depresses me more is that I'm not going to do anything about it.

"I would if I lived on a busier street," he replies. "I don't get any trick-or-treaters out where I live."

There's no such thing as a busy street in Morris. We're so small, you'd be hard pressed to find us on a city map of Wisconsin. We only have two stoplights.

Headlights roll by, tires spitting up waves of water like Moses parting the Red Sea. If I were driving I definitely would have pulled into a parking lot forever ago and waited this out. But Leon is completely at ease. I wonder if he retains this same pleasant expression when he chops people up into bits and slides their oozing remains down a cutting board into his trunk.

Not that Leon has ever given me any reason to be particularly wary of him. I should be making polite inquiries about where he lives or something like that, but I've got one eye on the emerald numbers of his digital clock and I'm wondering if Nicholas is home yet, because I'm hoping desperately that he isn't. The Junk Yard opens at ten and closes at six every day except for Saturdays, when it's open from eleven to seven.

Nicholas is a dentist at Rise and Smile Dentistry on the main road we're on now, Langley, and he gets off at six. Usually I beat him home because he stops at his parents' house to give his mother a coffee or to read over some confusing letter she got in the mail or whatever it is she's squawking at him about on any given day. If she goes more than twenty-four hours without seeing him her operating system fails.

This morning I found one of my tires completely flat. Standing there staring at it, I was transported to a year ago when Nicholas remarked that he ought to teach me how to change a tire. Offended by his assumption that I didn't already know how to change a tire, I set him straight and informed him that I've known for years how to do that. I'm a modern, responsible, self-sufficient woman. I don't need a man to help me with vehicular maintenance.

The thing is, I do not actually know how to change a tire. The weather this morning was pleasant and I had no clue it was going to rain, so I decided to walk—which is what brings me to my current predicament in Leon's car, because no way was I going to walk home. This sweater is cashmere.

My small lie about tires got a bit out of hand when Nicholas's dad, who has deplorably antiquated beliefs, commented that women don't know how to change their oil. In return I said, "Excuse you! I change my oil all the time." I said it for feminism. No one can blame me. Then I may have boasted that I once put my own shocks and brake pads on and have never needed assistance from a car mechanic, ever. I know Nicholas is suspicious and has been trying to catch me at it whenever my car needs work done. Conveniently, I am an expert mechanic only when he is at work, so he never sees me in action. I sneak into Morris Auto like a criminal and pay Dave in cash. Dave is good people. He's promised never to rat me out and lets me take credit for his labor.

Every building on Langley is a cold, bluish smear in all this rain. We pass a Claude Monet version of Rise and Smile, and I pray Nicholas doesn't have the vision of a hawk and can miraculously see me in the passenger seat of a strange car. If he gets wind that I didn't drive today, he's going to ask why. I have no legitimate excuse. He's going to find out I was lying about my car know-how, and his smug I-knew-it face is going to piss me off so bad that I'll get an acne breakout. He has no business being suspicious of my repairwoman prowess, anyway. It's sexist to assume I wouldn't know how to fix leaky hoses and sanding belts and whatever else makes a car go vroom. He should assume that all of my lies are true.

I want Leon to hurry up, even though it's slippery and I would very much prefer not to die in this car that smells like it's huffed an entire forest up its grille. I wonder how I can phrase the request to put his life in mortal peril so that I'll have time to look up YouTube tutorials before Nicholas gets home. Is it worth the possibility of skidding off the road in order to maintain this con? Yes. Yes, it is. I haven't been cultivating it for this long to have it blow up in my face over some rain.

I pick up a to-go cup off the floor and turn it over. "Dunkin' Donuts, huh? Don't let Brandy find out."

Brandy's sister owns a coffee shop, Blue Tulip Café, and

Brandy is her Junk Yard ambassador. She doesn't let anyone at work get away with patronizing big coffee chains.

Leon chuckles. "Oh, I know. I have to hide it like it's a dirty secret. But the coffee at Dunkin' Donuts tastes better, and then you've got to consider my allegiance to the name. When you share a last name with Dunkin' Donuts, that's where your loyalty goes."

"Your last name is Donuts?" I reply like a complete idiot, a split second before I realize my obvious mistake.

"My last name is Duncan, Naomi." Leon slides me a glance, and his expression wants to be *Are you serious* because this is a detail I should probably know by now, having worked with him since February at the Junk Yard, which is not literally a junkyard. It's a mom-and-pop store. But his manners are infinitely superior to mine, so instead his expression is *Oh, that's a perfectly understandable thing to say, I suppose.*

I want to open the door and roll out, but I resist. It's a monsoon out there and I'll have copper shimmer streaking down my cheeks. With this visibility, I'll wander into traffic and get run down. My black-and-white engagement photo will appear in the newspaper, with a notice that in lieu of flowers, my fiancé's family requests donations be made to their for-profit charity, Rows of Books, which sends dental hygiene textbooks to underprivileged schools.

I seethe for a moment because that is *exactly* what would happen, and I'm spiteful enough that I think I'd rather take the flowers.

Finally, finally we pull onto my street. I'm already unbuckling the seat belt when I point at the little white house with my dependable old Saturn and a gold Maserati out front, mismatched as can be.

YOU DESERVE EACH OTHER   13

Nicholas is home, goddamn it.

Standing on the porch with today's mail and a leather satchel tucked under his arm, unlocking the front door. The one time I need him to dote on his mother after work, and he comes straight home instead like a jackass. I check out my car and wheeze; the tire is so flat, the whole thing is lopsided. It'll be a miracle if Nicholas hasn't noticed. The Saturn looks pitiful next to Nicholas's flashy car, so out of place in Morris that everyone knows who it belongs to whenever it whizzes through the stoplight just as it turns red.

Conversely, Leon's vehicle is a Frankenstein's monster of Japanese parts. Most of it's a dull gray-blue, except for the driver's-side door, which is red and eroded from rust, and the trunk, which is white and doesn't close properly. It's been bumping the whole ride, which probably accounts for my visions of somebody bound and gagged back there. Poor Leon. I know they say it's the quiet ones you've got to watch out for, but he's never been anything but nice to me and doesn't deserve the side-eye. He is *probably* not Jack the Ripper.

"See you tonight," he says.

Brandy hosts a game night most Friday evenings. She invites Zach, Melissa, Leon, and me, with a standing invitation for our significant others. Nicholas has never gone to one of Brandy's game nights, Zach's barbecues, or Melissa's mini golf outings, which is just fine by me. He can go do his own thing with his own friends, whom he doesn't even like but hangs out with anyway because it's hard to make new friends when you're thirty-two.

I'm halfway across the yard when Leon unexpectedly yells, "Hey, Nicholas!"

Nicholas gives him a confused wave. My coworkers tend to

ignore him whenever they come into contact, and vice versa. "Hey?"

"You coming to game night?" Leon asks him.

A laugh that sounds like "Bagh" escapes me, because of course Nicholas isn't coming. Nobody there likes him and he'd just be defensive and sulky the whole time, which would suck all the fun out of it for me. If he went, my friends (I am still counting Melissa as a friend even if she'd rather I didn't, because I'm holding out hope she'll be nice to me again someday) might catch on that we're not the yin-and-yang lovebirds I've been pretending we are in my Instagram stories. In a way, it's convenient that Nicholas avoids my friends and doesn't stray close enough for them to inspect. Knowing that our relationship looks enviable from the outside is the only thing we've got going for us, since in reality what we have isn't enviable at all.

"What's that laugh for?" Nicholas asks, looking offended.

"You never go to game night. Why'd he even ask?" To Leon, I call, "No, he's busy."

"That's too bad," Leon replies. "You know you're welcome to swing by if your schedule opens up, Nicholas."

Nicholas's narrowed eyes never leave mine as he responds, "You know what? I think I'll go."

Leon waves cheerfully, which is at total odds with the shock I hasten to cover up. "Cool! See you, Naomi." Then he drives off.

Someone has said the simplest thing, *See you, Naomi*, and I have a strange thought.

It's been a long time since anyone has seen me, since I keep so much about myself hidden. *Me*, who I am really, an individual who has been alive for twenty-eight years, twenty-six of those not knowing Nicholas Rose existed. I've been slowly bleeding out the Westfield parts of myself to become pre–Naomi Rose. Almost Mrs. Rose. I've been one half of a whole for nearly two years and lately, I don't know if I'd even count as a half.

But when someone calls me Naomi with kindness in their voice, I feel like that girl I was before. During the brief time it takes for Leon's car to disappear down the street, I am Naomi Westfield again.

"You don't want me to come," Nicholas says accusingly.

"What? Don't be ridiculous. Of course I do."

I give him my biggest smile. To be convincing, I need to make the smile travel to my eyes. A true smile. Whenever I do this, I like to imagine that I'm looking at him in my rearview mirror, peeling out of Morris, never to see him again.

CHAPTER TWO

I'm on the sofa watching something that will rot my brain, half listening to Nicholas complain about a friend of a friend who joins his soccer games at the park a few times a month. It's the one who thinks he's a better player than Nicholas, the one who thinks he knows more about the game than Nicholas, and Nicholas is going to give him a piece of his mind one of these days. He's been saying that the whole time I've known him. At least he bought my story for why I walked to work: I'm taking steps to lead a healthier lifestyle and walking is my newest passion. Nicholas should follow my example and walk to work, too, instead of destroying our planet with greenhouse gases. Honestly, he could learn a thing or two from me.

I let him blow off steam. I nod and agree like the good little fiancée I am, but I am not a good fiancée at all because I feel like I might fall apart at any moment.

I'm a good actress. It's a point of pride. Nicholas's point of pride is that he thinks he knows every little thing there is to know about me. He tells people all the time that I can't hide anything from him. I'm transparent as air and intellectually just as substantial. The fact that he can look into my eyes and believe I am totally in love with him is proof that I'm a fantastic actress and he does not know everything about me, or even most things.

Ratio-wise, I would say that I'm forty percent in love with Nicholas. Maybe I shouldn't say I'm *in* love. There's a difference. Being *in* love is frantic. Fluttery. Falling. It's nervous sweats and pounding heartbeats and a feeling of tremendous rightness, or so I hear. I don't have that. I love him forty percent.

It's not as bad as it sounds, if you think about the couples you know. If they're being honest, a lot of them would list a lower number than the one they'd declare out loud. The truth is that I don't think any two people both feel one hundred percent in love with each other at the same exact time, all the time. They might take turns being seventy-five, their personal high, while the other clocks in at sixty.

I'm a miserable cynic (a newer development) and a dreamy romantic (always have been), and it's such a terrible combination that I don't know how to tolerate myself. If I were only one of those things, perhaps I would be nodding and agreeing with Nicholas, smiling brightly, rather than drumming up one of my favorite daydreams to focus on when I don't want to live in reality. In this dream, it's my wedding day and I'm standing at the altar next to Nicholas. The priest asks if anyone objects to this union and someone in the audience stands up, boldly proclaiming, "I do." Everyone gasps. It's Jake Pavelka, controversial season 14 star of *The Bachelor*.

In real life, Jake Pavelka isn't going to interrupt my vows, and Nicholas and I will be stuck with each other. I revisit my mental calendar and feel sick at how little time I have left. Right now, the thought of saying *I do* makes my pulse gallop like a runaway train.

I am falling apart and Nicholas doesn't even notice.

This is happening with snowballing regularity. Just when I think the odd feeling's gone and I'm complacent again, all feelings of dissatisfaction suppressed, the pendulum swings back at me. Sometimes the feeling hits me when I'm about to fall asleep. It happens when I'm driving home from work and when I'm eating dinner, which means I lose my appetite immediately and have to make up an acceptable explanation as to why.

Because of my excuses, Nicholas thinks I have a sensitive stomach and my PMS lasts three weeks. We frequently discuss my gluten intake and I pretend to consider cutting sugar out of my diet. This is what happens when you date a guy for eleven months, then get engaged six hours before finally moving in together and learning who the other person truly is on a day-to-day basis. Signing up for Boyfriend Nicholas and inheriting Fiancé Nicholas later on was some legitimate bait-and-switch business, let me tell you. I thought I'd won big-time when I landed him, but after sliding a ring onto my finger he relegated me to Eternal Second Place.

When I'm alone or when I might as well be because he's ignoring me in favor of spending quality time with his computer, I at least have the reprieve of letting my smile fall. I don't have to waste energy pretending I'm fine. I don't let myself indulge the dark, intrusive thoughts for too long, even though I want to, because I'm afraid once I start going full Morrissey, fixing the wall with a thousand-yard stare and reflecting on what exactly makes me unhappy, it will become impossible to fold those thoughts up and put them neatly in a drawer to reexamine another day.

I tune in to Nicholas's tangent long enough to grasp a few keywords: *Stacy, khaki ban, gas gauge*. He has found a way to combine his three favorite gripes into one blustery rant. He hates the new uniform policy his coworker Dr. Stacy Mootispaw is trying to implement, which is black slacks only and forbids his darling khakis. He hates Stacy. He hates his fancy car's gas gauge, which has been wrongfully blamed for not warning him when he ran out of gas last week while driving out of town.

I make a sympathetic expression and assure him Stacy is the scum of the earth and the khaki ban is discrimination. I'm a loyal fiancée, indignant on his behalf, ready to go into battle against his every grievance.

I think about how *actress* is another way of saying *professional liar*.

I'm lying to both of us all the time now, and I don't know how to stop. Our wedding is in three months and if I spill my guts to Nicholas about these mini bursts of panic he'll attribute them to cold feet, which is said to be normal. He'll write off everything I'm feeling with those two words. I haven't been excited about this wedding since it was taken away from me, all the decisions yanked from my hands, and knowing I'm not excited makes me anxious. If I'm not excited to get married, then what the hell am I doing?

But my problem is bigger than his interfering mother now; more than the age-old argument about where to go on our honeymoon and the size of the cake, which I no longer care about because I didn't get my way with lemon. *No one likes lemon,*

Naomi. I've been stewing in all the ways I've been wronged for so long now that my simmering resentment has outgrown itself to taint everything about him, even the innocent parts. In spite of everything, I'm such a caring person that I bottle up my negative feelings and don't share them with him. He'd never understand, anyway.

If he asks me what's wrong and my issue isn't one he can make go away with a few reassuring words, Nicholas gets frustrated. It reminds me of my mother once saying that you can't tell men about your unfixable problems, because they'll want to fix them and not being able to do so fries their wiring.

Is my problem unfixable? I don't know what my problem is. I'm the problem, probably. There are a lot of good things about Nicholas, which I have typed up in a password-protected document on my computer. I read it whenever I need to be reminded that Everything Is Okay.

I want to swallow a magic pill that makes me feel perfectly content. I want to gaze lovingly at Nicholas while he haplessly searches the bowels of our kitchen cabinets. We've cohabited for ten months and he still doesn't know where we keep anything.

Our names look so romantic together on paper. Nicholas and Naomi Rose. Have you ever heard anything lovelier? We'd give our children romantic *N* names, too, and make it a theme. A son named Nathaniel. His grandparents will call him Nat, which I'll hate. A daughter named Noelle. Her middle name will have to be Deborah after Mrs. Rose, because apparently it's a tradition going back exactly one generation. Nicholas's sister has been told the same thing, so if we all fall in line there's going to be a dynasty of small Deborahs someday.

I close my eyes and try to imagine growing up as that woman's biological daughter, and the picture is so horrific that I have to bleach it with happy thoughts of another contender for my heart—Rupert Everett in character as Dr. Claw from the 1999 *Inspector Gadget* movie—bursting through the doors of St. Mary's and fighting Jake Pavelka to decide who gets to marry me. One of them has a robotic claw, so it isn't a fair fight. "Not so fast!" shouts another voice. I look up to see Cal Hockley, *Titanic*'s misunderstood hero, rappelling down from the ceiling with the Heart of the Ocean clamped between his teeth. "This is for you, Naomi! The only woman worthy of it!" Nicholas shouts in protest, turning away from the altar, and promptly falls through a trapdoor.

With conscious effort, I look at Nicholas and try to make myself feel butterflies. He's responsible. We like the same movies. He's a good cook. I love these things about the man.

"Naomi," he's saying now, banging cupboards. "Where do we keep the Tupperware? I'm going to run to the store and get some cookies to drop off at the office tomorrow. How nice is that? I'm not even working. Nobody else swings by just to drop off snacks." Rise and Smile is usually closed on weekends, but once a month on a designated Saturday a few of them have to come in. To take out the sting of working on their day off, they all bring in snacks. "I want to make it look like I baked them myself," he continues, "or I'll never hear the end of it. Stacy says I never go the extra mile. I'll show her an extra fucking mile."

I do an unforgivable thing here and privately agree with Stacy. Nicholas does not go the extra mile, especially when it comes to me. He didn't get me flowers this past Valentine's Day, and that's okay because flowers are stupid, I guess. He reminded me that they're just going to die. On Valentine's Day we sat in separate rooms and tagged each other in gushing Facebook posts. We don't need to say sweet words in person because we know what Real Love is.

We have smarter things to spend our money on than over-priced jewelry (if the jewelry's for me) and plants that will slowly wilt for a week before turning to sludge (again: if they're for me). We could be putting that money toward something better, like a tennis bracelet and an entire garden for his mother.

He didn't get me flowers for our anniversary, either, and that's okay because we know what Real Love is and we don't have to prove ourselves to each other. He buys flowers for his mother while she recovers from a facelift because she expects it, but I'm reasonable. I understand. I know I don't need them, whereas Mrs. Rose *does* need them. He's so glad we'll never be like his parents.

On our anniversary, we don't even have to go out on a real date or take the day off work to be together, not marking the occasion in any way. We're relaxed and laid-back, nothing like his parents. Our love is so Real that we can sit on the couch and watch football like the day is no big deal, like it's just any other day. Every day is the same. Every day is like our anniversary.

Words are bubbling up in my throat. I push them down, struggle to find different ones. "Cabinet over the microwave."

"Thanks. Actually, do you have time to make cookies tonight? Stacy'll be able to tell if I haven't made them. I don't want to hear her bitch."

I give him a contemptuous look he doesn't see. "No. I'm going to Brandy's."

"So am I, but we've got plenty of time until then, don't we? And I need to jump in the shower, while you're not doing anything but sitting on the couch. Can you just whip up some cookies real quick?"

"Can't you just do it yourself tomorrow? Why do you need them right this minute, anyway?"

He's preheating the oven. He doesn't even know if we have all the right ingredients. He assumes I'll cobble it together from scratch like Cinderella's mice. "I'm not getting up at the crack of dawn to make three dozen cookies. It's easier to do it tonight." His voice lowers to a grumble. "Stacy's lucky I'm even doing this much, since I'm not even scheduled for tomorrow . . . we'll see how she likes taking her Saturday turn, for *once*."

I stare at Nicholas and my intestines boil because he thinks I don't know what he's doing. The only reason he's choosing to shower *right now* is so that he has an excuse to ask me to do this for him. It's like whenever we get home from a trip to the grocery store and he pretends he's getting an important phone call so that he doesn't have to help put groceries away.

He's pulling out mixing bowls, and that man is even more deluded than I am if he thinks I'm filling a sink up with mixing bowls I'll have to wash in order to feed someone he despises, while he takes the credit. Stacy can choke on store-bought sugar cookies like the rest of us. Why's he even bringing them? They're dentists. They should be eating celery.

I consider trying to persuade him to stay home tonight, but it occurs to me that I need him to drive me to Brandy's. I won't be able to take a crack at changing my tire until he leaves the house for a considerable period of time. I'm miffed with him for being such an I-told-you-so kind of person, which prevents me from coming clean. I'm forced to be just as stubborn as he is irritating.

"I bet if you told your mom you needed cookies, she'd have them ready for you in twenty minutes," I reply lazily. "In the shape of big red hearts, with your initials written in the icing."

"Speaking of Mom," he says, clearing his throat. "She was telling me how she talked to the seamstress about the flower girl's dress, making sure the measurements were right. And we were both so glad, we were just so glad, that they're able to help us out." I feel my soul shrivel up like dust and go *poof.* "Everyone knows it's usually the bride's parents who pay for everything, so we're lucky Mom and Dad have been so helpful."

Yes, so helpful. An image of my wedding dress pops into my head, one size too small because my future mother-in-law wants me to be ambitious, A-line and starchy, whiter than her husband's new veneers. I wanted cream and rose with an empire waist, which she said made me look four months pregnant. Nicholas told her we're saving ourselves for marriage because she's ridiculously old-fashioned and has to be coddled and lied to, and when she told me I looked pregnant I was sorely tempted to say it was twins.

I walked out of the bridal shop that day traumatized and broke, three thousand dollars charged to my credit card. To keep my integrity I insisted we split the costs, so Mrs. Rose paid the other three thousand. *Six thousand dollars for one dress.* I'm haunted by the scarlet word stamped in bold on the plastic sack that suffocates six thousand dollars' worth of material that will make it impossible for me to eat during the reception (which was the part I was most looking forward to): NON-REFUNDABLE.

Also, they offered their daughter Heather, who lives out of state and who I will meet for the first time on the day of my wedding, the role of maid of honor. When this made me upset, I was told that she's going to be my sister-in-law, so who else should the role go to? Brandy, my closest friend, was crushed when I told her.

Something else Heather gets for my wedding is a cream-and-rose empire-waist gown, just like all the other bridesmaids who hail from his side of the family.

Nicholas wants me to suck it up and endure being trampled just like he's learned to do, and raising a stink even to defend myself would be inconvenient for him. I've endured so much awfulness for the sake of keeping the peace that I ought to qualify for sainthood. I haven't voiced my resistance or my anger but I know he feels it, because he sure does love to avoid me these days. He dawdles at work after hours. He's at his parents' house more than our own. When he *is* home, it's like he can't wait for our minimal togetherness time to be over so he can scurry off to his study and hunch over the computer until bedtime. In my head I've named his computer Karen, after Plankton's computer wife on *SpongeBob*.

Nicholas's parents have money out the wazoo and they've thrown a lot of it at this wedding. I don't care what Nicholas says, they're not doing it to be nice or because they like me. I'm the uterus that will be carrying future Roses, interchangeable with Nicholas's ex-girlfriends.

Every step of the way, his parents have reminded me of how lucky I am to have their help, and how high the costs have been. I don't need the best champagne in the country served at my wedding. I'd be fine with wine from a box. No, no, only the best for their Nicky.

Don't you worry, Nicky. Mommy and Daddy will take care of it. I know Naomi's parents can't. Mr. Westfield was pushed out of his job, wasn't he? And Mrs. Westfield is just a school-teacher! How quaint. Mr. and Mrs. Westfield can barely afford the gas and the cost of their plates, the poor dears. Now remember, Naomi, don't slouch. Find a different expression, please. Maybe you should change your face altogether. Is that the color eyes you're going with? You're sure? You're wearing heels, aren't you? No, not *those* heels. Those are stripper heels. You're going to be a Rose, dear. That name means something. Sit up straight. Don't fidget with your ring. You're just like a daughter to us, we love you so much. Come stand directly behind us in this family portrait and suck in your stomach.

There's a smorgasbord of bullshit here to detest, but I think the thing I hate the most about Mr. and Mrs. Rose is that they still call their son Nicky. He won't even let me call him Nick. When they're not calling him Nicky and kissing his cheeks like he's five years old, they're calling him Dr. Rose and photocopying his dentist certificates to hang in their own study. They're vicarious dentists and lecture their friends about gum disease.

I can't possibly back out now. Everyone would be gossiping about me, spreading rumors. I'd look like a failure and an idiot. I'd have wasted thousands of dollars. There's no exit strategy, so I'm holding my breath and winging it.

I look at Nicholas and realize I am actually marrying this man. Forty percent because I love him and sixty percent because I'm too afraid to call it off. Everyone, including his parents, said we'd never make it down the aisle. I have so much pride that I'll do it just to prove them wrong.

"Fine, then, don't help me," Nicholas huffs, hurling an irritated look at me. I've ruined his evening. Stupendous. "I'll be rushed for time and I'm already stressed out, but what else is new?"

"Preach, sister," I mutter under my breath. He grumbles and bangs more cabinets, which gives me an oddly satisfying feeling. Misery loves company, after all. If I'm going to be thinking vindictive thoughts all night, I might as well drag him down into the trenches with me.

CHAPTER THREE

When we park in front of Brandy's, Nicholas sees Zach on the porch and eyes me sideways.

"Great. *That* guy is here," Nicholas mutters. He knows his name, but he's pretending not to. Tonight he'll pretend he doesn't know any of their names, like they're below his notice, as revenge for them not liking him.

Zach isn't doing anything but petting a cat on the porch railing, but I've complained about him ten thousand times to Nicholas for sneaking food from my lunchbox at work and regularly bailing on his shifts without any notice, so as much as I want to argue with every word that comes out of his mouth, I look down at my cards and decide not to play my hand.

"How long do we have to stay?" he grumbles. "Will there be food? I didn't eat before I left. And I don't want to be out late. I have things to do tomorrow." You'd think I forced him to come.

I try to remember what falling in love felt like and can't recall. It must have been over with very quickly.

I think he senses I'm losing my patience because when I slam my door, he doesn't say a word, just stuffs his hands in his pockets and follows slowly like he's on his way to the electric chair.

I have never behaved this way when roles are reversed and we're spending time with Nicholas's friends. I have perpetual purple shadows under my eyes and every time they see me they ask me if I'm sick. Every. Single. Time. One of these friends is an ex of Nicholas's, so I know she's doing it just to screw with me.

Zach's eyes sharpen when they narrow on Nicholas, who's stomping up the driveway with a scowl. Zach stops petting the cat and takes a long swallow of beer, one finger crooking around the glass neck. He never takes his eyes off Nicholas as he drains the whole bottle. "Well, well, well," he says with a smirk. "Look who's gracing us with his presence."

Nicholas tries not to break eye contact first because they're doing some kind of male standoff thing, but he's looking a little unnerved. Zach holds the door open for me, which is the first chivalrous thing I've ever seen him do. He slips in behind me before Nicholas can get up the last step and lets the door swing shut in his face.

I glare at Zach and open the door for my stricken fiancé, who has never been treated so rudely in his life. He will surely call his mother later and tell her all about it. Zach gives me his patented dead-eyed expression, shrugs, and walks into the kitchen without a backward glance.

Nicholas doesn't belong in this part of my life, and we both know it. He's here because he took my laugh as a dare, and he's every bit as spiteful as I am. Game night has lost its joy for me, and I know down to the bottom of my soul that this is going to end badly.

GET OUT HERE NOW, I text Nicholas. It's only been half an hour and he's taken five trips to the bathroom to pet Brandy's cat, which she's stowed away since I'm allergic. His excessive bathroom-lurking is stalling the flow of Cards Against Humanity and people are starting to get annoyed. When he scuttles out of hiding, he's so busy glowering at me that he accidentally steps on one of Brandy's masks that's fallen off the wall, and cracks it.

She has a row of beautiful carved wooden masks of animal faces in her hallway, celebrating her Yup'ik heritage. Most are of animals you'd find in Alaska, like bears, seals, and wolves. It's been her lifelong dream to move to southwest Alaska, where her parents are from, and we routinely scroll through real estate websites hunting for the sort of house we want her to live in. In the meantime, she's tried to give her house an Alaskan feel with cedar furniture and a faux fireplace.

"Way to go," says Zach.

Nicholas blushes, tugging a hand through his hair to cup the back of his neck. "I'm so sorry. What, uh, what is this thing? I'll replace it for you."

If Brandy's upset, she hides it well. "No worries. With a little wood glue, it'll be good as new!" She plucks up the mask and hurries away into the kitchen.

"I can pay for a replacement. How much did it cost?"

"Let him pay you," Zach encourages. "It's the least he could do. Wow, Doc, you really wanna leave, huh? Coming in here and breaking shit."

"It was an accident," I hiss, rubbing Nicholas's shoulder. Nicholas tenses and shifts aside. I notice that Melissa witnessed this, so I step closer to Nicholas again.

"No worries!" Brandy sings again, looking a bit frantic. "It's all good. Let's get back to the game." She takes her job as hostess very seriously, so she's eager to smooth this over. Nicholas could step on every mask she owns and she'd smile and apologize for leaving them out on the walls where anybody could step on them. "Is everyone having fun? Yeah? This is fun!"

Nicholas's eyes dart between Zach and Melissa, who trade whispers and grins. I'm not close enough to hear what they're saying, but Nicholas is. His jaw clenches.

Melissa giggles. Her eyes fall to Nicholas's polished loafers and she makes a low comment to Zach. I don't hear his entire reply, but he makes sure the last three words are audible. *Trying too hard.*

"How's that tooth?" Nicholas asks him in a tone that is not at all nice. Zach once went to Nicholas for a toothache, and when he said a root canal would be necessary it blew up into this whole ordeal with "Dentists just want people's money!" and "Dentists exaggerate minor problems to defraud insurance companies!" Someone in the waiting room recorded six minutes of the tirade and put it on the Internet, then linked it to Rise and Smile's Yelp page. My fiancé and coworker are now low-grade nemeses.

Zach gives him a disingenuous smile. "All better." Not true. Zach has refused to go back to the dentist and can no longer chew on the right side of his mouth. "I went to Turpin, which is where I recommend everyone go."

"Hey, I have an idea," I say. "Let's get back to the game."

Melissa ignores me. "The people at Turpin are more professional," she says.

Zach nods. "And not self-important quacks."

Brandy's starting to sweat. "Let's . . . ah . . . let's all get along. No problems, okay? Whose turn is it?" She sounds like a harried preschool teacher.

"I don't have a problem," Melissa says sweetly. Her stare cuts to Nicholas. "Do you have a problem?"

Zach looks elated. He loves drama and definitely wants someone to have a problem.

Nicholas's face darkens as he grows quiet. A storm cloud above my head begins to rotate, sucking all of my energy. When I want him around, he's never there. When I don't want him around, he's the devil on my shoulder. If he gets into a fight with my friends, my work life is going to suck. Will he care? No.

We're playing Clue at the kitchen table when Nicholas makes his next move. His ego is all bruised and battered now, so it was only a matter of time before he struck back.

He turns to Melissa. Cocks his head. "Didn't you use to go out with Seth Walsh?"

He knows damn well that Melissa used to date Seth. He also knows that Seth cheated on her with a married dental hygienist who works with him. Rise and Smile is a hotbed of scandal.

Melissa glares at him, then me. "Yeah."

"Hmm. Why'd you break up, again?"

Cyclops from X-Men has nothing on the burning fury in Melissa's stare. "We broke up," she says venomously, "because I was walking out of the West Towne Mall one day and I saw Seth's car in the parking lot. When I went over there, he was in

the back seat screwing another woman." She doesn't add it, but
we all think of the rest: *On top of Melissa's Lawrence University
sweater.*

I vividly remember the day she discovered them. At that
point, I'd been working at the Junk Yard, a shop of eclectic finds,
for roughly three months and Melissa and I were friendly. We
bonded over our mutual loathing of Zach's playlist, which he
subjects us to on Wednesdays when it's his turn to control the
music, as well as owning the same checkered shirt and red jeans,
which we used to purposefully wear on the same day.

I haven't worn my checkered shirt together with my red
jeans since our falling out, because I don't want her to think I
pine for the good old days when she didn't vibrate with fury at
the sight of me. *How could you not have known? Nicholas's BFF
getting it on with Nicholas's own coworker! He had to have known,
and he would've told you about it. You let me make a fool of myself
over that guy and didn't say anything.* I truly didn't know Seth
was cheating and still feel guilty for introducing them. Nicholas
says he didn't know, either, but I can't make any promises on
that front.

"Seth's an asshole," Zach says, rolling the die and moving
one space short of the kitchen door. The murder weapon has got
to be the rope, which is the only clue I've worked out. Zach's
going to guess everything correctly. He has a superhuman knack
for this game and won the previous two rounds as soon as he
edged his little Colonel Mustard game piece into a room.

Nicholas, who wouldn't play unless he got to be Professor
Plum, cuts Zach a dirty look. "You don't even know Seth, so
don't talk about him. He's my friend."

"Doesn't say much about you, then." Zach is honestly fearless and he will tell you exactly what he thinks about you, right to your face. It's a quality I find nerve-racking when I'm on the receiving end of it, and right now I'm somewhere between reveling in watching someone stand up to Nicholas and embarrassment that my personal guest is about to ruin this party. I forget to be an actress who pretends to be one hundred percent in love, and Nicholas glances at me, noting my silence, before turning his stare to Zach.

"What's that supposed to mean?"

Zach is a shark. "I mean that you choose asshole friends, and that reflects poorly on you."

Across the table, Brandy fidgets with her Miss Scarlet figurine and Leon's eyes flash to mine.

"Obviously, Melissa's still upset about Seth cheating," Zach continues. "You could easily keep your mouth shut, since you know she has every right to be upset, but instead you rush to his defense. There's a reason you're empathizing with the asshole, and that's because you see yourself in him. Ergo, you're also an asshole."

You could hear a fly land on the wall.

I'm supposed to reach for my poor fiancé's hand. Tell Zach to shut up. Declare that we're leaving. But Nicholas's expression makes me pause.

His mouth is pursed as he prepares his rebuttal, and he looks around the room with palpable disdain. He's seeing himself as the successful son of two wealthy pillars of this bite-size community, rescuing the oversugared population of Morris one cavity filling at a time. He's seeing my coworkers as lowly maggots crawling through the detritus at the bottom of the trash heap. They work at the Junk Yard, which sells alligator heads and novelty whoopee cushions with Whoopi Goldberg's face on them. Mexican jumping beans and mugs that say swear words when you fill them with hot water. When he judges my peers and finds them lacking, he forgets that I'm one of them. To Nicholas, it's Us versus Them.

Brandy looks anxious. She's so sweet and bubbly that I doubt she's ever seriously argued with anyone in her life, and people not getting along is the worst thing that can happen right in front of her.

"Zach," I belatedly warn through gnashed teeth.

"Can you try to get along with everybody?" Brandy implores him. "Does anyone want more pizza rolls? I have cupcakes, too. Everyone have everything they need?" She half rises from her chair. "Water? Soda?"

Zach pushes her back into her seat with two fingers on her shoulder. "I'm getting along with everybody just fine. Your turn."

Brandy's hand trembles as she rolls the die, and Nicholas is all finished deciding what vulgar thing he wants to say to Zach.

"I understand why you're so emotional. Having no real job security would put anyone on edge. Your store doesn't get more than, what, three customers a day? You've got to be hemorrhaging money." He flashes the same disingenuous smile that Zach has been giving him all evening. "When you're ready, I know a guy at the temp agency who can help you."

Zach raises two eyebrows at me, like we're sharing a private joke Nicholas isn't in on, then says to him, "You're aware that your girlfriend works at the same place I do, right? If it closes, we're not the only ones out of a job."

"I make plenty of money. Naomi doesn't need a job."

Anger steams off me like ultraviolet rays.

"The store's doing fine," I say, which is a big fat lie. The store's on its last wheezes. It's been around forever, since Mr. and Mrs. Howard got married in the seventies, and at one time was widely popular because we specialize not only in gag gifts but in bizarre curiosities. People used to make our store a road trip destination. But ever since the dawn of Amazon and eBay, you don't need to go out of your way to find weird, cultish knick-knacks. With one click, you can have them delivered right to your door.

Mr. and Mrs. Howard know they can't compete with online shopping, which is why our hours have been steadily scaling back and they finally sold their beloved Homer-Simpson-as-Elvis statue, who's been greeting customers in the doorway since 1997. They're so kindhearted that they can't bear to down-size the staff, even though two of us could easily be running the Junk Yard for them instead of five.

There's barely enough work to go around for everybody, and we're all desperate for more hours. The phrase *last to be hired, first to be fired* follows me around like the Ghost of Christmas Future.

"The store's on the brink of collapse," Nicholas says flippantly, waving his hand. "Won't affect you, Naomi. You'll be fine."

Brandy makes a strangled sound. "What do you mean, it won't affect her? Naomi loves the Junk Yard."

Nicholas says nothing, just taps his cards into a neat stack. It's the last straw.

"If the Junk Yard closes, I might ask the Howards if they'll hire me to work at their diner." Mr. and Mrs. Howard run a year-round haunted house up in Tenmouth as well as a diner for strange foods inspired by horror films, called Eaten Alive.

Everyone stares at me. The vein in Nicholas's forehead pulses. "Isn't that a long drive from here?"

It's perfect timing that I get to roll the die while I dramatically say, "Two hours."

His voice is deadpan. "You'd drive two hours to go to work. At a *diner.* Then two hours back home, every day."

"Mm." I pretend to consider. "If I move to Tenmouth, it would only be a five-minute drive. I could ride my bicycle, even."

I've captured the whole room, and it's magnificent. A sparkle of the old Naomi Westfield appears, blowing off ten months' worth of dust. At least, I think it's her. It's been so long since that Naomi and I have been in the same room together that I'm not sure I'd recognize her if we passed each other on the street.

My minuscule Mrs. White is in the library now next to Leon's Mr. Green, ready to accuse someone of murder. She's got a length of rope, and I pick over my options to see who I'm going to hang with it.

My eyes fall upon the pompous little fucker loitering in the billiard room.

Bingo. Professor Plum.

This Professor Plum is a particularly hypocritical incarnation who warns children away from sugary snacks while letting Skittles pool all over his side of the bed on a nightly basis. He's a villain escaped from Candy Land. He's the thief of my joy and future father of my children. Right now I love him twenty percent.

Nicholas's tone is frozen solid. "My life is here. I'm not moving to Tenmouth and giving up my life for you to serve grilled cheese to truckers, Naomi."

When he calls me Naomi, he definitely means Mrs. Nicholas. The diamond on my left hand is too tight, cutting off my circulation. The twenty percent shrinks to a ten, an all-time low that trips my self-preservation sirens. They're flashing and spinning, *Red alert! Red alert!*

"I want to make an accusation," I say at the precise moment he says with smooth authority, "I think we should call it a night." But my guess might end the game, so he waits and listens.

I draw it out, just to antagonize him. He hates when I let two ends of a sentence drift apart. "I accuse . . ."

Nicholas leans forward.

I pick up his game piece and float him over to the library. He'll like it there, where he can stock shelves with books about brushing your teeth in circular motions instead of from side to side. "Professor Plum."

Brandy gasps. Melissa scribbles furiously on her detective notepad. Zach's eyes glint with malevolent joy. Nicholas just looks annoyed. But Leon, I see, is smiling. Just barely, but enough that when my eyes rest on him, he gives me an interesting look.

It says *So this is where you've been.*

In a strong, bold voice, I march on: "I accuse Professor Plum of murder! He did it in the library, like a pretentious asswit, and he used the candlestick." I know it's not the candlestick because I've got that card myself, but I throw it in there anyway because: "It's the stupidest possible weapon."

Nicholas stares deeply into my eyes for an eternal spiral of time, and it's entirely possible that we are going to break up over a board game, which would be a hell of a way to go out. His mother's going to have a bonanza getting all her deposits back. The opportunity to call up small-business owners and yell that they'd better not charge her for an ice sculpture of roses will be the cherry on top of her year.

"Go on, then." His eyes don't leave mine as he jerks his chin to the center of the board. I realize that I've fallen asleep on the color of Nicholas's eyes, which for whatever reason I've been thinking are gray. Up close, fierce with challenge, they're every color of the rainbow.

Oblivious that I'm having an epiphany, he glares and his irises darken from pale silver to forest green like a mood ring. "Check the cards."

I do so as slowly and theatrically as possible, warming up to the old Naomi. He wants so badly to knock over his Professor Plum figurine and cross his arms, but he's trying to remain civilized. Dentists already have a bad reputation with phobics and he can't afford any more negative press, even among the crawling maggots of Junk Yard personnel.

I check the cards and let out a hiss. Zach looks at me knowingly.

Mrs. White, in the kitchen, with the rope.

"Well, wouldn't you know it! Looks like I'm the murderer," I say cheerfully. "Didn't think I had it in me." Nicholas casts me a distrusting look. I think he's going to be sleeping with one eye open tonight.

———

The worst part about this whole evening is how quickly Nicholas forgets it.

We're at home now, where I'm still irritated and he isn't. The man is baking cookies, and he's promised to wash up all the dishes, and now I have nowhere to point my anger because he's Over It, which means he's won.

He offers me a spatula to lick, which I refuse because maybe his trick is to use salmonella to kill me, and he plants a sloppy kiss on my hair and breaks away smiling down at me like I'm an innocent child.

He knows I can't argue with him now, because if I dredge up anything negative I'll look petty. So I stay in my well-worn position on the sofa (far right), where I've logged a thousand hours pretending to watch television and pretending to listen to Nicholas and pretending to be happy.

I snap a picture of him with his back turned to me and post it to my Instagram with a rosy filter. I caption it with three hearts and *Game night with my love! No better way to cap off an awesome day, and there's no one else I'd rather spend it with. xoxo. #LivinTheLife #MarryingMyBestFriend #TrueLovesKissFromARose*

#TrueLovesKissFromARose is our wedding hashtag and if you look it up on Pinterest you'll find one million pictures of bouquets, table settings, and bridesmaid dresses that I like (but am not allowed to have). Dopamine trickles in with the first response to my post: *omg you guys are so cute*; but the plush, pillowy feeling grinds down to metal on metal when Zach replies with *lmao. yeah right*. I delete his comment.

It's my own fault that I'm still in this mess, and I know it. I'm the biggest coward I've ever met. I'm doing neither of us a favor by refusing to back out. If Nicholas had half a brain he'd be calling it off, too, so maybe we're locked in some silent draw, waiting to see who bows out first.

I know why he won't. His mother's been nagging him to marry and give her grandchildren to rank from most to least favorite, depending on whose physical features our unfortunate progeny inherit. If Nicholas jumps ship now, Deborah will revert back to nagging him to procreate using the frozen, ten-year-old eggs of her friend from tennis, Abigail, who died a year ago and for whatever ungodly reason left her eggs to the Rose family. Heather, Nicholas's sister, is to be the incubator for this abomination of a child.

I can't jump ship, either. I've been shouting to the world that I'm perfectly happy in my perfect relationship, and if I run now I'm going to look like a fraud.

Aside from that, Mrs. Rose has hinted more than once that if I back out, she'll bill me for her troubles. If I leave her son, she'll undoubtedly take me to small claims court to be reimbursed for Swarovski crystal candleholders customized with the letter *R* (*everything* has been custom-ordered to feature the letter *R*), which I wasn't involved in picking out. I don't have a ton of savings, but I do have a little bit tucked away, and I'll defend it with teeth and nails.

"Mom's still going on and on about the prenup," Nicholas is saying from the next room. Maybe we've been here all evening and my imagination made up going to Brandy's. I'm sitting in the same spot, while staring at the same spot, and that uneasy churning in the pit of my stomach is a third, invisible member of our party. It materializes reliably whenever we talk about the wedding.

"I told her no way," he continues when I don't respond. "She and Dad never got one. Why should we? It's not like you'd ever leave me."

Nicholas loves to congratulate himself for not getting a prenuptial agreement. He thinks about it all the time, which I know because he won't stop bringing it up. He's waiting for me to jump in with a pat on the back, but I leave him hanging.

"Mandy's haircut looks awful," Nicholas remarks, darting a shrewd glance at me. "Those bangs. Ugh."

He knows her name is Brandy. I mention her at least once a day. I'm smoking at the ears not just over this, but because I had bangs when Nicholas and I met. He says all the time how pretty I was, and how he fell for me immediately, and yet for about a year now he's reminded me every time he sees a woman with bangs how much he loathes them.

"They look cute on her," I say defensively. It's true. Brandy's got these quirky piece-y bangs for her shag cut and she pulls it off so well. Her hair's always top notch. She experiments a lot with colors, and the style of the month is a mesmerizing blend of black and garnet. When she stands outside, the effect that sunlight has on her stunning hair belongs in a commercial. She never leaves the house without a full face of flawless makeup, and is the only person I know who can pull off a combination of electric blue liner, orange ombre eyeshadow, and fuchsia lipstick.

He whistles a low, innocent tune. It feels like *If you say so.*

I'm losing it so quietly that I am almost not even here. In my mind, I click the file on my computer that notes a list of Nicholas's positive attributes, running through each memorized line. They've lost their power to impress, I think because I've reread them so many times that I've become desensitized.

Nicholas holds the umbrella for me and makes sure I don't get wet. When it's raining and we park, he sidles up so that my passenger door opens to the sidewalk and not the muddy, grassy part of the curb. He has my order at all our restaurants mentally bookmarked, so he can recite exactly what I want to the waiter while I'm in the bathroom.

He has thick, beautifully rumpled chocolate-brown hair and

he gets side-eyed by a lot of women whenever we go out. He says my eyes are the color of champagne, which became his favorite drink after we met for that very reason, and I had a wonderfully bubbly, fizzy sensation course through my veins whenever he smiled at me.

He likes dogs. Not enough to get one, but enough to chuff a laugh while I kneel to pet someone else's dog, just before he says jokingly, "Don't get any ideas."

He doesn't sneakily watch our favorite shows without me. If a song comes on the car radio that he hates, he doesn't automatically change the station but first asks if I like it. He still wears a pair of socks with a poodle print that I got for him when we were first dating, even though it was a joke gift.

These might sound like minor traits, or even givens that I should take for granted, but I hold on to them like life preservers.

I love these things about the man. But I do not love the man.

I know this with all of my heart, sitting here in the house we live in together, the countdown to our wedding ticking louder and louder with each passing day. A doomsday clock. He and I are going to be a disaster, but whenever I think of taking proactive steps to avert the disaster, my tongue rolls up and my limbs paralyze. I can't speak out. I can't be the one to end this.

If he has a list about me, I'm sure it's much shorter. I have no idea what I'm bringing to our relationship right now aside from the fact that I'm keeping dead Abigail's frozen eggs at bay.

Thinking about this is prodding the wound, making it bigger, making it worse because I'm growing more aware of the breadth of my anxiety, the depth of my dissatisfaction. It is both therapy and torture. Something is not right. Something is missing. I am in knots.

I have no right to feel this unhappy, and I wish Nicholas were inarguably horrid so I could justify leaving. I fantasize about happening upon him with a dental hygienist in the back of his car at a shopping mall.

He thinks our relationship is perfect, or so he says. It's what I say to people, too. He tells everybody that I'm great. He thinks I adore him. We're the only ones who know what Real Love is.

"What do you want for dinner tomorrow?" I ask in a tone that sounds like I love him. It's an effort, and I'm exhausted.

"You pick."

"Chicken tacos."

"I was thinking stir-fry," he replies, and I know it's utterly unfair but my ten percent drops to nine. At this stage of the game, it takes nothing at all to dock points. If he breathes too loudly in his sleep tonight he'll wake up to a score of negative fifty. Keeping points like this is terrible. I'm terrible. Our relationship might be the worst thing that's ever happened to me, but when I go over it while in a positive frame of mind, it doesn't look that bad, so then I'm unsure.

How did I fall in love with Nicholas? How did we even meet? I can't remember anything good because it's been overshadowed by the intense dislike I feel now. Maybe we met on a dating app. Maybe I was getting a crown put on. Maybe we were both walking briskly around a street corner from opposing sides and ran into each other like something from a movie, loose papers and to-go cups and my purse clashing in the air. All I know is that a few months ago I woke up from a very long sleep and discovered I was engaged to someone I can barely stand.

"Sweetie," he says, which is what he calls me when it's payday or his favorite team won or he knows he's screwed up and needs to grovel. "I forgot to say. Mom had an appointment with the florist earlier and she wanted me to tell you she's changing it from delphiniums to carnations or something like that." He waves his hand in a circle. "You'd probably know better than me. Flowers are more important to women."

"You don't think I might have wanted a say in the type of flowers we have at our wedding?" I reply. "What about you? Don't you want a say?"

Nicholas blinks at me. There's an emotion hiding in his eyes, and I try to identify it before he turns his head to a sharper angle and it vanishes.

"It's already settled. She picked carnations, since you were so ridiculously adamant that it not be roses. Or do you think it's not too late to make changes? Think hard, Naomi. Anything you want to back out of?"

"What do you mean by that?"

"What do you *think* I mean by that?"

My eyes narrow. "Are you suggesting I back out of the carnations even though you literally just said that we're already settled on the carnations?"

"Maybe I'm not talking about carnations at all."

My spine snaps straight and I hold his stare, picking that emotion back to his surface. And I realize.

He's fraying my ropes.

"Oh?"

Nicholas lifts his shoulder. Lets it drop. "We could talk about anything. What do you say, Naomi? Anything you want to get off your chest?" He waits patiently for a response, but all I can do is stare at him. My mind is going a zillion miles an hour, zinging from revelation to revelation. I can't believe I've been so dense.

All along I've thought Mrs. Rose has been pulling the strings, but it's been Nicholas, using Deborah's nails-on-a-chalkboard powers to drive me to the point where I'll call this off. I'll be the crazy ex-girlfriend who snapped; I'll be at fault for everything and responsible for the steep costs of a broken engagement and lavish wedding. Everyone will feel bad for him because of what he had to undergo, jilted at the altar.

I can see him now, chin held high. *I just want her to be happy,* he'll say. A garden of Roses will sigh breathlessly and wonder how any angel could be so composed in such a dreadful situation. He'll screw up his eyes and think about that time a guy in a truck clipped his car, and squeeze out a single tear.

For the space of a heartbeat, I see our situation through his eyes. If I end this and he gets to pretend to mourn the death of our relationship, he can easily milk that for at least a year. A year of Deborah not riding his ass over giving her grandchildren because "the wounds are still fresh." Everyone around him will bend over backward to accommodate him. If *he* ends it, on the other hand, I'll come out of this looking golden. I won't be at fault; no one will call me a fraud. If anything, I'll gain sympathy points. People will say *How could he let you go?* and *If you ever need to talk to someone, I'm here.*

When you build a life with someone, so many of your building blocks prop up your partner, and you're propped up by theirs, until your foundations merge and walking away risks destabilization for you both. We have joint checking and savings accounts. Our phones are on the same plan. Both of our names are on the lease, and it stands to reason that whoever bails forfeits the house. His parents have invested in me, grooming me into Mrs. Rose material. We have obligations together. Long-term plans. I can't cut a line between Nicholas and me and float away free, because we have tangles.

Yes. I look at him and for once, I can see outside my own cloud of resentment long enough to see that he's got one of his own. He's perceptive, all right. He's already known for some time what I'm feeling. I'm not a good actress after all.

Our love percentage plummets to zero and a tremor shudders through the floor. Tiles and furniture tip into a crevice that snakes all the way down to the earth's core, separating kitchen and living room, him and me. The truth is plain, unfolding before us, but as usual I am late to catch on because I've been holding it all in and trying to rationalize away my gut instincts. Focused on myself, so wrapped up in trying to hide that I don't even notice which moves he's making.

My engagement to Nicholas Rose is a game of chicken.

CHAPTER FOUR

It's day one of being clued in on the fact that I'm locked in a battle of wills, and I'm lagging behind. Nicholas has enjoyed a leisurely stretch of uninterrupted time surveying our battlefield while I grapple blindly like a video game character stuck in a glitch. He's been strolling along, hands clasped behind his back, burying land mines with finesse. He's going to win this, like he wins everything. I think of his gold Maserati and my Saturn sharing curb space.

I groan and nearly give in when I sit up in bed and pluck off the Skittle he's left half-melted to my arm, leaving behind colorful mermaid scales. Nicholas doesn't work today but he's gone somewhere else after dropping off those stupid cookies, probably off to braid his mother's hair. Does he even eat the Skittles or does he simply dump them there, trying to piss me off?

I'm tempted to pack my bags and go right now, but that would be playing into what he wants. If anyone's going to pay

Deborah back for three hundred customized champagne flutes with *N & N* on them, it's going to be him, out of guilt, after he dumps me. Afterward, I'll hock my engagement ring and take a well-deserved honeymoon by myself in celebration. A singlemoon.

I'm thinking of ways I can get him to break first, like withholding sex, but truly I don't think that would faze him. It's been nine weeks since the last time he unenthusiastically gave me the business. If it weren't for the perks of shorter, infrequent periods, my strict adherence to a birth control regimen would be for no purpose whatsoever.

Maybe I can set up a fake online profile to catfish him. When he falls for it I can point at my handiwork and get righteously angry. I'll storm off. His mother will burst into tears. I'll take a picture of the moment and have it framed.

I'm going to blame the Skittles for what happens next.

I troop into the bathroom with a pair of scissors, pull down a hank of hair over my forehead, and snip it off before I can lose my nerve. The eyes in my reflection are wide and maniacal and I love it. I love the Naomi who can do things like this and not give a shit. Nicholas doesn't like bangs? Fantastic. I don't like Nicholas.

I notice my new bangs are slightly crooked, so I snip them to even them out. I end up overcorrecting so I have to snip again, and what I'm left with is not at all like Brandy's cute hairstyle.

I'm left with a sight that makes me mutter, "Ah, fudge."

It's even worse than being a kid and your frugal mom, who only goes to the salon to get her own hair done, puts a bowl over your head and cuts beneath the rim. I look like I got my hair cut by bending too close to a shredder. And there are two layers to the bangs, somehow. If I try to even them out any more it'll be chewed off almost to the scalp.

I stand in my empty house for a minute and listen to the whoosh of car tires spraying through leftover rain, estimating how far ahead of me Nicholas is, how many moves I need to make in order to catch up. I peer outside and observe a suspicious development: my flat tire has pumped up back to life. Either someone changed it for me or I imagined the whole ordeal. Right now, the latter seems more likely.

I see that he didn't wash the dishes like he promised, and I almost admire the evil touch. Neglecting to wash dishes is one thing. Voluntarily saying you're going to do it and then not doing it is an act of hostility.

He has, however, rinsed out his coffeepot, because he's the only one who uses it. More proof that he's being an ass on purpose. I place it back in the sink and decorate it with maple syrup. Then I write a message to him on the whiteboard, telling him I can't wait to marry him. I call him Nicky, which I've never done before, and after I get over the dry heaves that this gives me, I draw two interlocking hearts.

Let's see what you think of that.

Smirking, I tunnel into my closet and emerge from it in the most glorious anti-Nicholas costume I can find: a Steelers hoodie that belonged to my ex-boyfriend. I found it in my drawer two months ago, and I think it was Nicholas's remark that I don't know anything about sports and therefore had no reason to hold on to the hoodie that prompted me to tuck it away for a rainy afternoon.

The hoodie is a middle finger by itself, but to add insult to injury I shimmy into leggings he finds embarrassing because they're so old and worn that they're see-through in places and there's a quarter-sized hole on one butt cheek. These leggings and I have been through a lot together. Breakups. Bad dates. That time Tyra Banks yelled at Tiffany on *America's Next Top Model*. My parents/siblings canceling plans to come visit me, always and without fail, even though they'll gladly spare the time to drive to Florida to watch NASCAR races. These leggings are like comfort food and I'm never giving them up.

I top it off with the sort of makeup that his mother would call "unseemly" or "unbecoming." My lips are the color of fresh blood, making my mouth more eye-catching than the Babadook's. My eyeliner is a thick swoop of black that extends way past its cue, and my eyelids glitter all the way up to my eyebrows like a pageant contestant. It's not enough. I add pounds of blush and bronzer until my face is indistinguishable from a Mardi Gras float. I have bypassed "unseemly" and cannonballed head-first into Deborah's nightmare. I look exactly like her husband's first wife, the notorious Magnolia Rose.

I give myself a round of applause and send up a kiss of thanks to Magnolia Rose, my greatest hero for refusing to stop going by Mrs. Rose after the divorce even though her marriage to Harold only lasted a year and didn't bear any fruit. She's currently living in Key Largo with husband number five, who's twenty years her junior and nephew of the guy who invented Marshmallow Peeps. She has fifteen parrots living in an aviary that's the size of my bedroom and they're all named after murderers on *Law & Order*. I know this because she added me as a Facebook friend, probably to needle Deborah, who has twice tried to sue Magnolia for emotional distress caused by "ruining Harold." I want to be Magnolia Rose when I grow up.

Nicholas will obsess over who I'm wearing this kind of makeup for until it gives him an ulcer. My reflection in the mirror tips her head back and laughs like her skin is about to burst open with a hundred flying demons.

Yesterday I was listless and my favorite thing to do was wallow, but today I crackle with wicked energy. Everything has changed now that I have a plan.

Our wedding is set for January twenty-sixth, so I have three months to wear Nicholas down to a lifeless nub. I'm going to adopt ten dogs and turn Nicholas's study into my Dog Room. It'll be nice to avoid the hassle of getting my address changed at the post office or setting up Internet and cable somewhere new like Nicholas is going to have to do. Sucks to be him! The landlord gave us a great deal and rent is cheap enough that I'll be able to afford it on my own even though the Junk Yard pays peanuts. The economy's in the toilet and I need all the help I can get.

In my mind I hear him sneering: *The store's on the brink of collapse,* and I get an uneasy fluttering in my abdomen. He's wrong. My job's not in jeopardy and I'm going to be fine. If anyone's going to be out of a job, it's him. A new dental practice opened up at the first stoplight, Turpin Family Dentistry, and they accept so many insurance providers that Dr. Stacy Mootispaw has called it "grotesque."

I don't have health insurance, but the cost of paying out of pocket might be worth it to have Nicholas see me go to Turpin's for a cleaning. It's a scenario I dream about while scouring his baked-on veggie pasta from the casserole dish.

To pump up my courage for what I'm about to do next, I listen to three angry Eminem songs and then dial a number I have listed in my contacts as 666. I never call this number. My phone tries to save me by spontaneously shutting off and rebooting, but there's no stopping me now. I'm at least a hundred moves behind Nicholas on our battlefield. I'm surrounded by undetectable explosives and he's frolicking through the wildflowers without a fear in the world. He's been baiting me so long that I don't know how much of his BS is calculated and how much is inadvertent. I'm not sure I know him at all. But I sure as hell know his mother.

"Hello?" says Mrs. Rose.

"Deborah!" I fluff up my tone with sugar and honey, spinning in Nicholas's swivel chair. I'm in his office, where he doesn't like me being because he needs privacy for Calls With Mother. The two of them should run a motel together.

"Naomi?" She sounds uncertain. The third syllable of my name is muted; she's pulled away from the phone to check the caller ID and make sure my voice isn't an auditory hallucination.

"Hope you're not busy," I say with a huge smile on my face. It's Saturday morning. Deborah's got more activities on her calendar than the president, and I'm definitely interrupting something. "I wanted to talk about the floral changes that were made to my wedding without my consent."

I can tell she didn't expect any pushback on this, but she recovers quickly. Her voice is the soothing lullaby of reminding Harold to take his fish oil pill. "I hope you don't mind, dear. The florist couldn't schedule the appointment for any other time, and I didn't want to bother you. I know how busy you are at the . . . oh, I can't remember where it is you go all day. The Dump, it's called?"

"Yes," I say brightly. "The Dump." I burrow under trash

YOU DESERVE EACH OTHER

piles like a gopher. "I never did get that new florist's number from you, after you switched businesses for the third or fourth time. Do you have it handy? I want to tweak a couple of things."

"Tweak?" She sounds startled. "I'm *sure* it's much too late for that. It's all set in stone now."

"Deborah," I laugh. Deborah, Deborah, Deborah. "You saw the florist only yesterday! I'm *sure* she'll be open to listening to the bride. Who is me. I'm the bride." I twirl my villain mustache. I have never been more opposed to being a bride. They'd have to drag my unconscious body up the aisle, a ventriloquist throwing her voice to mimic my vows. "The flowers you picked just aren't my cup of tea."

"Delphiniums are out of season. Carnations will look so lovely at a January wedding."

"Carnations are outdated." All of my instincts are telling me that Deborah and Harold used carnations for their own wedding. "I'm thinking . . ." I see my colorless reflection in the glass of a framed picture on Nicholas's desk. He's six years old and a small fish dangles from his hand. Bluegill. He's smiling so big that his eyes are squinty, cowlick much more prevalent than it is now, two front teeth missing. His mother stands behind his shoulder, long melon-pink nails digging in. I envision her doing the same at our wedding, whispering into his ear.

"Magnolias," I finish.

Foam gurgles from my blood-red Babadook mouth and giddiness overtakes me. It's the closest to joy I've gotten in a long time. I'm going to follow this feeling straight down into hell.

She's so quiet, I have to check to make sure the line hasn't gone dead.

"Deb?" I prompt, biting my knuckles to keep from losing it.

"I don't think Nicky would agree with that choice," she eventually forces out.

"Nicky told me it's fine." I spin my chair again, knees to my chin. The seat is luxurious leather and marvelously comfortable, like sinking into a hot tub. My computer chair is two inches shorter than I'd like and made of wood. I got it from a yard sale. I put a lumpy pillow on it for comfort, but the disparity here is outrageous. This chair is mine now.

"Besides," I add. "It's my wedding, isn't it? I should get what I want."

"It's Nicky's wedding, too."

What does Nicholas care? He's going to marry at least three times in his life. When I'm sixty, I'll bump into him with a comb-over and a twentysomething on his arm, because men are terrible and they can get away with it. "You know what they say," I reply cheerily. "Happy wife, happy life! He'll do whatever it takes to make me happy. He's learned by example, watching how good your husband is to you."

I've never gone against Deborah's orders, even politely. It's easier to let her have her way. This is a brand-new experience for Deborah, and probably for her book club who's listening in. She's sitting opposite the mayor and her entire sorority, straining to keep a smile pasted on while spiritually strangling the breath of life from me. Her nasty habit of putting people on speakerphone so everyone present can share a laugh has come home to roost.

"That number, Deb?" I goad, crossing my feet on Nicholas's desk. A stack of files falls off, fanning across the floor like a royal flush.

"Um. Yes. Let me see." She's floundering. She can't give me

a fake number, but she can't give me the real one. This is not a
bluff and I will absolutely order a billion magnolias to adorn St.
Mary's. Imagine Harold's face when he sees the invoice.

Deborah stalls as she riffles through her Rolodex. I hear her
teeth clink together. I stay completely silent until she gets back
to me and spits out each number.

"Thanks!" I chirp. "While I've got you on here, mind giving
me the baker's number as well? I know I'd originally suggested
Drury Lane in Hatterson, but I believe you chose to go somewhere else? Is that correct? I'm sure you know best. Anyway, I'd
like their contact information, please."

Acid drips from Deborah's mouth. "Why would that be necessary, my dear? I've already gotten the cake taken care of."

"I want to thank you for that. You've been great! Just so
great. With your time, your money. Why don't I take some of the
burden off you? You deserve to relax and enjoy your golden years.
They go by so fast. I'm just going to take over a few moving parts
here and there, and don't you worry about a thing, Deb."

"But—"

"All you've got to do is show up for the wedding. I want you
to have a good time. Can't have a good time if you're busy organizing it all!" If my voice notches up any more octaves it will
become a whistle.

"I don't think Nicky—"

I cut her off. "That number, Deb? Thanks so much." No
one's ever dared to shorten her name to *Deb* in her life and I'm
abusing the unearned privilege with foam dripping down my
chin, soaking the front of my favorite Steelers hoodie.

When Deborah angrily recites the baker's contact informa-
tion, each clipped digit is code for *I'll kill you if it's not vanilla and*

chocolate marble. It inspires me to change the cake topper from our previously tasteful splash of flower petals. Nicholas's groom figure will be the knock-off Spider-Man from the dollar store, Tarantula-Boy. I'll be represented by a half-melted pillar candle with googly eyes, and everyone Deborah knows and loves will have to see. When Nicholas cuts the cake, one of my googly eyes will slide off like an omen. I'll smile at him with my red horror mouth and wild stare that will make him detest the color of champagne for all time, and his blood will curdle.

"Thaaaanks," I trill. "Deb, you're the best."

"I hope Nicky is all right with this," she says darkly.

"Don't you worry about him. I've got our Nicky covered. And soon he'll have his new mother-in-law to fuss over him, too. It's so cute, he was telling me the other day he's going to start calling her Mom after the wedding. My mother will lo-o-ove it."

A phantom hand reaches through the phone and wraps around my throat. "That's nice," she rasps.

"Isn't it? We're spending Thanksgiving with her. And Christmas. Nothing's more important than family, you know."

Deborah's rattled, but she's a pro. She reminds me that she mastered The Art Of Being A Bitch decades prior to my birth by replying, "Oh yes, I quite agree. But I'd reconsider those plans, because on Thanksgiving I was going to cut you both the check for the caterer, and Christmas happens to be the very day my seamstress needs to fit you again. If you don't show up, who knows what might happen? I'd feel just *terrible* if you walked down the aisle in a dress that couldn't zip all the way up."

In my mind's eye I see the bejeweled candelabra centerpieces at the reception hall detonate in an aerosol mist. I'm replacing them with foil confetti and ten-cent plastic doves. Everyone will think the elegant Mrs. Rose in her Louis Vuitton and Marc Jacobs selected it herself and wonder why the décor looks like Valentine's Day favors at a nursing home. They'll gossip that she's filed for bankruptcy.

I let out a short laugh. "That would be a disaster! Good thing I've got a long veil." I've been on my best behavior these past few minutes, but I can't resist throwing in: "See you for Sunday dinner, D."

I end the call and admire my chipped, uneven nails. I do another chair spin. A land mine over in Nicholas's end of the field explodes.

───

It's Sunday and Nicholas cannot believe I still haven't changed out of my best hoodie for dinner at his parents' house. I give him a disapproving look when he mutters under his breath. I'm a loyal fan of the Steelers. They're my favorite sportsball team and I would die for them.

He's still mad about the magnolias. Mrs. Rose tattled on me, crying to him through a sea of sodden handkerchiefs, and he appeased her by promising to keep the carnations and uphold the family name. Magnolias are utterly undignified. I am utterly undignified. He frowns at me to say *You're a disgrace*, but I know his real frown is due to the shrapnel in his leg. I'm a motivated soldier now, outfitted in full tactical gear. I've weaponized his unwitting mother against him: she's been calling him nonstop all day for comfort, and every time the phone rings I see him die a little more inside.

"I can't believe you," he says.

"I can." I sound much happier than he does, even though this is usually the part where he puts on his Good Little Boy grin and I mentally check out so that his family's rude comments have less power over me.

We're in the car on the way to see Debberoni and Harry. They live in the lone quasi-exclusive neighborhood Morris has to offer, big fish in a small pond, just the way they like it. They don't inhabit spaces where they'd let *just anybody* in. They have "a man" to do their gardening and "a woman" to do their cooking. Mr. and Mrs. Rose don't regard them as important enough to call by name. They put on such airs, the first time I visited I expected to see bars of gold used as doorstoppers. You'd think Harold had been secretary of state instead of an investment banker.

I hear the crinkle of plastic and look askance to see a bouquet of flowers resting on the back seat. For one stupid, miserable beat my heart leaps into my throat and I think they're for me—but then I see.

Of course. They're roses.

I can't help myself. "Wow, thank you for the flowers. You're so sweet."

"Oh." His cheeks turn pink. "They're for Mom, actually."

"What's the occasion? Is it her birthday?"

Her birthday was in January, same as Nicholas. He bought his mom a treadmill she circled for him in a catalog, and on top of that he proudly presented her with this little scroll of paper that said he'd gotten a star named after her.

"No. The flowers are . . . just because."

I shouldn't let myself be affected by this, but I am. This man sucks at being a fiancé. Imagine how much he'll suck as a husband. "It'd be nice if you treated me like you treat your mom," I say to the windshield, because I'm not quite brave enough to say it to his face. In my head I repeat what I just told him and my eyes bulge. *I'll take Things I Never Thought I'd Say for two hundred, Alex.*

"You want me to give you stuff because you make me feel obligated to, not because I want to?"

I consider it.

"Yes. At least then I'd be getting flowers. If I waited for you to *want* to give me flowers, I'd be getting as many then as I'm getting now. Which is none."

"Oh my god, Naomi," he sputters. "You told me forever ago that you don't want flowers. You said you didn't need them."

"Well, I didn't mean it! Obviously I want flowers. What girl doesn't? Can't wait till I have an adult son so I'll finally get some."

I can feel his burning stare. "If I told you I didn't want something, would you buy it for me anyway?"

I turn to him. "Why would *you* want flowers?"

His laugh is chilling. "Yeah, why would it ever occur to you to give *me* anything? A token of affection? Of course you don't think about that."

I *am* giving him something. Patience. It is a gift. I'm giving him a miracle in that I don't launch myself onto his seat and throttle him for insisting we hang out with his friends on my birthday and treat them to wings and cheese fries; for staying late at work on the Fourth of July when I wanted to go to a water park, but purchasing an enormous ball of fire for his mother— *him*, king of monologuing about the impracticality of gifts. If the galaxy imploded tomorrow, my last intelligible thought would be *Ha ha, there goes your fucking star, you bitch!*

"How long have you been stewing in this?" he demands to know.

An eternity.

"I'm not stewing. I'm fine."

"Sure." Another humorless laugh. "Mad at me for not bringing you presents. Meanwhile you ignore me at home, staring at the TV. You sit there like a doll on the shelf. You pout when we go to these dinners at my parents' house, but you don't have any family who live nearby and I'm struggling to give us some kind of family foundation here. It's amazing we still get invited over, frankly, because you exist inside your own head the whole time. No animation from you whatsoever from the second we get in the door." He shakes his head. "I might as well be there alone."

For a moment I'm stunned, because he's not supposed to know I'm inwardly pouting at these dinners. From my point of view, I've put on a convincing presentation of being happy and content. If he's known all along that I've been faking it, why hasn't he called me out on it before?

I spend the rest of our journey to Sycamore Lane thinking about how my next fiancé is going to be Nicholas's polar opposite. He'll have long blond hippie hair and a beard, an artist who rubs Pop Rocks on his teeth. His name is Anthony but he writes it &thony. He's indisputably an orphan.

Then we're in the driveway, narrowing in on what is sure to be two awful hours. I can't remember the last time Nicholas and I had fun in each other's company. We practice our in-front-of-other-people smiles and he hurries around the side of the car, reminding me of his one redeeming trait: there's something mesmerizingly fluid about the way he moves his body when he's not busy stomping to make a point.

His eyes snap to mine through the window, and his hand reaches for my door.

Then he smirks and chooses to open the back seat instead, grabbing the roses. He walks alone up to the porch. I follow behind him like a stray dog and wish that I could bark and snarl like one.

A Shakespearean plaque is bolted to the brick siding: A ROSE BY ANY OTHER NAME WOULD STILL SMELL AS SWEET. There's not supposed to be a *still* in that quote. I looked it up once to make sure it was a typo but never pointed it out to Mr. and Mrs. Rose because I don't want them getting a new one with the correct quote. I derive vicious pleasure from knowing their plaque is wrong.

I think about the first time I stood on this doorstep, nervous and optimistic, hoping so hard that I'd fit seamlessly into their world and they'd treat me like part of the family. Nicholas had wrapped his arm around my shoulders and kissed my cheek, grinning from ear to ear. *They're going to love you,* he'd said.

The door opens. Deborah bares all her teeth at me in a smile she doesn't mean, and I want to stick my finger down my throat right in front of her.

Nicholas and I exchange one last look of mutual loathing before we grin and hold hands. He squeezes. I squeeze back harder, but end up hurting my own fingers.

CHAPTER FIVE

Their lair smells like a postapocalyptic Bath & Body Works that has been stagnating in dust for ten years, with base notes of Aqua Net. The dusty odor has always confounded me, since I've never managed to find any actual dust. Each room is heavy and rich, trying hard to evoke French castles with Louis XV chairs while hoping you don't notice the stained pink carpet. If you're under twenty years old, you're expected to take off your shoes. There's one single television in the "salon"—a relic of the seventies that is never turned on and whose sole purpose is to reflect your shock that such a mammoth television set is still in someone's house.

Absolute silence falls over you like a hood once you cross the threshold into an Agatha Christie murder set and makes you want to speak quietly, which is translated through Mrs. Rose's human emotions processor as admiration.

It's her ode to a gilded age gone by, when children suppressed all their thoughts and emotions to make life easier for their boozy parents. Cherry wood, thick fabrics, onyx-on-charcoal damasks. Thousand-dollar bourbon, cork undisturbed, and crystal candy dishes that have nothing in them. Ornate frames of gold rope and eighteenth-century ashtrays you can Look At But Not Touch, enshrined behind backlit glass. A museum of Rose history that no one cares about except for the withered old Roses who grow here, and maybe me, the unwelcome and unsightly weed, if I end up having to marry into this mess.

Nicholas's honor roll ribbons from high school hang framed at the head of the dining room. Evidence that they have a daughter is scrubbed from everywhere except a tiny room they call "the *paaah*-lah," which contains one grand piano, a horde of porcelain cat figurines, and Heather's senior portrait. There are laser beams in the background and she's wearing braces with black rubber bands. Her mother sometimes talks about her like she's dead. Nicholas has told me that she's an EDM deejay, and just for that she's my favorite member of this family.

"Naomi! My dear! So very good to see you," Deborah cries, swinging forward to air-kiss one cheek, then the other. She learned from her own mother-in-law (a truly terrifying individual I got to meet only once before Satan called her home) how to be frigid and passive-aggressive. Honestly, this woman has no inkling where she is. We live in Morris, for crying out loud. Half our population has fur and nibbles on berries in the forest.

Meeting Deborah in person for the first time was jarring. She's persistently written in to the *Beaufort Gazette* with so many complaints about life in general that they gave her an advice column, *Dear Deborah*, where she doles out pearls of wisdom to loyal readers all over the county. I know Deborah's pearls for the costume jewelry that they are, because she's never come up against a problem that she didn't run to Nicholas to fix. The picture that accompanies her rants is at least fifteen years old. She's still got the same feathered bob, now with more highlights, but the skin around her eyes is stretched tight even though the eyes themselves seem to have shrunk to half their original size. The earrings she wears are so weighty that the lobes are stretched to two inches long.

She clasps my face between her soft, cool palms. I'm not sure she has blood. Sometimes she gets a little red in the face but that's only because she was left plugged in for too long and the outlet overheated.

"Goodness, Naomi, you cut your hair! And right before your wedding! What on earth were you thinking? Give me the name of your beautician and I'll have her fired for what she's done to you."

I ruffle my woefully short bangs and Nicholas hides a smile, pleased that he's got his mother insulting me for him. "It's a style. Like Amélie." Amélie's going to be my go-to reference with this hack job. I'll draw comparisons every chance I get.

She looks like she's holding back a mouthful of bees. "It really doesn't suit your face shape. Although I'm sure you already know that, and you've got an appointment booked to get hair extensions." She doesn't wait to hear a confirmation, eager to dive into her analysis of my appearance. It's what she does every time she sees me. "You're looking wretched all over, my dear. So washed-out and puffy. Are you ill?"

"Yes," I reply gaily. I hug her, which I've never done before (look at me trying all these fun new things!), and her bones shift and crunch under her prim clothes. Her clavicle protrudes so far, it's like someone buried her bones too shallow.

She skitters back, covered in my imaginary sick germs.

"Naomi's joking," Nicholas says plaintively. "She said she was fine in the car."

She pats her chest as though she's having palpitations, and we follow her to the living room so we can see her new coat rack (giant sequoia wood, twelve hundred dollars) and compliment it. I smell food cooking, and the promise of a free meal is the only reason I don't immediately impale myself on the coat rack.

When Mrs. Rose goes to check in with "the woman" about dinner, I pull out my phone and start tapping. "Potpourri," I say aloud. "Scribbly paintings. Creepy Hummel figurines of peasant children doing chores."

Nicholas gives me a wary look. "What are you doing?"

"Taking notes on how to make our house more enticing to you. You adore this one so much that you never want to leave, so I'm working out how to replicate the magic." I resume my phone tapping. "Bouquets of flowers bestowed by loved ones. Hmm, I'll have to find some loved ones."

He points to a crisp brown bouquet of last week's *just because* present. "You want that?" he whispers sarcastically. "An ugly handful of forty dollars?" He points next at a gaudy emerald brooch in a glass display case. "What about that? Would impractical jewelry make you happy, *darling*?" If I hear one more word from him about *impractical* I'm going to stuff him in the trunk.

"Steal it and we'll see."

His lips mash together. Knowing I'm under his skin makes my heart sing.

Mrs. Rose wafts back into earshot, so I pick up a vase that used to belong to Harold's mother and say, "I like this urn."

"That's a vase, dear." She pronounces it like *vahz*. There's no way she doesn't hate this vase, since legend has it that she and her mother-in-law once got into a physical brawl over where Harold would be buried—next to his wife or next to Mommie Dearest. Nicholas comes by his issues honestly.

"I'm surprised an urn this lovely isn't already occupied," I say as if I didn't hear her. "Although I suppose one day it will be." I give Deborah a contemplating look, up and down slowly from the top of her head to the tips of her pristine white shoes. "You have the nicest heirlooms. It's humbling to think that someday I'll have them all in my own home. Nick, can't you just see this pretty urn sitting on top of our fridge someday?"

His eyes sharpen when I call him Nick, but he doesn't have room to reply because Mrs. Rose says, "Nicky, what do you think of dear Naomi's new hairstyle?"

The only reason he keeps a straight face is that he's standing directly in front of a window. It'd be too easy for me to push him through it. "Naomi always looks great." Then he steps three paces off to the side before adding, "She has a large enough forehead that she can get away with short bangs."

They cover their bitchy grins with their hands in identical gestures. Nicholas notices and drops his hand. He looks a little shaken. I smile at him to confirm his worst fears.

Yes, Nicky, you're turning into your mother.

"Aren't those roses so nice?" I say to Deborah, gesturing at the dead brown ones from last week. "Very considerate of your adult son to bring you flowers all the time."

"Isn't it?" she croons. "Nicky spoils me so; he's such a wonderful boy. He does the same for you, I'm sure."

My smile twists at the corners and Nicholas has found something in the carpet to captivate him.

"Come look at these fresh ones!" she tells me, waving for us to follow her into the *salon*. Another forty dollars of Nicholas's regret stares mockingly at me from a small table. He's peeled the gas station sticker from the plastic wrap, and I muse that with cold weather approaching roses are going to be harder for him to find. He'll be forking out a hundred bucks a week for 1-800-Flowers.

"Aren't they precious?" Deborah thrusts the bouquet under my nose. I lean in and inhale.

"So *that's* what flowers smell like! I never get the opportunity to see them up close, so I had no idea."

Nicholas sighs at the ceiling.

"Look what else my Nicky got me." Deborah pops the lid of a small black velvet box, showcasing a glittering band of chocolate diamonds. I have never understood the appeal of brown diamonds. I don't want this monstrosity. If someone gave it to me I would never wear it. And yet I'm almost nauseated with jealousy.

"You're one lucky lady." I keep my gaze fixed on Nicholas. My tone rings so false, I know we all hear it. "What was the occasion?"

"Harold's and my anniversary." Harold is snoozing in a chair, hunched and lopsided. She wakes him up by yanking on his collar until he's straightened out. "What was it he got for you, dear? Golf clubs?"

Harold jumps and snorts. He's adept at speaking through his nose.

"Lucky, lucky, lucky," I sing. "So lucky that your adult son buys you diamonds and golf clubs to celebrate an anniversary that isn't even his! I can't imagine to what lengths he'd go for his *own* anniversary." This time, I don't dare glance at Nicholas. He'll want me to catch his eye so I'll know that he's seething, and not looking at him deprives him of this.

Conversation with Mrs. Rose is fifty percent listening to her swoon over Nicholas and fifty percent listening to her gripe, so it's about time for her to swing the other way. She asks why no one has received a wedding invitation yet, since she already had the type of invitation and wording ready to go. I stay silent while Nicholas puts together a reply, leaving him to twist in the wind.

The truth is that Nicholas and I can't agree on which engagement photo to attach to the invitations. Most couples attach engagement photos to their save-the-dates, but since we didn't send those out Deborah says we Absolutely Must Include Them With The Invitations.

The one I want to use has captured me at a magical angle. It gives the illusion that I have long eyelashes and fuller lips. My chest looks larger. I've absorbed all of the photogenic magic and left none to spare for Nicholas, whose right eye is shut entirely and his left is halfway there. We had the photos taken on a chilly day and the first thing you notice are his nipples pointing through his shirt. I laugh every time I see it.

The photo Nicholas wants to use makes him look like a *GQ* model, and my hair's blowing all over my face. Nicholas tells his mother, "Oh, I thought we sent those out already. My bad."

"You'd better do it," Deborah says warningly. "Or no one will show up."

Nicholas's ears perk up at this. He looks inspired. Those invitations are never going out in the mail. I have no right to be offended that he doesn't want to marry me, since I don't want to marry him, either, but I am. I console myself with the knowledge that I don't want to marry him even more than he doesn't want to marry me.

But when we're alone for a minute, the smiles fade away and he mutters in my ear, "Why don't you ever have my back? You always abandon me."

"You always abandon me first," I hiss.

———

"The woman" has fixed veal. Veal makes me cringe and Mrs. Rose knows it; it's why, up until now, she's offered an alternative dish if veal was going to be on the menu. Not tonight. It's a creative reprisal, I'll give her that.

She's watching me closely, craving a reaction, so I look her right in the eye and take an enormous bite. I don't care about my moral convictions tonight. I'll eat a bloody half-formed cow fetus with my bare hands if it'll get Nicholas to dump me in front of his mom like a total chump. What has my life come to, if that's my goal now?

Nicholas pins me with a glare. The angrier he gets, the more I feel like dancing. He's giving me so many nonverbal cues and they're fine encouragement that I'm going in the right direction. Muscle twitches. Clenched jaw. Fisted hands. Someone's got to teach this man about poker tells or he'll get his pockets cleaned out. Probably by me, in the inevitable divorce. My brilliant lawyer and I will ride into the sunset with everything he's got.

"Nicky just loves veal," Mrs. Rose purrs.

Nicky just does not, but he won't argue with her. "What else does your adult son love?" I ask. "You spend more time with him than anyone else, so you're the one to ask." I heave a dramatic sigh. "Even after all this time together, there's still so much I don't know. Our Nicky is surprisingly mysterious."

At that, his gaze snaps to mine, and there's a glimmer of amusement lurking there. "Don't sell yourself short, Naomi," he replies. "I think you're starting to figure me out."

"Yes, I believe I am. It's taken some time."

"We can't all be quick learners."

I swirl my glass of cranberry juice as we watch each other through narrowed eyes. "You should tell your parents our special news," I say at last, one corner of my mouth ticking up.

His eyebrows knit together and his mother is all aflutter. She probably can't believe something's happened in his life that she wasn't the first to know about. "News? What news? Tell us, Nicky."

"Tell them, Nicky," I parrot.

Deborah divides a stricken look between us. Clearly, she's terrified I'm pregnant. An out-of-wedlock baby! What would Pastor Thomas say? Just to scare her a little more, I absently drape a hand over my stomach. She makes a dry, rasping sound like the leg of a chair scraping across a wood floor.

Nicholas sees my game.

"Darling, I don't think I know what news you're referring to."

"It's unexpected news." I'm relishing this. "We weren't planning on it happening quite yet, but that's the way life goes."

"If you do have news," he grates, "I know it's not mine."

I tilt my head. "We haven't had anything newsworthy happen in quite a while, have we?"

"Speaking of news!" Deborah interrupts, dying to pivot the spotlight back onto herself. "I'm coming up on my fifth anniversary at the newspaper."

"We know," Harold mutters, spreading a cloth napkin across his lap. Deborah stares at him pointedly until he tucks a second napkin into his collar. I give it a year before she's got him wearing a bib. "We *all* know."

Deborah spoons more artichoke hearts onto his plate, much to his dismay. "*They* might not know."

She texted Nicholas three times this week about it, hinting that if he wanted to take her out for a celebratory lunch she's upholding boycotts with Ruby Tuesday, Walk the Plank, and Applebee's because of spats with the staff.

"Congratulations," Nicholas says automatically.

"Yes, it's quite an achievement, isn't it? I think I've solved more problems than the mayor! Lately I've been rescuing marriages left and right, but when you read tomorrow's column you'll see that even *I* can't save the lady who recently wrote in begging for my help." Deborah smiles like the cat that ate the canary. "She's having an affair with the handyman."

"I wish Nicholas were handsier—I mean handier," I say, stealing the spotlight right back. "I've been performing maintenance duties by myself. But I've been getting better results, interestingly enough."

Nicholas's stare is dehydrating. "Sounds unlikely."

"Maintenance duties?" Deborah repeats, turning to him. "Has something broken? Naomi shouldn't be trying to fix anything. She could make it worse."

"I have no choice," I tell her in a low, conspiratorial voice. "It's a desperate situation, and Nicholas won't use his tools." I tap my mouth with a fingernail, watching him go rigid.

"Nicholas has no use for tools," Deborah says emphatically, unaware that we are speaking in encrypted hate. "If something isn't working, call a professional."

"Good thinking. Do you know which handyman that lady was writing in about?"

Nicholas is fed up. "Being *handy* is unsatisfying when your fiancée is so obviously distracted and barely pitches in," he tells me with thunderclouds sweeping over his expression.

His hands are hot and sweating. I can tell by the way the fork in his grip fogs up. This is what he gets for calling me a doll on the shelf. I don't engage with his parents enough at dinner? He'll regret saying *that*.

"Harold," Deborah barks.

Harold jumps.

"What?"

"The kids are living in a broken-down hovel. Make them call a repairman."

The idea of Harold making Nicholas or me do anything is ludicrous. He can't make himself stay awake for the duration of a commercial. Harold only gets up from his chair if it means walking to another chair. He and his wife are presently wearing matching burgundy sweaters, fur from his back and shoulders creeping around a Peter Pan collar in a way that has me side-eyeing how Nicholas will age. He stopped having an opinion of his own in 1995 and lives for the moment he's told he's allowed to go to bed.

Trust this: you don't want to know more about Harold. He's like three-month-old lasagna left in the back of the fridge. With every layer it gets worse.

He drinks seltzer water with every dinner and his white hair sprouts from the top of his head in short tufts of cotton, same as his out-of-control eyebrows. If you're sitting directly opposite him, his hair is see-through and colors everything behind it with whimsical fuzz. He communicates chiefly through snorts,

grunts, and belches. Once, I walked in on him while he was leafing through a *Playboy* and he said, "Have you ever been with an
older man, Nina?"

My boss, Mr. Howard, says he knew Harold when they were
younger and Harold's "work trips" to Nevada in the eighties
were actually stints at Bella's Gentleman's Club. Like the innocent, naïve sunbeam that I am, the words *gentleman's club* conjured up genteel images of men playing cards and smoking
cigars. Then Zach told me what it actually was and it left me
equal parts traumatized and enthralled.

I still haven't let Nicholas in on this discovery. It's a pulled
punch I'm saving for after I've already knocked him down but
need to make sure he can't get back up again. *I'm getting my goddamn lemon cake and your mom is uninvited to the wedding.*
Roundhouse kick. *I'm wearing a tuxedo and we're eloping.* Jab
to the throat. *We're never naming our daughter after Deborah.*
High kick. *I haven't flossed in a year.* Uppercut. *Your dad goes to
brothels.*

"Call the repo man," Harold advises. "Tell him he's not taking anything unless he's got a warrant. Then go stash it at your
vacation home."

I wish I could exist in whatever world Harold is in right now,
holding an entirely different conversation parallel to ours. "Actually," I say, "our news is that we're thinking about getting
a dog."

"We are not." Nicholas's grip on his fork tightens.

I sip my cranberry juice. It's revolting. "Something small,
that yaps a lot. Maybe a terrier or a chihuahua."

A muscle in his cheek jumps.

"Maybe we'll get a cat, too," he suggests.

Deborah looks at me, frowning. "Isn't Naomi allergic to cats?"

"Is she?" He smiles at his clean plate. He's finished all his food, even the bits of creamy mushroom that I know he doesn't like. What a good little boy. I bet his tail is wagging in anticipation of being petted.

Nicholas pretends to consider. "Two cats, maybe, so the one won't be lonely."

"I've been thinking," I interrupt. Our dysfunction is growing increasingly evident. Even Harold is paying attention now. "About keeping my maiden name. It's what a lot of women are doing now."

This doesn't bother Deborah in the least. She's glad to hear it, I'm sure. Fewer women to share her name with. Unfazed, I change tacks.

"Actually . . ." I tease out the word. "Nowadays, sometimes it's the man who changes his name. *Nicholas Westfield* has a certain charm to it."

"He can't change his name!" Deborah cries.

"Why not? Women do it all the time. What's good for the goose is good for the gander."

Nicholas doesn't dignify this with a retort, shaking his head at me. "That's ridiculous," his mother huffs. "He has a lovely last name. Not that yours isn't . . . nice . . . but it's not quite as special as *Rose*, now, is it? *Dr. Rose* is how he's known in this community. He can't change it now. And I'm sure he'll want his children to carry on the family name, too."

"We're not having children," I declare. "I'm barren. I lost my uterus in a Ponzi scheme."

Nicholas throws his fork down with a clatter and stands. His business of moving around is loud, but not loud enough to disguise his mother's startled cry. "It's getting late." He scowls at me. "Come on, Naomi."

I wave a hand over my plate, feigning incomprehension. "But I haven't finished yet."

He grabs my hand. "Oh, you're done."

Nicholas all but throws me over his shoulder to get me out of that house. I can feel that my face is flushed with triumph and I know my eyes are bright and shining. A complete basket case. This is how I want to look in the picture we use for invitations. I wish I could fall down and laugh until my ribs crack, but he drags me out the door. Every muscle in his body is tense.

"Thanks for dinner!" I crow behind me. "Your adult son and I are so grateful!"

"Stop saying that," he snaps, tugging my arm when I try to dig my heel into one of the flowers in the yard.

"Stop thanking them for dinner? That's not very nice manners, Nicky."

He and I suffer each other in silence on the car ride home, preparing our arguments in our heads. As soon as we pull up under the halo of our streetlight we get out and round the car, doors slamming with hurricane force.

"Don't slam my car door." As if he didn't do the same.

He's in love with his status symbol of a car and would probably marry it if it were socially acceptable. "Your car isn't that good-looking and didn't even win the J.D. Power award. I hope a bird craps on it every single day for all eternity." Right on the windshield in front of his face, a big white splat.

"You're just mad because you drive a woolly mammoth."

"There's nothing wrong with my car."

"I'm sure it was in top form once. In 1999."

Listen to this man's privilege. He's probably never driven a car that was more than two years old. "I buy what I can afford. Not all of us have rich parents who paid our tuition at swanky New England schools."

"You want to go to college? Then go to college! Don't punish me for being successful enough to buy a nice vehicle."

And we've come to the crux of it. Naomi doesn't have a college degree. Naomi doesn't have a fancy car. How do we measure her value without these must-haves? I think about my parents saying I should have worked harder and applied for scholarships. I think about Nicholas's remark at game night that I don't need a job, and how no one believes in me. I wish I could go back in time and slam his car door twice.

I let his stride overtake mine so that I enter the house second; this way, I get to shut the door as hard as I want. The walls vibrate, floorboards shifting like tectonic plates. The ceiling fractures apart into a road map of jagged black lines. He and I square off, battle-ready, the room hazing crimson and pulsating with animosity.

"There's nothing wrong with your gas gauge," I tell him. It's one of the meanest things I could ever say. "You can't admit you didn't notice your fuel was low."

His eyes are crazed. At game night, I realized they change colors, and right now his eyes are the color of four horsemen heralding Armageddon, riding forth on beasts whipped from storm clouds. I can practically see the lightning flash, illuminating a rain of locusts. He drags a hand through his hair and messes it all up. A colorful wheel of insults cranks through his head and notches on one I didn't expect.

"I don't like your spaghetti. It tastes like nothing."

Whatever. He's just giving me an excuse not to cook. "I don't like your dumb *How to Train Your Dragon* tie."

He's so proud of that tie, because it features Toothless the dragon. A clever pun when you're in the teeth profession.

Rage burns a red rash across his cheekbones. "You take that back."

I shrug, smiling inwardly. It's a malicious smile all for myself, but I think he sees it because of the look he gives me.

"Sometimes I don't know why I try with you."

I agree. "Yeah, why do you?"

He combusts. "Giving me shit about my mother constantly, like I don't already know how difficult she makes our lives. You harping on me, and throwing me to the wolves all the time, doesn't make it any better! You're not such a peach yourself, Naomi. You think there aren't things about you that drive me insane? You think I don't feel held back from realizing my true potential?"

His chest is heaving and he looks like he might run out the door and never come back. To make him even angrier, I let out a pop of laughter. "Please enlighten me, Nicholas, as to how *I* am holding *you* back."

Oh, he's riled. He's hands on hips, tie yanked loose, so upset I can see his skin retracting as a shadow of stubble breaks through. His mouth is a slash of contempt. His eyes dip to the Steelers logo on my hoodie and he clenches his jaw so tight I know there's a hairline fracture there with my name on it. An X-ray technician will be astounded to see the word *Naomi* etched into his bones one day.

"For one, I hate this house."

My eyebrows arch so high, they nearly touch my bangs. "You picked it."

YOU DESERVE EACH OTHER   81

After eleven months of dating, we packed up our solo lives and came here to be one unit. It was the first rental house we looked at. We were dripping with vitality and butterflies, making grand plans. *We'll build shelves. Maybe the landlord will let us retile the bathroom. Doing projects together will be so fun!* Recalling happier times is like trying to remember a dream I had a hundred years ago—it's all a warped blur that no longer makes sense.

When we toured the house, we were so dreamy over our love nest that we didn't take into consideration that the limited street parking would make it a pain to accommodate two cars. We didn't notice the floors weren't level, which means every time I drop my ChapStick I have to chase it before it rolls under the furniture. We didn't think about the fact that there was only one spare room that could be turned into an office.

Which went to him, naturally.

"Sometimes my judgment's hasty," he shoots back, making it clear he's talking about proposing to me. "I don't like the street we're on, or this neighborhood. Morris is actually a scenic town if you're in the right spot, and we moved smack-dab where it's ugliest. There's nothing here."

He can see the question mark on my face. "I'd rather be closer to nature!" he blurts. "All these woods, all this countryside around us, and here we sit with a backyard so small you could spit across it."

"So, what?" I prompt. "You want to be one of those guys in a Nature Valley ad? Sitting on a mountain with your Labrador retriever, getting a hard-on over the smell of trees?"

"Yeah!" he nearly yells. "I want that. I think that's how I'd thrive. But you're not going to let me thrive, Naomi. I can already tell. You're content right here in your cement prison—"

"Oh god." I roll my eyes so hard, I see the spirit realm. "Take up hiking."

"—begging to get seasonal depression by locking yourself in a dark room and never going outside. Going to work doesn't count because you're still sitting in a car during transit. And I see you, Naomi. I see you never looking at the sky or taking the time to stop and smell the—" He sees how excited I am for him to finish that sentence and he kills it abruptly. "You're barely living, you know."

"I had no idea you were so thirsty to be one with nature." I use air quotes around *one with nature*. He hates it when people use air quotes. "What the hell kind of YouTube videos have you been watching in there on your computer wife? Seriously, where is this coming from?"

"MY HEART," he roars, and he's so sincere and agitated that I double over in a fit of laughter. "Shut up! Stop laughing." He's pacing now. He's been putting some deep thought into this. Who is this man in my living room with Armageddon eyes and a yearning desire to skip rocks across a lake?

"I want a helmet with a flashlight on it," he's raving. "I want a fireplace. A shotgun in case of coyotes. I want shovels and a shed to put them in. I want a canoe."

"Don't let me stop you from getting a canoe," I say, dead serious. "Nicholas, I'm here to support all your dreams. Please, go get a canoe. I'd love nothing more than to watch you paddle out into the middle of a lake."

"I need to feel *alive!*"

"I think what you need is a granola bar and maybe a trial run with the Eagle Scouts."

"I knew you wouldn't take me seriously. That's why I haven't said anything. But I'm not keeping it bottled up anymore, Naomi, I swear to god. I'm going to start living the way I want. I'm going to have the life I want, everything I want, no matter what it takes. I don't have forever; I'm already in my thirties."

"You're right, you're practically an old man. Your time is now! Start living your best life."

"I'm serious." He pinches a nickel that's sitting on the TV stand. "Heads, we start doing things my way. Tails, we stay the same."

"You want to plan our lives based on a coin toss? That sounds about right." I wish he'd flip a coin to decide the fate of our relationship while he's at it. Heads, we break up. Tails, we flip the coin again. We could quit each other right now and blame it all on the coin.

He flips the nickel. It lands on the back of his hand. Nicholas stares at the glimmer of silver.

"Well?"

"I guess you'll find out."

"Fabulous, be sure to keep me in the loop." I sprawl out on our three-seater, arrowing a lazy smile up at him. "Good night."

"Good night? If you want me to go to bed, then you're going to have to move. I'm taking the couch tonight."

"No, you can have your bed full of Skittles. I'm staying right here."

He storms back to the bedroom and closes the door with a barely audible *snick* that's somehow even worse than if he'd shut it violently. I hear the lock turn, and then it's just me alone in the silence.

We've never yelled at each other before. We're usually so wary of rocking the boat that we're maybe only eighty percent honest with each other. We've both dialed it up to one hundred for once, and logically I know I shouldn't feel better now but I kind of do. As the minutes tick by and I listen to his dresser drawers close, our mattress springs compressing as he rolls over them as furiously as he can manage, I have an intriguing revelation.

We've been together for almost two years, and this is our first real fight.

CHAPTER SIX

It takes eight strategically placed pins to make it look like I do not have bangs. The disguise requires twenty-six minutes to perfect, and I skulk into the Junk Yard on Monday breathing a sigh of relief that you can't tell I've butchered my hair.

Brandy notices immediately. "You gave yourself bangs."

"Things going that bad at home, huh?" Zach adds.

"I used to have bangs." I touch my forehead self-consciously. My forehead is the first thing I criticize when I look in the mirror. Is it normal-sized? Oilier than most? Foreheads are all I see now. Over the weekend I've come across nothing but pictures of beautiful women online and none of them have bangs. I only see pictures of beautiful women with bangs when I do not have bangs.

I Googled how to grow them out faster and ordered an emergency shipment of Mane 'n Tail shampoo and conditioner. I'm taking prenatal vitamins because a forum recommended it for rapid hair growth.

"I like my bangs," I announce. "This is the new me."

"Look out, world," says Brandy, my co-pilot on this adventure into delusion.

Melissa looks at me and bites her lip to suppress a smile. Zach nudges her shoulder and they share twin snickers. For the thousandth time, I wish that Melissa and I were still friends. I love working here, but I loved it even better before introducing Melissa to the man who broke her heart. She'll never stop punishing me for it.

In spite of her, I still feel lucky that I landed this job. I'd plastered the county with applications but didn't hear back from anyone except for Mr. and Mrs. Howard. Nicholas kept saying I didn't need to work, but after being laid off from my old job at the hardware store (which closed down), I got bored piddling around the house all day and needed purpose. A conduit through which I could channel all my free-floating energy before it started shooting randomly off the walls and ricocheted back to blast me.

Mr. and Mrs. Howard were both here for my first day, to oversee my training. It led me to believe they'd be here every day, and when they barely ever showed up again it left me confused as to who I was supposed to be reporting to. So I asked Zach, who *seemed* friendly, and he had me convinced he was my boss for three months straight. That asshole had me scrubbing toilets for his own sordid entertainment.

Without the owners here to keep us in line, the atmosphere is lax and easygoing. Even though Melissa can be frosty sometimes, our odd group has fun together, goofing off and doing nothing. And I mean *nothing*, because business is flatlining. Whenever a customer comes in, we end up eagle-eyeing them so intensely that they get weirded out and leave. One week, we were freakishly busy and high-fived each other when the shift ended with a fat cash register, thinking the ship was getting turned around. But nope, everywhere I look there are icebergs. There are holes in the ship. We're sinking.

I know the Howards can't hold out much longer. They're going to put themselves in debt just to make sure the five of us get a paycheck. We all feel bad about it, but we also want to keep our jobs for as long as possible, so none of us are willing to quit even if it means extending life expectancy for four other jobs. It's been brought up a few times, usually by Brandy, and we all fidget and avoid eye contact.

Today, it's me, Zach, Melissa, and Brandy on the schedule. Leon works by himself tomorrow, since he's the only one who prefers working alone. He isn't much of a talker, and embarrasses easily. I think maybe we overwhelm him, horsing around with taxidermied roadkill and quizzing each other to find out Which Sexual Position Are You on BuzzFeed.

About thirty minutes after I walk in, I'm proving my value to this company by fashioning paper clip necklaces for everyone (I make a lot of jewelry out of odds and ends here to pass the time) and listening to Melissa and Brandy negotiate the music schedule. Brandy usually chooses the music on Mondays, but Melissa's not going to be here for her turn on Friday so she's trying to get Brandy to switch. To her credit, Brandy isn't budging. I like to think I've been just the right kind of bad influence on her.

The bell to the front door dings and we all orbit to gape at whoever's come in. It's an eccentric billionaire who's going to save us. He'll buy out everything on our shelves and demand that the Howards replenish them. He'll pay us double what we're asking.

Actually, it's a gangly, pimpled boy no older than twenty, and he's pushing a cart of flowers. There are at least ten bouquets in plain glass vases, filmy red cling wrap protecting them from the rain.

"Naomi Westfield?" he asks, consulting a clipboard.

Brandy picks up my hand and holds it aloft. I can't speak. I have a bad feeling in the pit of my stomach and don't know why.

"These are for you."

When I don't move, he hesitates fractionally and then starts depositing bouquets on the counter. Melissa's face disappears behind a forest of green plumage and white petals.

The deliveryman leaves and still none of us have moved. I spot a white card sticking out and examine it. It's supposed to contain a message like I LOVE YOU or SORRY I'M SO AWFUL AND WRONG.

It's blank. But I know who these are from, and I've gotten his message, all right. He might as well have put it on a neon sign. HERE ARE THE FUCKING FLOWERS YOU NEEDED SO MUCH. ENJOY.

"What's the occasion?" Zach asks.

My mouth is dry. "Just because."

"This is . . . ah." Melissa grasps for words.

"Excessive," finishes Zach. "For a 'just because.'"

"How lovely! What kind are they?" Brandy asks me this like they must be my favorite. I don't have a favorite type of flower. I definitely have a least favorite, though.

"No idea."

We safari through our new botanical garden, but there isn't

any information attached. Not even one of those little tabs they stick into the potting soil that tells you how frequently you're supposed to water it.

"Looks kind of like oleander," says Melissa warily.

Zach cocks his head. "Isn't oleander poisonous?"

Suddenly the flowers make sense. It's an assassination attempt. We all whip out our phones and start looking up pictures of oleander, and it's true, I can see a resemblance. Five white petals, slightly pinwheeled, in clusters of greenery.

"Why would a flower shop sell poisonous plants?" I ask. "Is that legal?"

Melissa points out that we don't know for sure these even came from a regulated flower shop. None of us can remember if the delivery boy was wearing a particular kind of uniform. He could've been anyone. Maybe Nicholas hired him off Craigslist. WANTED: MURDER ACCOMPLICE.

We give our fingers a workout with frantic Googling. My ominous delivery sure does look like oleander to me, but it also looks like a million other types of flowers. They all look the same. We discover it would be really easy to kill someone with this kind of plant, and according to IMDb that very plot happened in a movie with Michelle Pfeiffer. Michelle's character used them to kill her lover, a man named Barry. I'm being Barry'd.

Oh god. I hear the pun and nearly faint.

"According to the language of flowers," Melissa says, "presenting someone with oleander is a way of telling them to *watch out*. Like, in a threatening way."

"'Watch out' like we're gonna *die*, watch out?" My voice is exceptionally high.

"I'm freaking out," Brandy cries, wringing her hands. "I'm freaking OUT, you guys. Are we sure it's from Nicholas? I mean, he seems . . ." She cuts me a sheepish look. "I'm sure he's nice."

"Of course it's from Nicholas," Zach bites, "and no, he's not nice. Dentists are monsters. He's probably still pissed that I won every round of Clue. When you're a monster, it takes nothing at all to trigger your dark side."

"You yelling at him in the dentist's office that one time could've been a trigger," says Melissa, who needs no convincing. "That's why you're on his list."

"And you're his friend's ex. You know how people are about their friends' exes." He points at me. "You're a loose end. Maybe he's cheating."

"What about me?" Brandy asks.

"He's got an insatiable taste for murder by now. You're collateral damage."

Brandy looks a bit disappointed that her demise isn't more personal.

I should be alarmed that we've devolved into *Nicholas is a cold-blooded killer* this rapidly, but weird, melodramatic afternoons are our normal. When you never get any customers, boredom creeps in and conspiracy theories sprout out of any tiny event, which we pass around until mass hysteria takes over. Zach is always the instigator, and he always turns out to be wrong, but the hysteria still catches on every time. When he waves his hands to gesticulate, all wide-eyed and passionate, he can make any bonkers theory sound plausible.

"The oleander," I whisper. "In the Junk Yard. By Dr. Rose. That's what this is! It's some kind of calling card, like all the big-league serial killers use. He's the Clue Killer." I inspect the blank message card again. No florist logo. It might as well bear Professor Plum's demented smile.

"He wants to kill us all because he lost Clue?" Brandy says doubtfully. "This can't be right."

We dive back into our research.

A different website proclaims that oleander means *enjoy what's in front of you and leave the past in the past,* which is a nicer alternative to *watch out,* but then Zach finds a site that looks pretty legit. It informs us that oleander is universally interpreted as *caution* in the flower language world. I hear the slow, somber bells of my funeral toll and hope someone competent does my makeup if it's going to be open casket. It occurs to me that I'm a little bit morbid.

"Can you die just from being exposed to it through the air?" I ask. "Do you have to touch it or is standing too close enough?"

Zach, hunched over his phone, mutters, "Yahoo Answers is a cesspit."

"Was the delivery guy wearing gloves?" Melissa asks. None of us can remember. At this point I don't remember a single detail about the deliveryman. Maybe it was a woman. A figment of my imagination. I'm hallucinating in the ER.

"Your fiancé might be a maniac," Brandy tells me. "Come home with me. Wait. I've got a date tonight." She pauses. "You could stay at my sister's place! She does have five cats, though, so you might sneeze a lot."

It's a sweet offer, but there's no way I'm sleeping with cats. Their hair gets stuck to everything and I'll get perma-red eyes that will make it look like I've been eating special brownies. I don't want to stay with my own sister, either, who lives forty-five

minutes to the east. We've found this to be a nice buffer distance, which is why my brother lives forty-five minutes to the
west. My siblings and I don't have much to say to each other and
interact mostly on holidays at our parents' house, which sits an
hour north.

"Actually, I think I should confront him." I'm so brave, I
impress myself. "Yes, that's what I must do. I can't let him get
away with intimidating me like this."

Brandy gasps. "No!"

"You've got to break it off." Melissa's eyes are black and
predatory. She leans in so close to me that I revisit the grapefruit
she ate for lunch. "Naomi. You have to break up with him.
There's no other choice. Do it now. Text him."

"Yeah, don't break up with him to his face," Zach advises. "I
once dated a surgeon and I drove across state lines before I left
a voicemail saying we were breaking up. This is the same shit;
Nicholas is right at home with sharp tools. Those tooth-scraper
things could be like a scalpel to the jugular if you know what
you're doing. He could turn out to be the Sweeney Todd of
dentists."

I know Zach doesn't believe a word of what he's saying, but
I get a flicker of slasher-film Nicholas in his white lab coat, eyes
glowing red over a hypoallergenic face mask, wielding doll-sized
weapons. He's high on bubble-gum-flavored laughing gas and in
the fog of his zombiefied brain all he can remember is that I insulted his tie.

"If you don't see me tomorrow, it's because I'm dead," I say.

Zach reminds me that we don't work tomorrow, Leon does.

"If you don't see me Wednesday, it's because I'm dead."

"Okay. We'll wait till Wednesday to call the police, then."

I chew my fingernails. Fuss with the flowers even though they might be poisonous. They're so pretty that it's hard not to. Nicholas is pretty, too. His pretty face will be the last one I see before I drift from this life. I'm only twenty-eight and I've barely done or seen anything. I hear his voice, my memory curling its edges into a taunt. *You're barely living, you know.*

I've got to destroy these murder flowers.

We're running around like animals escaped from the zoo, trying to figure out how to get them out of the store without touching them. Melissa, Brandy, and I are staunch feminists but today we turn our backs on equality by playing the help-me-I'm-just-a-girl card, and vote Zach to take one for the team.

He sets his mouth in a grim line and risks it all like a trooper. We package his arms in plastic bags, all the way up to the shoulders, and secure them in place with rubber bands. We pull up his collar to cover his nose and mouth.

He runs back and forth from the counter to a burn barrel Mr. Howard keeps out back for getting rid of leaves and twigs, and I think he might be a bit of a pyromaniac when he dumps a whole bottle of lighter fluid over the flowers and throws in a match. He stands there and watches the flames, hypnotized, while Melissa shouts at him that the fumes might be poisonous, too.

I know for sure that he doesn't believe anything we're doing here when he ignores her and starts tossing other stuff into the barrel to watch it burn. Old newspapers. A Dr Pepper bottle. Receipts from his jacket pocket. When he starts melting pennies, we give up on him and turn away from the back door.

Brandy and I scrub down the counter and floors with bleach, stopping every now and then to check each other's pupils and heart rates. It's too bad I couldn't keep the flowers. They were aromatic, almost like lotion or perfume. Even the burning smelled sweet before Zach topped it off with garbage.

He tires himself out after an hour and pours water over a smoking hill of debris before nudging it to the other side of the parking lot with a hockey stick. We pass the rest of our shift with games of tic-tac-toe we draw in the sand of a miniature Zen garden. We take a few BuzzFeed quizzes and I find out that if I were a supernatural creature I'd be a poltergeist. Brandy gets phoenix. I retake the quiz a few more times, experimenting with my answers, until I also get phoenix. By the time we clock out, we've forgotten about our brush with death.

Then I get a chime from my phone.

Did you not get the flowers?

Nicholas's text reminds me that he's the evil villain in my story and I should drive forty-five minutes in either direction to recover from my trauma at a sibling's house. I purse my lips and reply.

If you're asking whether I'm alive, the answer is yes. Nice try! I incinerated them.

He texts back right away.

WTF DID YOU ACTUALLY BURN THEM

"Of course," I huff to nobody, all alone in my car. The vents are still blowing out cold air and I've had the heat running for ten minutes. His damned Maserati has heated seats that make you feel like you're sitting in the devil's lap.

What else would I do with oleander?

He replies: You didn't do anything with oleander, seeing as how I gave you jasmine.

I squint at my screen, trying to decide whether I believe him. I didn't know until recently that Nicholas is a talented actor, so it's hard telling.

After a break of two minutes, he adds: If it HAD been oleander, burning it would've been a really stupid idea. JSYK. Oleander's toxic. He's Googled it, too. There's no way he knew that off the top of his head. Nicholas is fond of researching things and pretending that whatever obscure trivia he unearths is common knowledge. He watches *Jeopardy!* to show off (and because he's an eighty-year-old man trapped in the body of a Disney prince), getting a high every time he delivers the correct answer before a contestant does. Then he glances sideways at me to make sure I'm impressed. If I get up to leave the room, he pauses the show until I return so that I don't miss a moment of his genius.

Another text lights up my screen. It is ridiculously over the top, even for you, to make the leap from "Oh, my boyfriend sent me flowers" to "Oh, my boyfriend's trying to poison me." JSYK, if I were actually going to poison you I could find a cheaper method.

"Just so you know" is how he says "duh" to people without getting smacked. If I destroy him before he destroys me, I'm making sure his epitaph says JSYK, dummies, it's a myth that your hair and nails keep growing after you die.

I'm the only one left in the Junk Yard's parking lot, watching my breath puff out in this metal icebox and dreading going home. To stall, I look up the significance of jasmine in the language of flowers and hunt for hidden subtext like a sentimental Victorian paramour.

There are many different types of jasmine. I don't know precisely which strain he got for me. Most of the symbolism is typically romantic. I doubt Nicholas is aware that flowers even have meanings, or that he would choose one deliberately for a symbolic message I wouldn't know unless I looked it up. He probably had the receptionists at Rise and Smile find the closest florist and told them to choose whatever was on sale today.

I can see his frown. A shake of the head. *Impractical.* He knows exactly how much gas he could have put in his tank for the cost of that jasmine. He knows its conversion rate for groceries or our cell phone bill.

I catch myself lamenting that I didn't keep at least one flower before remembering there's no point. I never should have brought up the whole jag about not getting flowers from him. I'm not at all gratified by the jasmine, because I had to nag to get it, and he didn't send it out of love. He sent it because he felt obligated, just like he does for his mother. But where Deborah can somehow still derive satisfaction from that, I can't.

It's an empty gesture, a dark condemnation. In all the places it's supposed to please, it stings instead.

It's Tuesday, and something's up with Nicholas. He called the office to say he wouldn't be coming in, then left the house without a word to me. He's been gone all day. While I check my phone for calls or texts and wait for him to come home, I wander from room to room. It's a short tour, because our house is small. It fits two people if those two people love each other and don't mind being close. In the near future, it will fit one person comfortably.

My phone rings and I jolt, expecting to be told Nicholas surrenders and is never coming back, but it's Mrs. Howard.

I steel myself before answering. I love Mrs. Howard, but she has the voice of two bricks grating against each other from fifty years of chain-smoking Virginia Slims.

"Hi, this is Naomi."

I say that specifically because she always asks—and then she still does, anyway: "Is this Naomi?"

"Yes."

"Hon, this is Goldie Howard."

I smile. "Hello. How are you?"

"Dear, I'm great. Actually, not so great. You got a minute?"

My heart sinks into my stomach. *Last hired, first fired.* It's curtains for me. "Uhh, yes. Just, uhh . . ." I reach for a notepad and pen for some reason. My brain buzzes. Paranoia, anxiety, and nausea pull me into their familiar huddle and squeeze. "Yeah, what's up?"

She launches right in. "I'm sure you know that business at the Junk Yard isn't what it was twenty years ago."

"It's . . . not that bad," I squeak.

"Hon, it's that bad. Melvin and I have been going over the books, and it looks like we've got no choice but to clean house."

I can't cry. Mrs. Howard has been so good to me, and I won't make her feel any guiltier for doing what she has to do. "You're letting me go."

"I'm letting everybody go. We'll move some stuff around, relocating what's left on the shelves to our other businesses, but we'll be closed down by mid-November. I'd sell the Junk Yard the way it is to a new owner, but Morris real estate is in a slump."

She's right. After she closes the store, it'll probably sit there empty for ages before some optimistic sucker turns it into a bakery that won't last six months. All of our small businesses are closing and Morris will be a ghost town in ten years.

"We're trying to see what else we can do for you kids," Mrs. Howard says kindly. "We've always got a few different irons in the fire. I do burlesque, Melvin's an ordained minister. We go to a bunch of Midwestern fairs in the summer and do the carnie thing. And then there's Eaten Alive and House of Screams." She clears her throat, making me think of brick dust drifting loosely down a chimney. "I know Tenmouth is out of the way for that boyfriend of yours, but if you want to move here, we'll line something up for you."

I envision myself with a mask and chainsaw, jumping out at patrons in a haunted house. Or with a mask and chainsaw at Eaten Alive, gutting gelatin desserts inspired by *The Blob*. I think about my decision not to get a college degree and Nicholas telling me I don't need to work.

This is what my life has come to.

"Thanks, Mrs. Howard. That's a really generous offer."

"Think about it, okay? You don't have to let me know yet. Take your time, talk to your boyfriend. If you decide no but you eventually change your mind, give me a call. I think Melissa's interested in being a line cook at Eaten Alive, so there'll be somebody there you know."

The diner option dissolves before my eyes. House of Screams it is.

"I'm so sorry," she says. Her voice is even thicker than usual, and I think she might be crying. "We did everything we could. It's hard out there. There aren't many steady, decent-paying

jobs available, and I know we couldn't offer you kids any benefits or overtime, but at least there was *something*. You should've
seen us twenty years ago. Full parking lot, every day."

I try to picture that, and I can't. I've never seen the second
row of parking spaces occupied. The four or five employee ve-
hicles taking up room lends the illusion that we're semibusy.

"It's all right, I understand," I rush to say. "I'm grateful you
hired me in the first place. I've had a lot of fun there." Nostalgia
sweeps over me and my voice crumbles like Mrs. Howard's.
"Thanks for the notice."

"Take care, hon."

We disconnect the call, and I have no idea what I'm going to
do now. I've got one, maybe two paychecks coming that will
need to be stretched out to invisible fibers. I know what I would
do if there were no Nicholas in this scenario: I'd start packing
for Tenmouth and dedicate myself to a career of fake gore and
screaming soundtracks, strobe lights in the darkness. Mopping
up vomit and scrubbing graffiti. It's a depressing prospect, but I
can't afford to be picky.

Even if I manage to get Nicholas to dump me and I end up
with the house, I'll have no way of paying rent. I desperately
need to find a job close to Morris. I'll get a roommate. Two
roommates—we'll become best friends and everything will be
fine, just fine. That's my plan A.

Uprooting to Tenmouth is plan B. Plan C is impossible with
the noxious state of my relationship with Nicholas, so I don't
even consider it. I throw it out. Plan C is identity theft. I'll enjoy
a few relaxing weeks as Deborah Rose in my Malibu beach
house before the feds track me down.

I'm still fretting over my quarter-life crisis when Nicholas barges in, big smile on his face. If I didn't hate him already, that smile would be enough to seal the deal.

"Hello, Naomi," he says gloatingly. Maybe he's already heard about the Junk Yard.

I turn away. He walks to the fridge and opens it, whistling. I think about shoving him inside. He closes the fridge without pulling anything from it and stares in my direction; I know this because I can see him in my periphery, a smudge of browns and tan. He waits until I look at him, then starts laughing.

"What," I snap.

My attitude thrills him. He angles a smirk at me, and it's insufferable. He knows something I don't. I know something he doesn't, too. I've put a squirt of Sriracha in his shaving cream.

"What," I repeat, this time in a growl. He laughs louder, bracing a hand on the door frame like I'm so funny, he can barely hold himself up. This man is a lunatic. How did I wind up here?

The thought is so loud in my head, it ends up coming out of my mouth. Nicholas takes a moment to consider it thoughtfully. "If memory serves, I asked a question and you said yes."

And thus began my tale of woe. At least memory only serves one of us—thankfully, mine has been inked out with amnesia.

"How'd we even meet?" I marvel.

He wipes one eye with a knuckle, grinning crookedly. "I picked you up at a farmers' market. From the top of the pile you looked nice. Wasn't until I brought you home that I found out you were completely rotten on the inside."

My mouth is shaped like a kiss, which sends the wrong message. I arrange it into a frown and say, "I'm telling your mother you say the F word. She'll make you go to church."

He throws his head back and laughs some more.

"Where *were* you all day?"

He winks. "Miss me?"

"Not even." My glance slides to the window, where I notice a Jeep Grand Cherokee parked in his spot. "The neighbors' visitors blocked you out again. Too bad." I don't see his car, so he must be parked way down the street. Poor Dr. Rose had to walk in the rain.

He steps into my personal space to check outside. His hair is a little bit damp and smells fruity, like my conditioner. I'm going to start hiding my toiletries.

"Nope," he says.

"Huh?"

He tucks a finger under my chin and lifts so that my mouth closes. "So beautiful," he murmurs, eyes glittering. They're the color of morning frost, and they're having a laugh at my expense.

My heart starts thumping erratically from the way he's looking at me. I've been tuning out my attraction to him and suddenly it comes pounding back with a vengeance, until all I notice is the adorable curl of his hair, the sensual curve of his smile, the delicious notes of his cologne. He's gorgeous and I hate him for spoiling it with his personality.

He follows up with, "Just as beautiful as the moment we first saw each other from across the room. On visitor's day, at the prison."

I swallow. "I'll be headed back to prison soon, I'm sure."

"I hear they offer classes. You could finally learn what the word *regardless* means."

"It'll be worth it, sleeping in the same room that holds my

toilet, knowing you're not around to ruin anyone's life. Regardless." I pause. I want to let this go, but I can't. "Tell me where you were all day."

"Take a guess."

"Cheating, I hope. Make sure you leave evidence for me to find."

His smile bends. Dries that way. I pick up a stack of junk mail and flip through Super Saver coupons, hmm-ing approvingly over discount items. My favorite soap is two for one this week. Frozen pizzas are five for ten dollars. Nicholas is going to strangle me with his Toothless tie.

"What are you making for dinner?" he asks. Not *What are we having*. It's *What are you making*. The laugh is gone from his voice.

I don't glance up. "It's in the oven."

I hear him pivot. There's no timer on. No red light. He pulls down the oven door and it's just as he suspected. "There's nothing in here."

I allow myself a tiny smile. I deserve it, after the day I've had. Not knowing what my fiancé is up to. Being let go from the best job I've ever had. The dreadful bangs that don't look anything like Amélie's. "That's what I made. A whole feast of nothing, just for you."

He grumbles all the way into his study. The lock clicks. Thirty minutes later, he emerges and stands at the front door.

"What are you doing?"

Nicholas casts me a disdainful look, like I've just asked the nosiest question. I hear a car door shut and seconds later, he's got a box of pizza in his hands. Pizza for one. Well played, Nick.

He kicks the door shut and goes back to the study. I hurry to hide all the paper plates, hoping to inconvenience him, but he doesn't care. He takes one of the good plates down from the cabinet and smiles at me as he rolls up a slice of pizza and eats half in one bite.

When he's finished, he leaves his unused plate in the sink for me to wash.

CHAPTER SEVEN

Nicholas and I are one for two. I won Sunday, ruining the Roses' dinner. He won Monday by making me think I was going to die, even if that wasn't his intention. He won again yesterday by forcing me to smell his pizza through the wall and not offering to share.

It's fitting that today happens to be Halloween, because I'm so focused on breaking this man's spirit that my scary eyes are like those little electricity balls in science centers that make your hair floof when you touch them. I'm going to zap everybody in a fifty-foot radius.

When a Jeep Grand Cherokee sidles into Nicholas's parking spot, I'm settled on the porch, clutching a plastic cauldron of goodies for trick-or-treaters. Nicholas climbs out of the Jeep and wears a smug expression as he trots up the walkway. He's hoping I'll ask what the hell he's up to, but I'm committed to figuring it out on my own. Last night I found his keys and noticed that the

Maserati fob was missing. I plugged an unfamiliar key into the Jeep experimentally and sure enough, it's Nicholas's. What a bizarre purchase for him. According to the Carfax in the glove compartment, the Jeep's not even new—it's like ten years old and has had two previous owners. Harold would be rolling in his tanning bed.

Where's the Maserati? I have no idea. I'm dying to know but I would rather lick a fiberglass lollipop than ask and give him the satisfaction of not telling me.

There are a couple things amiss about Nicholas today. For one, he's wearing his old glasses instead of his contacts. I like the glasses because they fit his face well and they make him seem sophisticated and down-to-earth at the same time. Whenever I tell him this, he scrunches up his nose and shakes his head self-consciously.

Also, he's wearing jeans and sneakers, which are outlawed at Rise and Smile.

"Skipped work again?" I surmise.

He just pats me on the head and skirts around to go inside the house. Cool. I have no idea what my fiancé has spent the past couple of days doing. He's lording his secrets over me like a Scrooge. This is a totally normal, functional relationship we're in.

I think about Seth and a dental hygienist going at it in the back of his car and my eyes narrow to slits.

Nicholas joins me on the front porch right as the trick-or-treaters start to arrive and doesn't say a single word in relation to my latest effort to tick him off: I've added his business card to every single Ziploc bag of candy with the highest sugar content I could find. Pixy Stix. Sour Patch Kids. Candy corn. Fun Dip.

The concept of a dentist handing out teeth-rotting substances to children will look vulgar to the parents rummaging through their kids' bags and buckets tonight. *What a gross move,* they'll mutter. *Turpin Family Dentistry, here I come.*

But Nicholas isn't fazed as he passes candy into tiny hands, bowing to the princesses and pretending to be scared of the monsters. Maybe he doesn't notice the business cards because he's too busy remembering a romp in his back seat with a dental hygienist. In my mind she looks like the hot nurse from that old Blink-182 album cover.

I look at him and think *I'll kill you.* It shows on my face.

He raises his eyebrows and smiles. I recognize it straight away as his polite liar smile, the one he puts on when we visit my parents twice a year and they ask how well we're liking living in sin. The smile he gives my brother when Aaron corners him for a presentation of Please Give Me Rent Money; I've Spent My Paycheck On Another PlayStation. The smile he gives my sister, Kelly, when she stands too close and stares too long, winding a lock of hair around her finger in a way she imagines is seductive.

I want to hiss *Where were you all day.* I grind my teeth together to keep the words trapped. *Don't ask, don't ask, don't ask.* It's what he's waiting for, lounging in jeans and glasses, hands interlocked behind his head. That's the beginning and end of his focus right now: *Ask, ask, ask.* I hear the telepathic chant.

Children come and go in thin herds, makeup smeared, half their costumes covered up with coats and hats. The temperature drops with the sun, and I go inside to get myself a throw blanket. As I pass him, traces of some aroma I've smelled before greet me. The answer to my déjà vu sits in a locked drawer, just vague and faded enough that I can't pinpoint where I've come across it in the past. I wouldn't ask him even if he tortured me. When I return, he exhales loudly, then goes inside for his own blanket.

What'd you do with the Maserati.

Where in the hell have you been.

We ignore each other. I take keen stock of every virile man who happens by and wonder what else is out there. I'm surely settling.

I think maybe I've won this round, because I've decided on my own to hand out candy instead of asking him if he wanted to go to one of his friends' parties. But he's so at peace right here next to me in his chair, telling every kid he loves their costume and increasing the odds that their parents will pay him to drill holes in their small mouths, that you'd think this was his plan instead of mine. He has a way of making me feel like that, like I'm just tagging along.

"I have a surprise for you," he says finally. I look over to see that his eyes are closed. The tips of his ears and nose are red from the cold, and I watch his Adam's apple work down a swallow.

He's going to say something nasty next, so I don't reply.

"Did you hear me?"

"Mm-hmm." I stand up. I don't want to hear what his surprise is. It's a horse head in the sheets. He's put asbestos in the sandwich I'm taking to work with me tomorrow. He's gotten the dental hygienist pregnant. He's breaking up with me. I've won, but he's still kicking me out of the house. I have five minutes to gather my things before he calls the police.

"I'll show you the surprise Friday after work."

I go inside without responding. There's no way I'm coming home Friday after work.

———

It's November second. Friday. "Text me every hour," Brandy urges. "If I don't hear from you, I'm going to assume the worst, so Do. Not. Forget."

It's just Brandy and Leon with me here today. Zach has quit. He peered into his crystal ball weeks ago and saw the end was nigh, so he already had a new job lined up ready to go. Melissa has today scheduled off, and I bet it's for a job interview. I'm a moron for not taking any precautionary measures.

The atmosphere is subdued. We're scouring help wanted ads and promising to refer each other to our new bosses if we find anything good. Morris is a dead town, commercially speaking. Not bad for living in, but you're going to have to commute to a better town to literally *make* your living. Half of us are going to end up moving to Beaufort, the next town over, to work at a dog food factory. The other half will move back in with their parents. None of us can decide which camp we'd rather fall into.

Brandy's very emotional. She's worried we're all going to drift apart after this, and she's probably right. I'll stay in touch with Brandy, but I'm not sad about letting go of Melissa now that we aren't friends anymore. Zach will likely move on at an offensive rate and forget any of us ever existed. He's funny and whip-smart, but he's also a prick half the time and uses his best qualities to be mean-spirited. He plays keep-away with my purse and will spend hours mimicking everything I say, even if I'm trying to ask him something important. Whenever I leave my phone sitting on the counter unlocked, he sends texts to my mom that say I've joined the army or I'm pregnant and don't know who the father is.

Leon's expressed an interest in buying the shop from the Howards and turning it into an outdoorsy restaurant. He'll put a stuffed grizzly bear in the doorway where Homer Elvis used to stand sentry. "If either of you wants a job, I'll hire you," he tells us. "I want to get the restaurant up and running by spring." We nod and say, "Sure, sure," knowing it won't happen.

"If I could afford it, I'd take the plunge now and move," Brandy laments, toying with her choker necklace. "I wouldn't even take anything with me. I'd just go."

"When I win the lottery, I'll buy you an island off the coast of Alaska," I promise her. "With a guest suite for me to stay in when I visit."

"Win the lottery as soon as you can, please. Half of my savings dried up this summer when my refrigerator broke and I had to loan my sister money for her school books."

I lay my head on her shoulder. "You'll get there. Before you know it, you'll be shivering in negative-sixty-degree weather, wearing snowshoes and talking to me on the phone while you drive a team of sled dogs to the grocery store."

"I heard you guys all thought you were going to die on Monday," Leon announces, transplanting jars of pickled rattlesnake eggs and BBQ weevil larvae into boxes for Mr. Howard to pick up later. Mr. Howard's going to ferry half the merchandise away to Tenmouth and dramatically clearance the rest. There are fluorescent blue signs stapled to every telephone pole on Langley: GOING OUT OF BUSINESS SALE. EVERYTHING AT THE JUNK YARD MUST GO! Including the people who've made a life here.

"It was a close call," I sniff.

"Death by jasmine."

Brandy and I give him questioning looks for knowing my flowers were jasmine, but he shrugs and smiles. Goddamn it, Zach. This is just like him. I wish he were here so I could yell at him for knowing it was jasmine and letting us believe otherwise. Instead he is somewhere else, ensuring his own financial security like a total jerk.

I think about moving to Tenmouth, which would suck. I think about staying in Morris and not being able to find another job, which would suck. I gaze miserably at Leon's grizzly-filled lifeboat, which is already pooling with water. The only thing that could make this day worse is if I spontaneously started my period, so that's exactly what happens.

"I'm going to miss you guys so much." Brandy trumpets into a Kleenex. "I hate this."

"It's the end of an era," I say gravely. The lights have been on the fritz for two days, but we don't bother changing the bulbs. There's hardly anything left to sell, so lasting even another week would be a miracle. I examine my surroundings and hope I wake up from this nightmare. The blank shelves are particularly depressing.

One of my favorite parts of the job has been rearranging our displays, setting up elaborate live tableaus with marionettes playing Frisbee or re-creating iconic movie scenes with pop culture figurines. I'd dress our faithful old stuffed raccoon, Toby, in dog sweaters and berets and place him in a new position every day: by the register, reading a magazine; smoking a pipe on top of the jukebox; on the windowsill, peering outside through a pair of small binoculars. Brandy and Leon love looking for Toby when they clock in, and say my talent for devising full scenes out of the merchandise is being wasted somewhere we don't ever get customers. That talent is useless now, since all the merchandise is gone.

"I don't think I'm ready for the next era," Brandy sighs.

Me neither.

"You're going to forget all about me by January and won't invite me to the wedding."

"Of course you're invited to the wedding!" There will never be a wedding.

She blows her nose again. Her hair looks fantastic and I hate myself for not asking her a week ago which salon she goes to. I could have bangs as cute as Brandy's right now if it weren't for my impulsiveness.

"I've been keeping an eye out for your invitation," she tells me as we put our jackets on. It's not quite six yet, but staying here any longer is useless. "Maybe it got lost in the mail?"

"Oh." I try not to squirm. "Haven't sent them out yet."

"Don't you need to do that, though? To give people time to RSVP? Your caterer will want to know how many heads to expect."

Leon saves me from answering. "She's still got time. Anyway, what do you think the surprise is, Naomi?"

I open my mouth and can't think of a single nice thing this surprise could be. Whatever it is, Nicholas has the edge on me. I'm racked with nerves.

"Dinner," I say. "He'll serve me to a mountain lion." In a boiling cauldron of lettuce and carrots, like a Bugs Bunny bit.

Leon laughs. "I think that's a little dramatic."

Maybe so, but Nicholas has a dramatic streak as well. He got it watching daytime television in grade school, pretending to be sick so he could stay home and avoid bullies who called him Four-Eyes and made fun of the ascot his mother made him wear. Nicholas knows precisely what he would say to his childhood bullies if he ever came across one of them now. He's perfected his speech in the shower, which he must think is soundproof. Too much *One Life to Live* in his formative years turned him into a vindictive diva.

To be honest, I hope he gets the opportunity to deliver that speech someday. It's incredible.

"I'm going to put off going home for as long as possible," I tell them. Brandy nods sagely. "I might go see a movie. Then grab something to eat. Then see another movie. By the time I get home, the mountain lion will have gotten so impatient that it'll have already eaten Nicholas. We'll watch Netflix together on the couch. A wildlife documentary."

I laugh at my own joke, but the noise lodges in my throat when the door opens and a version of Nicholas from the Upside Down strolls into the Junk Yard. He's wearing hiking boots and a secondhand jacket the color of the woods. It's so wrong on him that it takes me ten whole seconds to process that it's camo. Nicholas Rose is wearing camo.

My jaw drops when my eyes reach the top of his head. His hair is stuffed under one of those old-fashioned winter caps that has fleece-lined earflaps. Its colors are ugly orange and brown plaid. It's hideous. The whole ensemble has proved fatal to a handful of my brain cells and maybe my retinas.

"Oh my god," I say in a hoarse whisper. "You're going to drag me into the woods and shoot me, aren't you?"

I'm *not* being dramatic. He's dressed like one of Morris's many avid hunters.

Nicholas rolls his eyes, but I sense a shift in his mood. There's a calmness about him that unsettles me. "I'm picking you up. Remember that surprise I told you about?"

Brandy clutches my arm, and I can almost hear her thinking *It's more oleander!*

I don't know why, but I lie. "No. What surprise?"

He frowns, which must be why I lied to him. My subconscious is cruel and wants him to think I don't listen to anything he says, which is only true half the time. I feel bad about it until I remember that he completely checked out of wedding planning the second his mother stuck her interfering nose in, and he didn't stop her from trampling my every piece of input. We're all invited to Deborah's wedding in January.

I have been taught not to get into cars with strangers, so I wisely say, "My car's here. I'll just drive home."

"Nope." He takes me by the arm and leads me outside before I can blink *SOS* at Brandy and Leon in Morse code. I drag my feet on purpose, but he holds me against his side and lifts so that he can kind of glide me over the blacktop. I kick my dangling feet to leave scuff marks. This is how I'll die: slightly unwilling but ultimately lazy.

I throw a pleading glance at my car across the way, but it doesn't spur to life like Christine and avenge me. Soon enough I'm locked in the passenger seat of his Jeep, which he still hasn't explained, and I'm split down the middle between curious and pissed.

"You're pushy."

He buckles me up and starts the engine. The Jeep smells like his Maserati's crazy uncle. It drinks too much and plows over mailboxes. It had Taco Bell for lunch.

"What about my car?"

The question emerges as a whine, and he rewards my surrender of dignity with an indulgent smile that doesn't make it to his eyes. "We'll come back for it."

"But why don't I just . . ."

There's no use finishing my sentence. He's grit and steel now and won't give me a straight answer. The weird outfit has toppled my grasp of him irrevocably. I don't know this man. I'm at a severe disadvantage. If this bewilderment tactic is retaliation for my pancake makeup and Steelers hoodie, it's working.

"Are you having a midlife crisis?" He's a bit young for one, but then again he reads all the boring parts of the newspaper and there are usually Werther's candies in his pockets. He mentions his 401(k) a *lot*.

The corner of his mouth tilts. "Maybe."

We pass the turn to the street we live on and keep going. I desperately hope Deborah drives by and gets an eyeful of what her son is wearing. Actually, she wouldn't recognize him right now. She'd assume I'm having an affair, which, I've got to admit, is what this is starting to feel like. There's no way this is Nicholas. A thousand-year-old witch has hijacked his body.

Nicholas's placid body language is freakish next to the apprehension seeping from my pores. I don't know this car at all. I knew where everything was located in the Maserati, napkins and sunglasses and a mini bottle of Advil. For whatever reason I'm hung up on a bottle of sweet tea in the cup holder closest to the dashboard rather than the one close to the center console. That's backward for him. Such a tiny detail, but it fascinates me. *Why?* Also, he never drinks cold tea. Only hot.

I tap the lid. "Whose is this?"

"Mine."

My jaw unhinges. He feels me gawping at him and can't hold a smile back. He tries, though, sinking his teeth into his bottom lip.

There's an umbrella on the floor I've never seen before. I open the console and find Tic Tacs, a case of old CDs, and a plastic fork from Jackie's still in its wrapper. Jackie's is a tiny hamburger place with no drive-thru and barely any sitting room, so customers have to walk inside and order their food to go. The only item on the menu worth a second look is the fries, but their fries are legendary. Hands down, best I've ever had, and we used to swing by and grab dinner there before heading to the drive-in to watch movies. I haven't eaten Jackie's in nearly a year, ever since Nicholas and I stopped being a perfect couple. It's blasphemous that he's still able to enjoy our favorite date food without me.

The cup holder not cradling anomalous tea is occupied with wadded-up mail, one envelope incorrectly addressed to both of us: Nicholas and Naomi Rose. I want to toss it out the window. His regular jacket is an ivory lump in the middle of the back seat, the same color as his flesh. It makes me think of the witch who shucked him from his skin and is wearing him like a bodysuit.

He just got this car and already there's a full life he's lived in here that I haven't been part of. I don't think I like it.

I repress a demand to know where we're going. Outside my window the houses have stopped whirring by in dense packs and pare down to sparse flickers every quarter mile. Brown fields rear up taller and wilder. The sky is a white mist that stretches for eternity, unnaturally bright given that it's evening. The road careens right, swallowing us up between walls of towering maple, scarlet leaves ablaze. We rumble over a potholed bridge and my teeth chatter.

This is it, then. He's going to drive us both off a bridge. Voldemort and Harry Potter's quandary pops into my head: *Neither can live while the other survives.*

Nicholas slows down and leans forward just a hair, paying close attention. I don't even see the driveway until after we've made the turn, it's so obscured by woods. Gravel crunches under the tires of Upside Down Nicholas's car, leading us along a winding path to a house on a hill.

It's surrounded by a forest of blue spruce and Eastern white pine, which I bet looks like a pretty Christmas wonderland when it snows. The front yard hasn't been raked in a century, layers upon layers of dead maple leaves rising flush with a pile of chopped wood carefully stacked. There's an ancient car with a tarp pulled over it, tires half sunk into the earth.

"That'll be gone in a couple days," Nicholas tells me when he sees what I'm looking at after we both exit the car. "He has to find someone with a hitch to help him haul it."

"Who?"

I don't think he hears me over the crunch of leaves underfoot. It's firmly packed in some areas and loose in others, so I have to choose my steps wisely or I'll break my ankle. I catch my balance on a little evergreen sapling. It's a runt of a thing, malnourished and crooked. "Aww." I brush the needles. "It's a Charlie Brown tree."

He makes an indulgent sound. *Hum.* I want to pinch him. He's doing that thing again, where he belittles what I'm saying even if I'm right.

"Before we go in," he says, halting my stride with a hand on my sleeve, "what do you think of it from the outside?"

"What?" I blink up at him.

His arm gestures to the house. I follow the swing. It's . . . a house. Old, probably. Dark brown strips of horizontal wood and spring green shutters, one hanging crookedly. A deep front porch with tipsy steps illumined by the pinprick of a glowing doorbell. The chimney's a column of lumpy round stones and the windows are the merry orange squares of a Tiffany lamp. A high tide of leaves swells up against the siding on the eastern wall, all the way up to a wide leaded glass window that must be the living room.

"It's fine, I guess. Whose is it?"

"Ours."

Ours. It echoes. Insensible gibberish. Undeniably false.

I snap my fingers and freeze time. Wheel to face him dead-on. The creature inhabiting Nicholas's body looks down at me with the most peculiar mixture of pleasure and solemnity, and I get the feeling he is wide, wide awake while I am just beginning to stir from my hibernation. He's skipped his contacts again, eyes sparking with intensity behind slate-gray frames. The ends of his hair curling out from his hat are so soft-looking, I almost want to touch but snatch my hand back because it feels too forward. He's my fiancé, but not. I don't know what we are. Who we are.

I unfreeze time and he smiles. "Welcome home."

CHAPTER EIGHT

A Renaissance painting of us invents itself in midair, capturing my bafflement and Nicholas's triumph. The second hand trickles at the slow drip of two million years, and then—

"What do you mean, 'ours'?"

"I bought it." His eyes never leave mine.

This—

But—

I—

!!!

The world flips as Nicholas turns our mind game on its head. I'm lost. It makes no sense whatsoever that he would buy a house and expect me to move in. We've been fighting for custody of the squat white rental. We've been fighting to push the other one to wave a white flag and get lost forever.

"Are you malfunctioning?" he asks, mildly entertained.

He's twelve steps ahead of me. He's twelve steps above.

Behind. Everywhere. I don't know where to turn and I don't know what his objective is. He's right, I'm malfunctioning. My circuit board is smoking. I have a *house*.

No, I don't. I hastily remind myself that I don't have anything that's part Nicholas. He doesn't belong to me, so neither does this. He's termite Midas. Everything he touches turns to rot.

The only lucid thing I can think to say is, "I take it you won the coin toss."

"Yes."

"But." Speech is not coming easily. My brain is continuously rejecting messages coming in from my eyes and ears as impossible. "A whole house?"

"I tried to buy half of one, but couldn't find any that are gaping open on the side or missing a roof."

I barely hear the joke. "How. Why. I don't—"

"I bought it from one of the guys you work with. Leon. I ran into him a few days ago and got to talking about the sort of place I wanted to live in, and he told me about wanting to move out of the place he's in now, and we realized we both wanted the same thing and could help each other. Turns out, he's actually pretty cool. He let me play with his bow saw and we've got plans to build a couple of chairs."

"Leon?" That's what I'm stuck on right now. "You bought this house from Leon? Leon *Duncan*?"

He chuckles. "I'll let him know you haven't forgotten his last name yet. He'll be shocked."

Great, they've been swapping stories about how rude I am. Maybe blanking on Leon's last name is the reason he didn't say a word to me about this all day. What a Judas.

"He knew this was the surprise and he let me think I was about to get murdered!"

"You really need to stop telling your coworkers I'm out to murder you." Irritation flits across his features. "Doesn't give me a good rep."

"We've never discussed the kind of house we'd buy together," I sputter. "I wasn't involved here at all."

"I wanted it to be a surprise."

"*You* wanted."

He just stares, not getting it. "This isn't the sort of surprise you spring on your fiancée! Couples do this shit together, Nicholas! One of them doesn't go behind the other one's back to do something of this magnitude. First you get rid of your car and bring home that—that *behemoth* over there—" He's laughing, which exasperates me even more, but I forge on: "I've asked you where you've been. You've refused to tell me. Do you have any idea what that's like?"

"Yeah!" he cries. "I do. I don't know where you've been all year, Naomi. Your body's here, but your head's somewhere else. You've gone and left me all alone."

If anyone's been left alone, it's me, fighting the War of the Roses all by myself. No way am I vaulting into *that* pool of lava, so I pick a milder topic to complain about instead. "We're in the middle of nowhere."

He shrugs. "So?"

I cast around for another complaint. What comes out of my mouth boggles even me. "I've always wanted a front door that's painted purple. The color of magic."

"That's a terrible reason to reject a house. Naomi, I bought us a *house*! Take a beat here and let that sink in. How many of your friends can say their boyfriend bought them a house?"

1. He's not my boyfriend, he's my fiancé. (Sort of.)

2. He didn't buy this house for me. He bought it for himself,

without asking or wanting me to be a part of that process. Am I supposed to be grateful that he's letting me tag along *after* he made all the decisions? If we're supposed to spend our life together as equal partners, this doesn't bode well.

3. My only real friend is Brandy, and at this moment in time she thinks I'm bleeding out in a ditch.

This is madness. I should go back to the white rental house now that he's apparently living here, but I can't give in yet. The war's still on. He's trying to pull the wool over my eyes, but I know we've simply relocated to a different battlefield. I'm not going to tell myself what I've been inwardly repeating for months now: It could be worse.

That's what I've been doing. Justifying staying with him by reminding myself it could be worse. *Look at her. Look at him. Look at those people. They're alone and have nobody. They're in terrible relationships. They're so unhappy. It could be worse. That could be me.*

Except, it *is* me. I've been unhappy.

"Okay," he huffs. "Except for the front door, which isn't purple, what do you think?"

Truthfully? There are a lot of dead, dirty leaves and it's out in the middle of nowhere and I so badly want it to be mine. I barely registered there *was* a house here when we pulled up, but after hearing him say the word *ours*, it was like the lights of a stage washed over the scene and made it all so beautiful I could cry.

It's the sort of place I'd like to settle down with my one true love—that is, somebody who isn't Nicholas. I want Leon to take back the house and save it for me to buy myself someday when I'm in a relationship that's loving and healthy. With a man I love at *least* eighty percent. Sharing it with Nicholas now will spoil it, the same way that some of my favorite movies we've watched together are now tainted, and so is the band we used to listen to together, Generationals. One of their songs was playing on the radio during our first kiss and after that, it became "our band." We've even seen them in concert. Now I can barely stand to listen to their music without resurrecting a thousand unwelcome feelings.

This property will forever be known as the house my ex-fiancé bought without my participation. It's the future Mrs. Rose's house, not mine. Which chafes a little.

"I don't want to live here."

He's losing patience. "I don't really care what you want, to be honest. I don't like you again yet. But I'm going to. And you're going to like me again, too. This house is going to save us."

"Save us?" I don't bother downplaying the ghastliness of his assertion. "I thought we were trying to kill this thing?"

His expression is so scornful, I flinch. "Naomi, if the point were a meteor hurtling straight toward the earth with the power to destroy us all, you'd still miss it somehow." He turns his back on me and marches determinedly inside the house. He's going to be a mountain man, come whatever, and I'm just along for the ride.

I think I see his new angle. It's even more disturbing than trying to get me to leave him.

It's cheaper and easier to mold me into the kind of woman he can stomach marrying rather than break up with me. If he does, he'll have to field a hundred surprise dates his mother sends him on to find the next broodmare contender.

My baby oven and I have been primed and vetted. I'm already familiar with his odious parents, who haven't managed to run me off yet. A compartment of my brain reluctantly hosts a glossary of dental terminology. I tolerate his satanic ritual of removing a banana wholly from its peel and laying the banana on the bare table without a plate, touching everything with his fingers and setting it down between bites.

I'm an investment. If he pulls his stock now, he'll bleed money and lost time all over the place. He'll be starting over, two years of his youth down the drain. But I've got news for Nicholas Benjamin Rose: if he thinks I'm not the biggest waste of time that's ever happened to him, he's got another think coming.

For long moments, I merely stare at the part of the house that ate him up. Details I still haven't noticed properly are swimming to the forefront for attention—the wooden roof shingles all bowing at their centers; the dingy welcome mat with a Scottie dog on it; the silhouette pacing behind the wide leaded window. He wanted nature? He's got it. English ivy swarms the chimney, trying to work its way down inside the house. The air is fresh and crisp. I don't hear any traffic, any sound of human civilization.

The house he's bought on his own, guaranteeing it will never feel like *ours*, sits up on a crest between two gently sloping valleys, and I think he's picked a hell of a hill to die on. We'll both be buried here. Our ghosts will haunt it, torturing each other and any misguided home buyers hoping for a country experience.

I'm still trying to orchestrate plan A, and Nicholas is subverting my efforts with plan C. Only one of us can win, but I'm no longer certain what the winner keeps and what they lose.

My favorite thing about the house that's mine but not mine is that it's dim and small and cozy, which doesn't sound appealing when I put it that way, but each room has a very particular feel to it, which makes my imagination go bonkers.

The living room is exactly where you'd want to relax in a comfy armchair with grandchildren strewn at your feet in a semicircle as you read them old stories of faraway lands. Swashbuckling pirates and flying trains, masked bandits and elvish royalty. The books are leather-bound, spines crackling in your aging hands. You sit quietly in front of a flickering fire with your soul mate as raindrops patter the glass, more contented than a cat stretched out on a windowsill.

The living room is where your grandchildren's fondest memories of you will be born, and that's where they'll always picture you long after you're gone. Every time they smell wood smoke or hot chocolate, it will pull them back in time to the sound of your voice rising and falling like a melody as you read to them.

"What do you think?" Nicholas asks.

"Hmm." I saunter past him into the kitchen, dissolving him with my mind powers so I can take it all in without his hovering.

The kitchen is airy and light, with exposed wood beams traversing the ceiling. Copper pots and pans and watering cans dangle from them like wind chimes. Green explosions of ivy burst from planters. The fragrance of freshly baked bread and sun-kissed linens on a clothesline perfume the air. In the summer, this is where you bite into a blackberry and feel the ripe flavors rupture on your tongue. In the spring, you lean over the sink and water the tulips kept in the window planter.

A kitchen witch lives here. She keeps a cauldron in the hearth and lays bundles of dried herbs across the overhead beams. There's a scrubbed wooden table and mismatched chairs painted all the colors of St. Basil's Cathedral. Toenails of the family dog go *clack-clack-clack* on the pine floors and everything about this room makes your heart lift into a smile.

"Doesn't come with any appliances," Nicholas says, "but that's fine." I stop walking and he accidentally bumps into me from behind. "Whoops. Sorry."

"You wanna give me some space?"

"Well, you're not saying anything."

"I'm talking to myself right now. Give us a minute."

It's his turn to mutter "Hmm." I'm glad when he ducks into the (one and only) bathroom, giving me a break from him.

The drawing room contains three tall, magnificent windows facing the woods out back. The yard beyond grades steeply, providing an excellent view of a pond with a long dock. This is the best room for stargazing. You part the luxurious red velvet curtains and watch a sickle moon arc over the forest, reflecting off the pond. This is where you keep your Christmas tree and a family of nutcrackers on the mantel. The walls are papered in midnight blue with silver foil stars and birch trees. Everything washes gold when the fire's lit.

A replica of Grand Central Station's clock is mounted to the newel post of the stairway right outside the drawing room, and in the middle of the night when you pad through the hushed house to curl up in a rocking chair on a thick woven rug, you pass the glowing face of the clock and hear its hands tick. The

world is quiet save for the ticking of that clock, and the soft
snores of your one true love sleeping upstairs, the rustling toss-
and-turn of your small children, and the whispering of branches
in the forest.

It.

Is.

Magical.

I can envision all of it so vividly and I want it. I want it bad.

Nicholas enters the drawing room while I'm mentally placing where my stash of sugar cookie and peppermint candles
would go and jars me out of my own little world with his voice.
"I think I'll take this room for my office." He spreads his fingers
at the bank of glittering windows. "I'll put a big-screen TV right
there, so I won't have to divide my time between working and
watching football."

The nutcrackers in my fantasy topple off the mantel and into
the fire.

"Ugh."

"What?" He does a double take at me, then the mantel,
which was where my gaze had been fixated. "You don't like the
fireplaces? I figured that'd be one of your favorite parts. There's
forced air, too. We won't need to light an actual fire to get heat if
we don't want to."

"The fireplaces are fine," I reply blandly. I'm surprised my
nose doesn't shoot across the room like Pinocchio. I love those
fireplaces more than my blood relatives. I want to nail two
mother- and father-sized Christmas stockings over them, next
to two child-sized ones. I want to buy a flock of flameless candles and take three hours tediously arranging them just so while
a pained Nicholas looks on.

Nicholas studies me, and whatever he sees in my face makes his eyes soften. "Come upstairs?"

"Sure, whatever."

There are three bedrooms upstairs, largely the same in size and layout. Plain walls, wood floors. The center one's half a foot narrower than the other two, and a lightbulb goes off in my brain before I can smash it: *Nursery.*

I'll never forgive myself for the thought.

"Which room's mine?" I ask, mostly to provoke him. He's seen the whole house before, so he doesn't look at any of it now, keeping his focus pinned on my every reaction. It's why I'm straining not to react: I can't let him see how much I love this place. When I enter a room, I think it's all right. By the time I'm walking out of it, it's become the best room I've ever seen. I'm going to be devastated when I inevitably have to leave. I've been living in that white rental all this time like a total idiot.

"Take your pick."

I can't discern by his tone whether he's agreeing to sleep in separate bedrooms. I haven't slept in our bed since the coin toss, and I'm not about to change that now. I don't know what would be worse: sleeping with him when I'm trying so hard to push him away, or making a move on him and then having him reject me because he's trying to push *me* away. I'm still confused about Nicholas's endgame here. His strategy's fuzzy.

"A house like this is full of stories. It should have a name."

He gives me a delighted smile. "Name it."

Wind batters the roof like we're in the eye of a tornado. We're so far removed from everything we've experienced as a couple. I shouldn't love it. We're Heathcliff's and Catherine's ghosts, marooned in the wilds of Morris. I blurt out the one thing I can think of. "Disaster."

His smile slips. "I'm not living in a house called Disaster. That's inviting bad luck."

"Buddy, we've got that already."

He sighs through his nose, a trait he picked up from Harold. I used to think all of his little mannerisms were cute until I saw the broader template they were cut and pasted from. Watching Nicholas push his drinking glass three inches to the right of his dinner plate stops being adorably quirky after you've seen his mother do it. Being acquainted with Deborah has killed so much of what I loved about her son.

"I'm getting a U-Haul over here tomorrow."

"Tomorrow?"

"That's right." He looks so pleased with himself.

I think he's testing me. Trying to break me, maybe, with all these unexpected changes happening at once. I decide to test him, too. "And if I don't want to move?"

"The U-Haul place is closed on Sundays, but if you want to rent a truck for Monday, be my guest. Until then, all our stuff's coming here."

There's that misleading word again—*our.*

Unfortunately, neither of us held on to much of our belongings from our single days. My old furniture is long gone, as well as his. We'd wanted to pick out everything together for our joint life, test-driving every couch at Furniture Outlet and bouncing on mattresses until we found The One. There are exceptions, like his desk and my toaster, but by and large our collection was curated as a couple. It'll be a bitch to divvy it up.

I can't afford to replace these possessions. He can. Or could, anyway. I don't know what the situation is now that he's bought a fricking house.

"And if I stay?" I prompt. "Do I get my name on the deed,

too? Or is this the place you'll share with whichever woman you happen to be with? There's no guarantee you won't toss me out in a month."

"This house is *ours*, Naomi. Why would I toss you out?"

"Why wouldn't you? I would, if I were in your shoes. I'd leave you at the old house and say adios."

Nicholas glares at me. He turns and stomps down the stairs. I'm still standing in the bedroom when he stomps back up, complexion a shade redder. "If you want to stay at the old house, fine. I'm not going to force you to come live here. But I know the Junk Yard's closing. Leon told me. So good luck paying your rent without me, sweetheart."

"I don't want your money. I'd rather sell my own liver. I'd rather work at one of the brothels your dad used to go to before your mom melted his brain with Dr. Oz supplements."

It's a kill shot, but he raises a laugh like a shield and my blow glances right off. "Am I supposed to be shocked? I've known about that for years."

It's inane, but I'm mad he knew about this and didn't tell me. It's such a juicy tidbit to hog all to himself. I'm supposed to be his fiancée! He should share these humiliating stories about his parents with me.

"You're the reason we're still living in Morris," he rants. "If it weren't for your ludicrous attachment to a gas station gift shop trying to be Ripley's Believe It or Not, I would've accepted that job offer in June. Bigger city, better pay. More opportunities for both of us. But *no-o-o*, you didn't *want* to move. You said your minimum-wage job was every bit as *important* as mine. Outright refused to even consider moving. Made me give up what is basically my dream job, so now I'm stuck out here forever. I knew at

the time that the Junk Yard was dying, and I was throwing everything away over you. Well, now you're going to throw away
something for me, too. You're going to throw away a little bit of
your pride and give this house a chance for one goddamn minute
before making a decision about whether you want to stay or
leave. You will at least give me *that*."

The last string of civilized feeling between us snaps.

"So you've been pissed off since June about not taking that
job, then," I shoot back. "I'd only been working at the Junk Yard
since February and I was just starting to feel settled into my new
routine. I loved my job. Why should I be the one to sacrifice?"

He's breathing fire. "Why should *I*?"

"I don't get what you're doing." I throw my arms up. "Why'd
you bring me here?"

"I thought this would be a nice surprise. I thought you'd
love it. Just like with the flowers you complained I never get for
you. But then when I do get you flowers, you SET THEM ON
FIRE."

"That's ancient history! How dare you bring that up. You
already admitted you don't care what I want."

He lets out a savage, animalistic roar and stomps back down
the stairs again. I hear him banging doors and nearly yell at him
not to bang the beautiful doors in my beautiful new house.
"Let's go!" he calls up after a few minutes. "We have to go get
your car! What the fuck do you want for dinner?"

"I fucking want pizza!" I holler. I've wanted some since the
son of a bitch got it delivered.

"Fine! I've got a fucking coupon for Benigno's, anyway!"

"Great! I fucking love Benigno's!"

We pile into his car as angrily as we can muster and don't

speak until we're inside the pizza parlor. When a lady comes over to seat us, a different Naomi and a different Nicholas smile our in-front-of-other-people smiles and our tone is so calm it's scary, but our insides are boiling.

When I'm in the bathroom, he orders me a Dr Pepper, which he knows is my favorite.

Before we leave, I wipe all the crumbs and used napkins from the table onto our plates and stack them, which I know he appreciates because he tries to be helpful to the busboys.

When we get back out to the car, we plot how to ruin each other's lives.

———

I don't know how Nicholas can expect me to take him seriously.

I mean.

It's just.

A pop of laughter bursts in my mouth before I can swallow it.

I woke up to three strange men in my living room this morning and squawked, flailing to cover myself, but luckily a blanket had found its way over me while I was asleep on the couch and no one saw my bare legs in boy shorts. When I stood up, I kept the blanket wrapped around me and almost tripped over it, yelping when Nicholas gave me an unexpectedly playful swat on the bottom to get me moving.

"Hurry up!" he said cheerfully. "Got lots to do today!"

That was hours ago, and I still don't know what mood I'm supposed to be in. Moving has been a real bitch, and I'm avoiding helping as much as I can. Lots of time has been spent hiding

YOU DESERVE EACH OTHER   133

in the bathroom, pretending it takes ten minutes to change a tampon. After my third faked tampon run in an hour, I emerge to find that Nicholas has made a daring wardrobe change. When he sees the evil smile on my face, his expression gets prickly and defensive, but I can't be held accountable here.

Nicholas is wearing this ridiculously baggy . . . I don't even know what to call it. Coveralls? He's head-to-toe khaki, which he must be *loving*, and his brand-new work boots probably weigh twenty pounds each. I think he's going for *hale, rough-hewn man of the wilderness*, but instead he looks like a Ghostbuster.

The plaid hat with earflaps is back, even though he must be hot what with all the refrigerator lifting and shelf maneuvering and anything else I'm pretending I wouldn't be any good at because I'm a fragile-boned female whose delicate knees buckle from carrying a box of tissues. If he wants to buy a house without my help, he can very well move everything into it without my help. I think he's waiting for me to throw that in his face, which is why he bites his tongue whenever he sees me sitting down, doing nothing.

This new look is unnatural on Nicholas. He's trying so hard to fight his own genes, bless him.

No matter what he wears to disguise it, Nicholas was bred to host balls at Pemberley. He's got an aristocratic, pretty-boy face, all sharp angles and quiet allure with pale skin, delicately disheveled dark chocolate hair, and a widow's peak. His gaze should be wicked to reflect the type of man lurking beneath, but instead it projects wide-eyed innocence, an inborn predatory trait to allow the wolf to roam among sheep undetected.

The architecture of his face is intriguing when he smiles: skin stretching over enviable cheekbones with hollows carved beneath, making him look like he's perpetually sucking in his cheeks. It's a pouty, prissy sort of beauty that screams *drape me over a leather chaise to contemplate ennui.* The idea of him strutting into a forest to chop firewood makes me choke. Rugged, this man is not.

"Are you Nicholas's evil twin?" I ask. "Or are you the good one?"

He scowls.

"Seriously, why are you dressed like that?"

"Shh." He glances at the doorway to the adjacent room where the movers are loading up the washer and dryer onto dolly carts. Their work boots are scuffed and dirty, whereas Nicholas's gleaming kicks emit a fresh-from-the-box chemical odor. "Can you just be cool? God."

"Nope. Are you trying to impress those guys or something?"

He changes the subject before the cool kids hear us. "Why do you keep running into the bathroom?"

I waffle between two disgusting possibilities, trying to decide which he'd find more repulsive. "Period stuff."

He looks skeptical.

"Do you want details? If you prefer, I won't flush next time and you can see for yourself what I'm doing in there."

"What is wrong with you?"

"You. You're what's wrong with me."

He stalks off and I'm feeling pretty great, I have to say. One of the movers clomps heavily my way and I rethink my strategy to slink off to a hidey-hole. The air is buzzing with testosterone, and I'm starved for a hit of it. Have I mentioned how excellent it is to have professional manly men come do physical labor right in front of you? Strapping men with sun damage and large, coarse hands and veiny forearms with hair. One's got a tattoo on his leathery bicep of a pinup girl reclining on the hood of a convertible.

Supervising is a tough job, but someone's got to do it. I stand in positions where their lifting, bending, and groaning is most advantageous, watching their muscles bulge and strain. Back muscles! Who knew there could be so many muscles in a person's back? I do now. Forget Tinder; after Nicholas throws in the towel I'm going to hire a batch of movers and find my next boyfriend that way.

Nicholas has a nice body. It's elegant and toned—the sort of body you could see mastering a piano as well as running across a rugby field. Currently, I'm not privileged enough to enjoy the benefits of his nice, elegant body, so men who were not previously my type are all hot to me now. I'm in a bad way. Boulder-size men with ZZ Top beards and face tattoos. Balding mad scientists. Count Chocula. The silhouette from *Mad Men*'s credits. If this drought goes on any longer I'll be lusting after the featureless figure on men's restroom signs.

I watch one of the men with a little too much interest and feel the heat of Nicholas's glower. I clear my throat and excuse myself from the room.

Later, he tracks me down and throws dirty looks in my direction until I give in and sigh. "What?"

"Could you be a little less conspicuous, please? How would you feel if you saw me ogling other women?"

I assume he ogles other women on the daily. I know they ogle him.

"I wasn't ogling anyone. I don't know what you're talking about."

He rolls his eyes. "Please. I've never seen a human go so long without blinking."

"I was . . . observing," I say primly. "Don't make something out of nothing. Anyway, no one could blame me even if I was looking, which I wasn't. It feels like it's been forever since I've gotten properly laid by someone who *wants* it."

Nicholas's mouth is a thin line. His stare is unwavering. I start to get a little apprehensive and break the silence with another "What?"

His shake of the head is curt. "Nothing."

Nicholas is lying. When he says *Nothing,* what he really means is *I need time to come up with something devastating to say.*

I'm all braced for it after the movers have left and we're standing outside our new house that's actually his house, which I'm still calling Disaster.

I'm watering the Charlie Brown tree because I have love to give and nowhere meaningful to dump it. This tree needs me. I'll feed him and sweep away his dead needles and he'll grow to be the best and biggest tree in the yard. He'll give pollination-birth to a hundred new trees, which I'll string with tinsel. He'll be the patriarch and general of my new tree army.

His name is Jason. Right now he's my number one priority on this earth.

Nicholas watches me closely as I pat Jason and murmur affirmations. I've heard from science that it helps the plants if you talk to them.

When I'm certain Jason is taken care of, I march up to the house. I haven't even taken off my shoes when Nicholas starts in on me.

"There's a difference between being needed and wanted. In some things, I like to be needed. With sex, I need to be wanted. I can't be just some guy in your bed getting the job done. I'm not having disconnected, going-through-the-motions sex with you. Not you. You're supposed to be the person I connect with the most deeply."

"We do connect." Oh god, is that my voice? I sound so blah. My lying skills are taking a beating from all the brutal honesty we've been engaging in the past few days.

"You stopped seeing me, Naomi. You stopped wanting me. You're going to figure out one of these days that I can tell when you're starting to disassociate, and it's the most heartbreaking experience I've ever had. It's nonstop. It keeps on happening. I try to bring you back to me every time you go to leave, off into your own head where I'm not allowed."

"I don't know what you're talking about." I feel deeply uncomfortable, and the intensity with which he's speaking makes my skin burn hot.

Nicholas continues as though I never interrupted. "I can't be intimate with you when you disassociate because I can't let that become our new normal. But being distant from you as punishment for being distant from me doesn't seem to motivate you to change. So I don't know where that leaves us. All I know is that it's a bad idea to fulfill your physical needs if you won't fulfill my emotional ones."

I'm not going anywhere near the subject of emotional needs. I cross my arms and rush straight to the defensive. "Motivate me to change how? What exactly would you like for me to change about myself, Nicholas?"

I can see he's shutting down. Of course, now that he's said his piece he wants to turn tail and flee, but I'm not letting him.

"I just want you to care about me," he implores, gesturing with both hands to the space between us. "I want you to listen. I want you to give a shit about my feelings."

Guilt knocks at my door, one single tap, before I remember

what we were originally arguing about: Him going behind my back to buy a house. Him low-key resenting me because he didn't take a job offer in Madison, assuming it was a no-brainer that I give up my job here in deference to his superior profession and superior goals. Him showering his heinous mother with gifts while neglecting me, and never taking my job or my friends seriously, and not standing up for me when his friends and family belittle me. This man gazing into my eyes with such torment, who looks so genuinely aggrieved, has been pushing me to leave him for months.

He's reframed the dialogue to make me the bad guy, and I almost tripped and fell for it.

"Two can play it that way," I hiss. "You think there aren't any changes I'd make to you?"

He flinches. "What changes?"

"Figure it out," I say, turning and heading up the stairs to the right-hand bedroom. I've given him the box spring and directed the mattress to what will be my bedroom for the duration of my visit. "You have until January twenty-sixth."

CHAPTER NINE

It's Sunday, the worst day of the week. Or it used to be the worst; now Sundays are the perfect opportunity to rub my hands together and see how far I can push the Roses. Sunday is the new birthday.

It's not bragging to say that my next move is a masterpiece. I check the clock and count forty-five minutes until my grand reveal. Forty-five long, excruciating minutes in what's been the slowest day on record. It's getting hard to hold it in, especially since it's no coincidence that my Steelers hoodie went "missing" during the move.

I don't want him to expect what's coming, so I'm generous with my smiles today. I slip Nicholas polite inquiries, pleases, and thank-yous like Trojan horses. This might have backfired on me, because he looks more suspicious than ever and all his suspicion has put him in a bad mood.

"You're still in pajamas," he tells me. I check the clock again.

Forty-three minutes to go. If time were moving any slower, it would be going backward.

"So? I've got time."

"*So*, we're meeting my parents at the restaurant in forty-five minutes—"

"Forty-three."

"—And it takes you an hour to get dressed. Simple math, Naomi."

It takes fifteen minutes to get dressed, if I haven't already picked out an outfit. It takes another fifteen minutes to do my hair, followed by fifteen minutes for makeup. Then I have to account for other last-minute stuff like tweezing my eyebrows or clipping my nails. Switching out snagged pantyhose. Foraging for a missing shoe. Getting *ready* takes an hour. Getting ready encompasses more than the simple act of pulling on clothing.

I decide to be offended. It's been a while, and it's so much fun, so I guide him in the right direction to give me some material I can misconstrue. "It's fine, I'll just throw on a sweater and pants a few minutes before we leave."

"You're not going to take forever to do your hair and makeup?"

Perfect. Thank you, Nicholas, you're such a dove. "You think I need makeup, then?"

"That's not what I said."

"You're implying that I'm not presentable in public unless I have a full face of makeup on."

"No. I absolutely did *not* imply that."

"I suppose I should take three hours to curl my hair, too, right?" I make my voice tremble. I am the victim of horrendous misdeeds. "Because I'm not pretty enough the way I am? I suppose you're embarrassed to bring me around your family unless I conform to society's impossible beauty standards for females?"

His eyes narrow. "You're right. Your hair's an embarrassment in its natural state and your face is so anti–female beauty
that if you go out like that, I'd insist on you walking backward
and ten feet away from me. I want you to go upstairs right now
and paint yourself unrecognizable." He arches his eyebrows.
"Did I do that right? Are those the words you'd like to put in my
mouth?"

My chin drops. He lowers his gaze to a newspaper and flicks
the page. He did it for dramatic effect. I know he didn't get a
chance to finish reading the article he was on.

"Actually, I'd like to put an apple in your mouth and roast
you on a spit," I say.

"Go ahead and wear pajamas to dinner, Naomi. You think
that would bother me? You can go out dressed as Santa Claus
and I wouldn't care."

Now I genuinely am insulted. "Why wouldn't you care?"

He raises his eyes to mine. "Because I think you're beautiful
no matter what."

Ugh. That's really low, even for him. I spin away from the
liar and go to wash another load of bedclothes. All of our blankets and pillows got streaked with grime in the U-Haul, so
Nicholas has been spending all day washing everything while I
scrub the rest of the house down with wipes. I have nothing
against Leon, and he lived cleanly, but I do feel a little like I need
to scrub him out of the house. His eyes are in the walls, following us wherever we go.

I check the dryer and holy god, this man is going to burn us
to the ground. "You need to clean out the lint trap! Letting it get
this packed is a fire hazard."

"You're a fire hazard," I distinctly hear him mutter under
his breath.

"I know you're used to having a woman do all the housework for you, but I might not always be around. You should listen to me. I'm trying to educate you and help you to grow as a person."

"How about you put your advice in a pamphlet and I'll take a look at it when you're finally gone?" he replies.

I make the trip upstairs as violently loud as I can. Maybe I go a little overboard, because I slip on the edge of a step and save myself by hugging the railing. I glance down, hoping he didn't catch what happened, but of course he did. His quiet laugh sucks one year from my life span. "Are you all right, honey?" he calls up, sweet as cotton candy.

"Shut up. Go draw your mother a bubble bath."

"You're obsessed with my mother."

I'm sure we've traumatized the house. It's used to quiet, sensitive Leon. It's probably never had to deal with this level of vitriol before. Nicholas and I are monsters nowadays and I don't like either of us, but I definitely don't like who I was before, the Naomi who kept her mouth shut and didn't speak her truth, so there's no going back. Nicholas and I are in a free fall.

I grumble obscenities into my closet, chucking Snoopy and Woodstock pajamas over my shoulder. I'm tempted to keep them on, but I've got applications circulating and knowing my luck, a manager at someplace I'm trying to get hired would see me. No one wears Snoopy and Woodstock pajamas to a steakhouse unless they're Going Through Some Shit.

I do, however, carefully choose a bumblebee-yellow shirt that washes me out. I tug my hair into an unflattering low ponytail, bangs sticking straight up like I've been electrocuted. I don't bother to dab concealer under my eyes. As a matter of fact, I dab some faint purple eyeshadow there. I look like a pilgrim with cholera. Mrs. Rose is going to have a field day with my appearance, which I'll punish her son for after we get home. My feelings are already so hurt, I can't help but smile at my reflection.

"Hurry up!" Nicholas complains outside my door. He jiggles the knob and it's locked, obviously. I've just gotten back the luxury of having a bedroom all to myself after a year of sharing and he's not invited in. "You waited until the last minute, like I knew you would. It's irresponsible to arrive late! I'll have to text Mom and tell her what our drink orders are, because you were dicking around all day and couldn't bother showering or putting on actual clothes until it was almost dark out!"

"I'm basically ready!" I yell back. "All I have to do is put my shoes on and . . ." I fill the rest of the sentence with low-volume nonsense.

"And what?"

"Get off my back. We'll get there when we get there."

"That's not how civil society functions. How about you grab your makeup bag and put all your crap on in the car?" It's adorable how he assumes I'm in here making myself pretty instead of smearing a pentagram on the floor in my own blood and casting hexes on him.

I turn fully around to face the door. "How about you go iron your socks like a complete psychopath? Anyway, leave if you want. I'll meet you there."

This has been the goal all along. I want him to leave without me.

"If we take separate cars, Mom and Dad are going to think something's up."

"Your dad probably doesn't even know what year it is. Your

mom will be grateful for something new to talk about. She's been beating that Heather-didn't-send-a-card-for-Mother's-Day dead horse for eons."

He hesitates. "Are you sure?"

It's Sunday evening. The wait for a table will be ridiculous. I picture a line of people trailing out the door, wrapping around the building. Two of them will be in matching sweater vest combos, fuming over the mysterious cancellation of their reservation.

"Go on."

I watch his Jeep pull away from the house before flying downstairs and grabbing my keys. Leon said he'd meet me at the Junk Yard. After that, I've got fifteen minutes to book it to Beaufort and make a spectacle of myself. Nicholas is too good a soldier to bend his will to my plan A and give up on his own. He won't submit unless his commander forces the order. Up until now, whenever I needled Deborah, it was for the purpose of annoying Nicholas. I knew she'd whine at him about me in private. Whining at him just isn't going to be enough. Luckily, I can get way worse! I'm going to make myself so obviously unfit to have around that Mrs. Rose will threaten to write Nicholas out of the will if he doesn't call off the wedding.

My ploy is a beautiful seven-layer cake. I don't have to cancel the wedding, and neither does my beloved fiancé. We're going to get his parents to do our dirty work for us: plan D. I'm casually setting fire to everything and it feels awesome.

———

Plan D is the stupidest thing I've ever done, which I realize about halfway to Beaufort. In all of my scheming, giddy over

the visual appeal of me rolling up to dinner in this Frankenstein's monster of a car, I failed to remember that my new whip
is a stick shift.

I had to feign confidence about this to Leon, because by
then he already had the keys to my Saturn and was elated
about the trade-up. ("Are you sure? Your car's in much better
shape than mine. Why do you want it? Are you sure?") In my
head, it looked like this: Nicholas bought Leon's house without
consulting me, so I'd go and buy Leon's car without consulting
him. I'd stun Mr. and Mrs. Rose, who are so snobby about cars
that they make the landscaper park his rusty pickup in the ga-
rage to hide it from the neighbors.

They'll see Nicholas's Jeep and know something's wrong
with his brain. When they see *my* car, they'll believe that whatever's wrong with his brain is *me*. I'm a lower-class nobody with
no shame who doesn't deserve their son. I'm a madwoman, and
I'll drag him down to my level. No country club in Wisconsin
will admit their precious boy when they see what kind of wife
he's shackled to.

I paid attention during Leon's mini lesson, but even though
he told me I have to accelerate at the same time I let off the
clutch, when I first tried to get going I didn't release the clutch
quickly enough and the car shot forward, knocking over a dumpster in the Junk Yard's lot.

The poor start got me rattled, I'll admit. As I drive jerkily
down the road in a car that still smells like pine forest, white-
knuckling the wheel and gearshift, my nerves start to clash with
the endorphin rush I get when I visualize Deborah's face as I
squeal this monstrosity into a parking space.

I begin to think I've made a grave error of judgment here.

I know for sure I have when I clatter and shake into Beaufort

and the car stalls at a stoplight. I've forgotten to either hold
down the clutch or shift into neutral while braking. Or something. I can't remember Leon's instructions anymore because
there's a line of twenty cars backed up behind me and the light's
green, but my vehicle is throttling me like I owe it money. I
brake and put the car back into neutral, but I'm stressed and my
other foot hits the gas. Everything is bad. Panic overwhelms. It's
fight or flight.

I abandon the car at the intersection, leaving the door wide
open. People are honking. Someone rolls down their window
and yells. I want to go back and shut the door, but adrenaline is
burning up my veins and I can't go back there; I'm never going
back to that car for as long as I live, or to Morris, and all I know
how to do now is run. Straight down into a ditch and up the
other side into the parking lot of a shuttered Kmart, running,
running, my nervous system on fire. I'm going to keep running
all the way to California. I'll change my name and start a new life.

This is the sunniest prospect I've had in ages.

I don't pause to catch my breath until I'm on the other side
of the Kmart, November air solidifying into ice cubes in my
lungs. I'm so thankful for the big, empty building shielding me
from all my problems. One of the drivers who honked at me is
undoubtedly on the phone with a 911 operator. The situation
will be eagerly described to an officer Who Has No Time For
This Shit by ten bystanders, and everyone on the scene will deduce that I'm high on bath salts. They'll call a tow truck while a
cop chases me down with a Taser.

Frankencar's still registered to poor, well-meaning Leon and
he's going to take the fall for me. I have to go back. I'm never
going back.

My thighs are cold and chafed, so the buzzing in my pocket doesn't catch my full attention until the fourth time it happens. It's Nicholas, of course.

You're VERY late. Where are you??

I'm out of your reach, Dr. Rose. I'm in no-man's-land. Good luck trying to find me out here behind the decaying husk of a superstore.

That's what I want to reply. But according to my phone it's fifty-three degrees with RealFeel of forty-eight, and I'm not cut out for a life of consistent exercise. I'm so out of shape that I'm still wheezing, dreams of California dissolving into the wind. I'm going to get stabbed out here. I'm so glad I'm wearing real clothes instead of pajamas.

Save me, I reply instead. I whine it aloud, too.

From what?

You. Your mother. Frostbite.

I snap a picture of the parking lot and send it. Car broke down. I'm stranded.

His phone call cuts me off midsentence: I've got Dots candy in my coat pocket. I'm going to leave a trail like Hansel and

"Naomi?" He sounds afraid. "How far into town are you? What happened?"

"That car is crap!" I exclaim. "It tried to kill me."

"I told you a million miles ago to change your oil and you said it was none of my business." In his mind, he's twirling through a field of I-Told-You-So's. That's his idea of heaven.

"Not that car. I traded it for Leon's clunker. It's a stick shift, Nicholas. I don't know how to drive a fricking stick shift! Bad things happened and I left it in the middle of the road. Now I'm in a Kmart parking lot." I kick a rock and squint up at the gray building, then a scattering of other dark buildings with empty parking lots along the same strip. I'm in a retail graveyard. "Maybe it's a Toys R Us."

"Jesus Christ." I can hear cars whooshing by on his end of the line. He's out on the sidewalk.

"Don't let me die here. I want to be somewhere warm when I go."

"Yeah, better ease into those warmer temperatures. It'll get a lot hotter once you arrive at your destination." I'm about to wail. "You need to tell me exactly where you are."

I wring my hands. Nicholas is on the phone, which makes him feel close, so it's okay to freak out now. He's going to remain calm no matter what. We've always been balanced that way: when one of us loses it, the other can't. Whoever didn't call dibs on instant hysterics has no choice but to keep it together.

"The first stoplight when you get into town. I went off, uh, into a ditch. Not in the car, I mean. I left on foot."

"Why did you leave your car?"

"I don't know! It all happened so fast. Give me time to think of a better excuse."

"I'll be right there. Go back to the car."

I don't go back to the car, but I do tiptoe out from behind the building and stand at the side of the road. There are flashing lights—a police officer and a tow truck. Oh lord, I'm going to jail.

Someone spots me and points, and my instinct is to crouch down. There's nothing to hide behind, so I'm crouching for no reason whatsoever. Forget jail. I'm getting a padded cell.

Out of habit, I'm scouring the road for a flash of gold Maserati, so when Nicholas steps out of a Jeep it takes me a second to recalibrate.

"Nicholas!" I hiss in a loud whisper. It's no use. I'm drowned out by the commotion of cars whooshing by. I wave my arms like an air traffic controller. He doesn't see me, striding straight into the heart of the chaos to take charge.

He checks over the abandoned vehicle and shakes his head to himself, seizing my purse from the passenger seat before shutting the driver's-side door. Holy cow, I left my purse.

Men in uniforms converge on him. I hide my face behind my hands from a safe distance, not wanting to overhear what is sure to be a humiliating story of my stop-and-run. Someone nods in my direction and Nicholas whirls to face me. Even from this far, I discern the odd glint in his eyes and read his mind like it's typed in a thought bubble over his head.

Well, well, well. How are we feeling about our choices now, Naomi?

Not good, is how I'm feeling. But at least I'm standing on the less policeman-y side of the road.

He says something to the officer, who looks at me, too. Identity confirmed. I'm leaving here in handcuffs, which will tidily accomplish my goal of getting Mrs. Rose to catapult me out of the family tree.

Nicholas calls somebody on his phone and chats for a minute before handing the phone to the officer. They chat for a minute, too; all the while, Nicholas is just looking and looking at me, and there's nowhere to hide from him. He's my only ally. He's my worst enemy.

He's walking across the road right toward me, wearing the coat I call his Sherlock Holmes coat. It was expensive and the

nicest gift I've ever gotten him. He wears it from the very beginning of autumn until the very end of spring, with a scarf looped
beneath the wide collar. The fact that he hasn't burned it yet and
danced around its ashes seems aggressively kind in my current
frame of mind.

His face isn't grim or smug, but neutral save for the tiny
crease between his eyebrows. Concern.

"What happened?" he asks when he approaches.

I shake my head. I can't talk about it. I'm already pretending
this never happened. "Am I going to jail?"

"No." He looks down at my purse in his grip. "Do you need
to grab anything out of the car?"

"No."

He wants to ask more questions, I can tell. Nicholas gives me
a long, searching look, then removes his coat and puts it around
my shoulders. His fingers play with the top button, as if to fas-
ten it, but he lets his hand fall.

He steers me to the Jeep without another word. I break into
a speed-walk when we pass the police car and tow truck, half
waiting for somebody to reach out and snatch me. After I dart a
paranoid peek over my shoulder for the umpteenth time, Nicholas smirks. "Relax."

The single word unlocks the deadbolt on my ability to form
coherent speech. "Is Leon going to be in trouble? I haven't gotten the title switched yet. What's going to happen to the car? It's
not actually broken down."

"Of course not. If it were broken down, you'd just fix it
yourself," he says, giving me a sly sideways look.

"Uh."

"Or maybe not. Wouldn't want Dave from Morris Auto to

start missing you." He observes my stricken face and turns away so that I don't see his smile, but I still hear it in his voice. "When Dave had his wisdom teeth removed, the first thing he said when coming out of anesthesia was 'Don't tell the dentist about Naomi's car.'" He pauses to let it sink in that I've been had, and my chagrin threatens to shrivel me up into a pocket-sized Naomi. Dave's really going to hear it from me the next time I get a *Rate our service!* email from Morris Auto. "Anyway, a tow company's taking the car home for us. I could drive it myself and let you take the Jeep, but you look a little shaken up."

My mouth is dry. "It's a stick shift."

"I know. I can drive a stick shift."

The world tilts. "What? Really?"

"Mm-hmm." The amusement is faint, but it's there.

I slide into the passenger seat and lock my door to keep out any cops who might change their minds last-minute. "I miss heated seats."

"I thought you hated the Maserati."

"I do. Did. Loved the heated seats, though. Just like—"

"Sitting in the devil's lap," he says before I can finish, sliding an arm behind my headrest as he turns to check the rear and backs out. He's so close, I can smell his aftershave, and my heart pangs with an emotion like homesickness. It's not the same aftershave he's been wearing lately. It's Stetson, which I gave to him as a Christmas present. Wrapped in gold foil paper he kept for so long, I can still hear the crinkling.

I love it, he'd said with a big grin. The scent of Stetson will forever link directly to the memory of that grin, and the adoration I'd felt for him. What if someone I date in the future wears Stetson, and I have to think about Nicholas and his grin every time I look at another man's face? He's invaded so many of my levels, there's no getting rid of him.

Later, after he opened his present, I saw the sort of grooming products he kept in his medicine cabinet and blushed at how nice and expensive they were. The price of his cologne rendered my gift an embarrassment. But he wore the Stetson every day from then on, even when his grin faded and our relationship transitioned from Before to After. He used up every last drop and didn't throw away the bottle.

"Did you get to finish eating?" I ask timidly.

"We'd literally just gotten seated when I texted to ask where you were. They lost our reservation and Mom went ballistic. Made the manager cry."

I can imagine. Deborah Rose has never exited any establishment without introducing herself to the manager.

"What'd you tell your mom?"

"That you were having car trouble and I needed to go pick you up."

Oh no. I loll my head from side to side. "I don't want to go to the restaurant. Please don't make me go. I have a headache. I have cramps. And blood clots. They're the size of golf balls." I begin to list more ailments but he pats my knee.

"All right."

I straighten in my seat. "Really?"

"Yeah, I don't want to go back there, either. Dad left us to go sit at the bar because he couldn't wait for a table. And Mom . . ." He shifts. A dark look creeps over his expression. "It's better if you two aren't in the same room tonight. She's had too much time to obsess over that comment you made about never having kids."

The fact that I struck a nerve with her makes me all warm and fuzzy inside. Anyway, I stand by it. Nicholas's and my DNA are incompatible for procreation. Mother Nature would never allow it.

I reply with a noncommittal "Mm."

He swings another look at me. It's fleeting, and the car's so dark that I can't be sure, but I think he's a little bit sad. The notion makes me itchy.

"We never discussed kids," he says at length. "That's probably something we should have done before we got engaged."

"At the time we got engaged, only one of us was prepared for the proposal to happen, so you're taking the blame for that one."

He huffs a laugh. "That's fair, I guess."

I don't want to talk about this. It'll only make both of us sadder, because there's no way we're having kids together. Pregnancy for me at this point would indicate immaculate conception. "I didn't know you could drive a stick."

"I've told you before. You probably just weren't listening."

I don't want a lecture, either. You Never Listen is the title of a story about my many flaws and failings. There's no safe ground here.

I try again. "It feels great to be running away from Sunday dinner, not gonna lie."

He almost smiles. I can see it flirting at the edges of his mouth. "It's a shame we didn't get to show my parents your new car."

"You would *hate* that."

"I'd record their reaction on my phone. Messing with them could be fun, Naomi, if I were in on the joke, too. You forget, I know better than anyone what it feels like to be smothered by Deborah Rose."

I study his profile. He keeps his eyes on the road, but he must be aware of the heaviness of my stare. "You'd mess with them?"

"Of course. They've earned it. I mean, they're my parents and I love them. I'm grateful to them for a lot of things, but they're also a huge pain in the ass. When I asked you to marry me, I kind of . . ."

His lips press together.

"What?" I hedge.

Nicholas swallows. "I kind of hoped we'd be like partners in crime, sort of. When Mom's trying to sink her claws into me and I can't get away on my own, you'd have my back. The two of us, a team."

"I wanted that, too," I manage quietly. Past tense. "I didn't know you did. I've felt second place for a long time."

"I never wanted you to feel like that. But . . . you didn't step up. You didn't become my partner. You left me to fend for myself."

"Yeah, kind of like when your mother openly insults everything about me and you say nothing," I say waspishly. "That sound she makes when I say yes to dessert. *Tut-tut.* Looking down on me because of where I work, and the fact that I only have a high school diploma. A million other things."

I gaze miserably out my window, but all I see is the reflection of Nicholas, stretched and rounded. The lights of Beaufort are far behind us, and now we're traveling through a black expanse of nothingness until we reach Morris.

Talking has gradually relaxed my body. Coming down from the high of going full Ricky Bobby running from nonexistent fire has left me with a headache that I'm not making up this time.

"My mother's difficult," he says. "It's hard to stand up to her; she's had my nerves twisted since childhood. I don't know how to do it alone."

I feel for him, I really do, so I stroke my thumb over the back of his hand. Just once. "I know it must be hard to have her as a mom sometimes. She runs off all your girlfriends and then gets on your case for not being married with five kids already. You're not alone in that, either. Imagine being the poor daughter-in-law who's supposed to supply those five kids."

A passing car's headlights illuminate Nicholas's smile. Another car following right behind flashes by, and by then the smile has vanished. I know he's wondering if I'll ever be Deborah's daughter-in-law. I'd have to be crazy to voluntarily marry into his circus, and he knows it. If this goes bust like we both anticipate, he'll need a mail-order bride. I'm the only woman in the country dumb enough to try my luck with Deborah's offspring.

My mind keeps rerouting back to the incident at the stoplight. I see myself through Nicholas's eyes, standing on the other side of the street, hands over my face. Knees bent. A royal messmaker. I hear what he's going to say during our next argument so clearly, it's like it already happened.

You cut off your nose to spite your face. Got rid of a decent car, willingly, and now you have to drive around in this piece of junk you don't know how to operate. You're so backward, you'd try to catch honey with flies. Wow, you sure have stuck it to me.

Real Nicholas hasn't said any of this. But Imaginary Nicholas is an amalgamation of realistic predictions based on callous things he's said to me in the past, so I easily hear his voice shape those words. It's not fair to be hurt or angry over something he didn't even say, especially since the words I put into my own head are all true, but knowing he potentially *could* say it—and probably will—is enough to make me sink into a dark silence that I don't rise from for the rest of the ride home.

CHAPTER TEN

Since neither of us had dinner, we both head straight to the fridge when we get home. Or some version of home. I'm still thinking of it as Leon's place, just with our stuff in it.

The bare shelves of our refrigerator wink back at us.

We each rush to blame the other. "Did you not go to the store?" he says, like it's to be expected. "You forgot to go to the store," I say, as if we'd already decided he'd make a grocery run and he'd neglected to do so. Then we frown at each other. Our methods aren't covert anymore. Our bullshit radars are fine-tuned.

He checks the microwave clock. "There's still time for you to run to the gas station for frozen pizza." He hands me his keys.

"I'm all pizza'd out." I hand the keys back. "When you go get us some burritos, I want the chicken and cheese, not beef and cheese."

We commence a fierce stare-down. I'm doing him a big favor

by staying here with him in this house that's probably haunted, saving him from miserable dinners with his mother where she'll criticize every single restaurant employee in the most devastatingly personal way possible. "Go get the burritos and I'll be nice to you forever," I say.

"Go get them yourself and I'll be nice to *you* forever."

Not worth it. "Nah."

"Don't you want to see how the Jeep drives? You'll like it better than the Saturn." His lips twist. "Much, *much* better than the . . . ah . . . what kind of car did you trade it for?"

"It's a monster, and I love it like it's my child. Besides, I can't go anywhere because I'm still shaken up."

I'm not shaken up, because being far removed from Deborah has revitalized me. He can tell.

"Fine." He relents, performing another inventory of our fridge. "I'll fix something for myself, then."

"So will I." I open the cupboards and hope to god there's an entire Thanksgiving meal up there. "For myself."

He gets out bread crumbs and eggs. I've seen this pattern before: he's making mozzarella sticks. They sound amazing.

My first thought is to make spaghetti. He doesn't like my spaghetti? Then I'll cook enough for a banquet and let it overflow from every Tupperware container we own.

Nicholas watches me retrieve a box of spaghetti noodles. "I see you're still mad about the spaghetti thing."

"Not mad." Just holding on to it forever.

"Sure, sure." He smiles, because the idea of successfully pissing me off makes him just as gleeful as I'm going to feel when he realizes I ate all the mozzarella cheese.

I scavenge for a big jar of tomato sauce and come up with nil.

I do find a leftover plastic tub of marinara from Benigno's and plenty of ketchup, so I say what the hell and squirt it into a saucepan. I find that the spaghetti box only contains four noodles, so I have to supplement with half-empty boxes of gluten-free fettuccine and organic brown rice farfalle. I put them on to boil and wish I lived with someone less nutrition-conscious when it comes to carbs.

"What are you making?" he snickers.

"Farfaccine."

"That's not a thing."

"It's my favorite food ever. I talk about it all the time; not my fault you don't pay attention."

He rolls his eyes and turns to root through the fridge. My body coils tight like a jack-in-the-box, waiting. Finally: "Have you seen the mozzarella?"

"Nope."

His gaze falls onto the trash can. He pops the lid and sees the crumpled mozzarella stick wrappers. Busted.

"Darned Leon," I say. "I bet he kept a spare key and snuck inside last night. We should change the locks."

Nicholas glares, then dumps his prepared breading into my saucepan.

"Hey!"

"It's going to suck, anyway."

"It is not."

"Your pasta's overcooked. And you forgot to stir."

"Fudge." I hurry to drain it. There are clumps stuck to the bottom of the pot. Gluten-free anything is already atrocious. Boiling it just makes it worse. While I'm fussing with the pasta, the marinara-ketchup combo starts spitting. I rush back and stir, then throw in some seasoning. I'm a regular Alex Guar-naschelli.

"Interesting choice."

"Huh?"

Nicholas taps one of the spice bottles I just used. Cinnamon.

"Oh. Yes." I stand tall. "It's the secret ingredient."

Nicholas is still hunting for a mozzarella replacement. It's no use. We have nothing. He gives up and eyes my pasta with res-ignation. "Farfaccine, eh?"

"A traditional Italian dish passed on from grandmother to grandmother." It smells like raw sewage.

"Maybe if it were creamier?" he says helpfully. "Looks a little dry."

We're out of milk, so we do something dubious here and dump in half a cup of coffee creamer. It does look better after-ward, even if the foul smell intensifies. Nicholas gets cocky and adds a sprinkling of pink Himalayan salt.

Our stomachs are growling. We ladle slop into our bowls and prod it with our forks to make sure it's not still alive. There are so many weird textures at play. Our low food supply reflects our carelessness, and the only place in Morris that delivers is closed. I'm stricken by a thought: Benigno's might not deliver all the way out here. I think their policy is delivering only within city limits.

Morris sucks. Nicholas should have taken that job in Madi-son.

We take a bite on the count of three. I want to spit mine out but he bravely chews his mouthful, so I make myself do the same.

Nicholas takes another bite. "This is the worst thing I've ever had in my mouth."

Nicholas thinks Warheads are haute cuisine, so he doesn't

get to pass judgment on farfaccine. "The cauliflower you poured buffalo sauce all over and told me was a chicken wing," I say. "That's the worst thing I've ever had in my mouth."

"It's going to be a drill next, what with all the Butterfingers you eat. Storing them in your cheek like a chipmunk and letting them slowly erode your molars. You'll be in dentures before you hit forty."

"You'll be right there with me, pal. You and your Skittles." I can't believe we're still eating. We're going to end up in the emergency room. "My tongue is numb. Is that normal?"

"I can taste this in my sinus cavities. *Taste.* Not smell."

I dig out a can of La Croix and we split it. The taste pairs horribly, so it's right on theme.

"We should mark today on the calendar and memorialize it by eating this travesty every year," he remarks.

"I'll copy down the recipe. Cinnamon, bread crumbs with egg in them. God, did we really use coffee creamer?"

"We're artists. No one understands." He slurps his sauce, a ring of red around his mouth.

I hear the crunching of gravel and we poke our heads into the living room. The tow truck driver is here. He must've had trouble finding the entrance to our driveway, because we've been waiting on him for close to an hour. I have to run upstairs and hide if I want to preserve my delusion that this never happened.

"Peace out," I say, and vamoose.

"Coward!" he yells after me.

Nicholas finds me in the kitchen on Monday morning heating up farfaccine in the microwave. He falls against the doorjamb laughing, straightening his cuffs. He's heading in to work. To-day, the Junk Yard will only stay open from noon to three, and Brandy and I are the only ones scheduled. Brandy texted this morning to say that Melissa's quitting, and I feel like we're the kids in Willy Wonka's factory, dropping off left and right.

"You're eating a bowl of food poisoning, Naomi."

"I'm hungry. Don't judge."

He takes down a bowl for himself and chisels out a congealed glob from the storage container. The microwave beeps, but I go ahead and press three more seconds onto the timer. When it beeps again, I press three more seconds. Nicholas stands there and lets me get away with it two more times before bumping me out of the way with his hip.

"We really need to go to the store," I inform him. "There's nothing here for dinner."

"I'll probably have dinner at Mom and Dad's tonight." He admires his reflection in the shiny oven door and smooths his hair. "You don't have to come."

This has never been optioned to me before.

I try not to be sulky. "Fine, then."

"I thought that's what you'd want."

"To eat dinner alone? Here all by myself? Sure, that's the dream."

"You don't *want* to go to my parents' house," he points out in a deadpan.

"No, I don't. But I think you should try making it three days without going over there."

"You know how my mom gets. Especially since we blew her off last night. I want to please everybody, but I can't, and in somebody's eyes I'm always falling short. Don't put me in this position where I have to choose."

I never make him choose, but he always does, anyway, which puts me in a position where I'm forced to be crabby. I press the release button on the microwave to open the door thirty seconds before his food is ready, then walk away.

"Real nice."

I scuttle up to my bedroom so that I don't have to say good-bye to him when he leaves, pondering what I'm going to do with my life. I check my phone for missed calls from potential employers, but I have no notifications because no one loves me and I'm a failure. I don't even have any spam emails.

I scroll through Instagram for five minutes and then have to shut my phone off because everybody else's lives are amazing and mine is a black hole. I have zero job offers and one fiancé too many. I have an abundance of odious fiancé. How am I going to get rid of him? I cannot marry this mama's boy.

Every time I picture the wedding I break out in hives. Deborah will want to come on our honeymoon with us, and she'll switch out my birth control pills for placebos. When baby Nicholas Deborah Jr. comes, I'll walk into the house one day to find all her belongings stuffed in the right-hand bedroom. *I've come to stay with you*, she'll threaten with a nightmarish smile, head spinning all the way around. *Forever!*

I'm putting a pin in plan D and picking up the lost momentum on plan A. I can do this. I can convince Nicholas to call it quits without getting his mother involved. I never want to see her again. I think about eating dinner by myself tonight in this empty house while Nicholas scarfs down a three-course meal cooked by "the woman," Deborah petting his hair and telling him he's special. There's no doubt in my mind that at some point in his teenage life she subjected him to a public mother-son dance.

You can't pick your parents or your grandparents, but you *can* pick your children's parents and grandparents. I don't have kids yet, but I think it's failing some kind of morality test to give them Deborah as a grandmother. It's particularly important that my kids have sweet, attentive relatives on one side of the aisle because they won't be getting any from mine. My parents are as distant and withholding as Deborah is smothering and omnipresent, and haven't expressed much interest in my life's developments aside from "Aren't weddings supposed to be in the spring?" They didn't even come down when I was being shuffled in and out of bridal boutiques with Deborah and her four closest girlfriends, which is supposed to be a momentous mother-daughter experience. Naïvely, I'd hoped for a close relationship with Nicholas's family, to give me that warm, supportive, grounded sense of belonging I've long been missing out on. I have so much unused love sitting inside me with nowhere to direct it.

I like the Nicholas who drops everything and runs when I'm freaking out at the side of the road. The one who wraps his coat around my shoulders and eats a bowl of food poisoning with me. But I can't wait for that Nicholas to pop up every now and then, leaving me a different version of him to deal with regularly: the man who abandons me in more ways than one to placate his demanding mother.

That's the Nicholas I need to be focusing my energy on. I can't let myself forget.

———

It's November twelfth and I've got to hand it to him, Nicholas is upping his game. I have a new document on my computer that keeps score. Sometimes I catch myself regarding it too objectively and from that point of view, we're immature children who need to grumble forced apologies at each other and shake hands. It goes without saying that I try to stay as unobjective as possible.

The past week looks like this:

Point Naomi: pirate b-day, lol
Point Nicholas: Instagram pic
Point Naomi: Brownie
Point Nicholas: Brownie
Point Naomi: Toothpaste
Point Nicholas: Shoes
Point Naomi: Shoes
Point Nicholas: Underwear

If you think about it, it's all Deborah's fault.

After Nicholas ditched me to have Family Fun Night at dear old Mr. and Mrs. Rose's house, he brought home an ugly set of salt and pepper shakers that Deborah gave him. They're porcelain babies. If you've ever seen a medieval painting of a baby, they look like straight-up demons. They have scary little old man faces and their necks are twisted at unnatural angles.

Deborah's salt and pepper shaker-babies look exactly like that. I shuddered when I saw them. I was all set to bury her gift in the back of a closet, but Nicholas was all: "They're family heirlooms! What if Mom comes over and asks where we put them? We have to keep them on the table." And I was all: "Are you friggin' kidding me? These things are repugnant."

At any rate, I ended up sticking one of them under Nicholas's mattress. The lump was just unobtrusive enough that I didn't think he'd realize there *was* a lump, just that his back felt achy in the morning. If I'd hidden both shakers, Nicholas would know something was up, so I kept the ugly pepper baby on the kitchen table and threw a potholder over it.

The following day, the saltshaker was back on the table where I clearly did not want it. I was still stewing when we went out to dinner at Walk the Plank, a seafood restaurant. I pretended I needed to go to the bathroom, but instead I flagged down a waiter and told him it was Nicholas's birthday. I asked if the staff could sing to him, which they did, while he wore a tricorn pirate hat of honor and nearly collapsed from mortification. On Facebook Live. (It was INCREDIBLE—they put a lobster bib around him that had this little plastic parrot on the shoulder, and when he blew out the candle on his cupcake everyone yelled "Tharr he blows!" Lmao forever.)

I thought, *Okay, we're even now.* Not so! I woke up to a notification on Instagram. He'd posted a picture of me while I was passed out on the couch. It's brutally zoomed in so that you can count my every pore, and I do not look remotely cute. I've got a six-inch string of drool dribbling out of my open mouth, glistening in the half light. He uploaded the shot in black and white and captioned it with three hearts and *Aren't I lucky? I get to gaze upon this absolute work of art every single day. #LivinTheLife #MarryingMyBestFriend #TrueLovesKissFromARose*

That picture has accumulated more comments than anything I've ever posted, and when I think about it I want to watch his blood drip into a bedpan. I want it to coagulate into a gelatin that I pour over a lemon cake, which I'll consume using utensils carved from the stone that resides where his heart should be.

My next move wasn't premeditated. I'd been driving home

from work when I saw a little brown dog in the ditch licking the cardboard box for a Whopper Jr. He wasn't wearing a collar and there weren't any houses nearby, so I assumed he was a stray. Anyone would assume that! When I picked him up and gave him lots of pets and nuzzles, Nicholas's voice ran through my head: *Don't get any ideas.*

I got *lots* of ideas. My ideas had ideas.

I brought him home and cooked a frozen hamburger patty for him, since we didn't have dog food and he appeared to like burgers. He fell asleep on my lap. According to the Internet, he is probably a mix of Jack Russell terrier and beagle. I decided to name him Whopper Jr. and I loved him more than any human I've ever known. When Nicholas came home, he found me carrying Whopper Jr. in one of Nicholas's nice work shirts, which I'd fashioned into a baby-wearing sling. He said "Oh my GOD, where did you get that," and I said "You're a daddy! He looks just like you," and Whopper Jr. sneezed on the pinstriped shirt-sling. It was so cute.

Nicholas didn't care about the dog's cuteness. All he cared about was that we'd have to get him neutered and vaccinated and chipped, and *dog food's not cheap, just so you know,* blah blah blah. Whopper Jr. peed on Nicholas's Sherlock Holmes coat (it was his own fault for leaving it on the floor) and Nicholas L O S T it.

Unfortunately, Whopper Jr. turned out to be Brownie, who'd escaped his backyard. The next day (after the dog and I bonded all night and I took over a hundred pictures of him wearing hats and sunglasses, sitting in baskets) Nicholas brought home a sign he ripped off a telephone pole that featured my new dog's adorable face, surrounded by three smiling children. He reunited

Brownie with his owners for me, because I was too emotional to do it, and when he got back into the car his eyes were red. He'd already fallen in love with the dog.

"We should go adopt a dog from a shelter," I'd said.

"Now is not the right time to get a pet."

Something that sucks about being part of a couple: Your partner has veto power and you don't get to just flow wherever the wind takes you. You're not allowed to have kids or pets unless both of you are on board. You can want a dog more than anything in the whole world but if your partner says no, you're out of luck.

Which brings us to the pettier half of the list.

I replaced our dentist-recommended Sensodyne with charcoal toothpaste, which earned me an incredibly gratifying rant. He was ten minutes late to work that day because he had to lecture me about charcoal toothpaste, which he doesn't believe in using. That's how he says it: "I don't believe in that." Like it's the Easter bunny. When I started to laugh, he got even madder. "DENTAL HYGIENE IS NOT A JOKE, NAOMI."

In retaliation, he hid all of my shoes, which meant I had to wear slippers when Brandy and I went out for brunch. To get back at him, I took the dress shoes that he wears every day to work and tied the laces into a tight bow, then dabbed the middle of each bow with super glue. Watching him try to untie his shoelaces and getting progressively more and more pissed ranks right up there in the top five of Naomi Westfield's Life Highlights. I don't regret it even if he did end up nailing all of my underwear to my bedroom ceiling with a staple gun.

The Junk Yard is officially dead and I'm officially unemployed, so I have no reason to wake up in the morning anymore except to exact Nicholas sabotage. The effort has absorbed one hundred percent of my focus. Honestly, if it weren't for the prospect of ticking him off I'd probably be steeped in a deep depression right now.

I contemplate this as I stick my sleeping fiancé's hand in a bowl of warm water and tiptoe out of the bedroom.

Ten minutes later I hear a fabulous yell. I smile and stir my Fruity Pebbles. It's going to be a great day! I check my phone for the fiftieth time in an hour, hoping for a missed call—a voicemail from Print-Rite, a paper store in Fairview looking to hire a receptionist to work four days a week, six hours a day. The pay's a joke, but at least they're not demanding I have fifteen-plus years of secretarial experience and a bachelor's degree. I can't tell you how many entry-level positions I've been circling in the newspaper, getting hopeful and calling them up for details only to hear I need a PhD and half a century of experience in their specific field.

Suffice it to say, the job hunt isn't going so hot. Every now and then Nicholas makes a comment under his breath about myriad job opportunities in Madison, and how different our lives would be if he'd accepted that job, and it fills me with the stubborn desire to prove him wrong. I *will* find work here. I'll find fulfillment. I'll be so damn fulfilled, it'll make him sick.

Nicholas stalks into the kitchen holding an empty bowl. He looks deranged.

"Something wrong?" I purr.

"I didn't piss myself, if that's what you were hoping for. But I did knock the bowl over in my sleep, and it fell on my phone." He shows me his phone's screen, which has more cuts than the diamond on my ring finger.

Oh, shit.

"I didn't have anything to do with that," I say quickly.

"I had everything on my phone! All my pictures, my contacts. Important information."

"Isn't it synced to your computer? You should be able to—" I start to ask, but his dark look shuts me up.

"This is over the line, Naomi."

"*This* is the line? I think taking someone's pet home with me was worse than this, to be honest."

He's an avalanche of rocks, crashing through the house. He crashes upstairs and grabs some clean clothes out of the hamper, which I haven't folded and put away yet because I am Extremely Busy checking my phone for missed calls from employers. I don't have time to sort socks. My career is at stake.

He crashes into the shower, where I and all the ghosts who live here listen to one half of an argument he probably thinks he's winning. Some of the points he makes are valid, but I holler back anyway. He's even angrier when he emerges. It's too bad nothing fun came out of the warm-water trick; I've been dying to try that one out since I was a kid and I've got to say, I'm disappointed.

"I can't believe you," he thunders, shaking his head.

"You're really mad for someone who didn't wet his pants. What's the big deal?"

He waves his cracked phone screen at me. Oh, right. I'd already forgotten. The fact that I've forgotten and I'm calmly spooning Fruity Pebbles past my lips is more than he can handle. Nicholas reaches out and swats the box of cereal, like a spiteful cat. Fruity Pebbles rain off the table.

"Hey!" I stand up. The kitchen's a mess now (after I *just*

swept it four days ago) and all that's left inside the cereal box is an inch of rainbow dust. "You wasted the whole box! How am I supposed to have a balanced breakfast tomorrow morning?"

"You don't deserve a balanced breakfast tomorrow morning! You can eat butterless toast and think about what you did." His feet are cinder blocks as he marches off for his wallet and keys.

I'm still frozen in surprise, half-standing, half-crouched. "But my nutrients!"

"You think I care?" he hollers from another room. "You put my hand in a bowl of warm water."

Seriously, this is not as bad as taking someone's dog. I stole a *living creature*. Who is part of someone's *family*. I didn't get this bent out of shape when I had to rip my underwear down from the ceiling, even though he'd punctured holes in all my favorites. Nicholas is a giant baby.

"But it didn't even work!" I yell back. Or so he says. I'm not totally convinced I didn't succeed, with the way he's reacting. I turn to go paw through the mountain of dirty clothes piling up against the side of the washing machine. The dryer door is swinging wide open, and you could see the clog of lint from outer space. I recognize the turquoise fuzz from a sweater he only wears for Visits With Mother.

Fucking hell. "Clean the lint trap or I will seriously, literally murder you," I threaten. "With an axe. Your blood will spray the walls. There are a million places to hide a dead body out here."

"Oh my god, please do," he responds. "Kill me and put me out of my misery."

"My anger is way more justified than yours. You're just mad about your phone, which isn't my fault. I've been telling you forever that it's stupid to keep your phone on the floor all night, next to the bed."

Nicholas materializes in the kitchen, three feet away from me. He looks like he wants to push me down a very long flight of stairs and I'm sure I've got an expression to match. I feel alive and awake, adrenaline surging through my veins. Everything is falling so wonderfully apart, I hope.

"My charger is short! That's why I have to leave the phone on the floor. It won't reach the nightstand because my cord's not long enough."

I don't have to crack an immature joke, because my smirk says it for me.

He throws his hands up. "God! Sometimes it's like I'm engaged to a ten-year-old."

"What does that say about you?" I muse.

"Stop distracting me. I'm late. Again." He glares at me like it's my fault he stapled my underwear to the ceiling and forced me to hit back. "Stop making me run late for work. I get that you're bitter I still have a job when you don't. Take out your aggression some other way."

I make sure he sees me drag my gaze over his lunchbox when I reply, "You bet."

Snarling, he tosses all of his pre-packed food (which I didn't even tamper with, but the fact that he can't be sure is a point for Naomi) into the trash and pulls his coat on. He skipped a shave and his hair's a bird's nest since he forgot to style it with pomade after his shower. The brightest hope in my life right now is that he won't remember, so that he'll get a glimpse of his tragic hair in the bathroom mirror after lunch and want to punch a wall. The two nosy receptionists at Rise and Smile, Nicole and Ashley, will whisper that he's having "trouble in paradise."

Lol.

He shakes his head, doing up the buttons on his coat. "You are just . . ." Words aren't adequate to convey his feelings, so he growls in his throat. He's so mad that he keeps missing buttons, skin burning from the roots of his hair all the way down past his collar.

"I'm just what?"

"Unbelievably self-absorbed." He walks backward to the living room, glaring daggers. He still hasn't realized he forgot his hairstyling products and his hairdo's going to air-dry like something from an eighties music video. The cold, moistureless air will not be kind. I sneakily check outside. It's windy as all getout. Somebody up there loves me.

"Self-absorbed?" I repeat in my highest register. What absolute slander! "Do you have any idea how many Livestrong bracelets I've owned? Oh, and I've stopped killing all those bees! What have *you* ever done?"

I follow him to the door. He slams it shut but I open it up again, beaming at him as he terrorizes the poor driveway. Leaves have never been stepped on so hard. He realizes too late that a puddle is hiding beneath some of the leaves and a string of curses rips from his throat when he inspects the soaking hem of his trousers.

"If you'd used common sense, then you wouldn't have wet the bed, now would you?"

"If I'd used common sense," he shouts, getting into his car, "I never would've proposed!"

The remark is a direct hit on my pride. It's sharper than it looks, surprising me by tearing right through its target and lodging a few inches deeper. I cross my arms. "Oh, shut up. Anyone would be lucky to have me. I'm a prize."

"You're the trophy they give to last-place losers."

He hears his self-burn and bangs his head on the steering wheel.

"Good luck!" I shout over the rev of his engine. "Have a great day, sweet pea! Try not to think about how everyone is staring at that zit on your chin."

Through the windshield, he murders me with his eyes. He's got his entire soul compressed right up against his irises and they're the color of hatred. They desperately want telekinetic powers so they can blow me into the sky, through the fabric of our universe and into another one. I hope it's a parallel universe with a parallel Nicholas and Naomi. I want to torture him with two of me.

I'm so busy dreaming of teaming up with my parallel-universe self for evil purposes that I don't notice he's backed over the baby evergreen poking crookedly out of the earth. The Charlie Brown tree. Jason.

He plows forward over Jason and backs up again. Weakling branches snap and crunch. It's twenty-two degrees and I'm standing in the yard in a tank top and an old pair of Nicholas's boxers that I laid claim to long ago. Yesterday's mascara clumps in my eyelashes and my cheek is wearing the pattern of my wristwatch. We belong on *Jerry Springer*. I inhale half the oxygen in Morris and bellow: "NICHOLAS ROSE, YOU UN-FORGIVABLE LITTLE SHIT."

He arches a brow at me. Then, to test my nerves, he puts his car in park and revs the gas. I try to convey with my stare exactly how deceased he's going to be if he runs over Jason one more time. Poor Jason. He's leaning so pitifully that another punch will do him in.

Nicholas smiles. Then his Jeep lunges forward, dragging up Jason by the roots.

Nicholas and I are a parable about bottling your frustrations. We've been inflicting a quiet violence onto our own feelings by confining them to tiny spaces with only a teaspoon of oxygen, fermenting them into an ugly chemistry incompatible with love. We've felt the glass trembling from the increase of pressure but continued suffering through our smiles.

I look at his smug, stupid face, and *BOOM*. The bottle combusts, releasing word shrapnel in the form of screamed nonsense.

"What was that?" He cups a hand behind his ear. "Was that . . . *what you get* for destruction of my property?"

"I didn't break your phone on purpose! You know how much I LOVE THAT DUMB FUCKING TREE."

He tips his head back and laughs, harder than he's ever laughed at anything: sharp and surprised and peppered with necessary gasps for air. I think I spy a tear running down his pinkened face. I want to throw a rock at him but I can't move, I'm so fascinated by this strange and magnificent new laugh. The hood of his car dazzles with sun, which pings off the gaudy diamond on my left hand and spins light into my eyes. I hate this damned ring. It's a symbol of possession, of love and eternity, declaring to the world that I've been taken over. The man who gave it to me is still laughing, reflected in the side mirror as he winds out of sight, out of our lawless frontier and back into the real world we're so detached from.

CHAPTER ELEVEN

Nicholas isn't laughing anymore when he storms through the door after work. I'm lounging on the couch in mismatched socked feet and a cherry sucker in my mouth, channel-flipping with glazed eyes. He's sharp and ready for blows, while I'm about to nod off. I've got half a second to reach the number he's dialed up to if I want to be any good in this fight we're about to have.

Excellent. It's been getting boring around here.

He strides over to stand between my feet, eyes flashing. His hair should look awful, but it's raining outside so it's doing this unfortunately sexy thing instead, falling across his forehead in damp, gleaming waves. I narrow my eyes and bite down hard on the candy. "What's up?" I drawl.

"Give me your phone."

I make a sound like *Pah!* "What? No."

"You ruined mine, so it's only fair that I get yours."

"I didn't ruin your phone, dum-dum. I have no idea how a

bowl fell on it. Maybe you should stop putting bowls in your bed."

He pats my pockets, which makes me giggle. "Where is it?"

I shove him off, but he just starts grabbing at the couch cushions. I've made myself a nice little nest of peanut butter chocolate bonbons, blankets, Kit Kat wrappers, a paper plate from the Toaster Strudel I ate for lunch, and two of Nicholas's watches. I've been gradually removing their links to make the fit tighter but forgot to put them back in his room.

"All day!" he exclaims. "The phone rings but I can't swipe on calls. My mom can't reach me on my cell anymore, so who do you suppose she calls next?"

"Hold on, let me guess."

He doesn't let me guess. Rude. "The office! And not my personal extension, either, since I have my phone set to voicemail. She's been calling the front desk nonstop over every goddamn thought that wanders into her head. Wasn't so bad when I had a working cell phone, because I could send her to voicemail and text back my replies. Short and simple. But no! Instead I get Ashley running in to interrupt me every five minutes, crying because she knows she's not supposed to interrupt me for unimportant crap like this but my mom won't give her a choice. *'Dr. Rose, your mother wants me to send her a PDF of your calendar so she can mark down what time you're taking her shopping this Saturday.' 'Dr. Rose, your mother's on the line again. She needs you to come by after work and tell your father he has to see a doctor about a cyst on his back.' 'Dr. Rose, your mother wants to know if you'll have time on your lunch break to go find those walnuts you brought to her Christmas party in 2011. Her friend Joyce needs them ASAP.'"*

"Sounds like a busy day for Dr. Rose," I snigger.

"I looked unprofessional in front of everyone! I could lose patients over this."

"And yet you're blowing up at me instead of, say, the person who's been calling your office all day?" I pop a bonbon in my mouth and give him a look like *Yeah, I make way more sense than you.*

"I expect you to be the bigger person! You know Mom doesn't understand. I tried to tell her she couldn't call the front desk unless it was an emergency, but everything's an emergency to my mother."

He growls, messing up his hair. He's wearing his navy blazer today and wow, the effect is quite something. His eyes are demon-black, and I'm not hating the whole day's-worth-of-scruff thing he's got going on. Nicholas has a very nice jaw; when it's lightly shadowed like it is now, coupled with the slate-gray frames of his glasses, he reminds me of a tormented English literature professor who's just hit rock bottom.

I am learning at this very moment in time that *tormented English literature professor who's just hit rock bottom* is my specific type. He doesn't even notice me checking him out because he's busy hunting for my phone amid a sea of candy wrappers.

The inappropriate timing of my epiphany is classic Naomi Westfield. If Nicholas knew what I was thinking right now he'd get so frustrated with me that he'd probably get on an airplane and leave the country.

"Your first mistake was expecting me to be the bigger person," I reply. "Deborah gives you shit twenty-four-seven and you shower her with attention. It gets results! You know what doesn't get results? Being understanding all the time and saying

'Whatever you need, babe. Walk all over me! Forget I'm even here.' Being the bigger person gives you permission to put my feelings second every time. I have to be *understanding*. I have to be *patient*, and keep my mouth shut while you coddle her. So I'm going to change tactics, because continuing to do what I've been doing while expecting different results is stupid. Debbie's playbook works. Being a whiny pain in the ass works. Maybe I should start calling the front desk, too."

Look at how well I've turned this around on him. Some of my best improv! I think all this fresh forest air and uninterrupted hours for plotting his ruination has beefed up my capacity for evil. I feel divine. Living in the wilderness is truly a form of self-care.

His mouth opens, ready for a retort, but he's interrupted by a low buzz. My phone's on silent but I've just gotten a notification. We both glance at the mantel where my phone's plugged into a charger. We both dive.

I'm swaddled in blankets, and the two beats it takes me to detangle are crucial. He's at the mantel by the time I'm free, and his hand closes over the dark screen. A tiny green light flashes. An email? A text? It could be Print-Rite responding to my application, and the contents of my stomach pitch wildly when I lay out my track record. I'm one hundred percent on nos and zero percent on yesses. *You're promising, but you're just not what we're looking for at this time. You're good, but not good enough.*

If I'm a millimeter from hitting my goal, that makes it even worse when I fail. I'd rather hear *You weren't even close. We never considered you for a second.* Anxiety kicks in and my brain fractures, thoughts splintering in a hundred directions. I'm drowning in midair and my body burns hot, a physical reaction I have to conceal. It's a no. It's always going to be a no.

The odds are not one in ten or fifty-fifty or any ratio I can latch on to optimistically. The odds are this: I've most certainly just been rejected by somebody. I can't let Nicholas see a rejection email. I can't let him count my failures and recite the number out loud. He doesn't understand what it's like to not get the thing you want; he's one of those people who believe that if you work hard enough, you can have anything.

To him, I'm a thoughtless slacker who doesn't have enough ambitions to start with, and when I *do* get an ambition under my skin, I lowball myself to take the sting out of the unavoidable letdown. *Underachieving.* It's a mortal sin for a Rose and the root of all my problems. I'm sure they whisper it behind my back.

What he doesn't know is that I do try, and then hide my failures. It's one of the reasons why I can't completely hate him when he makes digs about my not going to college: He doesn't know I ever tried getting in. He wasn't there when I shredded the rejection letters, proof that my parents were right and I should have focused more on studying than passing notes in class.

This was before I steeled myself and changed my attitude with the only coping mechanism available. Who wants a degree, anyway? Not me. I'm glad I didn't go. Look at all these suckers with student loans, in debt up to their eyeballs and no one's even hiring.

"Give me that!" I scream, kicking him in the back of the knee.

He holds the phone out of my reach. I hate it when he does that, using his height advantage against me. "I'm going to borrow it until I can get a new one. It's only fair."

"Give it back!" I jump up, grabbing ineffectively. "That's mine!"

His mouth purses, suspicious eyes calculating my flushed face and high-pitched voice. "Why are you so scared to let me see your phone?"

"I'm not scared." He hears the lie, I'm sure of it. "Give it back." I scrabble desperately, but it's no use. He's too tall and I'm trapped in some sort of Benjamin Button cycle—I feel myself getting shorter with every jump. "I mean it, Nicholas. I'm sorry your screen got cracked. I'll get you a new phone. I'm sorry, okay? Just give it back."

His expression turns downright lethal. This close up, I see my own terrified face imprinted on each of his pupils, two black mirrors. I see what he's seeing, and I know what this looks like.

"You just get a message from someone?" His voice is silky. The tip of it is so sharp, it could nick your artery without pressing.

"No. Why would you say that? Give me my phone." I hold out my palm expectantly and infuse as much authority into the command as possible. "Now."

His nostrils flare. "It's *him*, isn't it?"

"Who? What are you talking about?" I shake my head, snapping, "Hand it over! I'm serious. This is my personal property and keeping it from me is illegal."

Nicholas's gaze slides to my phone and his thumb moves, as if to tap the screen and bring my notifications to light. I freak out way more than the occasion calls for and next thing I know, I'm hanging off his back. My arms are around his neck, which gets me closer to my target, but he's squirming to get me off. "Give it!" I shriek. "It's mine!" I lose all sense of which words are coming out of my mouth and which ones are nonverbally exploding in my frantic brain. "Do what I say, or else!"

Nicholas backs up against a wall. He doesn't do it softly, either. I yank his hair and he spins, falling backward onto the couch. It's a move he shouldn't have made, because I lock my arms and legs around him with an iron grip and he's now a turtle on his back. I expend a burst of precious energy launching him off the couch, facedown on the floor, and revel in my moment of triumph before he starts fighting back.

"Get off!" He rolls us, but I'm scrappy and I've been storing up my energy all day with bonbons and *Real Housewives*. He's stressed. His mother has called his office fifty times. I've got an edge on him.

I'm straddling him now and I've got my hands on his throat. "Give me my phone!"

He throws my phone at the armchair across the room. I consider diving for it but my elbow still hurts from where he squished me against the wall, so I pull his shirt up over his face like a fifth-grade bully and pinch his nipples. Nicholas shouts.

Eyes obscured, he fights for use of his arms and smacks his own glasses askew when I yank his shirt back down. "Lie still!" I command. "I deserve to win this."

"You deserve tapeworms." His face is red and he's struggling more than he'd like to admit. I feel a rush of power to know that I'm actually a decent foe here.

"You bumped me into the wall on purpose."

"I did not, you little goblin." I bounce up and down, which makes him wince. "You're not a goblin, actually. You're a changeling. You've taken over the body of that nice girl I met."

"Her name was Naomi, wasn't it?" I say, tilting my head. "Too bad for her."

"Yes. Too bad for us both."

"You'll never see her again." I shift for better purchase on his squirming lap, and a jolt of surprise electrifies me when I discover he's hard.

All the air punches from my lungs as I burst out laughing. "Oh my god, *why*?"

His cheekbones burn. "Your top is low and you're writhing all over me. What do you expect?"

I expect him to be single-minded in his quest to end me, is what I expect. I'm amazed by man's ability to think about vengeance and penis contact at the same time. What I've been regarding as a savage WrestleMania showdown has been more like foreplay for Nicholas. I should have known. Men are trash.

The harder I laugh, the more I unintentionally rub on him, and the further into darkness his eyes slip. He's incredibly turned on and absolutely furious about it. At this moment, I have more control over his body than he does. The delicious power trip goes straight to my head.

His hands shoot out and catch me in the ribs. I have approximately one second to wonder if he's going to kiss me or kill me when he draws a wild card and starts tickling me. My hands are still around his throat, but when he tickles all my weak spots it's like pressing an eject button. I flop over onto my side, flailing uncontrollably.

"Ahh, stop!" I gasp. "I'm very ticklish!"

"Are you? I couldn't tell." He's getting back at me for making him horny and embarrassed.

I kick his shin and wriggle away, making a break for my phone. He seizes my ankle and pulls me back, but the smooth motion of gliding across the floor against my will is like an amusement park ride and instead of irritating me it just makes me laugh.

The laugh dies when Nicholas pins me. His hair's hanging down on either side of my face, breath fanning over my lips. He holds very still, just watching, closer than he's been to me in ages. My body remembers him and shivers.

His eyes are so black, I think I can see hell in them. For someone whose gaze has the power to compress souls into diamonds and diamonds into dust, I know he'd taste like spun sugar if I licked across his tongue. He's the poster boy for high-fructose corn syrup and I want to take a bite out of him. Peel off his shiny wrapper. Count how many of my teeth marks I find beneath.

The air is mountaintop-thin. "You're a demon," I tell him.

"And you've been a ghost," he breathes. I need the upper hand here, but I'm smaller than Nicholas. I use one of the only weapons at my disposal: surprise.

I reach between his legs and give him a firm, not unpleasant squeeze. His eyes widen, and the involuntary reaction of pupil dilation is mesmerizing. In the time it takes him to blink, a galaxy of colors dances across his irises: jade and brown and every flavor of blue, from summer rain to the midnight flash of moonlight on ocean waves.

I've got him on his back before he can register what's happened. "This is your downfall, right here," I say tauntingly. I squeeze my thighs on either side of him and he bites his lip. "You're supposed to be pissed off, not turned on."

"I can be both. You're not the boss of me."

"I could get used to this Nicholas," I say, toying with him. "You're actually present." Unlike the way he was the last few times we slept together, barely looking at me. He hates how excited he is right now and can't figure out which emotion he wants to let lead the charge. For logical, practical Nicholas who must keep his head in every situation, lust is terrifying.

"I'm always present," he bites out. "You're the one who's never present."

I ignore him, stroking his cheek. The atmosphere quivers, stretched so tight I could tap thin air and hear the resounding thump of a bass drum.

"You feel alive," I say. I lay my palm over his pounding heart. "Yes, very alive, like a real human man. I wouldn't have known it, since you never touch me. Have you forgotten how?"

He cups a palm around the back of my neck and simply rests it there, reminding me he could change the score at any moment if he wished it.

"Tell me you're sorry and I'll let you find out."

"Sorry for what?"

"Your half." His chest rises and falls deeply. I recognize all the signs, but it's as if they're from another life, they've been lying dormant for so long. I keep finding myself wondering, *When's the last time I saw this Nicholas?* because I'm forgetting that this Nicholas is new to me. He's uncharted territory. I want to explore the parts that are a surprise and punish him for the reincarnated parts he's trying to bring with him from his old life with the old Naomi. They don't belong here.

"My half," I repeat, sitting up straighter. I feel him beneath me and it's been *so* long; anything we've done in the last few months doesn't count. The last time we had sex, the space between us was dead air, unbroken by any emotion whatsoever— not love, not attraction, not tension. Right now, two out of three ain't bad. My body wants to trickle into liquid and spill forth all over him, but I venture to say, "Half of what?"

"Of what went wrong."

I swallow. It feels like someone's scratched my throat with talons. "We were never right to begin with."

He arches a brow. "No?"

"No. Changeling Naomi is the same person as First Date Naomi, just with all the shiny new penny rubbed off. We got too used to the best version of each other, so neither of us ever got to relax and show our normal selves. We've been hiding."

He stares up at me from the floor. He's slack-jawed but his muscles are strung tight. When he finally speaks, what he says catches me off-guard. "Who texted your phone?"

Before I can answer, he gently places a hand over my mouth. His skin is warm and smells like my conditioner. It's been a long time since he's slipped his fingers through my hair long enough for the scent to wear off on him. It's been a lifetime since we've smelled or tasted like each other. Been hungry for each other.

"Tell me, please?" His voice is velvety and compelling. Dangerous. "Be honest and you can have whatever you want."

He lets his hand fall from my mouth. I'm reeling. I think he might be laying a trap. Either that or I'm paranoid after laying so many traps of my own. Traps are all I see now.

"No one texted me. Who would? The only ones who text me are you and Brandy, and Brandy's busy with orientation at her new job."

"Can I see your phone, then?"

I bristle. "No. It's private."

"Even from me? I'd let you see mine."

I don't believe that for a minute. "So? I wouldn't ask to see yours. Your phone is none of my business."

"*I* am your business." He sits up, bringing our faces closer together. I slide off his lap immediately and insert a healthy amount of room between us. "Or I'm supposed to be."

"You don't trust me," I say.

"You don't trust me, either."

We watch each other. We've been watching each other so long, whenever I shift my glance I see a faint shadow of his silhouette thrown over every surface, like one of those black-and-white optical image tricks that you continue to see imprinted on blank spaces even after looking away. The sky has grown dark without our awareness. Through the living room window I can see a dash of stars, so much brighter here than anywhere else in the world. We're in our own bubble out here in the country.

This house is a place outside of time. It's so easy to spin around each other and lose track of hours, days, weeks. How long have we been here? It's got to be years.

I strain to remember how I wound up sharing intimate space with this other human being. I think I remember a zing in my bloodstream, a click of magnets. Laughter. Hope. The beginnings are so sparkly, so effortless. You can imagine the other person to be whoever you want. In all the gaps of your knowledge about them, you can paint in whatever qualities you like as placeholders. You can paint the other person into a dream impossible for them to live up to.

We met at a charity triathlon and struck up a conversation when he stumbled and I helped steady him. We met while volunteering at a homeless shelter. We met at a bank, depositing millions of dollars into our respective accounts. Braiding lanyards with at-risk youths.

He's right, I don't trust him.

He's kneeling at the other end of the rope bridge, hacking away at my lifeline with his knife. It's going to collapse before I can safely passage over. His eyes gleam as he watches me panic. He can't wait to see me fall.

Nicholas rises to his feet and checks the window, surprise

flitting across his face when he sees that it's already dark outside. I think he's realizing we're in a place outside of time, too. He shrugs back into his coat.

"Are you going out?" I ask, shadowing him.

"There's a freeze warning tonight. With as heavy as it's been raining, I should get ahead of this and go salt Mom and Dad's driveway now."

Suppressing the urge to roll my eyes is like trying to hold in a sneeze. How could I have forgotten this particular habit of the golden son? Anytime there's a freeze warning out and there's been precipitation, Nicholas goes over to his parents' house and salts the driveway. When it snows, he shovels their driveway. They could easily hire someone for this task, but darling Nicky takes up the mantle because he's Such A Good Son and craves their approval like it's cocaine.

"We should do our driveway, too," I say. By *we*, I mean him. It's freaking cold out there and I'm in my daytime PJs.

"Our driveway won't get as bad as theirs, since it's not paved." He slides his gloves on and flexes his fingers, admiring the quality of leather. "I've got snow tires and four-wheel drive."

"I've got . . ." My monster car flashes in my mind's eye. I'm afraid to have another go at it, but my only other transportation is an ancient bicycle Leon left behind. "What if I want to go somewhere?"

He knows I'm fishing for him to say something wrong, or that maybe I'm hoping he'll pass my impossible tests and say something right. *Fire your shot and find out, Nicholas.* "There's a bag of salt in the shed."

I follow him to the door. It feels like he's always leaving right when I want him to stay. When I need him here and he leaves, I lose something every time, over and over. He takes it from me when he goes. Always going. He's never going to belong to me. He's never going to want to stay with me. I'm never going to be enough. Even when we're not together and I'm away doing something else, it bothers me when that rigid sense of duty to his parents snaps its fingers and off he goes running. It's easier if I decide I don't want him around, because then at least he can't disappoint me.

"Nicholas," I say when he steps off the porch. Each blade of grass is an iceberg in miniature, crunching under his new work boots. I'm going to be the most honest I've ever been with either of us, out loud. Right now.

"I love you eighteen percent."

It's not a great number, but it's been worse. Those glasses and the messy hair are unfairly handsome on him and he's been more open with me. And more brutal. He killed a baby tree out of spite.

He stops in his tracks. Turns. "What did you just say?"

"That's the percentage." I clear my throat. "Eighteen."

He's so still, I think a strong wind might knock him over. "There's no such thing as loving someone eighteen percent."

"Yes, there is. I've done the math."

"You can't measure *love*." His voice sharpens on the last word before twisting. There's mockery running all through it now. "But if we're going to play the numbers game, then I guess I would have to say that I tolerate you eighteen percent, Naomi."

"So you don't love me, then."

"I didn't say that."

He didn't *not* say it. I cross my arms and wait for him to say something else. "Well?"

But he doesn't reply. His expression is so stormy that my pulse skips, and he leaves without another word. I go inside, a little wobbly after our conversation. I'm wobbly all the time now, but it's a step up from my fugue of before, half seeing and half listening to my surroundings. I pick up my phone, my heart a jackhammer in my chest. But it's not a rejection for one of my applications. It's a text from my mom, which is rare.

> I notice we haven't received our wedding invitation yet. Have you forgotten our address?

I compose a reply: I haven't mailed them out. We're not settled on a photo to include.

Gnawing on my cheek, I backspace all of it and type: They're ready to go. We'll send them out soon.

I backspace again. Then I delete the text without responding.

CHAPTER TWELVE

It's Saturday, which has a new meaning now that I'm still getting used to.

In our old life, if I wasn't scheduled to work we never spent Saturdays at home. I'd go browse flea markets and thrift shops while Nicholas hung out with his friends: Derek, Seth, and Kara—the ex he's "just friends" with and who loves to tell me I look tired. I don't care that she's married and blissfully devoted to her husband. I'm never, ever going to like her.

Seth's indifference toward me evolved into jealousy when Nicholas and I got engaged, as if I'm a usurper stealing Nicholas away from him. One-on-one, he's all right. Get him into a large group setting, and he tries to be a comedian. When this happens, all of his jokes are about Nicholas. He takes little jabs at him constantly, smiling while he does it, which disguises his put-downs as playful ragging. Nicholas's appearance takes a lot of hits. *Nice jacket. You stopping by the country club later?* Every time he makes fun of an item of Nicholas's clothing, it vanishes from his wardrobe circulation. He's stopped wearing the Cartier watch his parents got him as a graduation present and leaves his Ray-Bans in the car. If he uses a big word, Seth laughs and asks him if he thinks he's smart. *You think you're at a spelling bee or something?*

Since I'm not allowed to rip Seth's throat out and have been instructed to keep my mouth shut whenever he "jokes around" (Nicholas is in denial that the remarks bother him), I've stopped going to social events if I know Seth is going to be there. I've asked numerous times why he puts up with this, and reading between the lines of his bullshit responses I got the true gist: Seth was the first guy who wanted to be his friend in college, and now he feels like he owes him eternal loyalty. Since Nicholas wants to be the confrontational type but definitely isn't, he's let all the comments slide with an "Oh, c'mon" and an embarrassed laugh.

Offending people who treat him badly is not in his nature, so I'm proud of Nicholas for growing a backbone and ignoring Seth's recent texts: Come over and help me move, asshole. BYOB. Seth demanding that Nicholas help him move is pretty ballsy, considering he was nowhere to be seen when the shoe was on the other foot and Nicholas had to hire professional movers. People always go to him when they need something because they know he can't say no. I'm stunned that he hasn't given in to his guilt yet and skipped off to Seth's with a case of beer and a large pizza.

Weirdly enough, Nicholas has met up with Leon of all people. To go hiking. *Twice.* He won't tell me what they talk about and has called me conceited because he thinks I assume they're talking about me (which is true, but I bet they do).

Besides getting a ride from Brandy to Blue Tulip Café to discuss her new boyfriend (an optometrist single dad named Vance who I am rooting for because he's sweet and she deserves someone sweet), I haven't felt like hanging out with anyone lately, either. Today we're feeling particularly antisocial. Nicholas and I are too busy torturing each other to leave our little house of hatred.

It starts with the joke I can't stand.

We're on opposite ends of the couch, playing on our phones. (He's gotten a new one for himself.) I'm reading a news article because I need to stay on top of current affairs. This way if Nicholas starts talking about a subject he just heard about, I can say, "Oh, I already heard that." It's an excellent thing to do to someone you despise when the object of your . . . despisement? . . . is a pretentious know-it-all. 10/10, would recommend.

I mutter and murmur about the news article. When he doesn't ask what I'm reading about, I just go for it with a gasped *"Oh my god."*

"Yes?" He raises his eyebrows questioningly, like I just spoke his name. He often says this when I talk to a deity. He knows I hate it, and I think this gives him life. I'm adding minutes to his life span with my annoyance.

"I hate that joke."

"Some people find it funny."

"Nobody finds it funny."

"Gets a laugh from Stacy every time."

Dr. Stacy Mootispaw, crusader against khakis and accuser of him never going the extra mile. With as often as Nicholas has mentioned her, I won't lie to you, when I met her for the first time I was hoping she'd be a grandmotherly type, smelling of baby powder. Twice his age, in self-knitted sweaters with cats on them. A proud furbaby mom with a jolly old husband she loves so much she calls him on every break.

As you might guess, that's not what Stacy's like at all.

Her brain moves faster than Usain Bolt. She's got a million college degrees and could basically do whatever she wanted. The world is her oyster. If she ever gives up the dental game, she could easily model for J.Crew. She's got the shiniest black hair I've ever seen and a dazzling smile that must be half the reason she's in this particular industry. Perfect figure. Glowing skin so blemish-free, it's like she's been airbrushed. She doesn't wear a stitch of makeup but looks amazing anyway and I hate her for it. People who wake up looking glamorous can't be trusted.

Rolling my eyes, I go throw a load of clothes from the washer into the dryer, then end up doing a bit of vacuuming and organizing. I guess I'm a housewife now. Or house-fiancée.

"Whew, it's warm in here. Let's turn down the heat."

"You're just warm because you're up and moving around."

"No, it's definitely warm in here." I fiddle with the thermostat. It says it's seventy-two degrees, but there's no way it's not at least seventy-five. This thing is broken.

I sit back down and he stares at me, an irritable bear. "Speaking of Stacy," he begins, and I quash a rumble in my chest. "I got her for Secret Santa. Any suggestions?"

"Toothpaste."

He gives me a dry look. "Just because we're dentists doesn't mean we're in love with toothpaste."

"A gift card, then."

"Mmm, is that too impersonal?"

"Who cares? You're giving it to your coworker, not your best friend."

"I want to put some thought into it, though."

"If you want to put some thought into it, then why'd you ask me for ideas? I barely know this chick."

YOU DESERVE EACH OTHER   197

"I thought you might be helpful," he huffs. "You're both women!"

"Right, and we're all the same. We all like the same stuff, just like all men like the same stuff. I suppose I'll take the present I had in mind for my dad and give it to you for Christmas instead. Surprise, it's a model of the Brady Bunch house!" My dad's super into collecting memorabilia of older shows like *The Brady Bunch* and *The Partridge Family*.

"You know what I meant."

"I know you're sexist." I pull a throw blanket over me. "It's cold in here."

Nicholas glares. "That's it."

"That's what?" I ask as he gets off the couch and goes to find his coat and shoes. "What're you doing?"

"What I'm meant to be doing!"

What he's "meant to be doing" better not be Stacy Mootispaw. I follow him to the door and watch him march out to his car. Getting rid of the Maserati was a solid choice. It doesn't belong out here at all, whereas the Jeep looks like it was manufactured by nature. "Where are you going?"

He doesn't respond, peeling out without another word. I spend the next twenty minutes texting him. If he's in a dingy motel room with Dr. Sultry, the persistent vibration of his phone is going to be a real mood-killer.

Hey

Hey

Where are you

Nicholas

Nicky

Nickster

Nickelodeon

Heeeeeeeeeeeeeeeeeeeeeeeeeeeeeeeeeeeeeeeeyyyyyyyyyyyyyyyyyy
yyyyyyyyyyyyyyyyyyyyyyyyyyyyyyyyyyyyyyyyyyyyyyyyyyyyyyyyyyy
yyyyyyyyyyyyyyyyyyyyyyyyyyyyyyyyyyyyyyyyyyyyyyyyyyyyyyyyyyy
yyyyyyyyyyyyyyyyyy

Acknowledge me or I'm telling your mom you didn't come
home last night and you might be missing

Really? Not even for that?

I'm bowled over that my threat produced no reaction from
him, and starting to worry that he's incapacitated somewhere
when the Jeep comes clattering up the drive again.

He gets out without glancing at the house, which means he
knows I'm watching him through the window. What he hefts
out of the back of his car and lifts high above his head nearly
makes me faint.

It's. A. Canoe.

I'm in a lawn chair on the bank of our pond, snapping pictures
of Nicholas. He's maybe fifty feet out, in his plaid earflap hat

and Ghostbuster coveralls, trying to put a bobber on his fishing line. If Freud were sitting next to me, he'd probably deduce that stressors (i.e., me) have caused Nicholas to backslide into childhood to re-create his brightest moment in the sun. He's going to catch that bluegill again and hold it up proudly for the camera. Everyone will clap.

I call his phone.

He looks over at me in my chair, like, *You are ruining this.* We could be ten thousand miles apart and I'd still know what he's doing with his face. Telepathic waves beam at me, rippling the water like a helicopter's taking off. He's thinking loud and clear: *Go away. I'm becoming Who I'm Meant To Be.* It's a touch prissy and so familiar that I think I'm starting to love it on him.

This guy. Seriously.

I call him again. This time he answers. "What?" he snaps.

"Whatcha doin'?"

"What does it look like I'm doing?"

It looks like he doesn't know what he's doing. But I can't say that or he'll hang up. I need to monitor this situation as closely as he'll let me, for the sake of psychology. Science. *America's Funniest Home Videos,* possibly. He's still struggling to get his line baited because he doesn't want to remove his gloves.

"Aren't fish hibernating at this time of year?"

He pauses. "That's not . . . fish don't hibernate."

"I think I've heard they do."

"Shh. You're making me talk and I'm going to scare all the fish away."

"Did Leon say there's fish in this pond?"

His silence tells me he has no idea, but Nicholas is a prideful man. He'll stay out here until spring and catch a frog. Emaciated down to fifteen pounds, he'll thrust the frog in my face. *See!?* "Shh. I'm trying to catch dinner."

"I'm not eating fish from this pond. I don't know if the water's polluted."

"First of all, I didn't offer to share. Secondly, please stop talking. For multiple reasons." He hangs up and doesn't answer my next call. The call after that goes straight to voicemail. This is highly irresponsible of him. I could be having an emergency right now and he's made himself unavailable, which is the first thing I'm going to say to the nurses after rousing from my coma.

Nicholas tries to cast his line, but he doesn't press the release button at the right moment and the bait never leaves his own canoe. Sneaking a look over his shoulder at me to see if I witnessed that, he stands up and tries again. The poor lamb's unsteady on his feet and knows he has an audience, which undoubtedly makes this worse. I would hate to have Nicholas watch me try to fish.

It's like whenever I come upon him while he's doing push-ups and his body instantly quits on him. The simple fact of me standing there and observing transforms it into a public performance and his legs and arms turn to jelly. I bet video montages of his contributions to grade school plays will play on an endless loop when he gets to hell.

Nicholas eventually casts his line about five feet from his canoe and sits down, shoulders hunched. I know the precise moment he remembers his father's terrible posture, because he snaps straight again. He's got plaid flannel on beneath the coveralls and has been trying to coax his stubble into a real beard, but no matter how much he tries to be a burly lumberjack he still looks like he belongs in a boy band. The wind slowly revolves his canoe in a circle until he's facing me against his will, and he has to recast.

He's dying to look up at me. I'm a specter in his fringe. I'm to blame for the fact that he doesn't know how to fish. It's probably dawned on him that the little boy who caught a bluegill had somebody there to bait his hook and do all the arm work. Grown-up Nicholas is a prima donna. He uses rubber worms instead of real ones.

To avoid eye contact, he sets his pole down and starts to paddle his boat back around. His bobber tugs and he drops the oar by instinct to reel in his line. As the abandoned oar starts to tip over the edge of the canoe, he clumsily reaches for the pole and the oar and loses both. *Both.* Only Nicholas.

Oh. My. God.

(*Yes?* responds Nicholas, even in my imagination.)

I can imagine this cheapskate in the store prepping for self-actualization with outdoorsy equipment, debating whether to spring for a second oar. He's already dropping so much money on the state-of-the-art fishing pole, I know exactly how he rationalizes buying just the one oar. *I'll stroke on one side of the boat, then the other. Easy.*

Nicholas stands in the empty canoe, wind slowly spinning him, utterly decimated by this turn of events.

I stand, too, cupping my hands around my mouth. "How's it going?"

Nicholas takes off his cap and throws it down in a tantrum, raking his fingers through his hair. The oar is floating toward me. I can't help it. My laugh becomes the loudest sound in the universe. It echoes through the forest, sending up shocks of blackbirds. It thumps through Nicholas's veins, making him want to explode.

If it weren't for my laughing at him, Nicholas likely would have sat down and formulated a plan that didn't involve him getting wet. But I can push his buttons so well, coherent thinking falls to the wayside and his behavior takes a sensationally un-Nicholas turn.

He picks his hat back up and tugs it firmly down over his head, then dives into the freezing water. I laugh harder, giving myself rib pains, hiccupping. "What the hell are you doing?" I exclaim between vicious bursts. He got himself *stranded*. Actually *stranded*. And now he has to swim back to shore. This is the best thing that's ever happened to me. My body wants to give up, it's so weak from laughing, and I lean on my chair for support.

As Nicholas nears, my vision sharpens and I make out the ferocity in his eyes. His boots and clothes must feel like anchors, but he's swimming toward me with aggressive swiftness.

Oh, shit.

I'm backpedaling. "I would've helped you!" I call. "You should have stayed put."

It's true, I would've found a way to help him. After letting him sit there for an hour and posting a video of it online.

Nicholas's teeth are chattering when he emerges from the pond, sopping wet. He lumbers straight toward me. "Agh!" I squeal, ducking and crossing my arms like a shield in front of my face. He picks me up and throws me over his shoulder and my first thought is *holy wow*. He's stronger than he looks. Maybe it's adrenaline strength.

He turns on his heel and heads back to the pond. When I

realize what he's about to do, I clutch tightly to him for dear life while simultaneously kicking and thrashing. "No! Don't you dare! Nicholas, I mean it!"

He swings me around to tuck me under his arm, planting his boots two feet apart on the bank. I'm flailing like a snake but he doesn't lose his grip, tipping me over until my face hovers an inch over the water. Our reflected stares meet. My eyes are terrified, and his burn.

"Nicholas Benjamin Rose, I swear to god I will call the police if you don't put me down right now."

"Right now?" he teases, sliding me forward a centimeter. He's going to drown me.

"Not literally right now! On the ground! Put me on the ground!" I kick, but the movement just propels me forward. He's going to drop me on my face.

Nicholas hesitates. Considers. Then he does this impressive feat of strength in which he flips me like a pancake so that I'm right side up. He bends his face close, and it's like we're dancing and he's just dipped me, leaning in for a kiss. My lungs forget how to function and I'm frozen, wide-eyed in wonder as he leans in closer, closer, closer. His lips are almost brushing mine, and intention solidifies in his gaze. Accepting of my fate, I close my eyes for a kiss and he abruptly tilts me back until my hair is submerged. Icy water chases all the way to my roots.

I scream.

He laughs, setting me upright. "You ass!" I yell, slapping his arm. Nicholas laughs harder. My hair is the North Pole and I'm traumatized for life. "That's freezing!"

"Imagine how I feel."

"It's not my fault you jumped in the water, you idiot."

He turns and saunters away. "Shouldn't have laughed at me."

I snarl and jump on his back, bringing him crashing down to the ground. I'm not cognizant of what I'm doing, just that I must destroy this man. I reach out on either side of us and gather armfuls of dead leaves, furiously scooping them over him.

"What are you doing?" he asks, facedown as the leaves scatter over the back of his head. His chest seizes, and then I go *bump, bump, bump*, jostling up and down when he starts laughing. "Are you trying to *bury* me?"

"Shut up and stop breathing."

Nicholas howls with laughter. I'm so upset that he's not afraid of me and taking the end of his life more seriously that I hop up and down on him in reprimand.

Nicholas rolls and catches my hands before they can shoot out and strangle him. He laces our fingers together, grinning crookedly. "You should see what you look like right now," he tells me.

A murderous Jack Frost, probably. The image ignites another bout of anger, and I wrestle for control of my hands. He doesn't let go, tightening his fingers. "Stop stopping me from destroying you."

Tears leak down either side of his face as he laughs, cheeks pink, breath pluming up in white puffs. It hits me how much I like his laugh. His smile. His smile is ordinary when taken in on its own, but combined with the adorable laugh lines, the light that glows in his color-changing eyes, it's remarkable.

Some of the leaves I've been messing with have pine needles hidden in them, and they've prickled my palms, making them itchy. I rub my hands on either side of his jaw, using his stubble like a scratching post. Nicholas's eyebrows go up in disbelief, more tears leaking from the corners of his eyes. He stares and stares at me. "You're bananas," he says, not unkindly.

I snort. I have never heard him call anybody bananas. He's called me ridiculous half a million times, but *bananas* is so silly a term that I start cry-laughing, too.

He grins wider. "What?"

"You're a fopdoodle."

We both laugh. "I saw it on the Internet somewhere," I insist. "It's a real word."

"Your mom's a real word."

"Your mom's a real bad word."

He lets go of one of my hands so he can wipe his eyes. "Touché." Then he asks, "What does fopdoodle mean?"

"I assume it's a fop who doodles."

"Naturally."

I get off him. When he sits up, I shove him backward and hurry off to the house, cackling over my cheat of a head start. I know the first thing he'll want to do when he gets inside is take a hot shower, so I beat him there. I'm stripping off my clothes the second I get inside, shaking like a leaf with my wet hair, and lock myself in the bathroom. *Muah-ha-ha.* Now he'll have to wait. I'm going to take an hourlong shower and use up all the hot water.

The shower has just gotten hot enough to be pleasantly scalding when Nicholas unlocks the bathroom door and bursts inside. We've got one of those doorknobs you can pick by sticking a penny into the notch and turning it. I use this trick whenever I need something from the bathroom and he's shut himself in there to shave or admire himself in the mirror, but I don't think I appreciate being on the other end of it.

"Hey!" I squeak, trying to cover all my interesting parts with my hands. The glass shower door is all steamed up, so I'm probably just a flesh-colored blur to him. "I could've been going number two in here."

"With the shower running?"

"You never know."

My eyes are as big as pumpkins when he peels off his dripping coveralls and rips a flannel shirt over his head. Stomach. Chest. Arms. So much bare skin going on here and I'm not complaining about any of it. Being wilderness bros with Leon and playing with axes and power tools has been kind to him. "What do you think you're doing?"

"Taking a shower."

"I'm already in here."

"Good for you."

Nicholas completely ignores my shock. I'm a modest and innocent puritan lady, and he's out to steal my virtue. My mind flashes to previous episodes of not wearing clothes with Nicholas and it's a good thing the water's so hot, or he'd be able to tell I'm blushing. I remember how his mother has deluded herself into believing he's a virgin, and I smirk before I can help it.

Nicholas cocks an eyebrow at me as he slides open the door and steps inside. I wait for his gaze to lower, but it doesn't. He shakes his head in amusement, probably because I'm still trying to cover myself, then turns and starts lathering himself up with soap.

I don't move. I need to wash my hair but that would require the use of my hands. I decide to face opposite him, minimizing what he can see. The back's not as interesting as the front, I think.

I'm wrong about that, which becomes glaringly apparent when I catch our reflections in the shower door. He's looking at me. My gaze slides below his waist without my permission and it's clear he's found something about his view to appreciate.

"Don't look at me," I hiss.

His laugh is deep and rich-sounding in the acoustics of our foggy bathroom. "I'm not."

"Yes, you are."

"How do you know unless you're looking, too?" He reaches for my conditioner.

I spin around and take it from him. "This is mine and it's expensive. Get your own." He smiles like he wants to laugh because I've slipped up with the placement of my hands, so I quickly cover his eyes. He squints under my palm, nose scrunching.

"I can still see."

"Jesus." I turn around again.

"Yes?"

I want to stomp on his foot. My only course of action here is to hurry up so I can escape. I try to bend over a little to make myself smaller, because in my mind that gives him less to see, sneaking glances at him in the shower door. He's washing himself more slowly than he ever has in his life, staring openly. I think he's trying to get me flustered. If so, it's working. I slip a hand behind me, trying to span my fingers over my rear and block him from anything enjoyable, which just makes him laugh again.

"Close your eyes," I demand.

"Okay."

He doesn't close his eyes.

"Close them!"

"I did."

(He didn't.)

I need to rinse my hair, but he's standing directly under the spray, giving me very little room to maneuver. I plant a hand on his chest and he's immediately compliant, falling back. Nicholas's skin is hot satin under my fingertips, responding to my touch with goose bumps and a quickening pulse. I want to sink my nails into the slightest bit of give his flesh offers, but right now every flinch, every step and turn and tilt conveys a primal message. He's waiting for the signal that says *Help yourself to whatever you want. Don't be wasteful. Lick me up to the last drop.*

To prevent myself from extending an invitation I'm too much of a chicken to deliver on, I keep my eyes shut while I rinse my hair, hand motionless against his chest to make sure he can't come closer. When I open my eyes again, his gaze is flame, jaw white and set, and I imagine cracks running up the bone all the way to the top of his skull. Mist pearls in his lashes and brows, sweat cropping along the bridge of his nose and the hollows in his cheeks. He's a ripple of heat and with one gesture from me he'll gladly roast me alive. My heart goes *tha-thump*: a wild, winged creature in my rib cage. He looks like he's about to lose it and I won't lie, I'm a bit unnerved by what he might do.

It's been twelve weeks since I've had sex. Twelve weeks for Nicholas, too, if he hasn't been cheating on me.

The image of him sleeping with another woman and me catching him in the act doesn't inspire the same victorious feeling that it once did. It throws a bucket of ice water over all of my pounding, light-headed *need-you, take-me* while liquid fury chases through my bloodstream, synapses shorting out. If I

YOU DESERVE EACH OTHER   209

discover him cheating on me in a shopping mall parking lot I'm going to end up on the evening news. Stacy Mootispaw better stay out of my fiancé's dress-code-prohibited khakis or she's going to be putting her own teeth back into her mouth after I've kicked them out.

I can't let myself think about him that way, with me or anyone else. It's too dangerous and there are too many axes Leon left behind in the shed. If I conjure up memories of us in intimate positions, superimposing Stacy's face over mine, I'll black out and come to with holes smashed through all our walls.

I hurry up with my business, as if I can outrun these intrusive thoughts, and practically fall out of the shower while there are still suds in my hair. I dart a quick glance at Nicholas while grabbing my towel. He doesn't speak a word, but he might as well have an accusing thought bubble above his head that says *Coward.*

Running feels like surrendering a dose of my power to him, but I embrace my cowardly ways and hotfoot it up to my bedroom to get dressed. By the time I'm calmed down enough to tiptoe back downstairs, Nicholas is on the couch and his hair's already dry. It's so incredibly upsetting, how quickly a man's hair dries and looks perfectly fine.

"Look outside," he tells me.

I peer out the window, and my heart soars when a cascade of snowflakes swirls by and sticks to the glass. They melt one by one. "Snow!"

It's mid-November, but for me Christmas starts at the first snow. I get sparkly-eyed over the season, doing pirouettes around the house while I strew Hobby Lobby decorations left and right. I play all the classics on surround sound and set up

SARAH HOGLE

the tree well before Thanksgiving. I'm that person on social media you absolutely hate because I say stuff like *IT'S 224 DAYS UNTIL CHRISTMAS* in May. All the festivities of Christmas, and the joy and magic of it, make me happy, so I tend to stretch it out for as long as possible.

I turn to see what he's watching on TV, and do a double take. The television is turned off. He's watching me in the black screen.

Something about the way his eyes are following me feels intimate, making my legs watery. I'm conscious of the way my arms swing when I move, and the way I walk. It's similar to the way I sometimes move in dreams, where there's inexplicable resistance. Almost like I'm trying to walk underwater.

I go to the drawing room because I want to see the snow through those three beautiful windows, but his big desk blocks me. He sees the change in my expression when I walk back into the living room.

"What's wrong?"

"Nothing."

He doesn't speak, but his gaze narrows. He's got an ankle propped on his knee, fingertips drumming on the armrest of the couch.

Nothing.

It's a self-appointed martyr's answer. It ensures that the issue goes unresolved, and that I suffer all by myself. What do I get out of saying *nothing*?

"It's just . . ." I sit down on the other armrest, out of touching range. "When you first showed me the house, one of the things I liked best were the windows in, uh . . . in there." He calls it his office or his study and in my head I still call it the drawing room, because in a past life I was a duchess and I've never quite gotten over being reborn as a commoner in this age.

"I thought, *wow*, what a pretty view. You'd be able to see all the stars over the forest. I'd imagined putting an armchair right there, so I could sit and admire the view. I like that room. I'd put, I don't know, maybe a nutcracker on the mantel or something. I don't know." I shrug to downplay it. I sound insane. A nutcracker? Really? These are my gripes? I've been hyperfocusing on such minuscule details.

I'm immediately embarrassed that I admitted this out loud and I'm about to *never mind* the whole thing when Nicholas stands and walks into the drawing room. Standing on the other side of his desk, he slides his hands into his pockets and stares at the windows like he'd never gotten a good look at the forest beyond them before. "You're right," he says. He angles his profile toward me. His eyes are the color of a silver fir. They're fog and moonlight.

I'm not sure what part of my spiel he's saying this in reference to, but I'll take it. We fall into a pattern that is completely new but somehow already feels ingrained: We silently make dinner together and sit down in front of the television. We don't switch it on. We eat in companionable silence as the snow falls steadily around us and darkness smothers the world.

CHAPTER THIRTEEN

Our cease-fire comes to an end, predictably, twenty minutes after dinner when he hears my phone buzz on the mantel. I don't get up.

He glances at the mantel, then at me. It's a long, considering look. "Not going to see what that is?"

"Nope."

His suspicion is palpable, but I'm not mentally prepared to check my notifications. My heart is racing just knowing what it might be, and I have to give myself time to come down from the anxiety rush, bracing myself for bad news, before I brave a look.

One of the people I've secretly been in touch with about a job at a craft store I'd really, *really* like (and have already gotten my hopes up about) told me three days ago after I interviewed that she'd take three days to check my references and consider other applicants in the pool before emailing me with a decision. I've spent the day alternating between obsessively checking my phone (and my computer, in case for whatever reason the email doesn't pop up on my phone) and pretending the Internet doesn't exist. My nerves are shredded.

The longer I go on pretending I don't have a notification, the heavier Nicholas's gaze becomes. It weighs on me, distrustful. I see his problem clearly, because it's one I've been struggling with myself: he has questions, but with the state our relationship is in right now, certain information feels privileged. We're not in a position to demand answers.

It's like when two people are casually dating but haven't made it official yet. In this tender stage, they're not entitled to know everything they want to know about each other, so they can't behave with unearned familiarity. That's how it feels between us.

Nicholas is frustrated by his restraint. The whole situation is an annoying dance that breeds resentment.

"How did Brandy's orientation go?"

I'm surprised by his interest, especially since he didn't even pretend he doesn't know her real name. "She says her boss is sleazy. She's already looking for a new—"

"Melissa doing well?" he asks, interrupting me.

"Uhh . . ." Melissa and I are both grateful to be able to let our acquaintanceship drop. "I haven't talked to her."

"Still talk to Zach?"

I shrug. I wouldn't be surprised if Zach and I never crossed paths again. He's the kind of guy you can picture running off to Los Angeles on a whim, where he'll invent some simple gadget that becomes a daily staple you can't imagine ever going without, and in five years I'll see him on the Forbes list of billionaires.

Nicholas's gaze darkens. His foot jostles restlessly on his knee. "What kind of lotion do you wear?" he asks me.

"Huh?"

"I've been thinking of ideas for Secret Santa. Your lotion smells nice."

It's called Sweet Seduction, and I slather it on after every shower. The notion of him giving Stacy Mootispaw a present called Sweet Seduction and subsequently having that woman smelling like me makes me want to scratch my eyes out.

"I think what you're smelling is my shampoo."

"No, that's not it."

I sort through a stack of junk mail because I desperately need to break eye contact. I'm not as talented a liar as I used to think, and I don't want him seeing that this bothers me so much. I'm not giving him the name of my lotion even if he stabs bamboo shoots under my fingernails. Stacy can smell like latex gloves and antiseptic and stay in her own fucking lane.

My phone buzzes again. Is it the craft store job? Or somebody else telling me no? There's a zero percent possibility that it's good news, whatever it is, so why bother getting up? What's the point in ruining the rest of my night and getting myself depressed tomorrow? I'm never checking my phone again. I'll become an anti-technology recluse. I'll be wholly dependent on Nicholas, which he'll love. He wants to yank away all my safety nets before tossing me out to sea.

"I think someone's messaging you," he says quietly.

I shrug. "Probably a spam email."

"And you don't want to check? Might be Brandy."

"I don't think so. She's on a date with Vance the optometrist."

He hears the fear in my voice, the stubborn refusal. His eyes are lasers burning right through me; I can smell my skin heat up and start smoking. The fact that he doesn't know all my notifications are rejections means he hasn't tried to pry into my phone when I'm not looking, which I appreciate. No matter how much this bugs him, he won't invade my privacy.

"Maybe jewelry," he says suddenly.

I glance up. I haven't applied to any jewelry stores. But then, he doesn't know that's what's on my mind. He doesn't know my organs are being pressed in a vise. "What about jewelry?"

"For Stacy."

This topic is annoying. I am thoroughly, decidedly annoyed and there are thorns growing out of my flesh. Who cares what she gets? Does he ever put this amount of thought into presents he gets for me? I'll tell you the answer to that one: no. "I still don't see anything wrong with getting her a gift card."

"Jewelry would be nicer."

"Expensive jewelry would be, but isn't there a max on how much you're supposed to spend? Most offices that do Secret Santa keep it under twenty bucks or something like that."

"No, there's no limit," he says slowly. His eyes glitter, one corner of his mouth hooking back. I hold my breath because I can just tell he's about to toss a grenade. "Besides, I want her to know I care."

"She won't know it came from you," I remind him. "It's *Secret* Santa."

"I think she'll know."

"How? How will she know, Nicholas?" God, it's stupid for grown people to give each other holiday presents. When it comes to colleagues, anyway. It's undignified. People who work together shouldn't be forced to socialize unnecessarily. Whatever happened to professionalism in the workplace?

It's Nicholas's turn to shrug, but there's something pleased about his demeanor. "We know each other very well. We're close. I think she'll be able to sense it like *that*." He snaps his fingers.

"Giving jewelry to a woman you work with is inappropriate," I say frostily. "So is lotion. Get her a pair of socks, you pervert."

He turns his face away from me, covering his mouth with his hand. "Maybe a subscription service? A monthly delivery of flowers."

My blood froths. The image of him presenting her with flowers makes me homicidal. "Buy her a travel magazine. She should get out of the state more. Out of the country, even."

"Mmm, I think I'm leaning toward jewelry. A pair of earrings. What do women like, Naomi? You can be helpful here. Do women like diamonds?"

"Diamonds?" I screech. "For your coworker? What kind of message are you trying to send?"

"I don't see anything wrong with diamonds," he replies angelically, giving me a mock-puzzled expression. "Stacy's a valuable member of our team. I think Stacy deserves—"

"I swear to god, Nicholas, if I hear that woman's name come out of your mouth one more time, I'm gluing your lips together. I'll drag you outside and throw you back into that stupid pond, butt-naked this time. I'll go down to your office and chain myself to your wrist so you never get any private interaction with her. If you try to give her diamonds, I'm going to steal them back and bake them into your food. I don't give a shit how *valuable*—"

I pause.

Nicholas is laughing.

"Is this funny to you?" I'm shrill as a siren.

"Little bit," he admits, trying to hide a grin. "And it's *buck-naked*. That's the phrase, just so you know."

"If you give that woman flowers," I growl, "I'm going to—"

"Going to what?" He stands and comes toward me so fast I don't have time to react.

His palms sink into the fabric of the couch on either side of my head, face hovering over mine. I try to shrink back but there's nowhere to go. My blood pumps so forcefully, it makes my heart hurt.

Nicholas slants me a wild look, eyes blazing. "What are you going to do, Naomi?"

There's a frisson of anticipation and suspense in his tone; something that still hopes, in spite of our constant attacks. I reach for a sharp weapon but don't find any. Facing him on our battlefield, I drop all my armor.

"Cry," I whisper.

The strings of our reserve snap and he falls onto me, astride my lap, knees digging into the couch to support his weight. His fingers tangle in my hair and his lips find mine, soft and warm and inviting.

He isn't gentle. Nicholas's tongue darts along the seam of my lips in demand, and I open for him because my head is spinning and focus is a myth and he's kissing me *like this*. Has he ever kissed me like this? If he has, I don't remember it.

It takes me a couple seconds to catch up, but when I do I'm floored by how eager my body is to betray my better sense, forgetting the destructive things we've done to each other. All those thoughts slip underwater as I arch against him and he tilts his hips against mine, needing closer contact. We're kissing so hard that we keep forgoing the need to breathe. It's unimportant at this point. Minor details.

The longer we touch, the more confused I am, until I begin to think I've got my facts flipped. I think I hate him eighteen percent.

Nicholas repositions us so that I'm on his lap instead, which lends me a thrilling dynamic of power. I could derail this right now if I wanted. Or I could tighten my grip around his wrists and kiss, bite, taste. I can do anything I like. I can feel that he'll let me.

One thing needs to be cleared up right now, though. "You're never giving anything to Stacy for as long as you live," I inform him. "I don't care if she asks you for a stick of gum. I don't care if she asks you what time it is. She's not getting a single thing from you."

His wicked laugh shivers against my neck. "There is no Secret Santa."

I rip away to study him, my fingers curling around his collar. "What?"

He doesn't reply, so I tap his shoulder with the back of my hand. "No, seriously. *What?*"

Nicholas's eyes are lust-inked and volatile. His voice scrapes from his throat. "Tell me, and don't lie. Are you cheating on me with Zach? Have you ever, at any point?"

There've been a few clues so far that I'm stuck in a dream, but this confirms it. I stare at him closely, trying to figure out if he's serious. He cannot be serious. "Are you out of your mind?"

"Please don't. Don't make me feel like this is all in my head."

It's the tortured way he says it, and the *please*, that sways me. I'm not sure I've ever been tender with Nicholas before, and what a shame is that? I don't know how to be vulnerable with him, but there's no alternative here. I have to tread gingerly. I try to kiss him, but he doesn't move his lips against mine, waiting for the truth, breath releasing in small, staggered pants. He's just as jagged as I am.

"No," I say, gazing into his eyes so that he knows I'm being honest. "I'm not cheating on you with Zach or anyone else. I've never cheated. Why would you ask that?"

His reply tumbles out in a rush: "You don't like me being around any of your work friends. Zach hates me. Whenever I see him, he's hostile for no reason. You laugh really loud when you read his texts. And you've lost interest in me, which isn't in my head, either. I've felt you going away."

What he says actually makes sense, but at the same time it's so absurd I can't help the laugh that bursts from my chest.

It's the wrong reaction. Nicholas's eyes flash with anger. He tries to push me off, but I surprise him by locking my arms around his neck. Still shaking with laughter, I say, "I'm sorry. I'm just imagining the look on Zach's face if he heard you accuse him of messing around with me."

He's embarrassed and irritated and struggling in earnest now, so I hurry up. "He doesn't like you because you're a scary bogeyman dentist and he thinks you're on the warpath to give him twenty root canals without anesthesia. He'd *love* knowing he's been living in your head like this, because that's just Zach. He enjoys irritating people. But no, there's nothing going on between Zach and me. Ever. If you don't believe me, you can go ask him. He and his boyfriend will get a kick out of it, I'm sure."

Nicholas falls still, eyeing me skeptically. "Boyfriend?"

"Yep. I think he dates women, too, or he used to, anyway." I shrug. "It's none of my business. We've never been interested in each other like that." I narrow my eyes. "What about you? Have you ever cheated?"

"No."

He sounds sincere. He *looks* sincere. I want to believe him, but—

"Not with Stacy?"

He swallows and averts his eyes. My stomach bottoms out. "I was talking about Stacy to mess with you. I just wanted a reaction. I wanted to see if you'd even care if you thought I was . . ." He's at loose ends, trying to come up with a decent explanation. "I shouldn't have—ahh."

"You deliberately tried to make me think you might be into another woman? To hurt me?"

"Not to hurt you. To see if you were capable of being hurt by it. It sounds bad, but there's a difference." I'm not sure there is.

"You're right, that does sound bad."

But I'm not blameless in all this. Just a couple of days ago, I filed a millimeter of wood off the leg of his desk so it would wobble. I've tried to drive him nuts on purpose, too.

With that, I lean in and kiss him again. His surprise gives way to desire, hands grasping my hips. It's electrifying, how illicit this feels to me. I'm not the same Naomi and he's not the same Nicholas. It's like I'm cheating on my fiancé. The kiss keeps changing its name with new meanings. It's fast and quick, hard; then slow, exploring. We're in sync through every transformation, patient and then not, curious and testing and desperate. Above all, aware. I don't forget who I'm kissing. I don't tune out.

That's the element standing out to me so strongly now: how

alive this man is. Every piece of him, vivid, communicating with all of my senses. It's not that he's never looked like this, or felt like this, or tasted like this. It's that I've been asleep. I wonder what kind of revelations he's having about our kiss. What he's discovering about me now.

It's a wonderful relief that for these moments, we're on the same wavelength. Fighting him has been exhausting and it's a nice change of pace to steam up the room in other ways. I want to generate a fog of lust so thick that he'll never be able to find his way out.

He tastes like candy, the kind that starts off sour and dissolves into unbearable sweetness on your tongue. We're boiled down to base needs and nothing more. Hot, searing skin. Lowered lashes. Heavy breathing. Hands everywhere. I want him to touch me without wondering what I'm thinking—take the body, leave the heart. Being so close that he can't study me is a blessing, hiding right in front of him, distracting him with my mouth on his neck every time he hesitates and tilts, searching out my thoughts.

I remember thinking during kisses past that him being too close to see my expressions provided good cover. I'm not sure what those kisses meant to either of us. For me, maybe unsatisfying release. For him, I think reconnection that never happened.

I'm still trying to decide what this kiss means when we break it. We pull away slowly, watching each other. He might have weapons behind his back, but somehow I don't think so. Mine are within arm's reach.

The emotions racing through me are so bewildering, I'm grateful when he gets up to go adjust the heat settings. I'm not usually a jumpy person, but right now I'm hurtling toward a full-blown panic attack. I don't know what's happening and I don't know what's going on in Nicholas's head these days. I certainly don't know what's going on in mine. I run to my bedroom, conscious of him watching me all the way up the stairs. Again, it's like I'm moving underwater, under his microscope, Nicholas's clever brain decoding messages I'm unknowingly sending with my gait, how far apart my fingers are splayed, the color in my cheeks. It's never been so obvious that he can see right through me. The question is: how long has he been looking?

I can still feel his gaze pinned on me even while I'm lying in bed, heart thumping erratically, eyes wide open to absolute darkness.

It's very late when I think I hear the doorknob rattle. I've locked it out of habit. Maybe I'm imagining the noise. I close my eyes for a moment, meaning to get up and go see, but when they open again a second later it's dawn.

CHAPTER FOURTEEN

I get dressed in the frail morning light and creep onto the landing. Nicholas's door is ajar, so I tiptoe closer. His bed is empty, the comforter printed with palm leaves peeled back. I know what that blanket feels like against my bare skin. I regard it like an old friend I haven't seen in a long time, along with the headboard we picked out together. The curtains we picked out together. In those early days we would say yes to anything, floating on the high of trying to make each other happy. I would have slept on a sleeping bag if that was what he wanted.

His new bedroom is arranged the same way as our old one. The mattress is new, since I took our other one. Throwing a quick glance at the door, I sit down on the bed and do a little bounce. This mattress is so much better than mine. My room contains leftovers—the curtains that used to hang in our old kitchen, which means they're too short and don't block out enough light. My bedspread is a Christmas throw blanket.

I study the empty space beside his dresser and imagine mine next to it. My nightstand should sit on the right side of the bed, and its absence turns the whole room wrong. He keeps one of his pillows in the space where my head should lie.

It's a bad idea, lingering in here, but I'm too nosy for my own good. I rummage through his closet, touching all his crewnecks and dry-cleaned suits. The ivory button-down he wore at our disastrous engagement photo shoot. Our smiles were forced in every picture. Between takes, we muttered under our breath and accused the other one of not trying, of not wanting to be there.

One of those pictures is supposed to be in a frame on his nightstand. The nightstand contains only a lamp. My heart plummets, but then I spot the frame hanging on the wall. He's switched out the engagement photo neither of us was trying in and replaced it with a memory that takes me back to this past winter, days after he proposed. It's a bit blurry, and my arm is disproportionately wide because I'm holding it out to snap the picture.

According to the red paint in the background, we're in his friend Derek's kitchen. It's Derek's housewarming party, and as a gag we got him a gun that shoots marshmallows. Nicholas is right beside me, head on my shoulder. At the last second our eye contact abandons the camera, noticing a marshmallow stuck to the ceiling above us. My hand unconsciously strokes through his hair and holds his head to the cradle of my neck in what strikes me as an affectionate gesture I haven't done in forever. Just like that, a posed picture becomes a candid one.

As soon as the flash went off, that marshmallow fell on Nicholas's head, and everyone laughed. *Did you get that?*

No, I got the moment just before.

Too bad.

I wonder when Nicholas had this picture printed. Why this particular shot, out of the hundreds we've taken of ourselves? Why would he want it on his wall? Until now, I thought it existed only on my Instagram. Looking at the picture now, feeling these emotions, solidifies into a memory of its own.

I've already spent too long in his bedroom—his, not ours—and I need to slip out before I'm caught, but I need to know more. I'm on a mission to closely examine this man's belongings, the things he touches daily. I've seen it all so many times that I'm numb to it, so I have to focus. See through new Naomi's eyes.

I rummage in his nightstand, fingering each object. His contacts case and bottle of solution. A case for his glasses. Lube, which I might as well throw away at this point. An old charger that's no longer compatible with his current phone is next. Skittles. A pen and notepad from a Holiday Inn, top sheet containing a smiley face I drew. I pick up a disposable straw wrapper and am about to drop it when I see that the ends are tied together.

And I remember.

A few months ago, Leon went and got take-out Chinese food for everyone at the Junk Yard. Nicholas stopped by while we were eating, odd man out in his fancy black blazer and wingtips. I think the teasing he gets for his typically Rose-esque wardrobe is why he clings to the khakis: *See! I can be casual, too.*

He'd planned to take me out to dinner as a surprise and didn't understand that I didn't want to put aside cheap take-out that wasn't even that good in favor of driving an hour to an upscale restaurant. I was part of something here, this Junk Yard family. He was the outsider, annoyed that I'd undermined his plans. Annoyed that I had a new family and he wasn't invited in.

With the surprise dinner thwarted, he wasn't sure whether we wanted him hanging around. He strolled awkwardly about the shop for a few minutes, clearly tense, shooting us looks whenever we laughed. I didn't join him while he meandered through the aisles, painfully aware that half of my coworkers didn't like him. I didn't want them to tar me with the same brush. Joining Nicholas would be like declaring my allegiance to him, and then I'd be the odd man out, too.

So I stayed where I was and didn't try to alleviate his awkwardness. Didn't try to bring him into our conversation. I took everybody's straw wrappers and tied them into bracelets, which we all put on, even Melissa. Nicholas walked over while I was tying an extra straw wrapper, so I handed it to him. An afterthought.

And he'd kept it. He easily could have thrown it out when we moved, but here it sits. Nicholas's secret sentimentality.

My throat burns. My fingers curl around the piece of trash, preserved in this drawer like a precious treasure. I hear a fit of coughing from downstairs and return the straw wrapper bracelet to where I found it, then hurry from the room.

When I descend the stairs, I find Nicholas sprawled on the couch, coughing in his sleep. Used tissues clump on the coffee table and floor. He's twisted up in the blankets like he's been tossing and turning, shirt riding up to expose a gap of stomach. His hair's a mess and his glasses are askew on his face. He looks young and flushed and sweet.

I carefully remove his glasses and put them on the coffee table, then feel his forehead. He's clammy, but no fever. He doesn't know I'm watching him, which gives me free rein to have a closer look. His bone structure is so elegant, I almost hate him for it. He swerved all of Harold's genes while developing as an embryo and he's only going to get more distinguished-looking as he ages.

The tissue box is empty, so I go pull down a fresh one from a closet. Then I see he's had quite a night down here by himself, drugstore paraphernalia scattered all over the counter under the cabinet where we keep antacids and allergy tablets and the like. There's a plastic medicine cup in the sink with a drop of cherry-red liquid in it. It hits me that he probably slept downstairs so that his coughing wouldn't wake me up, and my heart makes a little tick, rolling over.

I root through the cabinets and come up with a bag of cough drops, so I leave those on the table for him, too.

"Just had to get that canoe, didn't you," I murmur to myself, padding into the drawing room. I sneak behind his desk to look outside and almost gasp.

It's a wonderland out there. A good four inches of shimmering white covers everything, even the pond, which means that canoe isn't going anywhere. It's stranded in the middle, surrounded by ice. The forest is breathtakingly beautiful with sunrise glowing up over the edge of the world, coloring the spaces between branches like stained glass.

I wish Nicholas were awake to see this, but then again, snow isn't as magical to him as it is to me. For him, snow means he has to go and—

Oh, crap.

My joy explodes to dust. Nicholas once left me in a bookstore to drive to his parents' house and carry groceries in from Deborah's trunk in the pouring rain. He did this because she called and asked him to. He mows their grass and fixes things around their house and worries about their memories and medical appointments and finances. He's incurably concerned, and will baby them for as long as he lives even if they don't necessarily need it.

I stare at his miserable form on the couch, back convulsing off the cushions with each coughing jag. He's so exhausted, the coughing doesn't even wake him up. This man is sick, but that's not going to stop him from going over to his parents' house this morning and shoveling their driveway. That's just Nicholas. He's That Guy.

I glance outside again at the snow, at the thermometer on the other side of the window that declares it's nineteen degrees, and I think with a vehemence that jolts me: *No.*

No way in hell.

There's only one way to stop him, so that's the way I've got to go. I reach for my coat and hat in the closet but see his coveralls and raise an eyebrow in consideration. It might not be a bad idea to wear something a little more heavy-duty. After I tug my Ghostbuster gear on and roll up the pant legs about a mile until the cuffs no longer drag, I decide to go the whole hog and grab his hideous earflap hat, too. It smells like him, which is oddly comforting even though he's right here, and the fleece is so soft and comfortable.

I need to get me one of these.

Once I'm all bundled up, I grab the keys to his Jeep and throw three different shovels into the back. Three shovels, because they're different sizes and I'm ashamed to say I've never shoveled snow before so I don't know which I'll want to use. Nicholas does all our shoveling. I don't think that's a fact I've appreciated until now: he always shoveled a pathway from our porch to my car when we lived at the old house. He never asked me to do it instead, not even once.

As a matter of fact, he scraped ice off my doors and windshields, too. He did it before he left for work, before I woke up.

Shame burns my face. When's the last time I thanked him for that? When's the last time I noticed he even did these little things for me and didn't simply take them for granted? I've been so hung up on him doing this for his mom and dad that I kind of forgot he does it for us, too.

I drive very, very slowly to Mr. and Mrs. Rose's house on Sycamore Lane. Only the main road has been visited by a salt truck, but the Jeep is a total champ and never slides. I am behind the wheel of Nicholas's Jeep that he bought without telling me and have entirely too much time alone with the disturbing revelation that I'm an asshole.

The lights are on when I nose up the driveway, which means Deborah's awake. Harold's got at least until noon before he rolls face-first onto the floor.

The beautiful, untouched snow blanketing their driveway sets me off. They've got no problem hiring people to power-wash their house and prune their rosebushes and arrange rock structures in the flower beds. And yet for whatever arbitrary reason, they depend on Nicholas to make this particular problem go away. They expect it. They say he's so *good*, so *kind*, and that pressure is a ten-ton weight, making sure he'll never stop doing it. If he does, they'll withdraw all their approval. He won't be the good, kind son anymore. He's heard the way they talk about Heather and knows that with one misstep, they'll be talking about him the same way.

I snarl at the snow, at the warm, glowing windows and Deborah's silhouette peeking out. Her maternal pleasure radiates.

Nicky is here to take care of everything! He loves to help us and feel useful.

Not today, dickheads! Today you're getting a substitute who's incompetent at best when it comes to manual labor, and you can just deal.

Their driveway is personally cruel to me right away, a crust of ice eating one of my shovels. I dig back in, nose dripping like a faucet, face a frozen block of "Why, god, why" while the rest of my body melts like a candle in these coveralls. This is the pits. This is some goddamn bullshit. I call my present situation every curse word I can come up with. Sometimes Nicholas is over here well before he has to go to work, and I mentally run through that timeline. In order to shower and get to Rise and Smile at seven, that means he's doing this in the dark. I'm so pissed on his behalf that I shovel faster.

It's frankly amazing that he has any goodwill left in his heart toward his parents. I want to drag them outside and bury them with my shovel.

There's so much snow to clear, I'm too daunted to be methodical about it and scoop at random, flinging it over my shoulder. Deborah and Harold aren't getting neat borders of snow on either side of the drive. They're getting carnage. It occurs to me that if I come back again next time it snows and do another piss-poor job, Nicholas will be off the hook. Mr. and Mrs. Rose will beg me to stop. They'll hire a snowplow guy.

When I'm about halfway finished, the front door opens and Deborah trundles out in a fur coat that's probably fashioned solely from baby animals, steaming mug in hand. She hustles over, a big smile on her face, until she gets up close and realizes that the person in coveralls and a hideous hat is me.

"Oh!"

Her horror is invigorating. I want to have it made into perfume. Clothing. Bath bombs.

"Naomi," she says gravely, like she's just heard the most terrible news. "I wasn't expecting . . ."

"Is that for me?" I reach for the mug. It's hot chocolate. Before Deborah can reply, I take it from her and sip. There are mini marshmallows swimming at the top, and I'd stake my soul she put in thirty-two of them, one for each year of Nicholas's life. This hot chocolate tastes better than the kind she supplies me with during winter visits, confirming my paranoid suspicions that Nicholas gets the good stuff while I'm offered store-brand.

Her mouth is a round O as she watches me drink. "Thanks," I say when I'm finished, handing the mug back.

"Is Nicholas feeling well?"

I'm not subjecting him to a pop-in visit from Mommie Dearest and chicken soup cooked by "the woman." "He's terrific," I tell her cheerfully. "Well, I better get back to it. Gotta lotta work to do!"

The rest of the driveway practically shovels itself as I zone out, thinking about Nicholas. Next time he comes over here to shovel, I should tag along to help out. We'll get it done in half the time.

Whatever muscles aren't numb are aching when I climb into the Jeep. I've been here for two hours. I'm positive it doesn't take Nicholas longer than an hour to achieve the same, if not better, results. When I pull out of the driveway, I honk twice for good-bye because I imagine that's what Nicholas probably does.

The journey back home is better than the journey out, since snowplows have cleared the roads. I can't wait to get home and shower, but I think about Nicholas's rough night. His coughing fit, and how he'll wake up hungry and pitiful with no motivation to cook for himself.

Most food joints around here are closed on Sunday mornings, but Blue Tulip Café, the coffee shop Brandy's sister owns, is thrilled when I pull up. None of the tables have patrons and there are no gaps between pastries in the display case, which means I'm the first customer of the day. This place is going to go the way of the Junk Yard and we all know it, so I buy extra. Breakfast sandwiches, soup, coffee. One of the workers helps me haul it all out to my car.

I make one more stop to restock on cold and flu medicine before heading home. For the first time since we moved, I visualize the house in the woods when I think the word *home* instead of the white rental on Cole Street.

When the Jeep shivers up the driveway, I can see Nicholas waiting for me behind the screen door. As I start to carry in the food and medicine, he runs out in his slippers.

"Get back inside!" I order.

"You need help."

"You need to sit down. You're sick."

He takes the coffee and soup from me, anyway. I'm amused at the way he keeps gaping at me, completely boggled. Deborah must have called him already with a full report. *Hills of snow all over the yard now, she just tossed it anywhere. And then she drank all your hot chocolate! The good kind!* "You didn't have to do that," he tells me when we get inside. "Shovel my parents' driveway. Why did you?"

"If nobody showed up to shovel their driveway, your mom might be forced to do it herself. Deborah's Gucci pantsuits? In *this* snow?" I chuckle dryly. "What a catastrophe. So I said, 'Not on my watch, snow.'"

His eyes are huge. If he thought I was a changeling before, I shudder to think what he imagines I am now. I pester him to go wait on the couch and bring him his breakfast, then test his forehead to make sure he doesn't have a fever. It's adorable how his hair is sticking out in every direction, and I run my fingers through it. He's speechless and I'm basically Mrs. Cleaver. I think I could get used to this whole surprising-him-and-making-him-speechless thing. It's delightful.

"Looks pretty out there," he manages after a couple bites of his breakfast sandwich, with a nod at the window. His voice is a touch hoarse, probably exacerbated by Deborah making him talk on the phone. It'll take a century to undo all the damage she's done to him, but I'll start with Vicks VapoRub and a humidifier. "All the snow. Like a holiday postcard."

He would think that, all warm and cozy in his flannel and slippers. I have no positive opinions about snow at the moment. Screw snow. I wish global warming would hurry up and abolish the whole season. I grunt noncommittally and trudge past him, shedding my layers as I go.

"I'm going to take a shower and maybe a quick nap," I say. "Will you be all right?"

He nods, still stunned. He shouldn't be this stunned by a nice gesture. It should be a given, but it's not, and that's my fault. I've been withholding nice gestures to punish him for not giving me enough nice gestures, and just look at how well that attitude's panned out for us.

I end up napping longer than I intended because my alarm never goes off. Maybe I imagined setting it. When I heave my sore body downstairs, Nicholas cries from another room, "Not yet! Hold on."

He clamps his hands over my eyes and nudges me into the kitchen, where I'm forced to wait in stupefied silence for ten minutes until he shouts hoarsely, "Okay! You can come in now."

"You need to save your voice," I say as I walk toward the sound of his shuffling. I stop dead in the doorway of the drawing room.

He's rearranged it: taken out the TV and relocated his desk to a different wall. My desk is in here, too, flush with his rather than squashed into a drafty living room corner. It doesn't resemble his personal office anymore, but a shared space. My shoes stacked beside his. My candles. His model train. His filing cabinet. My bookshelf, with a blend of my fiction and his non, his collection of fountain pens and my menagerie of Junk Yard curiosities. A marriage of personalities.

His eyes track me, absorbing every intricate change of my expression, so he notices when my gaze lands on the fireplace and my throat closes up. I feel a pressure in my sinuses, a punch to the chest.

There's a nutcracker on the mantel.

I picture him digging through our tubs of Christmas decorations in storage, remembering my throwaway comment, blowing the dust off Mr. Nutcracker's glossy black hat. How his mouth would kick up at the corner in satisfaction—*There you are.* What a silly thing to tear up over, a nutcracker. But I do.

"I'm taking tomorrow off work," he tells me. "We'll go pick out a sofa to put right here in front of the window, so we can look out at the view." Then he adds, "If that's, uh, okay with you?"

My head bobs a yes. It's my turn to be speechless. He smiles, and I think he likes doing this, too. Shocking me with an act of goodness.

Nicholas is feeling much better by the time evening rolls around, but he decides he doesn't want to push his luck by going out in this weather, so we cancel dinner with Mr. and Mrs. Rose. I make grilled cheese, he heats up tomato soup, and we sit side by side on the couch to eat and watch *The Office*. It's the best meal I've ever tasted.

Late that night, I wake up and need to get something to drink. When I pass his door, I reach out on impulse and touch the knob. I turn it—just to check—and find it locked. I'm not sure I'd go inside, if given the chance. I can't blame him for protecting himself from me because I've been doing the same, but right now our system of measure-for-measure doesn't infuriate or energize me. It disappoints, cutting deeper than any insult.

CHAPTER FIFTEEN

Rise and Smile is closed on Thanksgiving, which is fortuitous for us because Nicholas and I put off shopping for a centerpiece until the last minute. When Nicholas was in sixth grade his art class made centerpieces out of tissue paper and candy corn, and after that it became a Rose tradition for him to come up with a new Thanksgiving centerpiece every year. He usually goes all out with big, homemade displays, but he's spent all of November turning himself into the man on packages of Brawny paper towels and forgot.

I'm sitting at the kitchen table eating breakfast when Nicholas comes through the back door. He's in his coveralls, which I have a newfound respect for because I know how warm they keep you. He takes my favorite blue-green drinking glass down from the cupboard and fills it with two inches of water, then sets it beside my mug of tea. Inside it drops a wildflower. It's a little worse for wear, having endured several frosts and a snowfall, but most of its petals are still intact.

"Aww." I smile in surprise.

"It was growing inside the barn, up in the loft. Had to get a ladder to reach it."

I don't trust that barn. It's crooked and about five thousand years old. Picturing Nicholas scaling a ladder that leans on rotten wood is stressful. "Thanks. You shouldn't have."

"Yeah, well. Thought it'd be nice."

"I really don't need flowers."

His stare is a death sentence. "Never mind," I'm quick to add. "I still want them sometimes, probably."

His mouth twitches, and he eats half of my sausage burrito in one bite. When he leaves to go shower, I admire my half-wilted flower for unfathomable reasons. There is nothing particularly interesting about this plant. In an hour's time it will be most of the way dead. I think I'm going to blame society for wanting it, anyway.

Societal norms have conditioned me into thinking I need these dying plants in order to feel loved and appreciated. They're objectively useless and I know that. But it's the thought I'll remember, not the color of the flower or how pretty it is. The gesture of Nicholas seeing the flower, thinking about me, and going and getting a ladder in order to pick it is going to stay with me. Watching him drop it into my favorite blue-green drinking glass is going to stay with me.

When I'm finished getting dressed and ready, Nicholas is wearing a green henley I don't think I've ever seen on him before, and it makes the jade in his color-shifting eyes spark. The neckline is wide enough that I get a good look at his collarbones.

Good heavens. The man's got a fabulous set of collarbones. Then I notice the rounded caps of his shoulders. The heavens are very good, indeed.

He's whistling as he fills the sink with soapy water and starts washing dishes for the first time all year. I gape at Changeling Nicholas and give myself heart problems.

He's styled his hair differently, letting the soft curls fall loosely across his forehead instead of slicking them back. I helplessly draw closer, until I'm definitely invading his personal space. Is it the hair? The shirt? The flower? The fact that he's doing housework unasked? Whatever it is, he's a hundred times hotter today. If he starts sweeping the floor and cleaning out lint traps, I might need smelling salts.

Nicholas's busy hands in the sink fall still when I touch his face. "You have a nice jawline," I tell him, hearing the wonder in my voice.

He blinks as he looks away. "Um. Thank you."

"Your throat, too." It's a tragedy that I haven't noticed what a nice throat he has. Who knew nice throats were a thing?

My unabashed ogling is doing things to him; his throat turns red and splotchy before my eyes. I twirl my flower and watch him do the dishes like a total creep until I get myself together. Whenever I break my gaze I feel his moving over me, and I'm pulled back in again. He keeps catching me sneaking sideways looks at him, and I'm positive he's caught me silently mouthing *Oh my god*. The more flustered I get, the wider his smile grows.

I don't analyze it too deeply when I decide I need to change into a better shirt and touch up my lipstick. It's Thanksgiving, and that's the only reason I camouflage my micro-bangs with a headband and curl my hair. You have to look your best on the holidays. You have to switch out your beige bra for black lace and spritz yourself with body spray called DEVOUR ME. I don't make these rules.

I discover a unicorn in the bathroom: he's wiped down the sink after shaving. There isn't a single hair clinging to the faucet. It's the invasion of the body snatchers.

It's this detail that makes me generous enough to go start the car and get it warmed up for us. As I lumber out into the cold to switch on the ignition, I am a hero. I'm the most selfless fiancée who ever lived. I nearly slip on a patch of ice and for a split second I imagine myself in a hospital bed, leg raised up in one of those sling thingies, Nicholas fussing over me and fluffing my pillow. I don't even complain about my broken leg. *It's nothing,* I say stoically. *I'm just grateful it wasn't you who fell.* Nicholas weeps at my strength. He's never met another woman this amazing.

"Thank you," he says as we're pulling out of the driveway. "Nice and warm in here." He catches me goggling at his profile again and smiles. He really is something luminous when he shows his happiness, isn't he?

I need to get a grip. Sure, he presented me with a single half-dead flower and his hair is behaving quite seductively today, but we sleep in separate bedrooms, for pete's sake. It wasn't that long ago that I was fantasizing about rolling up my wedding dress into a ball and joyously watching it burn in the fireplace. In spite of any seemingly positive developments that surely won't last, I need to focus on the game plan here. Just as soon as I can remember what that is. He's sprinkling some kind of witchcraft on me to make it hard to think straight.

"Where are you going?" I ask when he turns on his right blinker.

"That craft place up here," he replies, confirming my fears. Let's Get Crafty is the job that I really, *really* want and was supposed to hear a decision on three days after the interview. That was last week, and the manager still hasn't contacted me. I think about following up with them every minute of every day, but if I have to nudge in the first place then I know they're probably leaning toward *no*. At least in limbo I can nurse my delusions.

"I thought we'd just go to Walmart in Beaufort."

He shoots me a strange look. "Haven't you been badgering me to shop more locally? Going to Walmart for everything is the reason why all our stores in Morris have closed down." We both think of the Junk Yard, which still smarts.

I'm a traitor to my principles when I reply, "Yeah, but the smaller stores are probably more expensive."

"It'll be fine."

I'm grasping at straws. "We're on a one-person income now."

"Relax, Naomi." He parks and squeezes my hand, then slides out of the car. I can't go into this store. They'll think I'm stalking them. They'll recognize me. Someone will mention the application in front of Nicholas, who doesn't know I'm still job hunting. He assumes I've given up because I don't talk about it. The only news I have to report so far is bad news, which I'm not raring to broadcast. I'd planned on telling him only when I received good news, which may never happen.

This day is dreadful. The sky is the color of illness and it's cold but all the snow's melted, leaving behind exhaust-blackened slush. My lipstick is too much and my skin is hot and itchy and I hate my car. My pulse is a battering ram.

"What's the matter?" Nicholas asks as he holds open the door of Let's Get Crafty. I tug between hating the store and loving it. If I get the job, I'm going to love it here more than anything in the world. If I'm rejected, I'll go buy every craft supply Walmart has to offer and put this store out of business. You don't have to tell me I'm a bad person for thinking this because I already know.

"Headache," I mutter.

"Got any Tylenol in your purse?"

"Meh." My shoulders hunch as I troop inside, endeavoring to make myself smaller and less noticeable.

"I was thinking about a cornucopia," Nicholas says. "Is that overdone?"

The answer is yes, obviously, but I'm not too concerned about the centerpiece for his parents' dining room table at this moment. My eyes are darting along the ceiling corners for hidden cameras. I think of a man in a back room somewhere, eating a sub sandwich and watching me on a tiny television screen. *Isn't she one of the applicants? Wow, isn't this sad. Coming in here to beg for the job, I bet.*

"Naomi?" Nicholas says. I get the feeling this isn't the first time he's said my name within the last thirty seconds. He snaps his fingers in front of my face.

"Shh!" I whisper, pulling my coat collar up to my nose. I look like a cartoon private eye. "Keep it down."

"Why? Nobody's in here." He looks around. "Imagine if we'd gone to Walmart. Aisles would be packed. We've got this whole store to ourselves."

Nicholas forces me to voice opinions on plastic vegetables, trying to determine if they're too fake-looking. "Should we use real vegetables instead? I thought plastic would be less wasteful. We could reuse them."

"For what?"

"Maybe a diorama at the office."

Right. *Eat your veggies, kids!* Quite rich, coming from this man. His breath is a Twizzler.

"Real vegetables would be better," I say. "C'mon, let's go to the grocery store."

"I want to look at everything they've got here first." His eyes are round and marveling as they take in way too many options. He's Martha Stewart now. I've lost him to the nuances between basket cornucopias and ones made of wire and we'll be in here for two hours deliberating.

I'm ruthless in my quest to leave. "Cornucopias, Nicholas? That's your pilgrim great-grandfather's centerpiece. Modernize it a little. Go minimal with a simple red apple."

He wrinkles his nose. "That won't be impressive. It'll look like I didn't try at all."

"Welcome to my life. It's easier over here, I promise."

I shouldn't make self-deprecating comments like this because they bolster the stereotype that I have no aspirations and I'm a thoughtless layabout, but it's become an odd habit.

He drags a finger up my spine, which he knows gives me the chills, and smiles when I jump out of my skin. He continues to browse at one mile per hour. Every time we round the corner into another aisle my stomach tightens with worry that the manager is going to come out and ask if we need any help. It's unavoidable. These small businesses are too darned friendly.

Twenty years later and with zero help from me, Nicholas has filled a basket with supplies to build our own birdhouse in the spring, which I can't wait to see him never touch, plus a bunch of random bits and bobs marked down to fifty percent off. He doesn't know what he's going to do with it all, but he's a sucker for those neon green discount stickers. "You never know," he says, whistling as he drops a package of blue buttons and rose appliques into the basket. He needs an intervention.

The next aisle is wedding decorations. We both freeze at the threshold.

"I think I saw pinecones back that way," I say, and he nods hastily.

"Yeah, let's go look at the pinecones again."

We're quivering cowards and we know it. We end up grabbing four mesh bags of pinecones (which we could get from our yard for free) as justification for avoiding the wedding aisle. I'm tired. My nerves are frayed. I beg him to just choose something and be done, so he gets a cookie jar that looks like a turkey. We're going to stuff it with the pinecones. It's a half-assed choice and he's heartbroken to show up to dinner with a centerpiece that doesn't blow everybody's minds, but I'm finding it hard to breathe and Nicholas's arm is probably stinging with red marks from my iron grip. I've been picking at him to get him to move it along.

"All right, you go check out. I'm going to wait in the car."

Nicholas doesn't hear me. I'm dragged up to the register and all the blood in my body flees the country when I see who's behind the counter.

Melissa.

I want to groan, but I force a smile instead. My skin is two hundred degrees. My organs are cooking like a casserole.

"Hey, Naomi," she greets me jovially. Straight away, that pleasant tone's got me shifty-eyed. Maybe her boss is close by. God, I hope not.

"Hey, Melissa! So great to see you! How've you been? New job, huh?"

"Just started Monday! I'm so lucky, you know? Nobody's

hiring." She gives me a great big smile that is totally alien on her generally hateful face.

I want to run out of the store. *Just started Monday.* The job she's got now is the job I applied for. Melissa was in the pool of contenders. Melissa beat me.

And no one called to tell me I lost the job. It hurts extra because the woman who interviewed me was so nice and sympathetic. Maybe she thought she'd wait until after the holidays to break the news, so that I wouldn't spend Thanksgiving crying in a closet.

"Congratulations," I make myself say. "I hope you like it here."

"Oh, I *love* it. In fact . . ." She takes her time ringing up the pinecones, hands moving in slow-motion. "I heard you applied here, too. Wouldn't that be fun, huh, if we both worked at the same place again?"

Nicholas turns his sharp gaze on me.

My voice is small. "I think they only had one position open."

Melissa knows this, of course. "Oh, that's right. Good luck with the job search." A gloating smile curves the edges of her mouth as she coasts a knickknack over the scanner.

"She'll find something," Nicholas inserts smoothly. "We're waiting for the right fit. Can't just accept *any* old job that'll have her—especially at businesses that will probably be closed within a year."

Melissa's eyes darken. I'm so grateful to Nicholas, I could cry.

"Luckily, I don't find myself in that position," she says, all uppity-like. "Let's Get Crafty is doing *superb*."

Nicholas makes a show out of glancing around the empty store. "Sure."

Her peppy tone falters, the ice showing through. "It's Thanksgiving. Of course we're not busy today."

Nicholas doesn't even have to reply. He raises his eyebrows, smiling guilelessly. It's more effective than a smirk. It's an expression I'm well acquainted with and it usually fills me with rage, but weaponized against Melissa I've got to say, it's looking more and more attractive.

"So . . ." She pretends to have trouble with a price tag, drawing this exchange out. "Burn any more poisonous flowers lately, Naomi?"

Nicholas stiffens. I'm going to stab her with the pin of her name tag.

"Actually, I haven't had time. Been pretty busy."

"Doing what? You don't have a job."

"Maybe we're having lots of sex," Nicholas cuts in, annoyed. "Maybe we lose track of the days because we can't stop banging." I let out an unladylike snort, both because what he's said is delightfully inappropriate and also so untrue that it kind of hurts. "Not really your business, is it?"

Melissa abandons all pleasantries. "That's about what I'd expect to hear from you. Lot of sex happening around your office, and I know that from experience. I wouldn't be shocked if you're screwing that dental hygienist, too. You and Seth both. The company you keep says a lot about you."

"Oh, for crying out loud," I snap. I've always been quick to lend my sympathies whenever she wanted to gripe about Seth (which was often), but seeing her here in this new setting, wearing a vest covered in trillions of craft-related buttons, it's just too much. I'm not rolling over and letting her punish us anymore. "This again? You dated the guy for, like, a month and a half. I've had to hear about this since May. Your grudge exhausts me, Melissa."

"Oh, my apologies! Have I not recovered from my heart-break fast enough for you?"

"If you need closure with your ex, then go tell *him* about it." Her mouth opens, but I raise my hand. "Listen, I'm sorry Seth is an asswipe who cheated. You didn't deserve that. Honestly, you could do way better and he isn't worth being this upset over. But nothing that happened to you is our fault." She gives Nicholas a dirty look and opens her mouth, ready to shoot off, but I beat her to it. "There will be no more attacks on Nicholas, you got me? I don't want to hear this shit ever again."

As for Nicholas, I don't think he's ever been more stunned in his life. He's giving me the same look I was giving him this morning. I'm being green-henley'd.

Melissa's movements grow jerkier as she stuffs our purchases into a bag. "Can you double-wrap that?" Nicholas asks, and we both derive sadistic enjoyment from watching Melissa double-wrap the cookie jar.

"And then double-bag it?" he adds.

The savagery is so skillfully subtle, you could almost call it art.

She triple-bags it. "Is that good enough?"

He flashes a charming smile. "Perfect."

Her glare cuts to me, and for once I don't do the thing I always do when she and Nicholas are having a clash. I don't chew my fingernails and apologize with my eyes. Instead, I give her airs like I am Extremely Important and have Places To Be. I invoke my inner Deborah Rose and scare myself to the core.

"Well, good luck with your life," Melissa says nastily after we pay and get our bags.

I decide to be the bigger person. "You, too, Melissa. Good luck. I hope this job works out for you."

Nicholas decides to not be the bigger person and takes a penny from the take-a-penny, leave-a-penny station as we walk away. I'm in awe of his cattiness.

"Enjoy your Thanksgiving!" he calls over his shoulder.

"You two are assholes!" she calls back. "You deserve each other."

I send her a thumbs-up. "Thanks!"

We're barely out the door when we can't hold our laughter in anymore. We throw our stuff in the car and tumble inside, peeling out like we're fugitives making a getaway. I give him a high-five. "You. Were. Awesome."

"Thank you, thank you." He grins. "You were, too."

"I'm so glad I don't have to hang out with her anymore."

He glances sideways at me. "She is right about Seth, though. I'm really tired of defending him. I feel . . . I don't know. I've never broken up with a friend before."

I'm not exactly a fan of Seth. He's nice half the time, but for the other half he builds himself up by tearing Nicholas down. "You're allowed to defend yourself when people hurt your feelings. You deserve to be around people who are good to you." Coming from me of all people, this statement is so outrageous I half-expect a lightning bolt to shoot down from the sky and strike me dead. I'm right, though: he deserves friends who actually act like friends. And so do I, for that matter. "You know that, right? Give yourself permission to put yourself first."

"I don't know how to do that."

"I'll help. And if Seth doesn't clean up his act, I still have the number for those movers. I'll set you up with them. We'll put you in some ripped jeans and . . . ta-da! BFFs in no time."

He smiles.

"Whatever you want to do about Seth is your choice," I say, "but if you ever need backup, I'm your girl. Say the word and I'll scare him so bad, he'll never step out of line again."

He picks up my hand. Kisses my knuckles. "Thank you," he murmurs.

All good things must come to an end.

It's the solemn decree ringing in my head as we sit down to Deborah and Harold's table. A feast spans before us, which should encourage some measure of happiness, but it doesn't because we're all about to have our legs trapped under a wooden slab together for the duration of an extra-long meal, and that means extra-long conversation.

I know what the topic's going to be. It's Deborah's favorite one. Nicholas and I have been doing a fine job of avoiding it when we're alone, as evidenced by our chickening out in the wedding décor aisle.

"Have you sent out the invitations yet?" Deborah launches right in, piecing bits of dark turkey onto her husband's plate. He's not permitted to make his own plate because he's "bad at portion control." The diet she's got him on now forbids stuffing, white meat, and potatoes, and he looks like he might cry. "It's nearly December." Her eyes flick to Nicholas, then me. There's accusation in them, clear as day. She thinks it's my fault the invitations haven't gone out.

Nicholas does exactly what I would do. He pretends he doesn't hear her. Then, when she repeats the question, he pretends he doesn't know what she's talking about.

"Invitations?" Like it's a foreign word he doesn't understand.

I shovel gobs of mashed potatoes in my mouth. I'm a lady. I have manners. No one can expect me to talk with my mouth full.

Deborah appraises Nicholas over her wineglass, eyes shrewd. "Your wedding invitations, darling. We still haven't gotten ours."

"Do you need an official one?" he asks faintly. "You already know the date and venue."

"I need three invitations: one for my memory book, one for your baby book, and one for the family records. Besides, everybody else needs theirs as well. All your aunts and uncles. Every day, it seems, I'm getting a call. *Where's my invitation? Am I not invited?* The men at your father's club, and all their wives, are in an uproar! They feel personally slighted. You can't leave anyone out, Nicky. It's rude."

I don't know any of those people she's referring to. Nicholas doesn't know most of them, and the ones he knows, he doesn't like. I don't think there's actually an uproar; more like Deborah's trying to gauge what's going on here, so she's making shit up.

"Frankly, you're putting me in a bad position," she goes on. "People know I'm orchestrating this whole operation, and when you neglect your duties it reflects poorly on me." She touches her necklace. It's a heart with four birthstones to represent everyone in her family. "So if you're not going to behave responsibly for *your* sakes, do so for *mine.*"

Nicholas withers. It's not a visible withering—for all outward appearances, he's fine. His face is calm, his tone bland. But I feel it like a sixth sense: he's hating this. We've just sat down and he wishes he could run out the door, but he can't. He's stuck being Nicholas Rose, Perfect Son, and after all these years the role is wearing him down.

"Harold," Deborah barks when he tries to steal a roll. "You know you can't eat that."

"You gave me too many green beans," he whines. "There isn't even any seasoning on them."

"Seasoning makes your bowels disagree with you." She turns curtly from him and says to Nicholas, "You'll come over sometime this week with the invitations. I'll help you address the envelopes myself, if no one else will." Nice little dig at me. "You've got to get those out if you expect your RSVPs in time. Some guests have to make room in their work schedules to be able to travel here for the wedding, and you waiting until the last minute to supply this information is extremely inconsiderate. I wouldn't be surprised if my friend Diana from college can't make it, now that there's barely any time left to prepare."

"You haven't just told your friend when and where?" he asks. "You've known it's going to be at St. Mary's on January twenty-sixth for months now. One p.m. You could've just told her yourself."

"That's not how things are done! You have to send proper invites. This isn't some trashy Las Vegas wedding, Nicholas. You'll conduct yourself accordingly."

She says this like Nicholas has failed her and ruined this wedding by not moving heaven and earth for some lady named Diana. Ten to one, he has never met Diana. Deborah just wants to show off whatever mother-of-the-groom outfit she's picked out for herself. A dazzling dress to outshine mine.

"I'm taking care of the invitations, Mom," Nicholas says amiably. "Don't worry."

"Don't tell me not to worry, Nicky. It's my job. And don't be ridiculous—I'm helping you get this matter settled once and for all. Come by Wednesday after work. We'll make an evening of it! I'll have the woman make those tiny pizza bagels you love, and we'll work until midnight if we have to." Note how she doesn't invite me to come, only him.

I'm all ready to tuck into my food and forget where I am when I'm suddenly transported back to Let's Get Crafty, and how awful I felt when I saw Melissa behind the counter. I had to process the loss of the job at the same time that loathsome Melissa was rubbing it in, and it might've killed my whole day were it not for Nicholas rescuing me. Instead of leaving the shop in a foul mood, I left laughing.

"Actually, Nicholas and I are booked solid next Wednesday," I answer for him.

Deborah eyes me curiously. "Doing what? Addressing the invitations?"

I can't commit to that. My relationship with Nicholas is a split hair. Sending out invitations makes the wedding all too real, and I still can't visualize walking down the aisle at St. Mary's. I can't visualize a priest's echoing, monotone instructions for how to treat each other during marriage, and I can't visualize myself in that A-line dress I don't love. I can't see myself staring up at Nicholas and hearing him say the words *I do*. I don't think Nicholas can picture any of this, either, which is why we've been dancing around it for so long.

"Fishing," I improvise. "In our canoe."

Deborah coughs on her food. Harold's hand shoots out, considers patting her back, but grabs a roll instead and stuffs it down his pants for safekeeping. I don't blame him. The green beans suck.

"You don't have a *canoe*, Nicholas," she says, like I've just told her we're shedding all material possessions and running off to join a cult.

Nicholas looks fatigued, so I answer for him again. "We do! It's a lot of fun. Nicholas took it out on the pond the other day."

She's aghast. "Whatever for?"

She's not addressing me, thirsting for a reaction from her son. I'm right about my hunch: this man's in need of a rescue. It requires a different strategy than him rescuing me in Let's Get Crafty. Mrs. Rose isn't Melissa. I don't give a single solitary shit what this woman thinks of me anymore, but Nicholas does, so I have to approach it with finesse. It's going to cost pride points.

"For canoeing in, of course," I tell her without a hint, even a whisper, of insincerity. Tonight, I am Shakespeare. "There's all sorts of studies that say canoeing is good for you mentally and physically. They call it a 'meditative sport.'" I don't know if I've made up that terminology myself or if I've heard it somewhere and kept it around subconsciously, but either way I'm proud of myself for producing it on the spot. *Meditative sport.* Sounds legitimate as hell.

I reach for the yams, but Deborah slides the dish away. "Don't eat those, dear. Your future children will come out orange." She leans over her plate until the ends of her bob come perilously close to getting in her gravy. "Nicky. Have you registered for wedding presents yet? I need to include it in the announcements at the church. I'm having them put it in every Sunday bulletin, and I'm thinking about asking the *Beaufort Gazette* to write a little something about you, too."

Nicholas sucks in a breath, but I squeeze his knee lightly under the table. I'm his knight in shining armor. That's my role here. I'm slowly understanding that it was always supposed to be my role, but I didn't realize it and missed my cue the first time my charge was under attack by fire-breathing mothers. I've got some lost time to make up for. "Deborah, this turkey is *sooo* delicious. What's your secret?"

Her secret is that she didn't cook it, someone else did, but she's so taken aback that she has to respond. "Oh. I . . . uhh . . . butter. And spices. And plenty of love!" She smiles dotingly. It's full of shit. "Love's the most important ingredient of all."

"I agree. Love is so important." I'm not going to leave her alone for a second. I'm going to occupy every square inch of space in this conversation and for once in his life, Nicholas will be able to finish his food while it's still warm. He won't be squirting honey into his tea tonight to soothe his throat after two solid hours of talking, talking, talking. "It's a shame Heather couldn't be here. I'd love to finally meet her." Heather split town on her eighteenth birthday and only comes home when she can't maneuver out of it. From what I've heard, she and Deborah have had an extremely tumultuous relationship ever since Heather was a teenager and Deborah was the horror of all parent-teacher conferences.

"Heather!" Deborah nearly fans herself. I've hit the jackpot. "Shame is right. It's beyond shameful she wouldn't come home for Thanksgiving. I've begged. Her father's begged."

Harold frowns as he shovels food into his mouth, probably

wondering if he did in fact do any begging. He gives up thinking about it and sneaks a piece of turkey.

"It's like we're nothing to her!" Deborah continues. "I always tell her on the phone that it's lucky we have Nicky, or else we'd be all alone. Our Nicky understands the value of family."

She pauses and looks at him, preparing to speak to him directly, so I say, "Yes, he does. Nicholas is a good man and I couldn't be prouder of him. You did a fine job raising him. Wow, this cranberry sauce is something else! I haven't had cranberry sauce this tasty in forever. The way my mom always made it was bleh." I make an exaggerated expression of disgust.

This gets her full attention. Deborah pounces on any opportunity to put herself above my mother. She hates that Nicholas is going to have a mother-in-law more than she hates Harold's ex-wife. And she literally had a priest come bless Harold's house after they got together, to rid it of Magnolia's essence.

"Thank you. It's true, not many people know how to fix it properly."

"Including you," Harold grunts too quietly for her to overhear.

I take a bite, then make a savoring noise. "Mmm. Divine. I'm not sure I've ever told you, but this dining room set reminds me of a French castle. I feel like Marie Antoinette when I sit here, if you don't mind my saying so."

Her eyes light up. "That's the inspiration!"

"You don't say! Solid job." I raise my glass and do a mock toast, which she reciprocates to my mingled wonder and horror. I don't dare look at Nicholas because I know if I do, whatever I see on his face is going to make me laugh.

She starts to tell me more about her table and chairs, which

I respond to with enthusiasm and a great many questions. I weave compliments about herself, Nicholas, and her knack for interior design wherever I can fit them.

Sucking up to Deborah was easy as breathing when Nicholas and I first started dating. I'd been out to impress, and I didn't know her very well. Everything's easy when your eyes are innocent and you don't spot the hidden dangers. My eyes aren't innocent anymore. I know exactly who this woman is. We have a history now. The sugary compliments still flow like they used to, but I'm summoning them through a different channel because my goal is different. My priorities are different. Nicholas deserves one holiday in which he isn't nagged to death.

When Deborah excuses herself to the kitchen to fetch the dessert, I gasp for air and gulp down all my cranberry juice, plus a glass of water. I brave a glance to my right and my heart skips.

Nicholas's eyes are resting on me. They're warm with gratitude, and that gratitude makes my exhaustion worth it. I'll go ten more rounds with Mrs. Rose if it means I get another look like that at the end.

When Deborah glides back in bearing a cake the size of a small island, I'm already laying the groundwork to pump her ego. "Mmm, that looks incredible!" I don't even have to lie. I didn't eat much of my dinner because I was so busy gabbing, and the cake smells like heaven.

"Doesn't it?" She's glowing from my praise. Deborah cuts two pieces of cake and slides them onto two small dishes. One she keeps for herself, and the other she gives to Nicholas. "Salted caramel apple cake. It's a Rose family recipe, passed down from generation to generation."

"I can't wait to try out the recipe myself."

Her smile is tight. "Someday, when you're a mother, I'll let you in on the secret."

Lovely. Using a recipe as leverage to get grandchildren. Still, I rub my hands together and say, "Until then, I guess I'll have to be content with simply eating the cake and not baking it!" I scan the table for another plate.

"I want some, too," Harold insists.

"Hush," Deborah scolds him. "You know you can't have this much sugar. Think of your bowels!"

I wish she would stop forcing us all to think of Harold's bowels.

I scrape cold food around on my dinner plate to make room for a slice of cake. But as I reach for the cutting knife, her hand closes over mine. Her skin is warm. Human.

But her eyes are cold. "I don't think you should, dear."

CHAPTER SIXTEEN

"Don't you agree?" she continues when I don't retract my hand. "You know . . ." Her eyes dip to my waistline. "For the wedding. It's tradition for brides to curb their appetites until the big day, so there aren't any rude surprises when it comes to the dress fitting. Normally I wouldn't say a word, you know I wouldn't, but you just ate an exceptionally large meal. Overstuffing yourself wouldn't be wise."

My mind spins, blinks, and shuts down. In the black vacuum, there exists a single word floating adrift. *What.*

"Mom," Nicholas says icily.

She places her other hand over mine, as well, patting fondly. My stomach revolts from all the polite, syrupy sentiments I've been feeding her entitlement complex over the past forty-five minutes. It doesn't matter how nice I am. It'll never matter. She'll always be horrible.

"When I was engaged," she tells me, ignoring her son,

"gluttony tempted me, too. My sister loves to bake and the house smelled like cookies and cakes every day. You can't imagine!" Her smile is chilling because she means every word that's coming out of her mouth. "But you *must* control yourself. Back in those days, girls had a way of taking care of the problem."

"The problem being . . . hunger?"

She nods, not hearing the incredulity in my voice. "Exactly. Can't be eating like a pig if you want to look trim in your wedding photos. Drink hot water with lemon and basil, and you'll get so full you'd swear you'd been eating all day long! I can go have the woman fix you a cup if you're still hungry."

"She's not drinking that crap," Nicholas interjects. "Let her have a piece of cake."

"I can't let her eat cake!" she exclaims. Even the torso of the Marie Antoinette she so admires rolls in her grave, like, *Girl, I wouldn't.* "I'm saying this out of love, Nicky. You have to believe that."

He's not backing down. "You're not her doctor, and what she eats is none of your business. If you're going to bring out dessert, you don't get to decide who gets it and who doesn't."

"I agree!" Harold pipes up.

Her cheekbones flush with high color. "Shut up, Harold."

"Don't you 'Shut up, Harold' me. I pay the salary of the woman who made this cake. I get to eat it." He reaches out. She slaps his hand, but he snatches the whole serving tray with startling agility and whisks it away to his lap. "Here you go, Natalie." He offers me an enormous chunk right out of the middle.

"No!" Deborah cries, rushing to intercept. "Don't eat that! You'll look like a sausage in your dress. After your last fitting, I had the seamstress take the gown in to a size zero!"

I drop the cake. It splatters magnificently onto the table. "You *what*?"

Deborah panics. She wrings her hands. "I was a size zero when I got married. It's not impossible—you just really have to start buckling down. No more desserts or—"

"I'm not a size zero." I'm mortified. I hate that I have to talk about this in front of Nicholas's parents. "I'm not even close. You'd have to remove my organs! I don't understand—why would you—why's it so—" I'm close to breaking down because I've been trying so hard to be courteous, and I should've expected this. I have whiplash. There is no part of me that desires to be a different size than the one I am, and I absolutely hate Deborah for trying to make me feel bad about myself for not meeting some bullshit standard she set over thirty years ago.

"How could you do something like that?" Nicholas thunders. "Whatever you told the seamstress, fix it." He rises to his feet, so severe and stone-faced that I'm rather intimidated. "Apologize to Naomi right now."

Deborah can't close her mouth. Her face is the same color as her raspberry blouse, a seamless match. The validation that he's siding with me zings through my system like a lightning bolt, and without thinking about it I stand up, too, and reach for his hand. His fingers slide smoothly through mine, locking. We've combined armies and we're a solid force field facing off against his mother's hail of word bullets.

"I mean well," she says soothingly. "How am I in the wrong here? I'm looking out for my future daughter-in-law. I know how nasty people can be. Imagine how it'll look when the dress doesn't fit right."

"The dress is made to fit *Naomi*," he snaps. "She isn't made to fit the dress. She's my fiancée, she's beautiful and perfect, and I won't have her spoken to like this by anyone, much less a member of my own damn family."

"Nicky!" she admonishes in a loud whisper, as if afraid the neighbors might hear.

"Apologize."

"But . . ."

She wants to lick her fingers and smooth his hair. Tuck him into bed. Push me from a tower. She'll steal our infant from his cradle and disappear to Mexico so she can be sure he's raised with an unhealthy attachment to her. He'll be christened at St. Mary's in a white gown monogrammed with roses.

Deborah sputters, eyes pleading, but when they move in my direction they're sharp as an eagle's. She never saw this coming. She never thought for a moment that he'd ever side with me over her, because to her I am unimportant. A necessary annoyance that allows her to throw a fancy wedding and get the grandchildren she wants so much, but other than that, I fade into her background. In this house, I have always felt unimportant.

"Pathetic," Nicholas snarls. "You can't treat my fiancée that way and expect to still be invited to the wedding."

I'm not sure whose gasp is loudest—mine, hers, or Harold's.

Actually, Harold's isn't a gasp. He's choking on his cake. "Oh, for goodness' sake," Deborah snaps, thumping him between the shoulder blades. "Chew! Don't you know how to chew?"

Harold is beet red, cheeks and eyes bulging. He coughs up flecks of cake that get all over the tablecloth and makes a hacking sound that comes out like *Shut up.*

"I'm invited to the wedding," Deborah declares while her husband is still struggling to suck air into his lungs. "Of course I am. Don't even say that."

"I'm not saying it, I'm threatening it."

"No!" Harold cries, interrupting his son. Deborah's trying to yank the cake away from him. "You don't let me have anything that makes me happy! I might as well be dead. I've sacrificed so much. I let you have Beatrice, now you can let me have a piece of cake or so help me *god* I will jump off the roof of this house!"

She lets him have the cake.

"Who's Beatrice?" I ask. This is the most bizarre dinner I've ever been to.

"A dog she had when I was growing up," Nicholas murmurs in my ear.

"How can you bring up Beatrice?" Deborah wails, eyes welling with tears. "You know what it does to me, especially at this time of year."

"Should have punted her into a lake." Harold picks up the cake in both hands and eats it like a barbarian. This is nuts. There's no way these people can try to angle themselves as being better than me ever again. "Fifteen years! Fifteen years, I wasn't allowed to sleep in my own bed because of that dog."

"She was my child!" Deborah yells.

"And I was your husband, unfortunately! Had to sleep in the guest bedroom! In my own house!" He leans toward me. "My ex-wife didn't like dogs. Magnolia." His eyes acquire a dreamy cast. "You don't know what you've got till it's gone."

"I'm not staying for this," Nicholas says. "I'm so sorry, Naomi." To our collective astonishment, he turns his back on the table and takes me with him.

"Nicky!" Deborah cries. "Don't leave just because of your father. You didn't finish your dessert."

"We're going. Happy Thanksgiving."

"Are you coming over on Wednesday, then? With the invitations?" Her voice is like a slap in the face, it's so unreal.

Nicholas is furious. I can hardly keep up with his power-walk, but I'm loving this. It's the sort of scenario I've dreamed about—him essentially telling his mother to fuck off and whisking me away. I'm still offended over Deborah trying to cram me into Slender Man's measurements, but it's rapidly being overshadowed by how wonderful it feels to have Nicholas stand up for me.

We duck outside without responding to her, and the head rush is giving me tunnel vision. Nicholas and I fly across the dark lawn, hand in hand. For the second time today, we're fleeing the scene of the crime and it's never been like this before with Nicholas and me remaining on the same side of it.

When we get to the Jeep, he braces a hand on the passenger door before I can open it and brackets me against the cold metal with his body. His eyes are intense as they peer down at me, so close I can taste his breath. He takes my face between his palms and says, "Don't listen to my mother. You are perfect."

I look away, swallowing. "Thank you." I offer him a small smile. "We made a good team back there."

"That's the way it's *supposed* to be," he says. He watches me for a moment, seeming to debate something. Then he closes in before I can wonder what he's thinking, and his mouth is on mine.

I turn to water, knocking back against the door. I barely have time to throw my arms around his neck before he lifts me off the ground, hands wrapped around my thighs. He kisses me fiercely, the sweetest candy, my body crushed between him and the car. Just as the words *oh my* float up into my consciousness, the front door opens and there stands Deborah, gawking at us.

I tip my head back and roar with laughter. Nicholas grins, eyes shining, and he laughs, too. I think he can't believe himself.

I don't know what's gotten into us, but I like it. From Deborah's view, Nicholas's hands have disappeared up the hem of my skirt, and the notion of shocking her like this almost makes me feel sorry for her. Almost.

When Nicholas lets me go, I have to make an admission to myself:

I have no idea what's happening anymore. It's terrifying.

I'm still hungry, and miracle of miracles: Jackie's is open.

"On Thanksgiving?" I exclaim to Nicholas after he climbs back into the car with a greasy paper sack.

"They're *always* open."

I look sideways at him. We grabbed so many meals from Jackie's the first year we dated, before we got engaged and moved in together and I lost my hardware store job all at once. "You still come here a lot, then?"

"Oh, you know . . ." He shrugs. But I don't rip my gaze from his face, and he eventually spills the truth. "Sometimes when things aren't going so great at home, I do. If I'm worried you're about to say something . . . uh . . . that I don't want to hear, I get in the car and leave. I'll say I'm going to Mom and Dad's, but most of the time I just drive around or I come here. Look." He opens the glove box, where a huge stack of extra-large napkins from Jackie's is crammed.

"You're worried I'll say something you don't want to hear?" I repeat, accepting a carton of fries from him. "Like what?"

He shrugs again, then starts to drive home.

Since it seems he doesn't want to answer this question, I come up with something else to say. "The plaque on your parents' house is wrong. The 'rose by any other name' one."

He laughs. "I know. I looked it up once. Don't tell them, okay? I want to see how long it takes them to find out."

We share a smile. Nicholas isn't so bad, maybe.

It's this goodwill that makes me say, "When we get home, there's something I want to show you."

He looks over at me. I feel his stare in the darkness, dividing between my face and the road. He's quiet but I hear his brain spinning the rest of the way home, wondering what I'm going to show him. I can't get a read on what his guess might be.

By the time we're walking through the front door, I'm already regretting this. Why am I so impulsive? I need to take back my offer. I strain to come up with a different secret to show him but draw a blank.

"So," he says, hedging. "What do you want to show me?"

I'm not sure I still would, were it not for the hesitation in his eyes. He's worried. He thinks that whatever it is, it involves him and me, and that it might be bad. I can't let him suffer, so I suck it up and summon all my bravery and then some. Never in a million years did I think I'd voluntarily show him this.

He's leaning against the kitchen counter when I hand him my phone. "Here." Then I retreat to the other wall, biting my nails.

He's even more worried now. "What do you want me to do with it?"

"Check my notes."

"Why?"

"Just do it."

He studies me for a handful of seconds like this might be a trap, then does as he's told. I want to snatch my phone back. My face is red and my heart's in my throat, and if he laughs at me I'm going to cry. His pity would be even worse. I am so certain that he's going to think I'm a pathetic loser. All the evidence is there in his hand. *No one wants me. Look at what you've thrown everything away over. A woman who can't even get hired as a waitress at Olive Garden.*

I watch him read the list that I've typed up in my notes, of every single establishment I've applied to. It's detailed: I describe if I applied online or in person, if I can expect to hear back from them over the phone, by text, or email. Places I had high hopes for are marked with smiley faces. The nos are followed by *X*s. The places I haven't heard back from yet have question marks beside them. There are no yesses.

It's a long list, and it's full of *X*s.

When several minutes pass and he still hasn't spoken, just staring at my screen as he no doubt decodes it all, I feel like I'm being strangled. When I was the only one who knew about all these rejections, I was able to handle it. Now that he knows, it's freshly humiliating. I know I'm not worthless, but god is it tough not to feel that way when you're in the middle of a never-ending streak of *This is hard to say, but we're going with someone else. We're very sorry we couldn't give you better news and we wish you the best of luck.*

I've got my face in my hands, so when a pair of arms wraps around me I'm not expecting it. His touch tugs all my threads loose, and I start crying into his shoulder. "It's stupid to cry over this. I'm sorry."

"Hey," he murmurs, nuzzling my temple. "It's not stupid. You have nothing to be sorry for. These places are stupid."

"They're not," I sob.

"They are if they turn you down. I want to get into my car and go throw eggs at all of them." My sob turns into a laugh, and the cheek he has resting against my hairline tightens, telling me he's smiling. But when he pulls back and examines me closely, his eyes are serious. "I had no idea you've applied to so many places."

"Yeah, well . . ." I wipe away my tears with my sleeve, averting my gaze. "It's embarrassing. Especially since you have a stable job. I didn't know if you'd understand."

"I would," he says softly. "And I'd want to be here for you. Support you and make you feel better. I want you to tell me when you get bad news so that you're not going through it alone."

"It's like applying to universities all over again," I confess. "I haven't told you about that, but about two years after high school graduation I decided that I wanted to go to college, so I applied to a bunch of universities all over the country. I was so hopeful; I thought for sure at least one of them would pick me. Then I slowly watched all the rejection letters trickle in. My parents suggested I apply to community colleges instead, because they wouldn't mind a lower grade point average, but by then I was . . . I don't know. Jaded, I guess."

He doesn't respond the way I think he will. He doesn't drill-sergeant me with a list of goals I need to set for myself and carry out, no matter what, no exceptions. He doesn't tell me I should have tried harder in high school, and paid more attention, or that if I'd been more focused I could have a bachelor's degree and a great-paying job by now. He doesn't say I planned my life badly and spent my twenties achieving nothing.

Instead, he asks, "What did you want to study?"

"I don't know, honestly. I thought I'd figure it out as I went along. Never had a specific major in mind—all I wanted was a workplace I looked forward to driving to every day. A small setting with friendly people, like having another family. Somewhere I fit in."

His eyes are so warm with understanding that I melt. "Like the Junk Yard."

"Yeah. I didn't even care that the pay was crappy. Having fun makes all the difference. Melissa sucked, but I got to hang out with Brandy every day. I liked the atmosphere and . . . I was comfortable. It was familiar. We got to listen to whatever music we wanted. I loved arranging displays and making the store fun for nonexistent customers. Moving around Toby the raccoon. I'm never going to find a job like that again."

He doesn't say *Yes, you will*. He hugs me tight and lets me sniffle into his shoulder. "I'm so sorry. If I'd known, I never would've made all those cracks about work and college. Shouldn't have made them, anyway. If there's any way I can ever help, will you let me?"

"I don't think there's any way you *can* help."

He heaves a deep breath. Wipes a tear away with his thumb. "I'm here, okay?" He grasps my shoulder and squeezes gently. "These aren't platitudes. I'm right here. And I want to listen. Whenever you're sad, I want to hear why. I want to know what you're feeling, all the time, so I can share those feelings with you."

I have to shy away from the emotions in his gaze, because

my heart is a tight fist in my chest and Nicholas shattering my expectations by being kind and compassionate is constricting it so much that it's like I'm wearing a corset. I can't breathe under the heaviness of his gaze. I want to trust that he means this, but I can't.

Right now he's sweet and empathetic, but what about a week from now? What if I'm having a bad day and when I tell him about it, I'm not met with this sweet, empathetic variation of Nicholas but the *other* one? The one who turned distant when issues arose that he didn't want to face? That Nicholas is going to come back, sooner or later, and he's going to make me sorry for being this vulnerable with him.

I can't forget what he's said in the past. *Naomi doesn't need a job. Don't punish me for being successful enough to buy a nice vehicle.* His bitterness that I held him back from that job offer in Madison. He can apologize a thousand times, but I'll always wonder if he meant what he said. If he believes in me.

"Whatever you want to do," he tells me, "I'll support you."

My mind flashes to the diner in Tenmouth. The haunted house. I say nothing.

"I'm sorry about my mom."

"Me, too."

"And my dad."

"I'm sorry for your dad and Beatrice."

This gets a chuckle out of him. "Beatrice. Her favorite daughter, Mom used to call her. It's a mystery why Heather never comes around."

"Poor Heather." Maybe she deserves the maid of honor role after all. I feed the errant thought into a wood chipper, because there won't be a maid of honor. There won't be a wedding.

Nicholas and I can't even walk down an aisle of wedding decorations, must less the aisle for our real wedding.

It's all going to fall apart, and this truth doesn't bring me any satisfaction at all. Right now, I don't hate Nicholas. I can pinpoint all the qualities about him I'll miss. But it can't go on. It would be so much easier if he hadn't started warming up to me again, if we hadn't started being honest with each other, exposing what we really think and feel. I want to be able to walk away at the end of this with strong resolve and the knowledge that I'm doing what's best for myself. For both of us.

I think Nicholas sees my confusion and inner turbulence but misconstrues it as disappointment over the craft store job, because the smile he gives me is not a smile he could put on his face if he knew I'm thinking about how I'll have to leave him.

"There's something I want to show you, too," he tells me, and leads me by the hand into the drawing room. My eyes pass over the nutcracker on the mantel and my heart pangs.

He perches on the edge of his desk and motions for me to sit in his computer chair. "I want you to see what I spend most of my time on the computer doing. It's not work-related."

Oh god. If he's about to click on Pornhub, I'd really rather just not. There's sharing and then there's oversharing.

"Relax, it's not bad." What he shows me wipes away all my melancholy, because I'm so astonished there isn't room for any.

"Are you serious?" I stare up at him.

He nods solemnly.

"This."

"That."

I blink at the screen. He's level 91 in a computer game called *Nightjar*. From what I can see of his home page, it's a fantasy quest featuring all sorts of mythical creatures. His account name is . . . "It's Al Lover?"

"Not *Al* lover. My name's *itsallover*, smartass." He pinches my arm. "As in *it's all over*. Those are Cardale's last words, and it launches the whole quest to find the . . . don't laugh!"

I'm fighting a smile. "Sorry." This is prime material. "Who's Cardale?"

He frowns at me.

"I'm not teasing you." I close my hand over his. "I'm just surprised, is all. But I want to know everything about this game. Level ninety-one? You must really love Al."

He rolls his eyes, but says, "Okay, Cardale is this ancient wizard who was in the middle of extracting a prophecy from the Dream Realm when he was attacked. That's how your journey as a player starts. Everyone's on the hunt for this prophecy, because his dying words were 'It's all over,' so people think something terrible is going to happen but they don't know for sure because the prophecy's gone. If you were familiar with the game, you'd have recognized right away what my name means—"

"Okay, okay." He's so sensitive about this, and it's kind of cute. "You're level ninety-one. That's pretty high. Are you close to finding the prophecy?"

"I've found the prophecy fourteen times. Every time I win, I restart the game and the prophecy automatically jumps to a different location with a different set of clues, so I get to find it all over again."

"When you find it, what does it say?" I'm actually getting into this.

"It changes every time. But on the forums—there are forums where we talk about the game—we think they all connect.

We get a simple sentence when we win, and it's kind of vague and fortune-cookie-ish and doesn't always make contextual sense, but when we compiled them in a database we found patterns. There are tons of theories, but personally I think there are hundreds of possible prophecies and if you arrange them in a specific order, it tells a story about who really killed Cardale."

He talks in an eager rush as he explains this to me. I cannot believe I've been so in the dark about this side of his life. It always annoyed me that he disappeared so frequently to his computer, but never once did I contemplate *what* he was doing on it. He's got a whole world of his own I didn't even know about! In hindsight, I'm a little miffed at myself for not being more curious. The man's a dentist. What did I think he was doing on the computer night after night? Staring at X-rays of people's teeth for hours? *God, Naomi. You are oblivious.*

"Who's this guy?" I move the mouse over an animated figure who's revolving in place on a platform, shifting his pose every so often so that he's flexing his biceps, then planting his meaty fists on his hips. He's wearing a black hood over his face and the whole effect reminds me of Man Ray from *SpongeBob*. I do not vocalize this.

"That's my character, Grayson."

"Grayson? Does that name have special meaning?"

"I named him after a comic book superhero, Dick Grayson." I snort and he pokes me. "Very mature. Back in the forties, they went around calling people Dick because they didn't know someday you would laugh at it. Anyway, I have other characters, too, but Grayson has the most experience points so I use him for the more dangerous quests."

I goggle at him. "Who *are* you?"

He gives me a lopsided smile, which I return. "A giant nerd."

I think maybe I have a thing for giant nerds. "Show me how to play."

His eyes light up. "Really?"

"If you wouldn't mind sharing this with me. I understand if you don't." I'm impressed by my own maturity when I add, "If you want to keep it for yourself, as an activity you do alone, I get that."

"No, I'd love for you to play with me!"

I can tell he means it. It hasn't been a secret that he uses his computer to escape, but here he is inviting me along on that escape with him. "In that case, I want an avatar with purple hair, three boobs, and a Viking helmet."

"You got it." He grins, then takes my seat and settles me across his knees. He starts tapping away at the keyboard, very much in his element while also being painfully aware of me and my reactions, my judgment. This part of him is new to me, but somehow it's so *Nicholas*.

"Why didn't you tell me any of this?"

He rolls one shoulder. "Thought you might make fun of me."

My heart sinks. "I wouldn't have. If you'd showed me this is what you were doing, I would've joined you. I'd be a level ninety-one, too."

"We'll get you caught up in no time. Prepare yourself for an all-nighter, Naomi. This game is seriously addicting—you have no idea. I'm going to come home from work tomorrow and you'll be at least a level twelve, I guarantee it. There's a ton to do, aside from the quests. You can wander around the villages and get sidetracked doing a million other mini quests, racking up points. It's an incredibly detailed, complex universe. They make it hard to get to the prophecy because there are so many distractions."

He sets me loose with my new character and within the first five minutes, I fall through a portal and randomly find a glowing trident that makes Nicholas gasp so loud I think I've done something wrong. He tells me the trident is rare, and when you stab a mythical creature with it you absorb all of its powers. He begs me to stab a dragon, but I gleefully bypass one in favor of stabbing wee mushroom people who give me the ability to bounce really high, like I'm walking on the moon. Ten minutes later, Nicholas is absolutely beside himself and is trying to bribe me with a trip to Sephora if he gets to be alone with the trident for half an hour. I hunch protectively over the keyboard to keep him at bay and moon-bounce into a hot spring.

I also ignore a demigod who can duplicate treasure in favor of chasing gnomes. Gnomes are delightful! Who cares about treasure when you can give yourself a small blue hat. I am amazing at this game and not at all surprised. Nicholas drags his fingernails down his face and groans.

He accidentally minimizes the page, which flashes to his desktop. Before he can click on it again, I cry, "Wait!" and point at an icon of a Microsoft Word document titled *Dear Deborah*.

I raise an eyebrow at him.

"Oh. Um." He flushes.

"It's okay. You don't have to tell me."

"No, you can see. It's, ah, a bit juvenile. Or you may get a kick out of it, I don't know."

It's a series of short letters sent to Deborah's column at the *Beaufort Gazette*. He ends each of them with signatures like ANGRY IN WISCONSIN or FED-UP SON. One of them, I see, is mistakenly addressed to Deborah Weiner instead of Deborah Rose.

"That's her maiden name," he tells me, biting his thumb to keep his ear-to-ear grin from transforming into a full-fledged laugh. "I thought the typo would be funny. Works out my frustration to get back at her in this small way, and so far, she hasn't guessed I'm behind them."

"Good lord!" I clutch a hand to my chest. "How could you give me access to nuclear codes like this?"

Dear Deborah, my mother fails to recognize personal boundaries. I'm in my thirties. How do I tell her to cut the umbilical cord and stop calling me twenty times a day?

Dear Deborah, my mother is overbearing and steamrolls my fiancée. She digs into our business with more determination than a dumpster diver, but whenever I express this to her face, she doesn't seem to get it. What am I going to have to do to make her get the point? Should I put it in writing?

Dear Deborah, I plan to propose to my girlfriend but I'm concerned my extremely interfering mother might attempt to hijack wedding plans. I hope she understands that this would be inappropriate, and I'm sure you'll agree.

"Does the newspaper ever post your letters?" I ask.

"They've posted six of the seven I've sent in."

"And your mom hasn't made the connection?"

He shakes his head slowly from side to side, a wry smile twisting his lips. "Nope. Total cognitive dissonance in her replies. She told me to just tell my mother nicely that I don't want her involved in my wedding plans, and the mother in question would likely say 'Okay!' and back off. You should have seen my face when I read it. I write these letters to get it out of my system when I'm really upset with her, but her replies just make me want to bang my head against a wall."

"Nicholas, this is the best thing I've ever seen in my life. For my Christmas present, I want you to write in and tell her your father used to go to brothels."

He clutches me close to him in reflex when he laughs. "Oh god, yes. I'm doing that for sure."

After we reread his letters several times, finding new bits to chuckle over, we go back to *Nightjar* and he familiarizes me with the game. He bounces me involuntarily on his knee, which won't stop jostling, and his fingers tighten around my waist. He's not mindful of his body language, absorbed in his storytelling, his tips and opinions. He's more animated than I've seen him in a long, long time, and he's loving this. He loves introducing me to a game that gives him so much joy.

I smile inwardly and pay close attention to every word he says. When we next glance at the clock, it's two thirty in the morning and I'm struck by the realization that my fiancé and I are becoming friends again.

CHAPTER SEVENTEEN

On Friday, Nicholas is the only one scheduled to work at Rise and Smile, having done the most Nicholas thing ever: he offered to absorb his coworkers' workloads so that they could go visit their families for the holiday weekend. (*How's that for an extra mile!* I can hear him thinking very loudly in the direction of Stacy's empty chair.) I torture him by sending gloating texts about all the treasures I'm discovering in *Nightjar* through sheer luck, which I can see from his account he's never found before in spite of the one billion hours he's played. He sends me GIFs of people with exploding heads and by five o'clock, he can't take it anymore and leaves early. When he gets home, I jump out at him from behind a massive pile of leaves I've raked, scaring him so bad that he topples into a different leaf pile. He chases me and I scream as loud as I want since we have no neighbors, zipping up and down the hillside until darkness falls.

We're covered in dirt and leaves. Nicholas's Toothless tie is ruined. He appraises it sadly, but I give the tie a light tug and say, "We'll get you a new one. *How to Train Your Dragon 2*: the sequel tie."

He smiles down at me. My heart does a somersault, and he begins to lean in, but we're startled away from each other by a spatter of cold white light, high beams fishtailing up the driveway.

It's Deborah's car.

Happy fun time disintegrates. "What's she doing here?" I hiss, backing up into the shadow of the house. I stare at Nicholas, panic rising. "Did you invite her? I haven't had time to clean anything. The sink is full of dishes and your mom is going to . . . eugh."

"No, I didn't invite her." His voice is hard.

The engine shuts off and both car doors fan open like the wings of a vulture. It must really be About To Go Down if Harold was brought along as backup. Deborah oozes out of the driver's side, slim silhouette appraising the house. Even in the dark, I can tell she's wearing a horrible frown. She's going to tell Nicholas he has to move. *Unacceptable home for my son. Unacceptable for my grandchildren.*

"Let's go," Nicholas says urgently, grabbing my hand and darting around to the back door. "We can't let them inside."

"We can't?"

"Never." I'm taken aback by how vicious he sounds. But I get it. Maybe the logic is nonsensical, but if we let Deborah and Harold darken our doorway, all the peace we've established here is going to go up in smoke. They'll taint it with their pessimism and judgment. When they leave, they'll take the magic with them, and it won't feel like our enchanted sanctuary in the wilderness anymore.

We run inside just as Deborah starts rapping on the front door. "Nicky!" She tries to turn the knob and knocks again, much louder this time. It's the most irritated sound in the universe; she can't believe we have the audacity to keep her out.

"Nicky, are you in there? Answer the door!" I'm reminded of vampires requiring permission to cross your threshold, and after you've let them in one time they're free to come and go as they please. Deborah sees our warm-blooded shapes through the door in infrared and bares her razor-sharp teeth, pupils expanding to fill the whites of her eyes.

Nicholas and I watch the door warily, neither of us moving. "Your mom needs to learn how to call ahead," I whisper.

"She called me three times while we were out back," he admits. "I didn't answer."

"Ooooh, someone's gonna be in trouble."

He nudges me with his shoulder. I nudge him back.

"Nicholas!" Deborah's using her I Mean Business voice. "Your father and I are here! Unlock the door." Harold distantly grumbles. Deborah's made him get out of his seat for nothing, and he hasn't had to remain standing for this long in five years.

"What do you think she wants?" I murmur in Nicholas's ear.

"She needs me to tell Dad he's not allowed to eat foods that begin with the letter *B*."

I cackle, then cover my mouth to quiet the noise. "It's the dessert you didn't finish last night. She's here to spoon-feed you the rest of your cake."

I notice the tension in his posture, how he tries to make himself invisible as he waits, almost audibly thinking *Please go away. Just leave me alone.* Stress lines his features and I want to reach out, smooth his problems away with my hands. Deborah is overwhelming even in tiny doses. Nicholas is exposed to her

nagging and emotionally draining diatribes nonstop. He gets no
downtime to recover.

"They're not home," Harold complains. "Let's go."

"Nicky's car is here and all the lights are on. I'm not going
anywhere till he opens up. If you want to leave, drive yourself
home. Nicky will give me a ride."

"Why on earth does he live all the way out here in the sticks?"
We're inconsiderate for making him travel a whole ten minutes.

For once, Harold's made a point he and his wife can agree
on. "This property is unacceptable," she says briskly. (Called it!)
"It's too far from home. The yard's a mess—we'll need to get a
landscaper out here to cut down all these trees. Nicky mentioned
a pond. What does he need a pond for? It's dangerous for small
children. First thing tomorrow, you're making calls to get a
fence built around it. You see those crooked shutters? They'll
need to go, too. Honestly, what was he thinking? He must've let
Naomi make the decision on this one. No wonder he hasn't invited us over—he's ashamed of it."

When it's beginning to look like Deborah will never leave,
Nicholas sighs and takes one step toward the door. I can't let
him give in. He's successfully ignored his mother for over fifteen
minutes now and I want to keep the momentum going.

"Come on." I take his hand and hurry toward the stairs,
dragging him along after me.

"What are we doing?"

I lead him into the empty middle bedroom upstairs and
open the window, which overlooks the front yard. Deborah and
Harold hear the groan of the ancient pane and tip their heads
back to gape at us. "What's up?" I call down.

Beside me, Nicholas drops to the floor like a sack of potatoes.

It's all I can do not to laugh. "What are you doing?" he cries again in a loud whisper.

"I'm your attack dog," I tell him. "I'm going to bark at these intruders until they go away."

Harold's gaze is fuzzy and perplexed. He squints, pointing at me. "Who's that?"

"That's Naomi, you idiot," his wife snaps, and he just scratches his head. His confusion is understandable. Harold likes to speak directly to my chest when addressing me, and thanks to this lovely window that conceals everything but my head and neck, my identification has been rendered a mystery.

Deborah cups her hands around her mouth. "Where is Nicky?"

I cup my hands around my mouth, too. "Nicholas isn't available to talk right now, but you can leave him a message!" Being an attack dog is more secretarial than one would think.

"But *where* is he?" she demands to know.

"Busy!" Jesus, lady. Take a hint.

She props her hands on her hips. "Aren't you going to let me inside?"

I think of vampires again and shiver. "Afraid not!"

Nicholas makes a strange keening sound. I glance down at him in alarm and wonder of wonders, he's *laughing*. It emboldens me to take this a step further. "I can't tell you what Nicholas is doing because it's a secret, by the way. A sinister secret. You should go now while you still can."

"I am not leaving until I see my son!" She pauses, voice dropping to a suspicious tone. "What have you done with him?"

"Nicholas?" I reply questioningly. "I haven't seen him in days. And that's the story I'm giving the police."

I check Nicholas's reaction and think he might be dead. He is keeled over, forehead on the floor, body shaking with quiet laughter. I can't believe he's letting me get away with talking to his mother like this, but after what she said to me yesterday I've got no qualms. I'm off my leash and I'll go as far as he'll let me. "He's not here. A spaceship took off a few minutes ago, so if you run you might be able to catch him."

I'm pretty sure I hear Harold say, "I'm not running even if a spaceship *did* take him." He stalks back to the car, but Deborah stays put.

"This isn't funny. I'll only tell you one more time to go get my son."

Nicholas sits up, deliberates for a moment, and then hollers, "I'm not home!"

"Nicky!" Deborah cries, pressing her hands together. He's alive! "Nicky, is that you?"

He pops up next to me at the window. "No! You have the wrong address."

"Nicky, I'm serious. Let me in."

"Nicky is gone forever. A dinosaur ate him."

"Excuse me?"

"He's a changeling."

"Nicholas Benjamin Rose. I'm losing my patience and do not find this humorous. It's freezing and I came here to speak to you like adults. I will give you until the count of three—"

"He's been Raptured."

"You do not talk to me this way! I am your MOTHER—"

Nicholas has never interrupted his mom before, and he's making up for it now. "This whole time, he was never real. All along, it was . . . Shia LaBeouf! Method acting!"

Deborah's figure is shadowy, but I can see her balled hands

and jutting chin. When her voice emerges, it's so guttural that it would make Lucifer lock his doors. "Nick—"

"I drop-kicked him out of a moving train and he's at the bottom of a ravine somewhere, busy being extremely dead. There is nothing for you here, then, so go on and be banished." He spreads his fingers wide and thrusts them outward like he's casting a spell. "I banish thee!"

I think he might be losing his mind a bit, because his giddy laughter drowns out whatever Deborah's down there squawking. She's spitting mad, Nicholas has thrown all his fucks to the wind, and it's *glorious*. The most beautiful display of childish behavior I've ever witnessed.

"Yeah, you tell her," I say goadingly. I love seeing him brave enough to give that woman a fraction of the hell she's owed. "You cast D-Money right out of here."

"I cast you right out of here, D-Money!" he yells at the top of his lungs, and I. Completely. Lose it. I can't breathe. Neither can Nicholas, who breaks down in the middle of his banishment chant and is laughing so hysterically that no sound escapes save for little gasping sobs. Tears stream down our faces.

"Look what you've done!" Deborah screams, shaking a finger at me. "You've corrupted my sweet boy! I know this is your fault, Naomi!"

I take a bow.

The spell is a success. Deborah gives up and stomps back to her car. Her tires squeal ominously when she tears off into the night, which is probably pretty close to the same sound she's making twelve inches from Harold's face right now.

I wipe the tears from my eyes and give him a high five. "Holy shit, dude!"

"I know!" He's got a crazed grin, chest heaving deeply.

"Unhinged" is my new favorite look on him. I think back to the conversation we had in the car after my stop-and-run fiasco at the traffic light in Beaufort, and how he said that messing with his parents could be fun as long as he was in on the joke, too. He really meant it.

I slide my palm over his cheek, matching his grin. "I'm proud of you. I wish I could see your mom's face right now."

"She's going to kill me." His smile freezes as he realizes what just happened. "Oh my god, she's going to literally kill me." He leans over, hands on his knees, breathing in through his nose and out his mouth like a woman in labor. I pat his back and a few anxious honking noises thump right out of him. "Did I seriously say all that? To my *mom*? Can we run off to an uninhabited island?"

"I like islands. Let's go. We'll have coconut pie every day."

"I can't believe I did that." More honking. "I got a little carried away, didn't I?"

"I want to see you get carried away all the time." I get a zap of inspiration and tap the windowsill. "Hey, can you go down there and stand where your mom was standing? Just for a sec? I want to check something."

He arches a brow at me but obliges. While he heads downstairs, I dash into my bedroom and fish a package of balloons out from under my bed, which I'd purchased when he and I were still sabotaging each other. I race into the bathroom, fill one up with water, and return to the window.

"Okay, I'm down here," he says, voice drifting up with a coil of white breath. "What did you need to check?"

"This," I say, letting the bomb drop. It doesn't land on his head as planned, but splatters all over his shoes.

Nicholas jumps back, arms out, staring at the dark spots on his pants. A thrill chases up my spine. Slowly, slowly, he lifts his head and growls, "I'd run if I were you."

With a gleeful scream, off I go.

I spend the weekend getting entirely too used to being on friendly terms with Nicholas. He teaches me how to drive Frankencar, which I'm initially resistant to out of nerves. But I get the hang of it pretty quickly and drive us to Beaufort to buy a canoe, which we strap to the roof of my car. We buy three oars and paddle out to rescue his wayward canoe. We spend Saturday on the pond, stabbing our oars at chunks of ice and playing bumper cars. Then we sit on the sofa in the drawing room, side by side, and watch the snow fall while we drink hot chocolate. He plays *Nightjar* (on my account, so that he can play God with my trident and exclaim, "Hey, you have to come look at this! I'm a unicorn! Look, Naomi, I have a *horn!*") while I read *Riverdale* fan fiction on Tumblr, and it's mellow and ordinary and achingly perfect. It makes me so sad that all the good parts in the story of us are rolling in right at the end.

An evil twist of fate: I don't think I want it to be the end. Not anymore. But while we seem to be learning how to treat each other's feelings with more care and making better choices, we're not what an engaged couple ought to be.

When he comes home on Monday all I want to do is gather up all my failures into a pile and sweep them under the rug, but instead I make myself share the parts of myself I'm not so proud of. I make myself say, "Today sucked. I spent half an hour on an online application before it got to the last page and they said a minimum of five years' experience in the food industry was required."

"What sort of position?"

"Assistant manager. It was the only opening they were hiring for."

He looks down at the rug as he toes off his shoes, and I wonder if he's thinking about Eaten Alive. Mr. and Mrs. Howard wouldn't even make me sit for an interview; if I said I could move to Tenmouth, they'd give me a job without hesitating.

"I'm sorry. Demanding a minimum of five years' experience is stupid. They miss out on so much talent by limiting themselves that way. It really is their loss." I can't help tearing up a bit at hearing such strong support from him. "If it cheers you up any, I stopped at the supermarket and saw a couple help wanted ads on the bulletin board." He hands me two flyers. They're for small, local businesses I've driven past but never patronized. Their parking spaces are always empty. They're the sort of workplaces I know Nicholas thinks are set up to fail because they can't compete against today's big retailers, but he still took the time to bring them home to me.

I start to drift off toward the couch, wanting nothing more than to escape into a television show until my eyelids are so heavy I can't keep them open, but he takes my hand.

"What are you doing?"

"Going to go make dinner. Come with me?"

I raise a mystified eyebrow at him. "Sure?"

He sends me a little smile that I return and doesn't drop my hand, lacing his fingers through mine. What world am I living in, that now I'm holding hands with Nicholas to walk from one room into another? His grasp is confident and sure, the sort you'd want leading you through a crowd. "You're a pretty good hand-holder, you know," I tell him.

"Just reminding you of all the things your Dr. Claw could never do."

Ahh, Dr. Claw. Evil villain of my dreams. With a limo, red suspenders, and a face like *that* (in the movie, at least), he could still get it even if he had two pirate hooks. "He's still got his other hand."

"Shh. I win."

"Yes, Nicholas, you are much better than an *Inspector Gadget* character."

Nicholas lifts his chin, mollified. In the kitchen, he tugs a chain that activates a strand of globe lights that run the perimeter of our ceiling, which casts a cheery ambiance. Then he taps a radio app on his phone and music infuses the room while he sifts through pans in the cabinet. "Where's the—oh, here it is." He twirls a frying pan and winks at me.

"What are we making?"

"Pecan pancakes."

It's barely dinnertime and the sky's already black. If it weren't for the glowing bulbs overhead that throw our reflections back at us in the windowpane, we'd be able to see the star-sprinkled forest. Familiar music wafts from his phone. Generationals. *Our* band. The song playing now is "Turning the Screw," which I haven't cued up lately because it reminds me of everything lovely that's disappeared from our relationship. It's been a while since we've listened to their music together. I wonder if he's favorited this song before, or if he's got it on a playlist. The thought of him listening to our band all by himself in recent times hurts my heart.

"Naomi."

His voice is velvet. I don't have to wonder if the choice of music is a coincidence, because I hear it in his deepened timbre. I see it in the feathering muscle in his cheek. I feel his atoms vibrating.

He looks sideways at me and my stomach drops. "Come here," he says, extending a hand.

I walk over so slowly that he laughs. I marvel at the impossible softness of the sound, coming from *him*, directed at *me*; the quirk of his lips, the warm fire in his eyes. When my hand slides into his, I've never been so aware of another person's physicality. All of my senses spike, picking out his details, the way he feels, smells, his body heat. He takes up the entire room.

Breathing becomes an effort.

The hand he doesn't have laced through my fingers lightly grips my waist. The top of my head rests perfectly beneath his jaw, which makes leaning against his chest irresistible. I didn't think we were the kind of couple that danced in a kitchen in the middle of the woods, but it turns out that's exactly the kind of couple we are. Two months ago, we would have done something like this only if other people were watching. Putting on a show.

I never want this dance to end. He won't let me press myself against him so that I can hide my face, gently tugging back every time I try to disappear. He tilts my head up and gazes right on through me to what lies inside. His eyes are bluer than a lake and they're gleaming with happiness. It dawns on me that I haven't seen him genuinely happy in forever. I've been so concentrated on my own unhappiness that I haven't noticed his. I've been fooling myself by thinking he's been content all along. How arrogant, to assume he was content with me when I so obviously wasn't content with him.

Our past is a string of disconnected memories I can teleport across. All of the golden, feel-good, light-as-air memories have been going dark, which has allowed the bitter poison ones to dominate the spotlight. But when Nicholas stares into my eyes like this, a few of those positive memories twinkle back to life and take the stage. When his palm slides over my cheek, fingers disappearing into my hair, it cauterizes a wound on my heart that's been festering untended.

Nicholas absorbs my attention so fully that I know I'll never forget how this feels. It's a peace and a comfort I haven't been able to find anywhere. It's how my heart pounds so loud I'm certain he can hear it. It's how his closeness makes my knees weak, and his skin brushing mine jolts me like a spray of hot sparks. It's how he knows me better than anyone else, and I never meant for him to.

I tried to keep him at a safe distance where he could only see the decent parts of me and it made us both miserable. I inadvertently let him in to see the ugly parts but instead of running away like I'd counted on him to do, he wrapped his arms around all of that ugliness and didn't let go.

———

We're on the floor, and Nicholas is asleep.

We had a picnic in the living room, the palm-leaf comforter from his bed serving as our picnic blanket. I can't stop running my hands over the fabric, remembering what it was like to sleep beneath it, next to him. Remembering him holding me close, breath stirring my hair. The memories make me ache so bad that my chest hurts and I want to cry, but I can't stop remembering. The floodgates are wide open.

It's warm and comfortable here in front of the fireplace, so

I'll let him sleep for just a bit longer before I wake him up. And it's nice, this sense of normality, lying next to each other. It's what most couples do, especially the engaged ones. But it hasn't been our normal.

Nicholas and I aren't touching. He's lying on his back, one arm bent behind his head, and there's a slight frown in his brow that makes me want to smooth it, so that's what I do. I think that's the place we're in now: I'm allowed to briefly touch him in innocent spots. For the purposes of caring. Soothing. Giving. We're not in a place where we can take. Greediness wouldn't survive. Moving too quickly might kill us stone-dead.

I hold my ring finger above me and watch the diamond sparkle. It's too forward for me to lay my head on my fiancé's chest. How absurd is that?

I don't touch him, but I think about it. I think his shirt would feel soft, fragrant with subtle notes of cologne you only catch when he moves. He'd feel like reassurance. Quiet strength. Security. The bright coals of a fire. He'd feel like warm arms on a cold starry night, breaths puffing up white. He would feel like a sturdy old house in the woods and a plaid winter cap.

Nicholas Benjamin Rose is a good man right down to his bones, and that is true even if he and I have been impossible.

I think touching him now would feel like plucking a flower from the barn and dropping it inside a blue-green drinking glass next to your breakfast plate. He would feel like blue spruce and wood smoke. Moonlight and glittering clouds. Pine, my new favorite scent. He's chinks of sunlight falling over a woven rug, warm to the touch, lazy as an afternoon kiss. Bare, tangled legs, napping together on the couch.

He's the cold, crisp air in fall and the sharp ice of a shovel's blade you run the pad of your finger over as you pass it, propped upside-down next to a dilapidated barn. He's in the trees. The pond.

I imagine him swimming in the pond this summer: bare, glistening skin. Jumping off the weathered dock. The lean muscles in his back bunching, every ligament springing to life.

Someday, for some woman, he'll feel like parting the curtains in an upper window, dust motes swirling in a sunny room, peering down on the curving back of a man building your children a swing set. He'll be a thick wedding band of solid silver, the only place on his hand that doesn't tan in the summer. He'll feel like two old trees growing together, branches plaiting into an embrace.

I wish I could see inside his head to know how he feels about me. I don't want to ask, because what if he says the past few weeks haven't been enough? What if he thinks we're unsalvageable? That's what I'd thought, but I'm not so sure anymore. I want to think that he's here with me because he wants to be, not because he's measuring all the inconveniences of splitting up and decided making it work is the easier option. He could be anywhere, with anyone, but he's here with me. That's got to mean something.

I'm staring at this man and thinking about the straw wrapper bracelet he keeps in a drawer.

There are hurts. I feel them all over, like stab wounds: the distance that we both allowed to settle in, ruining what should have been the happiest year of our lives. The ring that makes me feel like a fraud because it's so huge. As ridiculous as it might sound, in my mind he gave me such a big diamond as a way of saying *I love you THIS much!*; but how could he have loved me

THAT much when we still didn't completely know each other? When we'd never argued before and didn't live together and it was such smooth sailing. Way too good to be true.

He's seen me take it off a couple times. I told him the diamond is too gaudy, but in truth it didn't occur to me he'd care, because I didn't care myself. I bet he cared, though. I bet he hated that I took off his ring.

I hold it over my face again, flashing it from left to right to catch the blaze of the fire, and I see what he saw when he picked it out. I see my hand from his point of view, not mine. How it would glow with promise. I wonder what I feel like to him. What memories and possibilities run across his mind when he wants to touch me but feels that's not his privilege anymore.

For the first time since he presented it to me, I study my ring and think it's stunning. It's exactly the ring he should have picked. I'll never forgive myself for the moments I took it off.

He's radiant, lying here. Scintillating and golden. Nicholas is a rare, wonderful man, and I'm going to be so sorry if I have to give his ring back.

CHAPTER EIGHTEEN

In early December, Nicholas and I are still miraculously getting along. It's hard to trust, but all my reasons for feeling detached and resentful in the past have crumbled in light of Nicholas's newfound attentiveness. He's putting me first. He's been kind and reassuring. He stood up to Deborah on Thanksgiving, and the following night he literally banished her from the house.

I still can't believe he did that.

When these truths sink in, he doesn't feel like my adversary or the obstacle in my path to finding happiness. He feels like part of the path. Against all wisdom, I fall a little bit in love with pretending it *won't* fall apart. And in the spirit of this, I do a very scary thing.

I open up a new password-protected document on my computer and jot down ideas for tokens of affection. If this isn't a fluke, and if this is to work—*if*—I'll need to consistently make Nicholas feel cherished in small but significant ways. The most important and most challenging element is typed at the top so that I won't forget: *Keep doing this even if he doesn't reciprocate in an immediately obvious way.* I have to give while expecting nothing in return; otherwise, the gestures are empty. I hope I won't be the only one here trying.

One morning after Nicholas's shower, I draw a heart in the steamy bathroom mirror. He ducks back into the bathroom to brush his teeth and after he's left it again I find another heart he's drawn, interlocked in mine.

It's the world's smallest start.

Inside his lunchbox, I leave a note. *I hope you have a good day! I'm thinking about you.*

Reflecting on it, I die a bit because we haven't been genuinely sappy with each other in ages, so the barest of pleasantries is saccharine. We're in a sap drought. We've been complete idiots when it comes to understanding when a partner needs something they won't ask for.

At noon, he texts me. Thank you for the note. I'm thinking about you, too. When he comes home, he has a present for me: A plaid earflap hat to match his, because I've been wearing his so often that he thought I might like one of my own. It's the color of champagne and soft as goose down. I give him a kiss on the cheek, and where my lips touch him the skin glows pink.

I might be onto something here, so the next day I slip another note into his lunchbox:

Good morning! I think you're a terrific pancake maker and you always look and smell very nice. Thank you for supporting me. Have a great work day! Cavities everywhere are counting on you.

My nerves are this incredible mix of awkward *Gahh* and fluttery *Eeeee*, because what I'm saying is true. I hope to god he doesn't find it corny. I also leave a bag of Skittles on his driver's seat, which I'm less unsure about because Skittles are a home-run "just because" present and I know he'll have the bag empty before he parks at Rise and Smile.

When noon hits, I'm one hundred percent certain my note was corny and I want to fall facedown into a bank of snow. It's his lunch break, so he has to have seen it by now. I'm chewing my fingernails when my phone buzzes and I open a text message to see a picture of a piece of paper that I'm pretty sure is the one I wrote my note on. He's flipped it to the blank side and drawn a stick figure of a man with scribbles on his cheeks. Stick Nicholas is wearing a big smile and there are three wavy lines coming off him that he explains with an arrow and a caption: *My nice-smelling-ness.* There's a heart on his stick chest.

The next day, I leave this note for him: *I love our house.* It may not sound like much, but it's a big deal. In those four words I'm validating his decision to buy it, and I don't refer to it as *his* house. Apparently he checks his lunchbox an hour early, because he shoots me a text at eleven that says: I love living in our house with you. Look under your pillow.

I run upstairs and fling all my pillows off the bed. He's hidden a note for me! My heart lights up like a Christmas tree and I scramble over my mattress to devour every letter of the short message. Nicholas wrote me a note and took the time to slip upstairs and slide it under my pillow. Every step of the action resonates.

Good morning! You have excellent taste in music. (And men.) I'm so glad we stayed in Morris. I believe in you! You can do anything you set your mind to and I know you will achieve all your dreams. You are, and will always be, the most beautiful person I've ever known.

My smile's so wide it's hurting my facial muscles, and I lie on the bed and kick my legs and squeal. I'm certain that the ghosts who are watching think I'm a lunatic, but I don't care. I put the note back under my pillow and run a lap around the yard to work out my restless energy.

Beautiful! He thinks I'm beautiful. And he believes in me. *Or so he says*, the devil on my shoulder adds, but I flick the devil off. I'm going to let myself be happy about this.

I've forgotten what it's like to feel this alive. Colors are brighter, bolder. Sounds are louder. I brainstorm ways to thank Nicholas for his thoughtfulness and decide to have flowers sent to him at work. To my knowledge, no one has ever given Nicholas flowers in his life. To him, they're impractical and he probably associates them with the crushing obligation he feels toward his mother, so I would like to change that. After I call up the local florist and none of her suggestions sound particularly inspiring, I ask if she can put together an arrangement made entirely out of myrtle. Myrtle is generally used as filler greenery in a bouquet, too plain to be the main event, but in the *Nightjar* world collecting myrtle gives characters vitality points. I think the significance will make him smile.

Nicholas's car rumbles up the drive shortly after six, which means he hasn't made any stops after work, and I run to greet him right as he's shutting his door. He turns and looks down at me, a grin instantly appearing on his face. His eyes are bright and flickering like firelight, and a swarm of butterflies threatens to fly up from my stomach and right out of my mouth. He's holding my myrtle bouquet.

"Hey, you," he says, nudging my arm with his elbow.

"Hi." I take his lunchbox from him. (Look, I can be gallant!)

"Thanks for the vitality boost," he says. "It came in handy

when a three-year-old bit my finger." He shows me an indentation of tiny teeth on the tip of his index finger.

"I hope you bit the kid back."

"Her mom wouldn't turn around long enough for me to get away with it."

Has Nicholas ever looked this happy? No. What a shame, to know I've been accepting anything less than *this* smile he's giving me right now.

I think he wants to touch the way we used to. I think he wants to kiss me. But he's restrained. He leans his forehead down to mine. "You're cute," he half laughs, then pulls away and taps my nose. We stroll up to the house and if I'm not mistaken, there's a new spring in his step.

We pass our evening setting up the Christmas tree and making popcorn garland. He fashions me a popcorn necklace, so I make him one, too. We take turns tossing popcorn into each other's mouths. I'm marveling how every day is better than the one before it when he checks his phone and his face falls.

"What is it?"

"Text from Mom."

I pile a load of unsavory words onto a cutting board and dice them up into tiny pieces. Deborah has not called or initiated a text in days. When Nicholas texted her to test the waters, the responses he got were about as angry and self-pitying as you'd expect. "What'd she say?"

"Uh." He looks up at me, and his expression is so full of apology that I get a tug in my stomach and feel vaguely ill. "I forgot that I even agreed to do this. I told her yes weeks ago, and they've made plans for some big welcome, or else I'd try to back out."

"Back out of what? What did you agree to?" Ridiculously,

arranged marriage pops into my head and I'm ready to clash swords with some faceless woman in a bridal veil. I've got a ring! I saw him first!

"A trip to Cohasset, Minnesota. About fifteen years ago when Dad was still plugged into the investment world, he invested a chunk of money into a friend's start-up beer brewery, and it did well enough that he bought himself a partnership. Once a year he goes and checks out the brewery and they go over the year's figures in a meeting and decide how they want to grow the company. This year, though . . ."

He scratches his head. "Well, Dad says he doesn't care what happens to the company anymore and he's tired of long trips. He just wants to stay home. Mom's worried about missing out on potential investment opportunities, so she gave me a pile of spreadsheets to look over and begged me to go as his proxy."

"Oh." I pick at a thread in the rug. "What day is the meeting?"

"Mom says a man named Bernard is expecting me at ten a.m. this Saturday."

"Ten a.m.? How long does it take to get to Cohasset?"

He makes a face. "I don't know. I think, like, seven hours? I'll have to leave early. They'll keep me busy all of Saturday, and with a seven-hour drive back I'll have to stay in a hotel and leave Sunday morning." He checks the weather app on his phone. "Snow and precipitation all day Sunday. Of course. I have no idea how long it's going to take to drive back. I might get in late."

"That's the whole weekend," I reply glumly.

"You could come with me." Hope flares in his eyes. "You wouldn't have much to do at the brewery, but we could look up other stuff in Cohasset to entertain you. We'll play music in the car and get a ton of road snacks."

My focus zeroes in on the hotel part of this equation—
namely, if we'd share a room. Would he request one bed or two?
A bolt of excitement strikes, but it all goes dark when I remember: "I have an interview Saturday morning."

"Oh, right, at the campground."

I'm still not sure what the position entails. I'm trying to
avoid cubicles or small office settings, and the idea of being paid
to walk along nature trails holds a certain appeal. Our house in
the woods has converted me into Bear Grylls.

"Well." I pick at the thread until it unravels another inch. I
can't hide my disappointment.

Nicholas seems disappointed, too, but the ghost of a smile
lifts his cheek and the skin around his eyes crinkles. "Going to
miss me?"

"Not even," I mumble. It convinces no one. To distract from
the sudden gloom that's fallen over us I say, "So, will you be
making financial decisions on your parents' behalf, then? You
can invest their money for them? There's a GoFundMe to make
a movie about Pizza Rat, called Ratachewy. You should look
into that."

He laughs. "Nah, I don't get to do whatever I want with
their money. I'll mostly be listening and taking notes. Then I'll
report back to Mom and she'll decide what she wants to do."

I don't bother asking why Deborah can't just go herself. The
purpose of Deborah bearing children was so that she'd have
minions obligated to do her bidding.

"It's only two days," he says gently. "You'll have the house
to yourself. You can draw handlebar mustaches on all my pictures and jump on the bed naked."

"Sounds like my average day."

Once, this would have been a dream come true. No

Nicholas! I would have been rejoicing. It's such a bummer that now I have to miss his stupid, adorable face when he's gone.

I set my alarm on Saturday morning so that I wake up early enough to see Nicholas off. It's insane that they've scheduled the meeting for ten a.m. when he has to drive to get there. It's as dark as outer space and way too cold to be traveling. His engine and tires might blow up. On top of that, he's leaving right when I'm starting to come down with the stomach flu. There's a rising lump in my throat when I watch him tie his shoelaces, a leather bag with a change of clothes and overnight essentials at his feet.

"I don't feel well," I mutter.

He turns his head, scanning me from top to bottom. "What's wrong?"

"Stomachache. I feel like I'm going to be sick. I'm all sweaty and uncomfortable." I'm also pacing. For something to do, I unzip his bag and paw through his stuff. I dab some of his cologne on my wrists and rub them together, then bring the scent to my nose to inhale slowly. It settles my nausea a little. Then I raise my eyes to meet Nicholas's probing ones and my heart stutters. "What?"

"Nothing." There's a tremor in his voice and he looks away, tying his other shoe. When he stands up, I nearly shout.

"Wait! You can't leave yet. You haven't eaten any breakfast."

"It's too early for me to be hungry. I'll grab something on the road later."

"You want more coffee?" I drift toward the kitchen but he shakes his head, tapping a thermos.

"Got plenty right here."

Maybe he shouldn't drink coffee. It'll get him all wired and he'll speed. He'll fly off an overpass and his car will do sixteen rolls in midair. "I'm worried you're going to fall asleep at the wheel."

Nicholas chuckles. "I went to bed early, so I'm wide awake. I'll be all right."

"What if it starts to snow?"

"I won't fall asleep even if it starts snowing." I think I'm amusing him.

I frown. "Nicholas, I'm serious. I did some researching on Cohasset and I wasn't going to say anything because I didn't want to spook you, but in August there were three carjackings. Some guy came up to people at a gas station and said their gas cap had fallen off, and when they turned to check he pulled a gun on them."

He cradles my jaw in his hands. His gaze is molten and he looks almost like he could love me. I think about all the times I almost walked away and it's terrifying. I would have missed out on this. "Then I won't get gas in Cohasset."

I'm pathetic. A helpless newborn kitten. "You can't leave me here when I'm ill."

He puts a hand to my forehead. The gesture feels so intimate. I've slept with this man, but *this* feels intimate? I'm contagious. He can't go to Cohasset or he'll infect the whole brewery, and he needs to stay quarantined here with me.

"I think you're lovesick," he says with a curving mouth.

My stomach flips. My tongue is tied in at least three knots. I can't think of a response, so he steps even closer, until our bodies are just barely touching. "You are. Trust me, I know all the signs."

My mouth doesn't work. I try to form words and let out an unintelligible squeak.

He grins and leans in to kiss my temple. His lips pause at my ear, and I shiver so hard I know he feels it. "It's a condition I'm quite familiar with myself."

I clutch the arm of the couch so that I don't tip over when he withdraws. His back is turned to me, shaking slightly, and I'd swear he's trying not to laugh.

I'm such a mess over his accusation that I barely hold it together long enough to say good-bye. He says, "Good luck at your interview. I know you'll knock it out of the park. Be back before you know it, pretty girl." He winks, and then he's gone, in his Jeep that's going to crash, with a contagious illness and either too much or not enough caffeine.

I burn away the next few hours painting the front door purple, ordering Nicholas a new phone charger—one that's long enough to reach his nightstand—and setting up my new Instagram account dedicated to the gruesome salt and pepper shaker babies. I've named them Frank and Helvetica and I'm going to position them in a new location every day to bewilder Nicholas. It will be like Elf on the Shelf, and I'm calling it Demon on the Ceilin'. My favorite ideas involve suspending them from fishing line at Nicholas's face-level. The shower! The car! His office at work! It's going to be way more fun than my old Instagram.

My phone chimes with a text from Nicholas at 9:50 to say he arrived safely in Cohasset.

Good luck! I reply. I don't know what I'm wishing him luck for. He's not doing any of this for himself; he's doing it for his parents.

He replies, You, too! For extra good luck, drive by the Junk Yard on your way to the interview. Seeing an old friend might be just the boost you need.

My old friend died a slow, agonizing death. It will probably sit empty for at least five years, or maybe get bulldozed, which can only serve to bum me out. But Nicholas is trying to be sweet and encouraging, so I send him back a smiley face. He's so cute even when he's wrong.

I think about what Nicholas is up to today. His devotion to family, being the rock they all depend on. Being the man they call to come fix whatever's gone wrong, to smooth it out and make it better. I think of what these qualities will be like when transferred to a wife and children. I think how there's no way he'll ever miss a school play, a parent-teacher conference, a soccer game. How he'll want his wife to know he's capable of supporting her financially and she can work if she wants but doesn't have to, because that's how he shows his love—by providing stability.

It's a gesture I've completely misinterpreted, since it's loving but not necessarily romantic. You look at a love letter and it's clear as day—you think, *This is a love letter.* But when your significant other says, *You don't need to work. You don't need a job,* you might hear, *I don't think you'll find meaningful employment without a college education. I don't believe in you.*

In my head, I've been assuming that when Nicholas says I don't need to work, what he means is that any job I'd qualify for is so beneath his notice that I might as well not work at all. In Nicholas's head, all he's done is say, *Here I am, here I am. Be anything! It doesn't matter if you don't make much money, because I'll take care of you. I'll let you need me. I'll be your rock, whatever happens. Spread your wings, you can always fall back on me.*

Our communication has been so shitty, I don't know whether to laugh or cry.

I decide to put on Nicholas's hat and coveralls because wearing his clothes is the next best thing to bringing him with me, and I cringe to remember smirking at his big, durable boots and the button-down flannel, him wanting to change his stripes. Why shouldn't he be allowed to change his stripes? He can have spots, too, if he wants. I open the closet and find two pairs of coveralls: his, and a much smaller one. It's an initiation into his secret society.

On the drive to the campground, I repeat comforting phrases that remind me there's no use worrying about decisions not totally in my control. *If it's meant to be, it will be. If they don't want to hire me, that's their loss. Everything happens for a reason.* I'm lying to myself, but at least I feel better.

As the road rears up to pass the lifeless shell of the Junk Yard, I prepare for the usual twinge of anguish, but it's peppered with surprise when I spot my car in the parking lot. Or Leon's car now, I suppose. God, I miss that Saturn. If I were Nicholas, I would never let me live that down. The fact that I no longer assume it's a pulled punch he's saving gives me hope. We're making progress.

Maybe it's muscle memory, but I turn on my blinker and pull into the parking lot. A friendly face appears at the window and waves. I wave back.

"Hey!" Leon calls from the back room when I trundle into the shop.

"Hey, yourself!" I revolve in a circle. The store's gutted. There are rows of stains where shelves have sat without budging since the 1970s. A ghost of the Junk Yard still clings in the form of an aluminum sign on the wall above the register. It's been there since before I was born, I'm sure: a picture of a little girl bending to feed a mouse a wheel of cheese. Underneath it says *It's the little things.* "Wow. This place is empty."

"I know." He comes out of the back. "Weird, isn't it? Somehow it looks even smaller now that everything's gone."

"What are you still doing here?" I ask him. "Mr. and Mrs. Howard got you on cleaning duty until the place sells?"

"Nope! As of three o'clock on Wednesday, this place is officially sold." He leans against the counter and waggles his eyebrows, giving me a big, cheesy grin. "I was actually going to text you and ask if you wanted to swing by today or tomorrow to see it. I swore Nicholas to secrecy because I wanted to see the look on your face when you heard who bought it. I know you doubted me."

I gasp. "No way."

"And *there's* the look." He folds his arms, nodding. "You're standing in Backwoods Buffet. Coming this spring."

"Backwoods Buffet?" I repeat with a laugh. I can't believe Nicholas managed to keep this a secret. A few days ago Leon came over to fish in the pond with Nicholas and when I walked up on them to say hi, they clammed right up even though until then they'd been gabbing a mile a minute. Naturally, I assumed they were talking about me and I'm not entirely wrong.

He beams. "I've got other names if Backwoods Buffet sounds bad. The Grizzly Bear. Fireside. Timber! With an exclamation point, like you know how loggers used to yell . . ." He stops because I'm still laughing. "Hey, Timber!'s a good one."

"It is." I nod. "Fireside sounds cool, too." I gaze around the place, trying to imagine tables and chairs full of people eating.

"This is so awesome, Leon. I'm really happy for you! I'm trying to envision what it might look like, and in my head it's like Bass Pro Shops. Where's the kitchen going to go?"

"Got to have one put in when I have the addition built. I have a few uncles with their own construction business who are going to help me with that. Right now I'm working on rounding up a staff, which I was hoping you could help me out with . . ." He opens a drawer and pulls out a laminated plastic badge, placing it on the counter with a light thud. When I read it, I clap my hands over my mouth.

HELLO MY NAME IS NAOMI

CHAPTER NINETEEN

"Are you serious? Would you really give me a job here?"

Leon grins. "Of course! If you want one, that is."

"Hell yeah, I do! What would I be doing? I don't know much about restaurants, but I can learn. I'll learn how to cook anything you want. I'll listen to cooking audiobooks and become a gourmet chef. Or I can be a hostess! I think I'd like that. I could show people to their seats and give children crayons for their kids menus and say, 'Welcome to Fireside, my name is Naomi!'"

"You can do whatever you like," he says kindly, "but I'm hoping you'll help with the decorating."

I stare at him. "Really? Me?"

"Remember those *Rocky Horror* cutouts?" he says. "You made it look like they were holding a séance, which was so weird but also so awesome? Like, it's the sort of thing people would remember if they came in and saw it." I snort, remembering

how many hours I spent arranging that scene, which indeed nobody came in and saw. I'd forgotten all about it. "I'm counting
on you to make the place fun and memorable. A whole experience."

I'm so excited, I could bounce off the walls like a rubber ball.
"I can do that! Oooh, I have so many ideas already. If you're going to have fake trees, we can hide little birds in them, and play
nature sounds from tiny speakers. Maybe a waterfall feature
somewhere? It doesn't have to be big. Wait, yes it does! We'll put
FISH in it!" I shake his shoulders. "Real fish, Leon!" I'm chattering away, but then I think—"Brandy! Wait till she hears!
You're going to invite her to work here too, right?"

"I was going to, but I heard she got hired somewhere else."

"Oh, she hates it there." I've already got my phone out.
"Brandy!" I shriek as soon as she answers. Leon laughs while I
tell her to hurry up and get down to the Junk Yard.

Minutes later, she runs through the door. She's wearing
Golden Girls PJs, flip-flops, and a perfect smoky eye. Leon pulls
two more name tags out of a drawer: one that says BRANDY
and another that says MELISSA.

Brandy pins hers to her shirt and throws the other one in the
garbage. Leon arches a brow.

"I can't believe we're all going to work together again!" she
exclaims, tearing up. "My boss is so gross, you have no idea.
According to my five-year plan, I'm still three years away from
being able to move, so I need a win right now."

Leon looks pleased to know he's got two familiar faces on
board with this new venture. "I've got to warn you, I've never
run a restaurant before. Or any kind of business. But my aunt
has, and she's going to be joining us. There's always a possibility
it won't be as successful as I'm hoping, so you'd be taking a

chance. And in the beginning, I can't afford to pay more than minimum wage—"

"I don't care," Brandy interjects.

I'm in agreement. "I love this place. I want to be a part of whatever it is you're going to do with it." The more I think about it, the stronger the vision grows in my mind's eye. I'll affix large, mossy stones around the windows and hang a canoe on the wall. Maybe we can give it an Alaska-outdoorsy feel, which Brandy will love. First thing tomorrow I'm going into my backyard to collect sticks, which I'll twist into miniature trees with twine or use to adorn forest lanterns. I'm going to need some stuffed raccoons for sure. "I can't believe you're actually doing this," I say. "This is—*wow*. Good for you, Leon!" I slug his shoulder, then add, "Duncan."

"You remembered!"

"Yeah, yeah." I wave him off, but he's smiling. "How's the car?"

"Better than yours," he quips. "How's the house?"

"Wonderful. I can't tell you how glad I am that Nicholas bought it."

"Did it work?"

I'm not sure I heard him right. "Did what work?"

"The house," he replies. "Nicholas told me it was going to save you. *She's worth the pain of trying,* is how he put it. Worth the risk of failing."

My mouth pops open. "Did he? Well—yes. I suppose it did work. Or at least, I think it did. Hope it did." When Nicholas threw me a curveball with the purchase of that house and told me it was going to save us, I'd been ready to give up. I feel a rush of affection and appreciation for Nicholas, who held on.

"What?" Brandy pokes him. "Did I miss something?"

"We like Nicholas now," Leon informs her. She frowns, but he nods solemnly. "We do. He's a good guy."

She looks at me suspiciously. "Are you sure you're happy with him? Sometimes I've wondered, but didn't want to say anything in case I was wrong."

"I'm happy." I blink as it hits me how true this is. "Really, genuinely happy," I admit, and then I go "Oof" because Brandy envelops me in a crushing hug.

"All right, then. If we like Nicholas now, then I'm going to make nice. We'll double-date and do those wine and painting parties." This is one of the reasons why I love Brandy. She roots for other people's joy. "Nicholas'll like Vance. Did I tell you he's an optometrist?"

Leon and I both smile. "Many times."

"They can bond over long talks about health insurance and bad patients or something."

Leon watches me pin my name badge onto my shirt so that I match Brandy. "The way you're dressed, it's like you showed up today knowing you were going to end up working here." He motions at the hat. "Very Backwoods Buffet. It's hard not to suspect that Nicholas gave you a tip-off."

"He didn't. He *did* tell me to drive by the Junk Yard, though."

"Ahh. Sneaky."

I don't know whether to text Nicholas with HOW COULD YOU KEEP THIS A SECRET or BLESS YOUR GORGEOUS SOUL. "A mastermind," I agree. "Actually, I wore this outfit today because I thought it might suit the job interview I was on my way to. Which I need to call up and cancel . . ." I reach into my purse and pull out a completed application. "When did you say the job starts, again?"

"No later than April. Maybe March, if I can swing it. You still going to be unemployed by then?"

"I'm all in," Brandy says automatically.

That's a few months away. Well past January twenty-sixth, which in my head has signaled the time of death on my relationship with Nicholas. I don't think that's the case anymore. I think that come April, I'll still be living in that house in the woods.

"Yes, I'm going to wait for this job."

He shakes Brandy's hand, then mine. "Welcome aboard."

Brandy glances at the application in my other hand, then frowns and does a double take. "I wouldn't be using Melissa as a reference if I were you."

"I'm not."

She points at the number I have listed as my reference. "That's Melissa's number."

"No, it's—" I scroll through my contacts and stop dead. She's right. I'd meant to supply Melvin Howard's information and gotten Melvin mixed up with Melissa. "Oh, shit. This is the number I've been giving out everywhere I apply."

Her jaw drops. "No."

"Yes."

"Oh *no*, Naomi." She puts her hands over her mouth and snort-laughs. "I'm sorry, I shouldn't laugh. It's terrible. I'm so sorry, I really am."

The only reason I'm able to laugh along with her is that I've got a job now. "Laughing through my tears," I pretend-sob. "I don't want to assume that Melissa sabotaged me, but I also really want to think that now, because it'd be so nice to blame her for all those jobs turning me down."

"Melissa's the worst. Just for you, I'm gonna go to Let's Get

Crafty after this and mess up all the shelves. It'll take her ages to put everything back where it goes."

I give her a hug. "My sweet little protégé has come so far."

After I call my interviewer at the campground to cancel, we play Would You Rather and What's That Stain—the answer to which is almost always Zach, since he liked to secretly shake our sodas before we opened them. Brandy tells me he's busy forming a new religion in Florida. That absolutely sounds like something Zach would say, but whether he's telling the truth is anybody's guess. The man is an enigma.

Brandy and I head out to grab lunch for the three of us, and then it's just like old times again, minus Melissa and Zach. We're surrounded by sketches of what the Junk Yard is going to look like this spring, mocking up logos and a big road sign. Brandy uses a pencil to turn a hamburger grease stain on one of the papers into a lumpy rectangle. "And that'll be the karaoke machine."

"The *what* now?" says Leon.

"Oooh!" I squeal. "Karaoke! Brandy, that's a great idea. Five stars."

He stares at the grease stain with a look of revulsion. "Karaoke in a restaurant called Backwoods Buffet?"

"Yeah, and we'll do luaus! We'll put leis and grass skirts on your grizzly bears." I beam at him. "Don't lie. You love it. This is my decoration genius at work, remember."

He groans.

"All right, I've gotta go." Brandy wipes her salty fingers on my knee and I wipe mine on her back. Leon shakes his head at us. "Have to sit in a hot warehouse for the next eight hours while Bob, my boss, follows me around complaining about his ex-wife because he thinks women exist to listen to his problems. I can't wait to be out of there." She points sternly at Leon. "Don't you dare back out of this."

"I can't even tell you how much money I would lose if I backed out of this," Leon replies. "If I go down, you're all going down with me."

"Good. Because I'm going to spend the rest of the day dreaming about how I'm going to quit. I'm thinking it will be very dramatic. I'll throw a drink in Bob's face and say 'Go to hell!' and it will be amazing."

"Everyone will applaud," I say.

When she reaches the door, I call, "Text me info about those painting parties! Nicholas and I are going to drunk-paint with you and Vance the optometrist. Also, you guys are coming over to play Dungeons and Dragons sometime. I've never played before, but I feel like it will be an out-of-body experience for that nerd I live with, which I would like to witness."

Leon looks excited. "I like Dungeons and Dragons."

"You would, weirdo," Brandy says, just before the door shuts behind her. Through the glass, she yells, "Just kidding! Love you! Please don't fire me." Then she blows us a kiss.

I leave, too, still smiling from ear to ear long after I've climbed into my car. Who knows, the restaurant might only last a year. But I can guarantee it'll be a fun year. I couldn't ask for anything better than that. For the first time in a long time, my future unfolds before me bright with promise. I have dreams and goals and I will make them all come true. I can do anything, even learn how to change a tire.

I should probably learn how to do that, actually. Tomorrow I'm going to fire up the old YouTube and figure out how to do some of the stuff I've supposedly known how to do for ages. I'm going to symbolically adopt an endangered tiger and recycle my aluminum cans. I'm going to pay the library a sixty-five-cent fine I've owed for two years. I'm going to do three push-ups.

I come home to a purple front door and no fiancé. Or boyfriend, depending on whether he still wants to marry me. I'm not sure what to call him now. He's my friend. My partner. A selfless but complicated man who would drive seven hours because his parents asked him to, and he's a better son than they are parents.

He texts at six thirty. Finally done. Going to go grab dinner and find my hotel. How's your day been, Miss Backwoods Buffet?

That devious man. I'm going to kiss him so hard when he comes home.

I construct four casual, everything's-peachy replies but delete them. They're not the truth. The truth is this: I miss you so much. I wish you were here.

So that's what I send him.

I've been awake since before three a.m. and it's catching up. Upstairs, I pause at Nicholas's door. He could have locked it but he didn't. He could have shut it but he left it wide open, and I can't help the heartache that overtakes me when I see the palm leaves on his blanket. I miss that blanket terribly. I miss our headboard, and the glow of his digital clock. I miss our bed. The piece of furniture I've been sleeping on has never felt like my bed. How can it? There's no Nicholas there.

I snoop through his nightstand drawer to check if the straw wrapper bracelet is still there. It is. He's also got the notes I've packed in his lunch and the popcorn necklace I made him, stashed away like a teenage boy with a crush. He's pressed a stem of vitality-boosting myrtle between the pages of a book to preserve it forever. The tight, hibernating bud of a flower inside my chest yawns its petals wide open, taking up all the room until the pressure in my expanded rib cage leaves me airless.

Something is not right. Someone is missing. I am in knots.

I cross to my side of our bed and slide under the covers. I'll be long gone before he returns and he'll never know.

The bedclothes are cool and there's no dip of weight where another body should lie, but his scent is here. My eyelids are as heavy as iron doors and I finally let them roll closed, breathing in a million memories of Nicholas.

———

I'm asleep when it sinks into my consciousness that I'm not alone. I open my eyes to the darkness, fuzzy-brained and not quite out of my dream yet. It's late, after midnight. There's a man lying next to me, in exactly the place he's supposed to be. This is where he belongs, and yet it's a lightning strike straight to the heart to see him here.

"What are you doing home?" I blink several times, waiting for him to disappear. I'm still dreaming.

"You missed me."

"You came home because I missed you?"

He's got his elbow bent on the pillow, palm under the back of his head, watching me fathomlessly. His other hand drapes across his stomach. "Yes."

My pulse speeds up, because I'm in his room and he's caught me. He drove home all night in the snow and the dark and found someone sleeping in his bed. This is where he belongs, but he might not say the same about whoever it is he sees when he looks at me. Which Naomi? Can he tell a difference?

He sits up, leaning over me. My vision is adjusting to the dark enough to clear the shadows from his face, and now I can see that his gaze is liquid. His lips are a soft curve. "I missed you, too," he says, and presses those lips gently to mine.

I loop my arms around his neck and tug him closer, in case he has any ideas of retreating after one kiss. He smiles against my mouth, closes his eyes, and I melt into the feel of him against me. The kiss is a hungry, powerful force, but he breaks it so he can travel down and kiss my neck. My body reacts, breaking out into an inferno of heat, sensitizing, knowing he's the only one who can give me what I want. Into my skin, he murmurs, "I've missed you everywhere."

"Mm?"

"*Here*," he says as his lips brush where my heart beats, letting the pain and ache bleed into his voice. "I've missed you here." He kisses my mouth. "And here." My fingers tunnel into his hair, and his turn to fists that burrow into the mattress, lifting his body over mine. He stares deeply into my eyes. "Here."

The word is a pale breath.

"I've missed you, too," I reply, the edges of my vision going gray and blurry. Nothing else exists right now. The world begins and ends with this man.

I don't know I'm crying until he wipes it away and his own eyes shimmer with tears.

We deepen the kiss, and it says what we don't have to. I tug him closer, closer, until we align all over. When we part for breath, I ask, "Do you know you're my best friend?"

"Am I?"

His eyes are sapphires held in front of a roaring flame, glinting as they're turned. I know every microscopic detail of his face. I know the shape of his brows for every emotion. He is the most beautiful man who ever lived, and at one time I couldn't have said with any certainty what color eyes he had. He was no more memorable than a picture hanging on the wall that I'd long gotten used to. How many times did my gaze pass right over him, not realizing he was looking back at me? Always watching. Listening. Waiting.

"You are." My heartbeat is painfully strong and my torso is a twisted rag. My lungs claw for oxygen. Another tear slips over my cheek, which he kisses away.

I'm falling apart, and I think that Nicholas sees.

His hand is warm as it passes through my hair. His eyes are so tender that my muscles involuntarily relax, fingers uncurling. He buries his face in my throat and inhales. "God, I've missed you. Naomi."

My name trembles in the air, and speech has never been so hard to find. But he needs it. He needs me to give voice to my feelings, because he's not a mind reader and it's not okay that I soak up what he gives without offering myself in return. I can't let him think he's alone, not for one moment.

"I like it right here," I tell him, cradling either side of his face between my hands. "You make me happy. It makes me happy that you came home because I missed you; I'm appreciative of everything you do, for me and anybody else. I'm lucky to be with a thoughtful man like you and I'm sorry that I've taken you for granted and acted like a jerk. I'm thankful that you stayed put until I found you again. You supporting me, and making me feel valuable, is everything."

He smiles and leans his cheek into my palm. My throat constricts, more tears welling up. I blink and splash the pillow. It's not scary anymore to strip down like this in front of him. He's got me. He's right here, and I've got him, too. "Relearning you has been the best thing that's ever happened to me."

He rubs a thumb over my cheekbone, down to my jaw. "I'm thankful you've forgiven me," he says. "I'm sorry for every time I've ever made you feel unimportant. You are the *most* important, and I'm working on showing that better. You're my best friend, too. I have more fun with you than anyone else, and I like how you challenge me. I like being around you and when I'm not around you, I'm always thinking about you. I want you to know I'm thinking about you all the time."

It feels so lovely to be good to each other.

Being this close and not arching into him is an exercise in restraint. I'm starving, and I can feel that he is, too. He skates a heated glance down my body and his eyes haze, chest rising and falling more deeply.

I try not to let my voice shake when I say, "Where else have you missed me?"

He arches an eyebrow and a devious grin tugs at his lips. Actions, not words, are his reply. He divests me of my shirt and shows me *where* with his hands. My shorts and underwear follow, and he shows me with his mouth. Every little touch is magnified a thousandfold because it's been a hundred years and counting since we've been skin on skin. I'm on fire and this has got to be downright excruciating for him, so I pull him back up to me.

"Hey, there," he says softly.

"Mine." I don't have the mental faculties for conversation. I'm a single-minded cavewoman. "I need you. Now."

"You've still been taking the pill, right?"

"Yes."

I slam his mouth to mine and while our tongues are busy, I impatiently yank down the waistband of his boxers. He leans back somewhat to help, laughing against my cheek. I feel the vibrations all the way down and it makes me crazy; I'd shake him for his ability to be amused right now if his extremely urgent erection didn't tell a different story. He's multitasking again, being aroused and entertained at the same time. It's not fair that he can divide his attention and I can't.

I palm him between the legs, and am rewarded with a fluttering of eyelids, Adam's apple working up and down. His breath is sugar, the taste melting in my mouth.

"More?" I tease.

He lets his eyes fall closed and tilts his head back, surrendering to the sensations. "Yes."

"Yes, what?"

His eyes flare wide, holding me captive. He grates a word, low and guttural. "Please."

"Mmm, we'll see." I bite his lower lip gently between my teeth and scrape my nails down his chest, ending the journey with a tight stroke. I moan into his ear and steal away his hard-fought control. Nicholas groans when I undulate against him. His murmurs, too quiet for me to understand, track down my throat and chest until he finds something he likes.

His body is shadow, stardust, and moonlight. He angles his head in a studious way, scientific fingers exploring crests and valleys, burning slow circles with his touch. I whimper a plea and he smiles but doesn't oblige. He's in no rush, which makes no sense to me whatsoever. I'm impatient and if it were up to me, we'd already be going for round two.

Rather than heed my begging, he lets his teeth graze across the soft expanse of my stomach. His hand moves down between my legs and applies pressure, relenting for one single stroke. His lips blaze a trail from my shoulder to my hip bone in an agonizingly slow, languid process, curls tickling skin.

Darkness closes over me and I let my other senses assume control, light-headed from the rush of his wanting, his delicious weight sinking me into the mattress. I sigh his name while he touches and tastes at his leisure, and he rises over me, breath flaring across my naked chest like the smoke of a fire.

Saying his name is what topples him over the edge. It's the magic word.

He slams his wrists down on top of mine and is inside me before I can blink, swallowing my gasp down his throat. He feels *incredible*. He never stops kissing me as he moves in a measured, sensuous rhythm.

Nicholas smooths a hand around my waist, resting at the base of my spine so that he can hold me to him and do as he likes with perfect control. His face is tight in concentration, sweat gathering at his temples from the effort of holding back. He won't let me hurry him. Every time I try I'm chastised with a nip of teeth, the brand of his hand. His punishments are a reward of their own.

I kiss the soft flesh of a fluttering pulse on his neck, below his ear, and a deep rumble shudders through him. I take his chin in my hand and force him to look at me through half-lidded eyes that wrestle for control, to prolong this and make us suffer. His eyes are black as the night forest.

He rushes forward but his kisses are surprisingly gentle, halting the movement of our bodies. I want to protest, but he pulls back and I can see that he's thinking hard about something. Worry lines his forehead. He lifts my thigh and hooks it to his side, every muscle rigid as he starts moving again. I can trace the tendons in his neck and arms. "Nicholas?"

He gazes down on me. "Say you love me?" he whispers.

My heart bursts in my chest, white light popping behind my lids like fireworks. "I love you," I say, and watch it blaze through him. "Of *course* I love you, Nicholas." His thrusts meet every roll of my hips, and we both come apart.

My thoughts are impossible to sort through. My body feels amazing. Satisfied. It's never been like this, or if it was, I've forgotten. When our breathing evens out, I trace the shape of a heart on his chest. His hair is a dark halo on the white pillow, and his eyes are still burning when they fall on my face.

I grin at him. "That might be the one to beat."

"Even better than our first time?"

We both laugh, because our first time was a mess. He came to visit me on my lunch break at my old hardware store job and we ended up doing it in the storage closet. Standing up, he tried to position me against the wall and when we were done I came out to discover that hanging on the other side of that wall were tools, which now lay all over the floor. I'd forgotten to lock the front door, and the two customers browsing had likely gotten an earful.

"Remember that time in my car?" I snigger. "You got—"

"Hot coffee spilled all over us," he replies along with me. Nicholas groans. "Nothing kills the mood like scalding liquid on your crotch."

"*And he was never the same,*" I intone gravely. He smiles and elbows me.

"Felt terrible for ruining your sweater."

"I forgot all about that sweater. Hm. Worth it, though."

He twirls a lock of my hair around his finger. "Remember when we met?"

How we met is insignificant in light of how we met *again*. We met again while each trying our best to push the other one away. Whether we pushed each other too far remains to be seen. Can these past few weeks be real, and the past year a dream? Or is *this* the dream? We've been corrosive, and we can't undo it, only recover from it if we try harder at this than we've ever tried at anything. He's burrowed so deep beneath my surface, there's no separating him from tendons and bones, no getting him out of my blood.

Of course I remember. It's been sitting in the lost and found of happy memories, waiting for love to spin a revolution like the sun and light it up again.

"How could I forget?"

CHAPTER TWENTY

It's nearly two years ago and I'm at a bowling alley in Eau Claire for my dad's surprise party. Mom's got one of the tables bedecked with CONGRATULATIONS and HAPPY RETIREMENT balloons and a cake with a picture of his face in the icing. Aaron and Kelly, my brother and sister, are both in hateful moods for having to make the trip up. Kelly had to break plans with friends that she'd made after forgetting she agreed to come to this, and Aaron won't stop griping over the cost of gas. It's why he didn't bring a present. His presence is a present. Before he leaves, he's going to shake down Dad for twenty bucks.

Dad hates surprise parties and he didn't want to retire in the first place (his company forced him out, basically), so when he finally shows up he's in an evil temper to match everyone else's. Mom tries to be perky to save everything, but since she hates to bowl and spends the whole time talking on the phone to her sister, it just makes Dad grumpier and they all start fighting.

A man in the lane to our right is bowling alone. I know he can hear my family arguing, because even though I keep telling them to keep their voices down their hissing ends up being just as loud. Also, he's glanced in our direction a few times.

"Can I pretend I'm here with you?" I ask him jokingly. I'm holding a glittering nine-pound ball I got from behind the counter. I use children's bowling balls because my strengths lie in the mental arena rather than physical. I'm also not above requesting bumpers.

"Sure." He smiles at me, and my stomach does a little flip. He's got cute, wavy brown hair that curls slightly where it falls across his forehead, and an honest smile. Kind eyes.

"Thanks. My family never learned how to behave in public."

He chuckles and shakes his head. "My family could give them a run for their money, believe me."

Kelly's in tears. I hear her call Aaron an asshole for stealing five dollars from her purse to get a bag of weed from someone he just met in the bathroom, and I agree with her. He calls her an asshole right back because she once reported him to the IRS for not disclosing $125.00 he made staining our uncle's porch, so I agree with him too.

"Can't believe that, sorry," I deadpan, and we both laugh. I jerk my thumb at my siblings. "They probably haven't been great for your concentration."

"I have been a little distracted," he admits. Then he slides me a long look. "But it isn't because of them."

I think he's flirting. Is he? I become a cliché and turn around to make sure he's not actually addressing someone standing right behind me. Nobody's there.

His lips curve into a smile. "So, family issues aside, you seem pretty nice."

Do I? "I'm all right."

"And *I'm* nice," he says, hedging.

I'm cautious as I reply, "You might be."

"I've also been told I'm pretty cute." Yes, definitely flirting. My insides light up and play eight-bit music like I've won a game of pinball.

"You might be."

He grins, because I'm flirting right back. "You should go out with me tonight," he says casually, not breaking eye contact as he sends the ball skittering down his lane. I hear it break against a battalion of pin soldiers, but neither of us checks to see how he scored. We're staring at each other.

"On a date?"

"Yes."

There's nothing for me to do but laugh. I don't know this man. I don't live anywhere near Eau Claire. Our paths are never going to cross again. "Sure, I'll go out with you," I tell him. "If you manage to knock down all your pins right now."

He studies the pins he's got left. He's just bowled a split. His ball shot clean through the middle, knocking them all down except for the one on the far left and the one on the far right. Unless he's secretly a professional bowler who can curve gravity, there's no way he can bump off both foes. They're too far apart for him to ping one off the other, so the odds of getting a spare are astronomical.

His eyes glint. "You promise?"

I pause before I reply. I'd have to be an idiot to root for him, so that's what I do. "Sure, I promise."

As soon as the word leaves my mouth he starts walking right down the center of the lane and knocks over both pins with his shoe. He turns on his heel with a flourish, his reflection spanning over a shining, waxed floor, and sends me a devilish grin. I have to admit he's got me. The screen over our heads explodes with digital confetti and the letters for the word SPARE! tumble down with a cacophony like a bag of spilled coconuts.

He looks pleased with himself. There's an undeniable chemistry between us that tempts me to lean a little closer. Explore it. I should walk away, but I won't, because there's something here. It sucks that I live so far away. He won't bother once he hears I'm long-distance. But I have to let him know.

"I'm not local."

"I know," he replies, winking at a bowling alley worker who witnessed his stunt and is sending him a stern frown. "You're from Morris."

"When did I tell you that?"

"You didn't. I saw you there myself about two weeks ago loading groceries into your trunk. I live in Morris, too."

My mouth falls open.

He's delighted by my shock. "I wanted to walk over and say hi, but figured a strange man approaching you in a dark, mostly empty parking lot while you were alone wasn't the way to go." He lifts a shoulder like, *Hey what can you do.* "But I thought about it after that, wishing I could have another shot at it. How great would it be, to get a second chance? I've even gone back to that store a couple times, in case I might see you again."

I'm gaping at him, and I look over my shoulder to see if my family's eavesdropping. They're gone. They've left without saying good-bye, and it's just the two of us—me and this strange, increasingly dazzling man whose name I don't even know.

"Every year for my birthday, I go to my parents' house and my mom puts candles on a cake," he tells me. "Some Facebook friends from college write on my wall to say hey, and I wait until the day's almost over to reply because I want it to seem like I had better things to do all day than count how many happy birthdays I got. I never go anywhere else or really do anything. Today I woke up and felt like going bowling. It's the first birthday I've ever spent completely by myself. I didn't want to go to a bowling alley close to where I live because I didn't want to run into anyone I know, so I looked up other places online and found this one. Picked it at random. Eau Claire."

I am wholly riveted right now. His screen blinks in the periphery, nudging him to bowl another frame, but our eyes are glued to each other. We're standing close, but not close enough for me to clearly discern the color of his eyes. I think they might be gray.

"This is the first birthday I've been alive that I haven't blown out a candle and made a wish," he says, taking one deliberate step closer. All the oxygen in the building starts to evaporate, leaving me two insufficient gasps for each lung. "But you walked in here today, anyway. You ended up in the lane right next to mine, and you started talking to *me*, initiating conversation. What are the chances? Two people from Morris, meeting in Eau Claire? And the very one I wanted to meet."

I can't breathe. He steps closer and my pounding senses blur all of his features into a warm, rose-tinted haze. My brain kicks on and off, like I'm intoxicated. It's a struggle to stay upright. To not lean in that final inch. I don't know who this person is and I don't know what he's got planned for tonight but there's *something* here I've got to explore. If I don't, I think I'll regret it.

"For the first time," he finishes, "I've gotten my wish."

———

It's been so long since we've slept in the same bed together that when I wake up on Sunday morning all I want to do is stretch out and enjoy it. But Nicholas drove through the night to be with me, and I want to do something to make him feel special, too. The way to a man's heart is through his stomach, so I'm going to woo him with a home-cooked breakfast. And by home-cooked, I mean I'm going to buy one of everything on the menu at Blue Tulip Café.

Certain muscles that have been atrophying during our dry spell are stiff and sore from last night, and I stifle a small cry when I climb out of bed. I glance at Nicholas, who's lying on his back with his legs crossed at the ankles, sound asleep. Of the two of us, I'm the sprawler. He sleeps in a neat line like he's been laid in a tomb, taking up minimal room. I triple in size when I'm in bed, arms and legs fanned out, hair seeking his nose and mouth. These past few weeks of sleeping apart have probably been a mercy for him in this way, but too bad; his nights of rest and relaxation are over. I miss having someone to kick.

For a minute I merely stand there and admire him, a thrill shooting through my nervous system.

He loves me. He didn't return the words expressly after I spoke them, but I know he does.

On the kitchen table I spot a gift he's brought back from his trip: a glass paperweight with wildflowers preserved inside. He's found a way to make flowers functional and cost-effective. Smiling, I leave him a thank-you note.

I take Nicholas's Jeep so that I can fill up his gas tank for him, then top it off with a trip to the car wash. By the time I pull into the driveway with a huge haul from Blue Tulip riding shotgun, my head is buzzing with ideas for how we'll spend the day. It's too cold for outdoor activities, so maybe we'll do laser tag. Or go to the movies. I duck into my car real quick because I think I have a gift card for Beaufort Cinema in my glove box, and that's when I notice that the heap of trash bags next to the log pile has grown and the front door is open. It would seem that Nicholas has been busy since I left. He'd better not be in there making food.

We've been steadily clearing out junk Leon left behind in the shed, most of which was already there when he moved in. I glance at one of the trash bags, a gap in the opening from being too loosely tied. The powder-blue color inside sparks recognition, and I step closer. My heart beats a tattoo on my breastbone, but my brain riots against what I think it is, so I have to untie the bag. I have to be sure.

I take out the small box, one of many. There are five of them still in the bag, dented and smashed. A disposable plate smeared with ketchup has gotten on one of them, and I hunch over, lungs compressing to half their size. My ears are ringing with white noise and my eyes sting. I'm going to throw up.

It's the wedding invitations. He's thrown them all away.

Across the battlefield, Nicholas saunters gracefully forth, head held high. He twirls his sword. Contemplates. Then he spears me straight through the heart.

———

I leave the box on the ground and go back to my car without processing or planning any of my steps. I'm on autopilot. I'm a fatally wounded soldier crawling off to hide so I can die alone in peace. I dimly register Nicholas standing on the porch, and I think he might be calling my name, but every self-preservation instinct I have is kicked into full gear and I have to get out of here.

Instead of driving toward Morris, I hurry out of town. The twists and turns I make are like a paranoid criminal evading a cop car. I stop paying attention to road signs and choose the way at random. The only thing that matters is that he doesn't find me. I can't let anyone see me like this.

An hour passes before I find somewhere to park—a rest area enclosed by a crop of trees, the view through my windshield sloping down to a public lake. There's an RV ten spaces down the lot, but we're otherwise alone and I've got plenty of privacy. I press my forehead to the cool steering wheel and inhale deeply, releasing staggered breaths. It hurts. I'm hurting so bad, and I wish I could return to the Naomi Westfield who wanted Nicholas to throw out the invitations and call off the wedding. She would have been celebrating this.

The lake and trees swim. It's a misty, gloomy day, and I wouldn't be surprised if I keep on driving and driving, never to come back again. I'll leave Morris in my rearview mirror, bringing a long-standing fantasy to life.

The notification light on my phone is flashing. With shaking fingers, I toss it into the back where I hope it becomes irretrievably lost. I close my eyes but all I see is that smashed box of wedding invitations in my hands. When I lift my gaze to the windshield, my mind conjures up Nicholas standing in front of my car. A down-low heat ignites and ripples its way up, my anger a thundering roar. *Hurt me? I'll hurt you more.* Our old standby.

He has his feet braced apart as though he expects me to run him over but stands his ground anyway. I mouth a single word of warning. *Move.*

I read his lips. *No.*

We stare each other down. I let the car bump forward a few inches. Nicholas's eyes fly wide but he doesn't back off, calling my bluff. Not a wise choice. I honk my horn and he ignores it, planting a hand on my hood like his touch alone can stop me. To my undying frustration, I *feel* that touch. It's unforgivable.

I love him, I love him. I don't have to love every little thing about the man, but I love the man. He never said *I love you* back. *Say you love me?* That's what he said. But why would he say that if he didn't love me? What about the note he left calling me the most beautiful person he's ever known? What about the straw wrapper bracelet? He kept it. What a nothing thing that I made. What a nothing thing that he kept.

I refuse to believe we're still on opposite sides, but I also have a habit of ignoring reality.

The mist has thickened and it's foggy out as well, so I switch on my headlights as I reverse out of the parking lot. I can't sit still for too long or I'll combust. My conjured Nicholas dissipates in the high beams, gone with the flourish of my hand.

My soft, raw heart keeps presenting alternatives to what is happening. Defense mechanisms. *Maybe he loves you, but he just doesn't want to get married anymore.* That's not so bad. It'll stay the way it is now. It's finally feeling good again, even when it isn't always easy.

But then I remember Nicholas down on one knee, the rest of the world blending into oblivion. Peering up at me anxiously, heart in hand. *It's not enough for you to be my girlfriend. I need you to be my wife.*

Not anymore, it seems. Maybe he only loves me eighty per-cent. No. There's no such thing as loving somebody eighty per-cent.

Am I okay staying with this man if it turns out he *does* love me but doesn't want to wear my ring on his finger? Maybe he'll change his mind someday. Maybe he didn't mean to throw out six boxes of wedding invitations. Maybe he meant to put them in storage but got the bags mixed up. It's all an accident, a mis-understanding, and we'll laugh about this someday.

Either that or in a few months, Nicholas will have moved on to somebody else. This mystery woman will sleep on the palm-leaf comforter he and I picked out together. She'll have the purple front door, and the narrow middle bedroom that could one day be a nursery. She'll have Nicholas's smiles, his skin on hers, his breath coiling in her hair while she sleeps. She'll have Nicholas.

I could pretend I never looked inside the trash bag. I could drive home right now and come up with an excuse. I'll say that after I left his Jeep in the driveway with the keys still in the igni-tion, food on the passenger seat, I was gripped by a sudden, all-consuming desire to get in my car and drive to the mall. I'll say my phone died. I won't acknowledge what I saw in the trash and it'll be like it never happened. I can't remember if I shoved the box back into the bag before I left, or if I tied it up. I hope I did. If I just left it sitting there, he'll know I found out.

His actions last night make no sense today. How could I have misread him so wrongly? Maybe he only made love to me because he'd been driving all night and he was tired. He wasn't himself. He woke up regretting what we did, possibly feeling taken advantage of. He's mad at me. He thinks I tricked him.

The hours slip away as I drive and drive and drive. It's dark when the road inevitably takes me back to Morris, even though I beg it not to. I still have no idea what I'm going to do. I don't have any cash left after refilling on gas and keeping myself busy all day, which just leaves me with my credit card. The second a hotel charges me for a night's stay, it's going to pop up on his phone because we share the account and he gets a notification whenever a charge is made.

I'm hungry and haven't eaten anything today, so I park in front of Jackie's and go get two large orders of fries. I sit on the hood of my car and eat, the food warm in my cold fingers. I know what's coming. I knew it since I handed my card to the cashier, and I've accepted it, which is why I don't move a muscle when a Jeep Grand Cherokee rolls into the parking space next to mine.

I just stare straight ahead and eat another fry. I feel him watching me. Is this what he wanted? Either I know him better than anyone on this earth or I don't know him at all. There is no in-between.

Nicholas leaves his car. Out of the corner of my eye I see that he's clutching a dented blue box of invitations, and my throat burns like I've swallowed acid. "Naomi," he says.

I can't do this. "Please don't. You win, okay? It's over. I'll end it so you don't have to."

He sits down next to me, car creaking under his weight. He balances the box carefully on his lap, and just having it this close makes the splinters of my heart prick my chest walls. We'll never sit down and address them together. Our loved ones will never open them and smile, and say, *They're really getting married, then. They're really going to do it.* We'll never face each other across a flower-strewn aisle and promise ourselves to each other forever.

"What do you mean, 'over'?" Nicholas asks, quiet and throaty. "Don't tell me you're trying to break up with me after all we've been through. That's not happening."

"Isn't that what you want?"

"No." His fingers slide under my chin, raising me to eye level with him. His gaze radiates an emotion I'm convinced he doesn't feel, and it's agony. "Sweetheart . . ."

My eyes cut to the box on his lap and I want to throw it. "Stop. I don't want to hear anything else. It's not necessary."

"Oh, I think it's very necessary."

"It's over. Just leave me alone."

His eyes are smoldering. "Naomi, if you say one more time that we're over, I'm going to lose my mind. I've been going crazy all day, not knowing where you went. You didn't answer your phone, and when you drove away your driving was jerky and all over the place. Do you have any idea what that did to me? I was on the verge of calling up hospitals when I saw the credit card charge."

It's ridiculous that I feel guilty for worrying him. "I want you to go away. Please."

"Because of this?" He taps the blue box, and I flinch.

"Because I've had a change of heart."

I'm off the car before I know what's happened, caged between the cold metal of the hood and Nicholas. There's no room to dodge around him, nowhere to go. My senses reel, overpowered by him, collapsing into his touch to meld us perfectly together. His dark stare glitters with fear and fury, and something else that takes me another half second to translate. Need. Deep and burning. If I weren't pinned, my knees would buckle.

He places his hand over my thumping, traitorous heart, commanding every nerve ending, every desire. I am wide, wide awake. He shudders an exhale and his face descends so close that I think it must end with a kiss, which is why I close my eyes.

"Your heart is mine," he says.

CHAPTER TWENTY-ONE

Nicholas opens the box and removes an invitation. An RSVP card falls out and tears away, pinwheeling across the parking lot. "I've kept one of these folded up in my wallet for months," he tells me. "I'd take it out and look at it sometimes, and I'd smile because I was so excited to marry you. But then I stopped being happy when I looked at them."

"Because you stopped wanting to marry me."

He hands me the invitation. "How do you feel when you hold this?"

"Sad," I reply truthfully.

"Read it. Tell me then what you feel."

I'm so empty, you could hear the wind blow through me. But I sit back down on the car, Nicholas hopping up beside me, and have to read the fancy curling script twice before it digests.

DEBORAH AND HAROLD ROSE
Proudly present the union of their son Dr. Nicholas Benjamin Rose
At 1:00 pm on January the twenty-sixth at St. Mary's Church
To Naomi Westfield
With a reception to follow at Gold Leaf Banquet Hall
Black tie only
No children or service animals permitted

I haven't given these invitations a second glance since they arrived in the mail, and my response is the same flare of annoyance. Nicholas observes my reaction and nods. "Exactly. Do those look like they should be our invitations? Are those our words? Does any of that feel representative of our marriage? Your middle name isn't even on here."

"It's not what I would have picked," I admit, hearing the bitter notes in my voice. "But I didn't pay for them, so. Didn't get the final say."

"Isn't that insane, though? That you didn't get the final say?" He examines the invitation. "Never decided on a picture to put in these, either. It's just as well, since those pictures memorialize an unhappy day. I remember you weren't feeling well, and I didn't like my outfit. We were annoyed with each other, standing in front of the photographer with fake head-over-heels smiles."

"True."

"And these ribbons?" He touches one of the ivory silk bows on the invitation. There are tons of them, with faux pearls in the centers. "Does this resemble our taste at all? I've had a good long time to think about this, and when I look at these invitations they don't feel like ours."

"They're not. They're your mother's." I look him right in

the eye. "If you didn't like the decisions she made, you should have spoken up."

"I know. I'm sorry I let her take over everything . . . I knew how it was making you feel and I just let her do it because at the time it was easier for you to be upset with me than to have Mom upset with me. Which is screwed up."

"Yes, it is." There's no point rubbing his nose in it, so I add, "You're getting better, though. You've been defending me. You haven't let any of her insults slide. And for your own sake, I'm glad you haven't been going over there every day and taking all of her calls."

"It helps that I have you beside me, encouraging me." He rests his head on my shoulder. "You make it easier."

"I haven't always made it easier."

He takes my hand and squeezes. "I was sorting through things to throw away this morning, and found the boxes. It was the most natural thing in the world to toss them."

"Wow," I remark hollowly. "Don't bother to soften the blow or anything."

"Sweetheart, why would we have a wedding in St. Mary's? Why would we use a stuffy banquet hall for our reception? Do either of those places hold any personal significance for us?"

"No, but—"

"It should be about *us*," he continues urgently, taking both of my hands in his and turning us fully to face each other. "And the guest list! It's a mile long. I don't know most of the names on there. Why would we crowd all of these strangers around us for the most special moment of our lives?" He crushes an invitation into a ball, and I wheeze out a gasp. "These are for a fake wedding. I threw away the invitations because I don't want any of those people there."

My eyes are saucers. "None of them?"

"Why would I? This isn't about anybody but me and you. The only people I care to have at our wedding are those who have treated both of us well. That rules out just about everybody I know, including the person who designed these invitations."

I can't conceive of a wedding between us in which Deborah isn't the grand marshal. She'd never let us get away with excluding her. For Deborah, our wedding is a social event at which she can preen and trot around her son like a pageant mom. She can't wait for all the other moms in her circle to congratulate her. "What about our families?"

"Fuck our families. Fuck everybody." He throws the crumpled invitation at a dumpster. It bounces off the rim.

I burst out laughing. I know he doesn't mean that, but maybe for one day, he's right. On a sacred day that signifies putting each other above all else, celebrating a deeply personal commitment, maybe we shouldn't have to accommodate the wants or opinions of others. We should do what feels right for us and no one else.

"We'll make our own family," he says earnestly.

I shake my head and muse, "You've lost it." I take an invitation from the box, smash it into a ball, and shoot it at the dumpster. It misses.

"If I've lost it, then good riddance to whatever it was that I had."

Scrunching up our wedding invitations and vaulting them in the general vicinity of a garbage can is strangely cathartic. Once we get started, we can't stop. We pile them up like snowballs on the hood and take turns trying to make it in the dumpster. He scores eleven and I score nine.

"This one's my grandmother's," I tell him as I hurl a snowball of paper and ribbons. "For pressuring me to wear her veil even though she could tell I didn't like it, and for suggesting I might be too old to bear children." I land my shot and Nicholas cheers. "Suck it, Edith! You're officially uninvited!"

"This one's your brother's," he replies, swinging an arm around like a baseball pitcher and letting it fly. It misses its mark by a mile and ends up in the road. "I know you stole my sunglasses, Aaron!"

"I can't wait to throw your mom's."

"Oh, please, let me. I've earned it."

He's right, this honor belongs to Nicholas. I hand him a fresh invitation just so he has the satisfaction of crumpling it with Deborah's name in mind. He grinds it with precise ferocity and it arcs over the dumpster, pinging off a stop sign.

"If I make this one," I say, tossing an invitation snowball from one hand to the other, "you have to pick up this mess by yourself while I watch and eat fries. I'm not getting fined for littering." I squint and aim carefully, but miss. Of course.

"Ha!" he crows. "Sucker. If I make this, you have to go back inside and buy me a chocolate shake."

Nicholas misses, too. "Damn."

I snort. "Your aim's even worse than mine."

"Your face is worse," he mutters, to which I have to laugh.

There's one last invitation in the box. I wad it up with purposeful slowness. "If I make this shot . . ." I think of the craziest outcome to all this I can come up with. It makes perfect sense. "You have to marry me. Not someday, and not maybe. We do this now."

I swing my arm back and am about to let it go when Nicholas catches my wrist. He plucks the invitation from my fingers, slips down off the car, and walks over to the dumpster. He very deliberately drops it inside.

I raise an eyebrow at him when he walks back to me.

He stops a foot away, hands sliding into his pockets. His eyes are no longer teasing. "I'm not leaving you and me up to chance."

I stare at him. He's dead serious. "Really? You want to get married?"

"Really. There's no one else I want to torture but you."

I can't stop staring at him. The way he's talking, it sounds like he's offering me everything I want. I'm dying to take it on trust, but there's a crucial part of myself I've given him, which he hasn't yet given in return. "But you still haven't said you love me."

"That's not true."

"You haven't."

"I say it all the time, I just say it very, very quietly. I tell you when you're in another room, or right after we hang up the phone. I tell you when you've got headphones on. I say it after you shut the door behind you. I say it in my head every time you look at me."

He steps closer, until we're breathing each other's air. I don't know what the right thing to say is, but luckily Nicholas does. He's got me.

He cups my face in his hands and brushes his lips over mine, his gaze so soft, a smile curving the edges of his mouth. "Of course I love you, Naomi. I never stopped."

It takes six days for the marriage license to be granted after we apply, and for now we're just holding on to it until the right moment.

Nicholas and I are driving back from an afternoon of laser

tag, thanks to him taking a sick day at work. His hand rests on the gearshift, and he's facing straight ahead at snow gusting across the road. It's not snowing right now but it has been all day, white drifts rising twelve inches on either side of us. I cover his hand with mine and feel that barely discernible flex, an automatic response that feels like reassurance and unity.

"I vote we invite your parents next time," I say, imagining Deborah and her fresh manicure holding a laser gun like a dead spider. Harold huffing and puffing, trying to shoot her.

He cackles. This fits perfectly into our plan of changing up how we spend time with his parents—finding a way to make it entertaining for us so that family togetherness doesn't feel like a draining obligation for the rest of our lives. We have a long list of weird experiences we're going to subject them to, and last night we drank too much wine and fell off the bed (okay, maybe I'm the only one who fell off the bed) laughing at each other's suggestions while trading the notepad back and forth.

We haven't breathed a word about the marriage license to them. We'll break the news after we're already married and throw a reception at a bowling alley in Eau Claire. Or maybe we'll write a letter to *Dear Deborah* at the *Beaufort Gazette* and tell them that way. If she doesn't have a meltdown about our imperfect ceremony, she definitely will when she hears we're combining our surnames to create a brand-new one unique to us. Rosefield.

I shiver and crank up the heat. The paperwork that says Nicholas and I are legally allowed to marry within the next thirty days glows from the glove box, and I pick up the conversation where we left it off before laser tag. "Plane tickets this time of year are going to be expensive."

"True. I'm not sure I want to fly in this weather, anyway. I'm already such a bad flyer, and if it's snowing I'll be freaking out up there."

"That rules out Bridal Cave in Missouri and that glacier in Alaska." We'd been considering courthouse nuptials, but then I typed *interesting wedding destinations* into a search engine and the results inspired us to be more imaginative when it comes to eloping. Eloping is fantastic, by the way. I highly recommend doing it if you ever get the chance. All the fun of getting married, none of the stress of planning a traditional wedding.

"Do you have a favorite day of the week?" I ask. "For example, I would not want to get married on a Monday."

"Oh?" He slides me a brief glance. "Why is that?"

"I think it would increase the chances of anniversaries falling on a Monday. Which are never good days."

"I don't have a preference for the day of the week," he replies, "but I'd rather not get married in the morning. My hair looks best when it's had a few hours to breathe." I nudge him, and he makes a show out of combing his fingers through his brown waves. He's only half joking; his hair is indisputably peak-glorious in the latter half of the day.

I love talking about wedding details. I love hearing Nicholas casually discuss spending the rest of his life with me. I don't bother to hide my happy dance, and while I don't look over at him I know my elation is contagious and he's smiling.

"I have some of Wisconsin's waterfalls mapped," I suggest. "Might be cool to get married in front of a waterfall."

"Or on a scenic trail. Plenty of those around here."

"If we're going to get married on a scenic trail, we might as well just get married in our own backyard," I joke. Then we both freeze and stare at each other, because it's perfect.

"Why is that not the first place we thought of?" Nicholas says wonderingly.

"Right?" I'm dumbfounded that it's taken us this long. "The pretty trees. The pond. Imagine the barn in the background, all those icicles coming down. And snow everywhere! Oh, it'll be a fairy tale."

"Walking to our honeymoon will take thirty seconds. Free lodgings. We won't have to pack."

"Yes." I clap. "Yes, yes, yes."

"And to think, we were considering getting on a plane and flying all the way to Juneau to stand on a glacier and be just as cold as we are here. And we own the venue!" He swings a look at me and grins. "Naomi, we're getting married."

We pass the Junk Yard, and I crank around in my seat to peer out the back windshield. "Wait! Turn around."

"What? Why?"

I pat his arm repeatedly. "Turn around, turn around!"

"You turn around first, crazy lady, and then I will." He reverses in a driveway. "Where are we going?"

"Right here." I point at the Junk Yard. There are two cars out front—Leon's and Mr. Howard's. I don't know right away why we needed to turn around, but I *know* it, and wait for the reason to catch up to me. My instincts were right, because I remember:

"My old boss, Melvin, is an ordained minister."

Nicholas parks and stares at me. "Seriously?"

I'm so excited, I can't speak. All I can do is nod. It's not a Monday, it's not morning, and opportunity knocks. Mr. Howard walks out of the shop carrying the sign from above the register, *It's the little things*, and stops when he sees me. I wave, opening my passenger door.

"Hey! Do you have a minute?"

The best weddings are surprise weddings. I had no idea when I woke up this morning that I'd be getting married today, and I hope it's a sign. I hope our marriage is full of spontaneous surprises like this one, and plan Cs that go spectacularly right.

I dig through the closet of what's going to be a guest bedroom, now that I'm not sleeping in it anymore. Every article of clothing I own is swallowing the bed or scattered all over the floor. What do you wear to a spontaneous backyard wedding?

My nicest dress is sleeveless and about as thin as tissue paper. I'd turn into a Popsicle.

I try on a sweater and immediately rip it off. I try to layer a turtleneck and leggings under a different dress, but they don't mesh well. "How's it going?" Nicholas calls through the door. I bet it took him fifteen seconds to get dressed, the heathen.

"I have nothing to wear!"

"Go naked, then."

I throw a shoe at the door and he laughs. "Hurry up!" he says. "I want to marry you."

"Hush, go away. I love you."

"I love you, too. See you on the other side."

I hear the staircase creak as he heads downstairs, and resist the temptation to look out the window and see if he's out there yet. I open the door, thinking to tiptoe into our bedroom and plow through his wardrobe in search of something better to wear, but step in a puddle of fabric laid in front of the door.

Coveralls. I pick them up and shake them out. They're mine, the smaller of the pair. They're practical and they're not much to look at, but if you're going to be standing outside in seventeen-degree weather reciting your vows, layers aren't a bad idea. I smile and yank them on over ordinary clothes. Then I yell for Brandy, who bounds up the stairs with a hairbrush and curling iron. Brandy is one of the exceptions to our no-guests rule, since she's positive and respectful of our choices and won't cast a shadow on our day.

"Ready?" she asks happily.

"Good luck. You're going to need it."

"Oh, shush. You have nice hair." She shoves me into a chair and begins to fuss with my bangs, which have grown out a smidge. Nicholas thinks he doesn't like bangs, which goes to show he doesn't know what he's talking about, since he keeps falling in love with me whenever I have bangs.

She gives me a crown braid that I never could have pulled off arranging myself, and when she's finished I'm pleasantly surprised by the Naomi who blinks back at me in the mirror. My hair is actually pretty darn cute. "Stunning," she says, hugging me as she hops up and down. "Here, I brought you this." She opens her palm and shows me a breath mint.

"Wow, thanks so much," I reply dryly.

"It's my wedding present to Nicholas. Girl, no one wants to kiss a quesadilla."

I pop the mint and swipe on simple lip balm for a finishing touch. Leon, the other exception to our no-guests rule, is waiting downstairs. Mr. Howard must already be outside with Nicholas.

"Your husband-to-be made this for you," Leon says, handing me a bouquet of snipped evergreen branches. I hold them to my nose and twirl.

"How do I look?" I pose for them.

"Like you're gonna go spray somebody's crawl space for termites," he says.

"Excellent. That's what I was going for."

Brandy offers me her arm, which I accept. I thought Brandy was here to be my maid of honor, but evidently she's going to be giving me away. "You ready?"

"I'm beyond ready. Need to go lock that man down before he gets any ideas and escapes."

We all walk out the back door into lavender twilight, picking our steps carefully down the snowy hillside. There's no aisle. There are no flocks of bridesmaids or groomsmen, no flower arrangements, no flash of a photographer. It's as far from St. Mary's as you could get.

The forest retreats into a black smudge, cold air rushing into my lungs. The man I love is waiting for me at the pond's edge, and I feel his pulse as if it's my own. My senses kaleidoscope, collecting pictures and scents and sounds to preserve until my dying day. I've been holding my breath since the second I met him; how strange now, to exhale at last. Breathing will never feel the same again.

I'm sure the scenery is lovely, but it dawns on me that it doesn't matter where we are. Nicholas could be standing in a storm, a desert, a vacuum. I wouldn't know the difference, because he's all I see.

He hits me with a smile so beautiful that it swells me with more emotion than can fit inside my body. The word *love* feels like Nicholas. It's filled all the way up with him. One day that word will evolve, filling up with the people we bring into this world together. I can't wait to see what kind of magic we spin with that word, how many shapes it will take. I can't wait to see how many memories emerge from our decision to stand right here, right now, and take each other for better or worse. As far as that goes, I say: bring it on.

We already know each other's worst. We've battled right through it and come out the other side unbreakable. There will inevitably be arguments, concessions, and peace treaties drawn up in spilled blood, sweat, and tears. We're going to have to choose each other, over and over, and be each other's champion, never letting ourselves forget the good whenever we're stuck in a patch of bad. It's going to be work. But let me tell you something about Nicholas Benjamin Rosefield:

He's worth it.

Nicholas's eyes glimmer with unshed tears and his smile is luminescent. Like me, I know he's not taking any of this for granted.

How great would it be, to get a second chance?

The sun descends over the curve of the earth and plunges the sky into a brilliant spectacle of blues and purples that play off the snow like the northern lights. He takes my hands in his, examining my icy red fingertips. He blows gently across them to warm them up, then pulls me closer to share his heat. He's got a sprig of evergreen in the utilitarian front pocket of his coveralls, like a boutonniere, which makes me laugh.

The thing about a wedding is: you don't remember the vows. You forget them the second after your mouth utters the sacred words, because your brain needs the room to catalog every detail of your partner's face. All of my concentration is on him. Everything is wonderful. Every day is the same. Every day is like our wedding day.

Mr. Howard's words are so quiet in my ears, it's like they're coming from another world. Nicholas's mouth hitches at the corners, just a little, before he leans in. His gaze rises from my lips to my eyes, and whatever it is about the way I'm looking at him gives him pause. Makes him kiss my forehead softly before dropping to impart the kiss that will make me his wife.

Diamond twinkles of snow tumble around us as I tug my fingers through his hair and kiss him again and again, this man who belongs irrevocably to me.

How did Nicholas and I meet?

We met in a house called Ever After, the second time we were strangers. And I am one hundred percent in love with the transformation of us.

ACKNOWLEDGMENTS

It takes a village to give a book a pulse, and my village is incredible. To my literary agent, Jennifer Grimaldi, who changed my life in a nanosecond: thank you, thank you, thank you for championing my story, for helping me polish it until it gleamed, and for connecting me with my film agent, Alice Lawson (another genie who makes magic happen), and the publisher of my dreams, Putnam. If you'd told me when I started writing this novel that I was going to end up *here*, I would have laughed myself out of a chair. When I think of all the people who have said yes (and enthusiastically!) to this book, I still want to pinch myself.

To Margo Lipschultz, superstar editor: I offer thee a figurative garden of camellias, which according to one site means gratitude (but according to another means "longing" and "flawless beauty," so take your pick). I'm so lucky to have you on this ship with me, making my days brighter with your emails, your passion for this story and these characters, and your fabulous expertise. Thank you also to my lovely UK editor with Piatkus, Anna Boatman, and high fives all around to the wonderful Putnam team: Sally Kim, Tricja Okuniewska, Ashley McClay, Alexis Welby, Brennin Cummings, Tom Dussel, Ashley Tucker, Mia Alberro, Marie Finamore, Bonnie Rice, Ivan Held, Christine Ball, Amy Schneider, and the art team: Vikki Chu, Christopher Lin, and Anthony Ramando.

Enormous, eternal gratitude is owed to Marcus, my husband and dashing, dependable hero. I wouldn't be able to write a single word were it not for your support, which has never wavered. It's been my lifelong dream to be an author, and because of your hard work and sacrifices I get to stay home every day and write stories with the silliest, sweetest children on earth. Lillie, Charlie, and Baby Number Three: I love you all to the moon and back. You bring so much fun and joy to my life. Also, this is definitely the only part of the book you're allowed to read.

Something else: I think it's important to be transparent about what comes *before* the good news. While *You Deserve Each Other* is my official debut and my experience with it so far has been out-of-this-world amazing, it is far from being the first novel I've written. To my fellow writers in the querying trenches—worrying, revising, and starting over for the umpteenth time: never give up, no matter what anyone says. If you keep writing and keep trying, you'll uncover the story that's meant to be. Those are simply the odds.

Thank you to the lovely authors who agreed to read this book in advance, and who have generously spread the word about it online. Your support has been amazing! Thank you to Skypeland, my first readers, whose friendship, cheerleading, and caps lock feedback encouraged me to keep writing. You talented ladies have all been massive inspirations and I cannot *wait* to line my shelves with your books!

One last thank-you goes out to you, the reader, whoever you may be. You took the time to read my story, and for that I am forever grateful.

Keep reading for an exciting excerpt from
Old Flames and New Fortunes by Sarah Hogle.

CHAPTER ONE

BLACKTHORN: OUR PATH IS BESET WITH DIFFICULTIES.

Twin purple roses, one bud closed. *Love at first sight.*

A two-leafed red carnation. *I must see you soon.*

Eight-and-a-quarter inches of grape ivy. *I desire you above all else.* The magic hums to let me know I'm on the right track, and I smile, busily fulfilling a pickup order at my luckiest time of day.

It is late April, when flowers have begun to swallow up the stone walls, when it's just warm enough that I can take my coffee in the courtyard at dawn and watch blue chase pink from the sky, stars popping like soap bubbles. My world is alive with the fragrance of freshly turned soil and shivering mist, chickens clucking around my ankles and eating the bugs on the brick pavers before the bugs can eat my crocuses.

To my back is the carriage house I've lived in for the past three years, built in the French country style, with sandy stone and white shutters decorated with moss and ivy. Rows of elevated flower beds burst with riots of hellebore, bleeding heart, forget-me-nots, bluebells. This courtyard, with its five-foot-tall perimeter and the witch hazel tree that's even older than the neighborhood, flowering quince with peach blooms, the shock of yellow sunrise forsythia—is all my kingdom.

My heart tap-dances to a song in my soul, inherited from my grandmother, who inherited it from hers, and yes, I can believe it. Curious tourists in my family's shop ask me frequently: *Do you believe it, truly?*

I reach for buttercups—*What golden radiance is yours!*—but catch my hand drifting, landing inexplicably on blackthorn: *Our path is beset with difficulties.* My hand jumps back.

"No, it is *not*," I tell the flowers sternly, plucking a buttercup instead. "Your path is simple and happy, and ends in a September wedding, just like Cecelia dreams." Cecelia, one of my regulars, is determined to turn her boyfriend into a husband. Of course, my flowers won't *force* him to propose. They'll merely spark an idea in his mind, if magic agrees with the pairing. The spell is informed by the flowers' traditional symbolism and how each flower reacts to the others. The twin purple roses are representative of how they met, the carnation expresses urgency, and the ivy symbolizes how Cecelia feels. They tell a special story, one imbued with magic to help spur on Cecelia's wishes: *Once upon a time soon to come, Gustav will happen to be ten minutes early for work, so he'll decide to walk the long way around, passing a jewelry shop. He'll glance in the window, and right there in the front, he'll notice a gem that'll remind him of his beloved Cecelia.* Now, magic can tempt Gustav to the shop, but whether he chooses to walk inside is his own business.

I'm pretty sure I invented flora fortunes. I call myself a *flora fortunist* since "creating floral arrangements using the language of flowers to magically bring a person's romantic hopes to fruition" is a mouthful. Much like tarot or palm readings, I can't cast my own will over a person's destiny. I can only intuit what a person's love life needs and try to attract what they desire—to get the object of their affections to notice them, to get over an ex, or to encourage their ex to get over *them*. My spells never force love, only open up possibilities.

With the buttercup added to the mix, I'm overcome by a tingly slide of wrongness; whenever I make a misstep, I get a sensation like I've put one foot through a rabbit hole in a field, I've sat in something sticky, or there's dust in my eye. Itching and muck and bad tidings, the dread of having missed an appointment, a phantom popcorn kernel I can't get out of my teeth.

Tossing out the buttercup, I use my pruning shears to snip off six inches of blackthorn (which does *not* align with Cecelia's hopes for an imminent wedding).

Just like that, the wrongness clears away.

I hear an internal *click* of a door unlocking: In my mind's eye, light glows through a keyhole, and with it, a rush of air scented with greenery. The sensation of getting a flora fortune right is different every time—all I know to expect is something wonderful. I close my eyes, bracing—

And taste pumpkin buttercream frosting on my tongue. The image of my grandmother's beige apron with the red stars stitched on the front pocket, which she wore when I was little, comes rushing back. Licking the icing off my hand while leafing through an *American Girl* catalogue. Standing on a stool, mixing batter. Dottie's baked talismans! All in a moment, I've gained

access to every lost memory of the pumpkin treats my grandmother used to bake for the autumn equinox, and it's almost as
if she's here again.

Every time I weave together a flora fortune the way magic
wishes me to, it rewards me with a uniquely pleasant sensation,
a ray of happiness that can light up the rest of the day, sometimes a long-forgotten memory unburied. There is no physical,
provable indication that a spell has occurred. It all takes place in
the heart. And this is why, even though I feel magic's effects as
surely as I feel the brush of clothing against my skin, most folks
don't believe witchcraft is real.

Ironically, I have trouble explaining my particular magical
skill set to other witches, too, since as far as I know, nobody else
has this ability. I know a witch who can influence the weather
with their emotions, another who has lucky bakes. But magic
took note of my keen interest in garden spells and floriography
and combined them into a whole new branch just for me.

The symbolic language of flowers is greatly varied: There is
Victorian floriography, which is the most well-known. In the
Victorian days, you couldn't go around flirting openly with
someone you had the hots for because everybody had to conform to oppressive decorum, so they'd wear an apple blossom if
they hoped a certain suitor would try a little harder, and that
sort of thing. There's also Hanakotoba, Japanese floriography,
which, just like Victorian floriography, assigns symbolism to
popular plants and flowers. Sometimes, a plant has different
meanings across cultures, and sometimes it's more or less uni-
versal.

I go with whichever meaning feels right, favoring the more
descriptive, poetic ones I've cobbled together from books and

websites. Some of the symbolism I even make up myself, if I feel no existing meaning fits.

I stare at the arrangement in my hands. The composition of this magic doesn't strike me as being meant for Cecelia anymore, but I don't get the vibe that it matches any of my other customers' unfulfilled orders, either, so I'm not sure who it might belong to. Whoever it is, the poor thing's love story looks convoluted, with an undercurrent of imminence, of reunion. Cogs whirring, destiny underway.

Clutching the strange bouquet, I step through the back door of the main building, into the wraparound sunroom where more of my flowers grow, accidentally knocking over a planter and spilling soil across the floor. As I sweep it up, I elbow my toad-flax, which topples into the arbutus, two plants whose symbolism are total opposites (*Be more gentle in your wooing* and *Be mine, I beg of you*). These plants don't like touching each other, clashing energies like an angry cat's bottlebrush tail.

"You all right?" Luna calls out.

I need more room in here goes without saying. "Yeah," I grumble, finishing up the job and heading into The Magick Happens. Built in 1850, the shop predates the town's establishment. A great brick square with glossy black shutters, gas lantern sconces, and a gold, purple, and green medieval banner with a gold cauldron on it that reads THE MAGICK HAPPENS by the front door, it began its life as a stagecoach inn. In the 1970s, Dottie Tempest purchased what was, at the time, a music store, and abracadabra'd it into a boutique for candles that set your love fate in motion. Luna, my oldest sister, learned candle-making at Dottie's knee and has carried on the tradition, filling the main shop floor from top to bottom with candles.

The floors are rustic maple, walls papered with a misty forest pattern of pale grays, greens, and blues the color of dusty miller in early morning frost. A bright, polished staircase that leads to Luna's apartment above is roped off from customers, shelving beneath it occupied by crystals, velvet drawstring bags filled with stones or dried herbs, and talismans. Everything smells like old wood, a long history, and wax in every scent imaginable.

The room splits off to the right into a low passageway lit by electric torches, making a 180-degree turn before ramping steeply down, directly below the shop into three small rooms devoted to fantasy and paranormal fiction as well as witchy how-to books, which we call the Cavern of Paperback Gems. Signed copies of Zelda's cozy paranormal mystery series have a table all to themselves.

Even though Zelda, the middle Tempest sister, is eight hours away in Treasure Cove, Virginia, she runs the Cavern remotely. She sends us handwritten descriptions on note cards, monitors inventory, and purchases titles to have delivered to our doorstep. A playlist called "Ren Faire" sends trills of fiddle and cittern throughout my and Luna's domains, but not down in the Cavern, where Zelda plays either the *dark and stormy night* playlist or *Bram Stoker's Dracula: Original Motion Picture Soundtrack*, depending on her mood. A special old-fashioned phone rests on the wall beside an embroidery hoop that reads *Dial 3 for Recommendations*, which connects directly to Zelda's phone.

Do I believe in magic, truly?

In a place like this, it's impossible not to.

But lately, the magic's been changing. What once was a fluttery zing is a dense churning, manic and confused thanks to the chaos of plants I've got crammed in the sunroom, all the different energies mingling at too-close range. The state of our atmosphere is downright unpleasant. Ordinary customers don't notice, but to my eyes, nettles and lady's slipper three feet from each other spells palpable disaster. I've got dried flowers suspended from the ceiling, vines swallowing up every inch of wall space, live shrubbery overwhelming my workbench. As demand for flora fortunes has grown, I've had to keep more varieties on hand, and I've run out of room. Every day, the air between Luna and me is charged with *what if.*

What if we aren't able to climb out of the sinkhole we've crumbled into? Three months ago, the vacant lot next door went up for sale, and we figured it was the answer to our prayers. Not only does the property come with a greenhouse (albeit a pretty old one), but the lot is paved, so why not use that space for a magical night market? It was a competitive sale, so our landlord, Trevor, decided to waive the inspection, and we poured *all* of our savings into a property that has turned out to be a dumpster fire.

I still cringe, remembering how we'd celebrated when the other bidders stepped back, unwilling to match our offer. I imagine they are all laughing at us now.

Without glancing up from the computer behind the front desk, Luna tells me, "It'll happen." Even though witches only get one main specialty and Luna's is candles, she's uncannily perceptive. I think this is more of a Luna thing than a witch thing.

"Mm." I tie on my apron—green, purple, and gold, like the banner out front, our shop name emblazoned in a medieval font—and turn the hand-painted wheel of fortune until it clicks to Monday. On Mondays, our deluxe subscription box brings you eight grams of dried verbena, a bottle of honeysuckle oil, a Love Awakens candle (rose, amber, and cardamom), and a historical fantasy novel of our choice. For in-store purchases only, a fresh posy good luck charm can be added to the box for $2.99.

"Your aura has an interesting little dash of happy surprise in it." Luna tilts her head and smiles. "Which ones bloomed?"

I jiggle one of the ancient leaded windows unstuck, raising it as high as it will go. A cool breeze sails in, along with a whistling *eee-ee-ere, eee-ee-ere*. I glance sharply upward, where a lark watches me from a tree branch, head cocked as if he knows a secret. "The windflowers."

"Fantastic. Dry some out when you get a chance so I can throw them into a batch, will you?" She finally looks up at me, dark circles rimming her big blue eyes, chin-length corkscrew curls tugged into a tiny blond bun. Our eyes are the only feature that the three of us sisters share. Luna's taller than I am, more willowy. Zelda's shorter and curvier, with long ginger waves; my hair's naturally pin-straight brunette, but these days I keep it in a bleached bob—and usually under a hat. Straw boaters with silk ribbons are my favorite for spring.

"Do you think I should start making lotions and bath oils?" she asks.

I blink at her. "My darling Luna, you cannot be serious. You're stretched so thin."

Snapdragon is on her lap, rubbing his gingery face along her wrists. She bends her head to kiss him.

"I'm looking at a witchcraft store run by this lady in Little Rock, and you should see all the stuff on here. She does *all* of it by herself, too. Creating, shipping, processing orders, promotion, all of it. I feel so inadequate."

"Look around you. You've made this business *thrive*."

While she and I technically don't own this place, we're undeniably the ones in charge. Grandma handed the reins over to her son (our dad) when I was twenty-two. My sisters and I once looked forward to inheriting it from him someday, but he lost the shop to our mother a year later in a tumultuous divorce, after which she sold it for a pittance out of spite. The dream is to buy it back someday. As the store's success grows, though, so does its monetary value, and our dream of family ownership recedes that much further from grasp. I can hardly blame Trevor for not wanting to sell. He fell into the witchy business entirely by chance and has seen only profit since then.

Her expression is grim. "I don't know about thriving. Not anymore. If we can't put up the night market, I don't know how we'll recoup the price of the lot."

"It's too early to start worrying."

"Can't start worrying when you never stop."

I thrust my coffee mug under her nose, which she accepts, growling at the screen. Blue light slants across her freckled face, many of which are actual freckles and several of which are tiny rainbow dots tattooed across the bridge of her nose and cheeks. I grab the mouse, closing her browser.

"Hey! I was doing reconnaissance."

"Go back to bed." The shop is open from ten to five on weekdays, noon till four on weekends, but she rises at five to get an early jump on preparing the online orders.

She hand-waves.

I pass the giant fireplace with the emerald tiles, patting Grandma's crystal ball on its mantel for good luck. My niece, Aisling, says she frequently glimpses Grandma's reflection in its curved surface; says she sometimes hears her voice curlicuing down the fireplace like the notes of a song, or hears her snoring while a ghostly Dottie dozes in a rocking chair facing the hearth.

I open the front door wide to let in more fresh air and wander barefoot onto the cracked wet sidewalk, mentally scrolling through my lunar calendar to recall which moon phase we're in—waxing crescent—which means it's time for aboveground planting of annual flowers and fruits. There isn't room for anything new. I turn to go back inside, head full of strawflowers, but just as I do so, a red Nissan Cube with yellow rims whips into the empty space in front of the store, bass so loud that the boulevard vibrates.

Trevor jumps out, attempts to slide across the hood but only makes it a quarter of the way. "What's up, beautiful!"

"I'm covered in dirt." I show him my palms as proof. "My clothes smell like chickens."

He rolls his eyes. "Stop flipping over compliments before they've baked on one side."

"I don't know what that means."

"Have it your way. What's up, ugly! Where the hell are your shoes? The sidewalk is where all the bugs live. What's wrong with you?"

"The better question is, why're you here this early?" Trevor never drops in until well after opening. Punctuality, for him, means "an hour or two late."

He slips into the shop. "Go wash up, gross-o, then tie every lucky flower you've got to a crown, because it's happening. *Today.*" He raises his voice to shout past me. "Luna! Where you at?"

I frown. "What's happening? What is *it*?"

Knowing Trevor Yoon, this could be anything. One time, he showed up with an ear piercer, and he and I spent the day piercing each other's ears. Another day, he brought in a go-kart he said was "rigged with fireworks," as a birthday gift for Morgan. (Morgan wisely has not ridden it.) He makes Luna come unglued, always accidentally knocking stuff over or forgetting to file taxes or sticking candles with polarizing energies next to each other. He's a rocket ship with no navigation system barreling through the galaxy: the tall, lanky, Sagittarius brother we never had.

He's wearing a fancy suit and has paired it with a novelty tee (Cersei and Jaime Lannister with their arms around each other: *Bros 'n Hoes*). I can tell immediately that he's feeling himself. He's gotten a root touch-up on his white-peach hair, styled in an undercut with a forward sweep. He's wearing neon green sneakers, which he only busts out for special occasions.

"We're not getting a burrito bar," Luna calls out warningly. Snapdragon is traipsing across the slope of her shoulders, paws kneading her back, forcing her to hunch with her nose an inch from the computer keys. "Trevor, we've discussed this. It makes no sense to put a burrito bar in here, and we don't have the room, anyway."

He twirls dramatically, showing off the purple satin lining of his blazer. "We're tabling that discussion for later because you're so wrong that it's ridiculous, but that's not what I'm talking about. My dad just called. He's here, in Moonville, and he wants me to meet him for lunch at eleven o' clock."

Luna stands up; Snapdragon tumbles down her back and hits the floor with an annoyed *meow*. "Because of . . . ? To talk to us? To hear our pitch?"

Trevor nods, dark eyes aglitter. "What else could it be? He *never* visits."

"I didn't think he'd come through," I say in wonderment. "I thought he was gonna leave us hanging."

"So did I!"

The air is sucked from the room. Luna and I stare at each other, dumbfounded, which Trevor relishes with a shit-eating grin, before saying: "We might actually pull this off. Today. We could get the rest of the money *today*."

We all start jumping up and down. "It's happening! It's happening!"

© Marcus Hogle

Sarah Hogle is a mom of three who enjoys trashy TV and pro-
voking her husband for attention. Her dream is to live in a falling-
apart castle in a forest that is probably cursed. She is also the
author of *Twice Shy* and *Just Like Magic*.

🐦 witchofthewords
📷 Sarah_Hogle

SARAH HOGLE

**"Whatever Sarah Hogle writes,
I'll be reading it."**
—*BuzzFeed*

**For a complete list of titles and to sign up for
our newsletter, scan the QR code**

**or visit
prh.com/sarahhogle**